The

Virgin of Small Plains

Ballantine Books

New York

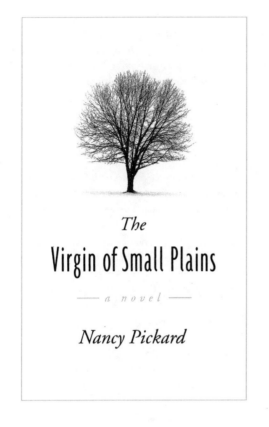

The

Virgin of Small Plains

—— *a novel* ——

Nancy Pickard

The Virgin of Small Plains is a work of fiction. Names, characters, places, and incidents are the products of the author's imagination or are used fictitiously. Any resemblance to actual events, locales, or persons, living or dead, is entirely coincidental.

Published in the United States by Ballantine Books, an imprint of The Random House Publishing Group, a division of Random House, Inc., New York.

BALLANTINE and colophon are registered trademarks of Random House, Inc.

Library of Congress Cataloging-in-Publication Data

Pickard, Nancy.
The virgin of Small Plains : a novel / Nancy Pickard.—
p.   cm.
ISBN 0-345-47099-0 (hc : alk. paper)
1. Cold cases (Criminal investigation)—Fiction.   I. Title.

PS3566.I274V53 2006
813'.54—dc22
2005055550

Printed in the United States of America on acid-free paper

www.ballantinebooks.com

2 4 6 8 9 7 5 3 1

First Edition

Text design by Laurie Jewell

For Mary and Nick

Acknowledgments

Special thanks to David Phillips for his expertise, to Karen Phillips and Denise Osborne for the Fridays that refresh, and to all my other friends—in person and online—who lift me out of the page and back into life. Special thanks always to my patient and wise editor, Linda Marrow, and to my agent and friend, Meredith Bernstein.

The

Virgin of Small Plains

Chapter One

Abby Reynolds braked her truck on the icy highway, startled by what she imagined she saw off to the side of the road. *That can't be,* she thought, as she squinted into the snow, trying to see more clearly. When the wind blew an opening in the blizzard, Abby realized that it was not a hallucination. It was not an impossible illusion sketched on the early morning air by the gusting snow. It was . . . *good grief!* . . . it was Nadine Newquist in a bathrobe, surrounded by swirling white, struggling through drifts on the old cemetery road, as if she were determined to visit a particular grave on this particular morning.

My God! It was Nadine: the judge's wife, Mitch's mom, Abby's own late mother's lifelong friend. It really was Nadine, a woman who was sixty-three years old and speeding toward early Alzheimer's at about the same rate that Abby's pickup truck was sliding sideways on Highway 177.

What the *hell* was Nadine doing out there?

She was all by herself, in a bathrobe, for God's sake, in a blizzard . . .

Abby pumped her brakes with a light touch of her foot, didn't slam on them like a fool, but her truck started to spin anyway, going round and round on the two-lane blacktop like a two-ton skater on ice.

She let her steering wheel alone, waiting for it to stop spinning before she touched it again. Coffee sloshed out of her lidless thermal cup in its holder by her knee; the smell of it filled the cab of her truck. She could still taste her last sip of it, along with the fruit and cereal she'd had for breakfast—all of which was now threatening to come back up her throat.

With a shudder, the truck came out of the spin and started sliding sideways again, skidding in a long diagonal across the yellow line into the eastbound lane. A heavy drift of snow slowed it down and changed the direction of the slide, until it was going backward. The skid went on and on, picking up speed as it backed into the crest of a rise, then dropped down again, taking the bottom of Abby's stomach with it. And still the truck stayed on the pavement, hemmed in by snow, avoiding the shoulders, the deep culverts, the barbed wire fencing beyond. People thought Kansas was all flat, but it wasn't, and especially not in the heart of the Flint Hills. The roads in this part of the state were long and straight, but they soared up and plunged down like curved ribbons of hard taffy.

Abby felt a wild hopeful moment of wondering if her truck could somehow manage to slide its way safely all the way back into town on the wrong side of the road. That would be a miracle. As she sat helplessly moving back the way she'd come, like a passenger on a roller coaster in reverse, she looked up the highway to the west, hoping not to see headlights coming at her. That way looked clear. In this strange, slow motion, made to feel even more eerie and timeless in the swirling snow, she felt as if she had all the time in the world before whatever was going to happen in the next few moments happened. She felt strangely calm, even curious about the possibility of crashing, but she didn't feel calm about Nadine out there in the snow.

She grabbed her cell phone from the seat beside her.

In the uncanny suspension of time, as her truck drew two long parallel lines in the snow on the highway, Abby realized she might be able to get out of her seat belt, throw open her door, and dive out. But if she did, what if her cell phone broke in her fall, or she hurt herself too badly to call for help? Then nobody would know about Nadine. Mitch's mom could fall out there in the cemetery, be covered by snow, she could die . . .

If I don't jump, I'll crash with the truck.

Nadine . . .

Heart pounding, stomach queasy, no longer feeling calm about anything, Abby gave up the idea of trying to jump to save herself. Instead, she punched in the single digit that called the Sheriff's cell phone. It was on auto-dial, because Rex Shellenberger was as long and close a friend to her as Nadine had been to both of their mothers, as close as Mitch had been to Rex and Abby, once upon a happy time, a long time ago.

"Sheriff Shellenberger," he said, calm as toast. But it was his recorded message. It went straight from those two words to the beep, wasting no time for people in emergencies.

"Rex! It's Abby! Nadine Newquist is wandering in the snow in the cemetery. Come help me get her out of there and take her home!"

She felt the truck veer left, and then felt it in her back and bottom first as the ride got rough and the rear tires slid onto gravel underneath snow.

Her roller-coaster ride, her trip back through time, was almost over.

Nobody would believe she had traveled so far on ice without crashing, Abby thought as the ride got rougher.

Panicked thoughts flashed through her brain, images without words. Should she call Nadine's husband, Tom? No, the judge was a notoriously bad driver in the best of weather, and a veritable menace at the first hint of moisture on the roads. Everybody knew that. Nobody with any sense ever consented to step into a car if Judge Tom Newquist was driving it, especially if it was raining, snowing, or sleeting. She'd only get him—or somebody else—killed if she called him out in this storm.

Frightened, Abby looked out the windshield just before it tilted up toward the sky.

In that split second, she glimpsed Mitch's mom again. Nadine's bathrobe was a tiny slash of deep rose on white, a hothouse flower inexplicably set outside on a winter's day. Abby knew the robe was expensive, soft and silky to the touch. She'd seen Nadine wearing it a lot lately, because she insisted on spending her days and nights in lingerie. It hardly mattered, since she didn't seem to be able to distinguish night from day anymore. When the judge or the nursing attendants he hired to watch her tried to get her into other clothes, she fought them. Abby knew the robe was made of thin material. The body under it was also thin, with hardly an ounce of fat to protect Nadine from the fierce cold that wrapped around her now.

At sixty miles an hour, Abby's truck hit the far side of the cement culvert with a crash that telescoped the exhaust pipes, flattened half of the metal bed, tore through the transmission, ripped out the gears, and shut the engine off. It was a ten-year-old truck with no air bags. Her seat belt saved her from being thrown into her windshield, but not from being slammed sideways into the window.

Chapter Two

January 23, 1987

"Mmmm."

Abby kept up a steady "mmm," while Mitch kissed all around her upper lip from the left side to the right, and then all across her lower lip from the right side to the left, and then again and again, around and around her mouth until she thought she might expire from the pleasure of it.

He was eighteen, a soon-to-graduate senior.

She was sixteen, the one who had to stay behind to finish high school.

She adored kissing him. Loved making out with him. Could have spent the rest of her life lying on her back in her single bed in her room with her head on her pillow and Mitch propped over her on his elbows, nonstop kissing her, pausing only for sweet little licks of his tongue between her lips.

She started mmming with such an intensity that he went *Shhh* into her lips. That made her lips tickle, which made her mouth curl up, which felt funny under *his* lips, which made him smile, which made both of them giggle, and then finally laugh so hard that Mitch had to fall away, onto his back, squeezed up against Abby on her narrow bed.

"*Shhh!*" they urged each other, and had to push their faces into each other's collarbones to keep the noise down. With her nose pressed down in the sweet hollow of his neck, Abby could smell his scent that was part spicy deodorant, part sandalwood aftershave, and all Mitch. He was laughing so hard at their attempts not to laugh that he snorted into her neck, which made her arch her back with her own less-than-silent laughter. Tears ran down both of their faces, moistening everything they touched, most of all each other.

Finally, when it died down, they snuggled in each other's arms.

Mitch had football shoulders, and eight inches over her five feet four, but his waist and hips were narrow and he had the long, slim leg muscles of a distance runner, so it was really only the top half of them that was crowded in the bed. Abby knew how to solve that by rolling toward him so he could wrap his arms around her while below their legs entwined. Wound around each other, they commenced plain old smooching again, silently meeting lips to lips again and again, working up to longer kisses, greater intensity, which was sure, eventually, to lead to more almost-out-of-control hilarity. Or, to more serious things, if they weren't careful. On this night, Abby didn't want to be careful, but Mitch didn't know that yet.

They were about halfway to something when there was a loud rap on the door to Abby's bedroom.

They froze in each other's arms.

The doorknob rattled as somebody tried to get in.

They were fully dressed, lying on top of the covers, with Bruce Springsteen in the background singing "Badlands" on an album turned up just loud enough to cover suspicious noises.

"Abby?" It was her mother's voice. "Why's your door locked, honey?"

"Don't come in, Mom!"

"Why not?"

"Because . . . I'm working on your birthday present!"

"Oh!" They heard her mother, Margie, laugh on the other side of the door. "In that case! I wondered where you had disappeared to. I haven't seen you in hours." Her tone turned teasing. "Mitch's not in there, is he?"

"Mother!"

"When did he leave? I didn't hear him go."

"Hours ago!"

"Are you sure I can't come in, Abby? Maybe you need some help getting those diamonds glued onto that gold necklace?"

"You wish!" Abby called back. "With *my* allowance?"

"Okay, then." Her mother feigned a martyred tone. "If you won't let me help . . ."

Mitch slid one hand up under Abby's sweater, over her ribs under her loosened bra, then onto her left breast, and she moaned softly.

"What?" her mother called from the other side of the door.

Abby closed her eyes in bliss, then opened them, and forced herself to say, "Mom?"

Mitch lifted her sweater, exposing her bare breast, and brought his mouth down onto it.

"What, honey?"

Abby felt as if her entire body was a single nerve cell vibrating from her left nipple.

"Is Dad here?"

Mitch's other hand began a slow descent under the waistband of her blue jeans, sliding lower, lower, stopping when it reached its destination. Unable to bear the torture, Abby put her hands on each of his and pressed, making him stop right where he was.

He grinned, and waited.

"Dad's back," her mother answered. Abby had seen her father leave the house on a medical call several hours before, and he hadn't been home for supper, but she hadn't paid attention to when he came back. Her mother said, "Hey, have you looked outside? You know it's snowing, don't you?"

"Really?" Abby turned her head toward her windows and then

Mitch did, too. Together they looked out at snow falling heavily in the glow of the driveway lights. Abby turned back to call to her mom, "How much are we going to get?"

"Enough to close school tomorrow."

"Yippee!"

They heard her mom laugh again. "You sound like a little kid when you do that. I'll have to take you sledding and give you hot chocolate in the morning. We're going to bed, sweetheart. You go ahead and work all night on my gift, if you have to."

Abby laughed, and called out, "Night! Love you!"

When she said the last words, she looked into her boyfriend's eyes.

"Love you, too," her mother's disappearing voice called back, as Mitch mouthed the exact same words to Abby. They didn't move until they heard the door to her parents' bedroom shut. Then Abby wiggled under him, encouraging him. "Let's take our clothes off," she whispered, and he didn't need to be asked twice.

They had never had intercourse. They had been boyfriend and girlfriend forever, stealing kisses when they were only eight and ten years old. By junior high, they were petting until they were both crazed. Through the years, they had made out as if they were going for advanced degrees in kissing. They had been totally naked together as many times as they could get the privacy to strip. Mitch's fingers had been inside of her, her hands had taken him to climax, but they had never had intercourse.

"I do love you," Abby promised him.

"I do love you, too," Mitch said, with as much fervor as if he was taking an oath on a Bible.

"Stay with me all night," she said, in a rush of words.

"I don't know if I can stand it," he said, and laughed quietly. "I'd better go."

"No." Abby looked directly into his beautiful brown eyes that were gazing so tenderly back at her. "Stay. You don't have to stand it anymore."

He raised an eyebrow. "Huh?"

"Let's . . . do it."

"You're kidding. Tonight?"

For answer, she stroked him where he could least resist her.

Mitch moaned, and said, "Oh God, Abby."

But he pulled away from her. "Listen. Are you *sure*?"

"Yeah, let's get it over with."

Mitch pulled back again. "Get it *over* with?"

"I didn't mean it like that," she said quickly. "I just mean, we've made it into such a big deal. Maybe that's a mistake. It kind of scares me, that it's such a big deal. I mean, maybe it's not that big a deal after you actually do it. Billions of people have done it, right? Millions of people are probably doing it right this minute, all over the world. In London and Paris. In Singapore and Bangladesh. And right here, this very night, in Small Plains."

"No way!" he exclaimed in mock shock.

"Even here," she assured him. "I've thought about this a lot."

"I can tell."

"So maybe we ought to just—"

Mitch leaned toward her and began to kiss her gently. Then he whispered, "I thought we were going to wait for a special time, so we could plan it and do it right. Candles and shit."

Abby laughed and covered her mouth.

"Candles and shit? Geez, you're romantic!"

Mitch laughed, too. "You know what I mean. Valentine's Day. Or New Year's Eve. Like that. A fancy dinner, then we'd go someplace where nobody knew us."

"And I'd be so nervous I'd mess everything up," she told him, confessing her fear.

He pursed his lips in thought, which forced her to lean forward to plant a kiss on them.

"Hm," he said, after a moment, "too much pressure, you mean?"

"Yeah, too much pressure for something that's supposed to be so natural."

"This isn't about me going to college, is it, Abby?"

"Cripes!" she exclaimed in a loud whisper. "I can't believe this! I have to convince you? I have to sell you on the idea of having sex with me?"

"Shhh! I'm sorry!" he told her. "I'm surprised, that's all. Of course I want to do it, but geez, Abby, your folks are right down the hall."

"With a noise machine that covers every sound but the telephone."

"Okay, but what about B.C.?" he whispered into her left ear.

Abby rolled her eyes. "I can't believe you!"

B.C. was their private shorthand for birth control. It had always felt sexy to talk of doing what they weren't allowing themselves to do. It had made them feel mature, superior, horny. Three girls they knew of had gotten pregnant in the last few semesters at Small Plains High School. Abby and Mitch knew they couldn't let that happen. They had to face parents who would kill them, or be horribly disappointed in them, if it happened to them.

"Don't you have one, like, in your wallet?" Abby whispered back to him.

"Me?" Mitch looked offended. "Do you think I carry them around?"

"I thought all guys did. Rex has one in his wallet."

"Oh, yeah? How do you know that?"

"I saw it one time when he left his wallet someplace."

"Well, you've been through my wallet enough times. You know what's in there."

"I just thought, maybe you had one—"

"Well, I don't," he said, and smiled at her. "I never wanted anybody to think that you—"

She kissed him. "Thanks."

They fooled around for a while, and then she said, "My dad has some. Downstairs. On a shelf in his office."

Her father was a physician, a general practitioner who practiced out of an office attached to the rear of their house.

Mitch pulled away again. "How do you know *that*?"

"How do you *think* I know? Don't you ever go through your dad's stuff?"

Mitch grinned. "Which shelf?"

"In the supply closet off the examining room. Fifth shelf up from the bottom on the left as you go in. They're in a box labeled—"

"Don't tell me. Trojan?"

She giggled. "Yeah. Super lubricated, supreme pleasure, maximum protection." But then Abby frowned in concern. "Is that bad? To have to use one? Do you mind?"

Mitch blushed. "I have no idea if that's bad. It all sounds good to me."

"Me, too."

"Abby—"

"Mitch! Yes, yes, yes. Now, now, now. You, you, you. And me."

"I love you," he said. "I think I'm in shock, but I love you."

They heard a toilet flush down the hall in her parents' room.

They froze again.

"I'd better wait," Mitch whispered, while Abby groaned with frustration.

"Let's make sure they're asleep before I go get it," he said. "I'll call Rex and have him cover for me in case my folks notice I'm not home."

"I can't stand waiting any longer!"she said.

"I'll take your mind off of it."

They started kissing again, but this time it had a nervous edge of anticipation that it had never had before.

Chapter Three

When Rex got yelled awake by his older brother, he shot out of bed feeling surprised and stupid. He had fallen asleep in his bed while he was doing his homework. Damn, he thought as he staggered to his feet, couldn't anybody let a guy get any sleep?

"What?" he called out, into the hallway. "What time is it?"

His brother Patrick yelled back, "Time to get your lazy ass out of bed and into the truck!"

"Why?"

"Look out your window, dumbshit!"

"Patrick!" their mother called reprovingly, and then coughed.

Rex turned toward his window and instantly understood the summons from his older brother. *Oh, shit.* The night was bright with snow. Lots of it. Flying, blowing, window-pinging, sleeting, blizzard snow. His dad was going to be furious. If the old man could arrest God for dumping this storm on them, he probably would. And then he'd arrest their neighbor to the north and string him up from the nearest barn door. Nine months earlier, that rancher had let one of his bulls get through the fence that separated his fields from where the Shellenbergers were grazing their heifers, the young females who hadn't given birth yet. The inevitable result was that instead of calving in March, when they were supposed to, they were due now, and at the worst possible time. A few calves had already arrived, but there were bound to be at least one or two tonight. If they didn't get to them in time, the calves, all wet from their mother's wombs, would freeze to death in minutes, and it wouldn't do the heifers any good, either.

"Mom? You coming with us?" he called out.

"No," his mother called back, sounding hoarse and really tired. "I've already half-got pneumonia." Between coughs, she managed to tell him, "Don't go out there without a coat, Rex." She knew him well, he thought, knew he'd run out of the house in nothing more than his boots, jeans, and sweater if nobody made him dress any warmer.

The ranch house was icy at that hour. His mom always turned the thermostat way down when she went to bed at night. Over the hours after that, the two-story white house got progressively cold enough to freeze your butt if you made the mistake of having a nightmare that woke you up and reminded you that you needed to piss.

Knowing his mother would get out of bed to make sure he was adequately dressed, Rex whipped off his jeans, pulled on long underwear, put his jeans back on, then put on an extra pair of socks. Sure enough, when he emerged from his bedroom, there she was, standing in the doorway of the bedroom she shared with his dad. She was short and plump, her men were all tall and lean. Rex pointed to his feet. "Extra socks, Mom." He pointed to his legs. "Long johns." He pointed downstairs. "Coat. Gloves. Hat."

"Good boy." She resumed coughing, and turned back toward bed.

With one hand on the railing and one on the wall, he vaulted down the stairs three at a time, grabbed the stuff he'd told his mom he would, and then raced outside. His father and brother were already waiting for him in his dad's truck, which was idling at the front of the house. Rex saw that Patrick was in the backseat, so he climbed in front. "I thought we were only supposed to get a couple of inches," he observed to his dad.

"Goddamn weatherman," his father muttered. "There oughta be a law."

In the dashboard lights, his dad's complexion, always red from high blood pressure and a choleric nature, looked dark and purplish, from the heat of anger and the cold of the weather. Nathan Shellenberger jerked the truck into first gear so furiously that the vehicle's rear end whipped from left to right and back again on the icy driveway.

"Whoa, Dad," Rex said, putting a hand on the dash to keep from banging into things.

In the backseat, Patrick laughed as he got jerked around by the centrifugal force.

They were still fishtailing as their headlights picked out the highway. It was going to be a slick, hazardous trip to their first gate. If his mother had been with them, Rex thought, she would have said, "Let's don't end up in a ditch, all right, Nathan?" But she wasn't there, so his dad continued driving too angrily and too fast for safety.

They knew which pastures to check, but the pastures were large, with many draws and hard-to-reach spots where cows wandered off to give birth to their calves. Fairly easily, they located one "girl" down in a draw where she was on her front knees, bellowing in pain and difficulty. Under their father's direction, the brothers dragged a metal Y-fork, winch, and chains from the back of the truck and used them, working together as a practiced team, to pull the bull calf from his mother. Within moments, after delivering the placenta, the mom was back on her feet, turning toward her new calf, nuzzling him, trying to get him on his feet, too. But the baby was soaked and shivering so much it couldn't stand. Patrick scooped it up in his arms and carried it into the truck with him—blood, excrement, and all. Rex and his dad led the new mother up a ramp into a narrow stall in the bed of the truck, where they shut her in. When the three of them climbed back into the cab, with the baby in Patrick's arms, and his dad turned up the heater, Rex smelled the rich, animal, comforting stink of new life all over them.

Slowly, this time, they made their way back to the barn, where they placed the pair together in a stall. When they saw the mother licking the calf and the calf starting to butt her in search of an udder, they hurried back through the cold and snow to the truck to repeat the process as many times as they had to that night.

•　•　•

"There," Rex's father said, and pointed to a mound of snow where there wasn't any natural reason for such a mound to be. "Look there, boys. What do you think that is?"

They had already found two more new calves, one doing all right, the other frozen.

This looked as if it was going to be more bad news.

Rex couldn't tell from a distance what it was that lay so still in the whiteness.

Even when his dad pointed the truck's headlights at it, they couldn't tell what they were looking at. "One of you boys go see, so we don't all have to get out again."

"Your turn," Patrick told him.

"Baloney."

"I don't care whose turn it is," their dad snapped. "One of you go!"

Patrick swatted the back of Rex's head. Because of the cold, it hurt worse than usual.

Rex whirled around and yelled at the backseat. "Stop it, Patrick! What are you—ten?"

"Go!" his dad said. "Or I'll leave you both here."

"No, you won't," Patrick said, sounding comfortable. "Mom'd kill you. Go, little brother. Mom won't be nearly so upset if Dad only leaves one of us behind."

Rex climbed out into the blowing snow and bitter cold again, thinking, *If I was the one who got to go to college this year, I'd have made sure I got to stay there.* Patrick—the good-looking one, the wild one, as he was known to the world—had managed to flunk out after only one semester at K-State University in Manhattan. He'd been back home only a week, and nobody but his family knew he was back. Feeling ashamed of his brother's failure, Rex hadn't even told Mitch or Abby the news that Patrick was home. *Hiding out,* in Rex's opinion, *mooching,* while he figured out what school might take him next, pretending to be helpful around the ranch while it was actually Rex who did the work.

The closer Rex got to the mound of snow, the less it looked like a cow or calf.

He was nearly nudging it with the toe of his boot when a horrible queasy feeling shot through him a moment before the awful truth seeped into his brain. His mind registered, *body,* before his eyes conveyed, *girl.* Before he could put all the pieces of the shocking puzzle together, he knelt on one knee beside her, looking down at her, not understanding.

She lay on her side, impossibly naked in the blizzard.

Her hip was the highest part of her, the snow-covered hump they'd seen from the truck.

Her skin was as white as the snow around it, her hair as brown as the earth under her.

Without thinking, Rex grabbed her thin shoulder, turned her over, and gasped as snow fell away to reveal her body and face. Her eyes were closed as if she had lain down and gone to sleep. He took in the full breasts, the mound of stomach, the pubic hair, the slim legs that were bent as if she had tried to curl up for warmth. For all of that, it was her bare feet that made her look the most vulnerable. Rex saw blood between her legs, down the inside of her thighs, and pink snow beneath her.

Even cold and dead, she was the most beautiful girl he'd ever seen.

Emotion whipped through him like a bullet, ripping his eighteen-year-old heart open.

"Rex! Is it a calf? What'd you find?"

His father came up behind him.

"My God," he heard his father exclaim in a loud, stiff, shocked voice.

Rex felt himself lifted and pulled to his feet, felt himself pushed away.

His father took his place, kneeling down in the snow to look at her.

"Dear God." Nathan Shellenberger turned around to stare up at Rex, as if his son could provide the answers. "Do you know her?"

Dumbly, Rex shook his head, denying her: *No.*

"Go get your brother."

But when Rex returned with Patrick, it wasn't so his dad could also ask his older brother if he knew her. It was only so the three of them could lift her and carry her between them back to the truck. They were all big men, over six feet, but none of them could do it alone because of the awkward, frozen posture of her body. His dad lifted her head and shoulders, Patrick took her feet and legs, leaving Rex to place his gloved hands under her hips. He had to force himself to do it. It was all so strange. And one of the strangest things of all was that nobody was saying anything. He had told his brother on the way back to their father what was going on, and Patrick had said, "Jesus!" and "What the hell?" and "Who is she, is it somebody we know?" Rex, his lips numb, his mind reeling, hadn't answered his brother's questions. When they reached their father and Patrick saw her, he, too, fell silent.

The snow was falling so thickly it was disorienting in the dark.

Rex felt as if they were moving through space, that they were giant spacemen threading in and out among trillions of tiny luminous stars. Several times as they struggled through the drifts, over the rough ranch land, Rex thought he was going to drop her, or be sick.

At the truck, they paused, holding her, unsure what to do next.

"We'll have to put her in back," their father said.

Rex hated that part of it, the handing of her stiff, bent body up to the bed of the pickup truck, the securing of her body by laying her down between the back wall and some fifty-pound feed bags. It felt ludicrous and disrespectful, even when his father covered her with empty burlap. But Rex knew the answer to the question, "What else could they do?" was *nothing.* Small Plains didn't have a hospital so there was no ambulance to send for, and his dad couldn't expect McLaughlin Brothers Funeral Home to send out a hearse to the middle of a cow pasture, not in this weather.

Back in the cab of the truck, his father said gruffly, "I'm dropping you back home, Rex."

"Why? Where are you going?"

"Well, we're not leaving her in the back of the truck all night, son." His dad's tone was sarcastic, but also gentle. "When you go in the house, don't say anything to your mother about this. I'll tell her."

"Yes, sir."

The "sir" came out unexpectedly, as it sometimes did when his dad changed from rancher to law enforcer.

"We disturbed the 'scene,' didn't we?" Rex asked, now speaking to the sheriff.

"Can't be helped. We couldn't leave her out there."

"Why not?" Patrick asked, sounding sullen.

His father snapped a glance in the rearview mirror and said, more impatiently this time, "Think. Coyotes."

Rex shuddered, sliding down in the seat.

"The snow's going to destroy some evidence," his father said, "like footprints, but it might preserve other things."

"Like what?"

"I don't know, Patrick. We'll see when it melts."

"Do you think somebody killed her, Dad?" Rex blurted.

Instead of answering the question, his father said, "It looks like she was raped."

Rex felt shocked to hear the word spoken out loud. *Raped.*

In his mind, he saw the red streaks on her thighs, the pink snow beneath her.

After his father said the loaded word, it hung in the cold air of the car, as if his dad was waiting to hear how his sons would respond.

"What about the new calves?" his brother asked, from the backseat.

"There's nothing we can do about them now," their father said.

"We'll lose some," Patrick persisted, as if that was the most important thing.

Suddenly furious, Rex turned around and glared at his brother. "She's *dead,* Patrick."

"So what? Shut up."

"So *what?*"

Patrick shrugged, turning his face away and staring out the far window.

"Asshole!" Rex whirled back around, violently shoving himself into the seat back.

His father didn't remonstrate with either of them, just let them stew in their own emotional juices while he navigated the hazardous roads back home. When Rex glanced over, he saw that his dad had a grim set to his mouth, which could have been because he was thinking hard, or because of the girl, or just because of the driving conditions. It was hard to tell, just as it was hard to tell how his father felt about a lot of things, unless he was angry about them. It was only anger that his dad seemed able to express openly and without reservation, and now and then a kind of patient, sarcastic affection. The more subtle ranges of feeling stayed locked up inside of him. Or, maybe, Rex thought, he had delegated all of those to Rex's mom, who had enough sensitivity for all of them.

When his dad pulled up into their driveway, Nathan Shellenberger bypassed the house and drove on to park in front of the barn.

Rex got out of the truck, and Patrick opened his door, too.

"Get up here in front with me, Patrick," his dad ordered him.

"Why?" It sounded whiny, and made Rex want to slug him.

"Because you're coming with me."

"Huh? Where? I don't want to. I'm tired, Dad."

"And I don't care if you don't want to. Get up here. Now."

Patrick slammed the back truck door, then just stood in the snow while their dad got out on his side and trudged toward the barn.

"What's he doing now?" Patrick complained.

"Probably going to use the barn phone."

"To call who?"

"How the hell would I know, Patrick?"

They watched their dad slide one side of the barn doors open, and then disappear inside.

Patrick took a step toward the truck door that Rex was holding open. He got right up in Rex's face, grinned, and said in a low voice to his brother, "Congratulations, asshole. You finally got to see a naked woman."

Rex shoved him into the truck.

Patrick laughed, and shoved him back.

Rex pulled back his right arm to hit Patrick with everything he had, but Patrick ducked under and slid into the front seat, so that Rex's fist landed on the metal divider between front and back. Pain shot up his arm like a lightning bolt, and blinded him. His teeth clamped down on his tongue, filling his mouth with pain, too, and with the bitter taste of his own blood. He fell back into the snow, grabbing at his broken fist with his other hand, then crying out in agony at the touch of his own hand.

Laughing, Patrick slammed the door shut, and locked it.

"Sucker!"

When their father returned, Rex had already gone into the house, cradling his fist.

* * *

"Rex, honey, is that you?"

"Yeah, Mom."

"Did you boys find any calves? Come in and talk to me. I'm too sick to get up."

Reluctantly, Rex went to her open doorway. "One dead, two live ones, Mom. We put them in the barn."

"Did we lose any cows?"

"No, just the one calf, but we didn't get around to every pasture."

"You didn't?" She coughed repeatedly, grabbed a tissue from a box on the floor, blew her nose a few times, and then said, "You've been gone a long time. Why are you holding your arm like that? Is something the matter with your hand?"

"Nothing. I hit it—"

"Come here, let me see it."

"Mom, it's okay—"

"Come here, Rex."

He went and sat down on the edge of her bed, and showed her his fist. In the glow of the bedside light that she had turned on, it looked viciously discolored. He saw he had cut it, right across the top of his knuckles, and there was blood. The snow and cold had limited the ooze, and kept the swelling down so far.

"Good grief. What did you do, hit your brother with it?"

He stared at her. How did she always know?

She sighed. "I won't even ask why. The two of you don't need a reason, do you? I want you to ice that down before you go to bed." She kept small plastic bags full of ice at the ready in the freezer, for tending the wounds of athletic sons and a husband who did physically dangerous work. But then she looked up from his hand, directly into his face. "What's the matter, Rex?" She frowned, cocked her head, as if listening for something. "Did you come in by yourself? Where's your brother? Where's your father?"

His dad had told him not to tell her. He was supposed to wait for his father to do it. But he hurt, and he was exhausted, wound-up, confused, and upset, and she was his mom, the best listener of any person he'd ever known.

Rex started at the beginning, and told her everything.

He didn't stop until his hand began to ache so bad that it was either go get some Tylenol for the pain, or start to cry.

Chapter Four

Mitch and Abby kissed and tortured each other until the coast was clear.

"Now?" he asked her.

Feeling equal parts shy, sure, scared, and excited, Abby nodded.

Mitch slipped out of her bed, and got back into his jeans and undershirt, leaving his boxers, sweater, shoes, socks, and winter coat behind in the room. When Abby saw how he had to struggle—carefully!—to get his half-cocked penis back into his pants, she giggled, and when he saw why she was laughing, he flushed as red as the valentine she had taped to the wall above her bed. "Very funny," he said with mock sarcasm, and they both laughed. He made a comedy out of walking bowlegged to the door. They both flinched when he turned the lock and it *clicked* open. After a tense moment of waiting to see if anybody else had heard it, Mitch sneaked through, turning around just long enough to flash her a grin.

She blew him a kiss, and mouthed, "I love you!"

Mitch left her door ajar, so he could slip back in later.

Abby quietly jumped out of bed and pushed all evidence of him under her bed, just in case. She slipped on his red-and-white football jersey that she slept in every night, inhaled the scent of him that clung to it, and let it slide down her body. Then she got back into bed to wait for him.

She didn't feel any guilt about lying to her mother. In her family, they lied to each other all the time, and only laughed about it when they got caught. "Don't tell your mother I ate that second piece of pie," her father might say. "Abby, don't tell your dad I threw his old tie out with the trash," Margie might say. Abby lied for her older sister, Ellen, and Ellen, when she was home from KU, lied for her. They were tiny lies, Abby thought, the lies that made it possible to live life without feeling totally chained down to other people's expectations, the lies that gave ordinary days a little spice and adventure. There was nothing wrong with it, in her opinion, though it boggled Mitch's mind when he heard them do it. His tiny family—the judge, Nadine, Mitch—lied to each other, too, Abby knew, but there was hell to pay if they got caught, which made them extra careful around one another. "That's the whole difference between our families," Abby had once told Mitch. "You guys are so formal, and you take everything so seriously, and we don't. And that's weird, because my dad's the one who's a doctor, where a lot of things really are life and death, but we don't act like it. Every time you do anything wrong, it seems like it's a capital offense."

"Well, my dad is a judge," Mitch had pointed out. "Guilt, innocence . . ."

He had drawn a finger across his neck, and made a sound like having his throat slit.

Abby had shivered, moved his finger out of the way, and kissed his Adam's apple.

But that was also the good news—the little white lies came easy to her, but no lies at all came easily to Mitch. Even listening to him ask Rex to cover for him, she'd heard how tense he had sounded, how quickly he'd hung up, as if he didn't want to dwell on it. Abby figured she would be able to tell if Mitch ever lied to her. She took it for granted that he was as loyal as he was honest. What he said he'd do, he'd do. And if he didn't, he'd tell her the truth about why not.

Which also meant, however, that if her mom or dad caught him on the stairs and asked him what he was doing there at this hour, in his bare feet, poor Mitch might blurt, "I'm going to get a rubber so I can screw your daughter for the first time!" At the thought of it, Abby felt contented laughter bubbling up from her heart, and before she knew it, she had to bury her face in her pillow to hide her giggles again.

Then she heard a phone ring, but not in her room, and her giggles died abruptly.

It was her father's medical emergency line, ringing on that phone in their bedroom.

"No!" Abby whisper-yelled into her pillow. "Please, please, please! Not tonight, please, please don't anybody need him tonight!"

.   .   .

Thank God the Reynoldses had wall-to-wall carpeting everywhere, Mitch thought, as he crept down the second floor landing, and then down the carpeted stairs to the first floor. And thank God Margie Reynolds believed in night-lights, so there was at least some illumination for his trek. As well as he knew this house, which was nearly as well as he knew his own, he still didn't know it well enough to move blindfolded in the dark.

He made himself think about what he could do or say if either of Abby's parents woke up and discovered him sneaking through their house in the dark. Mrs. Reynolds might forgive him, but Mitch had a feeling Doc Reynolds might not be so easy on him.

"Mitch?" he'd say in that bass, raspy, rumbling voice of his that made everything he said sound well-thought-out and important, even if he only said hello or good-bye or pass the pie. When Quentin Reynolds told people they were cancer-free, they took it as a pronouncement of Gospel truth; if he told them they had three months to live, they believed it, and tended to follow orders by folding their mortal tents on or about three months later. It was well known in town that you wanted to be real careful about what kind of information you asked Doc to give you, and make sure you could handle hearing it. Mitch's father said that when dealing with Quentin Reynolds, it was best to be a person of independent mind. Quentin also had a dry sense of humor that confused people who lacked one. Mitch could just imagine him saying, "I could have sworn that I got out of bed and that I'm not dreaming. But there you are, sneaking down my front stairs . . ."

Mitch crept through the kitchen toward the door that led into Doc's office and examining rooms. He'd eaten two pieces of Mrs. Reynolds's cherry pie in that kitchen that very afternoon while Abby's father worked on the other side of the wall, but it seemed a lot longer ago than that now.

Doc Reynolds kept to the old-fashioned tradition of conducting his medical practice at home, instead of at an office downtown, and so Mitch walked in the dark through a compact addition that had been built onto the house before he was born. Padding silently in his bare feet, he passed through a small waiting room, a reception and nurse's office, and then down a short hall where there were five doors leading to Doc's office, two examining rooms, one bathroom, and a large supply closet.

If he thought that explaining what he was doing in the house would be difficult, explaining what he was doing in the medical quarters was going to be impossible.

"Oh, just stealing amphetamines, Doc. Why, is that a problem?"

Mitch pushed open the door to the supply closet, and offered up a prayer to the god of young virgins. On second thought, he changed that line of defense, too. The god of virgins might not be too pleased that he was about to lose two of his best disciples.

That thought made Mitch's knees go so weak that he nearly sank down onto the tile floor.

When the phone rang like a tornado siren going off, he jumped as if a doctor had poked a needle in his ass.

•   •   •

For a few blessed moments after the phone rang, Abby didn't hear anything from the direction of her parents' bedroom. She let herself imagine that she and Mitch were still safe. But then she heard their door quietly open, and her heart managed to both sink and to race at the same time. She heard her father hurry down the hallway toward the stairs, and all she could do was hide her face in her hands. Her dad was being quiet, but not *that* quiet, so maybe Mitch would hear him coming and find a place to hide—

Galvanized by the need to warn Mitch, she sprang out of bed and raced to her door.

"Dad!" she called out. "What's going on?"

He barely glanced back over his shoulder long enough to say, "Shhh. Go back to sleep."

"Is somebody having a baby? There hasn't been a car wreck, has there?"

He didn't even bother to turn around to shush her, but just kept on going.

Abby retreated to her bed. At least she had tried to warn Mitch. He *had* to have heard her!

Holding her breath in suspense, Abby squeezed her eyes shut and prayed, *Please*!

When she saw light through her closed eyes, she opened them. But then, when she realized it was headlights coming up their driveway, she knew they'd lost their chance. The only good news was that she wasn't also hearing anything to indicate that Mitch had been caught by her dad. He must be hiding in the house. Or maybe he was already running home.

Oh, no! Through the snowstorm, without his shoes or coat . . .

Abby turned her face toward the ceiling, feeling horrible. She felt disappointed, mad, sad, scared, nervous, worried about Mitch, guilty, every bad feeling she could possibly have. Why did love have to be so *difficult*?

•   •   •

Mitch dived into the dark medical supply closet seconds before Abby's dad pushed open the door from the kitchen. Light from approaching headlights flooded the dark rooms as somebody drove up to the entrance to the doctor's office. For several moments, Mitch stood frozen in the dark, trying to catch his breath without anybody hearing him gulp it into his lungs. Abby's voice, calling "Dad!" had scared the hell out of him. Now, he cringed at the sight of the long sliver of light that came in at the edge of the supply closet door. He hadn't dared to close it all the way, since that might make noise. Would Doc notice it was ajar?

Oh, God, he thought, what if Doc had to get something in the supply closet?

Desperately, he stared around, but saw only open shelves, including the one with the box of condom packets. They looked like a bad joke now. *Ha ha. Not tonight, sucker.*

Mitch's heart pounded so hard in his ears that he felt deaf. As through a percussive din, he heard doors slam outside, then the outside door to the office opened, and then he heard the voices of men. With a shock that felt like a kick to his stomach, he recognized them. *Jesus H. Christ,* it was Rex's dad and Patrick. *Oh, great!* Was his own dad coming next?

Feeling as if he had little left to lose, since they were bound to catch him, Mitch inched closer to the crack of light. He might as well take a look. But what he saw shocked him more than his own predicament did: Preceded by Doc Reynolds, Rex's dad and brother were carrying a naked girl down the hallway, coming right toward him.

Doc stopped in front of the supply closet door and then flung open the door of the examining room opposite it.

"Put her in here," he told them.

The father and son turned into the first examining room.

As they did, they turned their burden so that her long hair hung down over their arms, and her face was revealed to Mitch.

His breath caught in his throat, and he thought, *My God, she's dead!*

Instinctively, he stepped back to get away from what he was seeing, but he could still see her. Her eyes open, she seemed to stare right at Mitch for an instant before they moved her face from his line of vision.

And then, belatedly, a jolt went through him, and he thought, *I know her.*

Through the blood pounding in his ears, he heard Quentin Reynolds say, "Lay her down on the floor, Nathan."

"The floor, Quentin?"

Rex's dad sounded angry, aggressive, but then, he almost always did.

"You've got to put her someplace," Abby's dad said with a kind of heavy patience. "Lay her down."

"Why not on the examining table?"

"Put her on the goddamned floor, Nathan!"

In the supply closet, Mitch's whole body jerked in surprise at the doctor's tone. He had never, *never* heard Abby's dad curse, or even talk like that to anybody.

"Keep your shirt on, Quentin," Nathan Shellenberger said.

There was a pause, and then Mitch heard Doc say, "Patrick, go wait in the truck."

When the asshole didn't move, as Mitch knew he wouldn't, because that was the kind of jerk Patrick was, his father shoved at his shoulder and said, "You heard him. Go."

Patrick didn't argue, just shrugged and slowly did as he was told, slamming the office's outside door behind him. It was only after he was gone that Mitch realized he was surprised to see that Patrick was in town at all. Why wasn't he in Manhattan, where he was supposed to be at college? Rex hadn't said anything about his asshole older brother being home.

It didn't seem important, especially not when Mitch heard Nathan Shellenberger say to the physician in a low voice, "What now?"

Abby's dad didn't answer him with any words. Instead, he surprised Mitch—and, from the expression on his face, the sheriff—by walking out of the examining room and back inside the house. He left the examining room door open. Mitch stood in the dark supply closet staring across the hall at a frightening tableau: The sheriff stood silently, a sentinel, seeming to guard the girl's body on the floor.

Doc returned within a few moments, carrying several plastic grocery bags in his left hand, and something else in his right hand. He walked back into the examining room. Still without speaking, the most respected and popular general practitioner in the county looked the county sheriff in the face briefly, and then squatted down and proceeded to place the girl's head carefully inside three of the bags. He then took some kind of twine from one of the drawers in his office and tied it tightly around her neck, securing the bags.

"What the hell are you doing, Quentin?" Rex's father demanded of him.

"What has to be done."

He left the office again, going back into the house one more time.

While he was gone, Mitch again watched Rex's dad stare down at her.

Slowly, almost not wanting to look, Mitch let his own gaze slide down to her body. They had put her on her left side. She was curled up as if she were asleep, and she wasn't moving.

When Abby's dad came back, he had a couple of sofa pillows in his hands. He squatted down again, only this time he lifted the girl's covered head, and placed the pillows under it, as if he were trying to make her comfortable on the hard, tiled floor.

Then Abby's father moved back a couple of feet, though he still squatted on the tile. He reached for the other object he had brought in along with the plastic bags. He lifted the girl's softball bat that he had carried with him into the office, and he brought it down on the plastic-covered face. Nathan Shellenberger cried out. So did Mitch, in the supply closet. But nobody heard him; their attention was riveted on the bat that just kept going up and coming down. The plastic bags contained the splattered flesh and blood. The pillows muffled the sound to thuds, though in the doctor's office they all heard the repeated and terrible cracking of bone.

The sheriff turned away, fumbled toward a plastic wastebasket, and vomited into it.

"Jesus Christ," he whispered, as he wiped his mouth off on the sleeve of his coat. "Jesus, God, Quentin!"

"Go home," Abby's father said, in a harsh voice. "We'll talk when Pat's not waiting for you."

The sheriff fled, letting a blast of snow and cold air in behind him before he shut the door.

In the closet, Mitch sank down onto the floor and stared wide-eyed into the light.

He watched Quentin Reynolds examine the surface of the bat, and then bend down to examine the floor. He seemed satisfied that the bags had contained the gore, because he didn't attempt to wash anything. Gently, he leaned the bat against a wall. He picked up the plastic wastebasket into which his old friend had thrown up and carried it down the hall to the bathroom. Mitch heard the sounds of a toilet flushing, of water running, and after a while Doc came back down the hall with the wastebasket in his hands and walked back into the examining room again. After putting the wastebasket back down, he put his hands on his hips and gazed around, as if checking to see if he had missed anything. And then, without any warning, he began to weep, a weeping made more violent by his efforts to contain the sounds of it. For several moments, the stocky man's shoulders shook as sobs wrenched him. Finally, he dragged the sleeves of his shirt across his eyes. Then he removed the cushioning pillows. He checked them, too. He left the girl with the destroyed face on the floor, and carried the bat and pillows back into his house, turning off the office light and quietly closing the door behind him.

Mitch waited until he thought he could stand up again.

Barefoot and coatless, without even a sweater to pull over his T-shirt, and on nerveless legs that trembled as he moved, he emerged from the closet. He paused for a moment in the hallway and stared into the examining room, but he couldn't bring himself to look down. Averting his eyes from the horror of it, he ran into the waiting room and then stumbled out into the snow. He could barely feel the cold. It was only when he inhaled sharp, painful air that he realized he had been holding his breath. As he shuffled down the driveway, he looked up at the windows in Abby's room. There was no light up there. Mitch felt as if all the light had gone out everywhere.

·   ·   ·

When the truck backed down the driveway and its headlights disappeared, when her father came trudging back up the stairs, when he had shut his bedroom door and a long time passed after that, Abby gave up waiting for Mitch to return to her bed that night. At least he hadn't gotten caught, she was pretty sure, or else her father would have thrown open her door to read her the riot act. So that was good. But nothing else was. Not poor Mitch having to run home barefoot in the snow, not Mitch having to take the chance of getting caught by *his* parents when he sneaked back into his house, and not the two of them being separated on the one night they should have been together most.

God only knew when she'd get the nerve to try again.

The tears started to come. Abby cried herself to sleep, feeling sorry for herself.

"This is just the *worst*," she told her wet pillow. It was *hard* to be sixteen. She just couldn't imagine how it could be any harder.

Chapter Five

When she padded downstairs in the morning, Abby wasn't surprised to realize that Mitch hadn't called her yet. Yawning, delighted that school was canceled, she took bread out of the refrigerator and put two slices in the toaster.

"Mom?" she called out in a sleep-hoarse voice.

"Doing laundry," came her mother's voice, up from the basement.

Abby was relieved not to hear any condemnation in it, no hint of, "Boy, are you in trouble when I get up there, young lady." She could hear sounds and low voices from her dad's medical office, meaning he was working in there this morning. When he didn't come storming out to confront her, either, she figured they'd gotten away with it.

Gotten away with nothing, she thought, ruefully.

Mitch would probably sleep in even later than she had, Abby thought, as she pulled out butter and raspberry jam, and he deserved to. She unscrewed the top on the jar of jam, ran a forefinger around the outer edge of it, and then licked off the tangy, seedy overflow. She hoped he hadn't gotten caught sneaking home. She didn't envy anybody who had to convince the judge of a false story. It was his profession to be able to winnow truth/wheat from lies/chaff, and it would be especially easy with Mitch.

Around the time that her toast was about to pop up and the room was filling with the warm, yeasty aroma of homemade bread, Abby got the delightful idea of getting dressed and stomping into Mitch's house and waking him up. If Nadine would let her into his bedroom, she could jump on him and surprise him awake. He'd hate it for about two seconds, until he saw who it was who was straddling him and tickling him.

Abby left the toast where it was in the toaster.

She ran upstairs, got dressed in warm layers of clothes, then raced back down to find her tallest, warmest boots and to toss on all the other layers of protection that made living in Kansas such a drag in the wintertime. She told herself that if she lived on a Caribbean island, she wouldn't get any snow days. But maybe she'd get hurricane days—

Abby felt goofy with the sheer pleasure of being sprung free for a day.

She flung open the front door.

God, what a gorgeous day!

The sun was so bright, reflecting off the snow, that she almost ran back into the house for sunglasses. Squinting hard against the glare at first, she barely noticed the presence of the sheriff's car in her driveway. But it was just Nathan Shellenberger, Rex's dad, her own dad's lifelong friend, no big deal. Abby was accustomed to all of the town's families running in and out of one another's homes. She didn't give it a second thought.

It wasn't even all that cold, really. By the time she had high-stepped the length of two front yards, and waved at neighbors who were shoveling, she was so hot she pulled her wool cap off her head and stuck it in her coat pocket.

Abby shook her hair loose, reveling in the crisp feel of fresh air, clean hair, being sixteen.

Yeah, she was disappointed they hadn't been able to go through with what she'd planned the night before, but it wasn't like it was the only chance they'd ever get. It had just felt that way to her in the middle of the night when any bad news seems worse that it really is. She certainly wasn't mad at Mitch about it. It wasn't his fault that her dad got an emergency call last night. Probably some woman delivering a baby and unable to make it through the storm to the hospital in Emporia. Abby hoped everything had turned out all right. Her dad hadn't been downstairs very long, and he hadn't called her mother down to help him make a delivery, so maybe the patient didn't make it in, after all. No, wait, there'd been the headlights and the noise of a truck in the driveway—

Abby shook off those thoughts, hoping for the best for everybody.

It scared her and made her giggle, all at the same time, at the thought of Mitch hearing her dad coming, panicking, and sneaking out of the house. He must have frozen!

Damn, why did the Newquists have to have the world's longest driveway?

By the time she had trudged all the way up, she had also peeled off her gloves, and unbuttoned her coat to let the sides flap free. When she reached the big front door, she rang the doorbell. Any other house in town, she could just walk on in, but not here. Nadine had heard too many crime stories from the judge. She believed there was a burglar around every bush and a rapist hiding in every backseat. Abby's own mother constantly kidded Nadine about it, but that never did any good. Year after year, there was some new security device added to the Newquists' house—a dead bolt, a chain, one year a security system (in Small Plains!). This past year, they had adopted a dog that barked so much they'd finally had to get rid of it before one of the neighbors got fed up and shot it.

"Abby," Nadine Newquist said, upon opening the door. She looked her usual elegant, unwelcoming self, Abby thought, only more so, if that was possible. How such a cold fish had given birth to a sweetie like Mitch was more than most people had ever been able to fathom. But she'd known the woman forever, eaten grilled cheese sandwiches in her kitchen, drunk lemonade in her yard, and so she made her usual effort to treat Nadine Newquist just like she treated every other adult in town, courteously and cheerfully.

"Hi, Mrs. Newquist! Can you believe all this snow! Is Mitch awake yet?"

"Mitch is not here, Abby."

"He's not? He's up already? Where'd he go?"

"He drove off this morning with his father."

Abby laughed, thinking his mom was joking. But when she didn't also laugh, Abby said, "They really did? This morning? Where'd they go?"

Nadine Newquist looked into Abby's eyes for a long moment, and then she said, "The judge took Mitch out of town, Abby. We're sending him away. He won't be graduating with his class. We're enrolling him somewhere else. He's not coming back."

"*What?*"

Abby blinked, not sure she'd heard the words she'd heard. They'd come so fast. There was so much weird impossible information in them. She couldn't grasp them. They slid out of her brain. Nadine was going to have to start all over and say them all again, slowly. That way, the words would turn out to be something completely different from what Abby was afraid she'd heard, words that nobody could ever possibly have said to her.

"What?" Abby asked, again.

Her mouth had gone dry, her heart was pounding.

"As you know better than I do, Abigail, my son came home very late last night from your house, when he wasn't supposed to be there. He lied to us. Apparently, it was not the first time. Perhaps lying is perfectly acceptable in your home, Abby, but it is not in ours. I don't blame Mitch. I blame your influence, and not just about the lying, either. He's feeling far too much pressure from you. Mitch doesn't know how to say no to you, Abby. And neither he nor we want him to ruin his future by hooking up with a girl who would get pregnant in order to keep him here with her."

"No! I didn't . . . I never . . ."

Nadine put up a hand, palm out, to stop her.

"We're taking him away from you, Abby, and you're just going to have to live with the fact that it's your fault that our son cannot remain in his own home. He agrees with us that it's the right thing to do. He will have a far brighter future away from you than he would ever have with you. You're just a small-town girl and he's meant for bigger things. You need to forget him. You need to get on with your silly little life."

Mitch's mother closed the door in Abby's face.

Abby stood there, in shock, for about two seconds. Then she rang the doorbell again. When nobody answered, Abby pounded on the door with her fists until it hurt too much to keep doing it. When that didn't raise any response, she yelled, "Nadine!" The first name slipped out, a personal, desperate plea. "Please, Mrs. Newquist!"

There was no response from within the house.

Abby didn't know what to do or how to react to the strange, horrible feelings inside her body. She felt as if she were going to explode from panic and grief. She ran around through the snow to the side of the house, trying to see in through the windows, but all the drapes were closed. She ran to the back, even tried the back door, but it was locked tight. For a wild moment, she considered dragging a ladder out of the garage, propping it against the house, and climbing up to Mitch's second-floor bedroom.

Not graduating with his class? Not coming back?

Feeling pressure from her, afraid she'd get pregnant to trap him?

That was impossible! It was a joke. They were playing a cruel joke on her. They were all inside, behind the curtains, laughing at her. It couldn't be true! No matter how serious Mitch's mom had looked, no matter how much her voice had quavered with anger, no matter how deep the contempt in her eyes, it just couldn't be true.

Is this really my fault? Abby backed away from the Newquist house.

For a long time, she stood in the snow, staring at the house that wouldn't let her in. Was this really happening because of what she had wanted to do last night? Were they trying to keep Mitch and her apart?

She couldn't believe Mitch had ever said those things, or felt those ways about her.

Abby ran to the back door and pounded on it again.

"Please! Whatever I did, I'm sorry, I'm sorry! Please don't send Mitch away! Please don't send him—"

Her voice trailed off, and she finally began to cry.

• • •

When her mother found her there ten minutes later, Margie put her arms around her sobbing daughter.

"How did you know where to find me?" Abby wept into her shoulder.

Her mother looked as if she had run all the way through the snow. She had on a jacket, but it wasn't even zipped, and she wasn't wearing gloves, hat, or boots. With her feet clad in nothing but loafers and socks, Abby's mother stood in the deep snow and held her.

"Nadine called, and told me to come get you." Margie tightened her grip on her younger child, and whispered back with a tearful vehemence that turned her vow to a hiss, "I'll kill her for hurting you like this!" She stroked the back of Abby's head with one hand, and wiped her own tears with her other hand. Pulling back just enough to be able to look into her daughter's brimming eyes, she said, "Come on, let's get out of here. Let's go home, sweetheart."

Chapter Six

When Rex staggered down to breakfast that same morning, he found his mother seated at the kitchen table with her head in her hands, instead of cooking breakfast as she usually did. No wonder he'd come down late, he thought; there had been no smell of bacon frying to lure him out of bed. The whole house felt cold and looked dreary, even though the snow had finally stopped and bright sunshine was coming through the windows.

He dragged himself up out of his own misery enough to say, "You okay, Mom?" When she looked up, he saw that she wasn't. "You look awful!"

"I feel even worse than I look, and please don't comment on that."

"Where's Pat?"

"Asleep."

"You want me to fix you something?"

She shook her head, but winced as if it hurt. "Your dad needs to see you in the barn."

"When?"

"He said, as soon as you got up."

"Have you talked to Doc Reynolds?" he asked her.

She looked startled at his question, but then seemed to realize that what he had meant was simply, "Did you call your doctor?"

"I'm afraid he'll send me to Emporia, Rex. To the hospital. I think I have pneumonia."

"Mom! If you don't call him, I will."

"I'll do it. Go to the barn." But before he could leave the house, she stopped him. "Rex? You asked if I'm okay, but I didn't ask if—"

"I'm fine, Mom."

He wasn't anywhere near fine, "fine" was a distant country he was sure he'd never see again, but he didn't want to talk about it. He didn't want to think about it, either, although he couldn't stop. He was surprised he had slept at all, and he felt as if he hadn't. His hand was definitely broken, no doubt about it. It was swollen to twice the size of his other hand, fluorescently discolored, and it hurt like holy hell. It was an indication of how rotten his mother felt, Rex knew, that she hadn't even asked about it. He was careful to keep it hidden behind him, so she wouldn't be reminded of it, and feel she needed to do something about it. And anyway, his hand was nothing. It didn't hurt at all, compared to the way his heart felt. It, too, felt swollen, bruised, broken.

The snow had stopped falling, leaving more than two feet of white covering everything. That was two feet that would be multiplied by the many square feet that Rex figured he was going to have to plow and shovel before the morning got much further along. How he was going to manage to do that with a broken fist was just something else he wanted to avoid thinking about. Everything felt like an insurmountable task. He was so exhausted that he felt like there ought to be a warning label attached to his body: *Do not allow to operate large machinery*. His brain was foggy with stress and lack of sleep, and he felt as forgetful as if he had never done chores before, never fed horses or mucked out a stall. He felt as if somebody was going to have to take him by the hand—the one that didn't hurt—and lead him from one place to another on this day of no school. How was he going to know where to go next, with no bells to ring in the hallways every forty minutes?

Clumsily, with his good hand, he slid open one side of the barn door, stepped into the warm, fragrant space, and then closed the door behind him.

"Dad?"

His father was in a stall where they had placed one of the cows with her newborn, and he was feeding the calf a supplemental bottle. When Nathan glanced up, and bestowed a tight, tired smile on his son, the unexpected warmth of it nearly undid Rex. Tears sprang to his eyes, and his throat filled. He had a suddenly overwhelming desire to confide his feelings to his dad, just as he had to his mom the night before, but long habit stilled his tongue.

"Won't she take the teat?" Rex said, and then cleared his throat.

"Yeah, she will. I'm just making sure she gets through the first twenty-four hours." His father pulled a long rubber nipple out of the baby's mouth, and the calf tried to follow it. Foamy white formula dripped from her pink tongue, and more formula from the big plastic bottle dripped onto the hay at his father's feet. Behind the calf, the young mother seemed to take it all in bovine stride.

"Sit down, Rex," his father said, pointing to a hay bale across the way.

When Nathan finished with the calf, he went over to the big metal sink they had in the barn, washed out the nipple and bottle, and set them on a counter to dry. Then he sat down near Rex on a second bale of hay, letting out a deep sigh as he settled his weight. Rex rested his wounded hand so that his father couldn't see it. His mother would be worried, but his father would be pissed at the stupid way he'd broken it.

Rex sucked air when his hand touched straw.

"What's the matter?" his father asked instantly.

The question made Rex wonder if his mother had talked to his father at all.

"Nothing." To take his mind off that pain he touched another one—his sore tongue. "Sorry I didn't get up in time to feed the calves."

His father waved it off. "I never got to sleep. Thought I might as well work."

"Where did you take . . . her?"

"To Quentin's office. Nothing else I could do." He paused a moment, seeming to gather his thoughts. "Son, do you trust me?"

"What?"

"I said, do you trust me?" It came out gruff, impatient, but Rex put that down to the fact that his father looked embarrassed to be saying the words.

"Sure," he said quickly, wanting to get the excruciating moment over with, so he could escape to something easier than talking to his father. Like shoveling acres of driveway with a broken hand. "You're my dad. Of course I trust you."

"Yes, but have I *earned* your trust over the course of your life?"

Rex thought this was becoming a very strange conversation. "Yes, sir."

"What if I told you to do something you thought was wrong?"

"You wouldn't do that—"

"What if I did? Would you do it, just because I asked you to?"

Rex was just about to complain, "What are you talking about?" when his father quickly added, "Would you trust me to have everybody's best interests at heart? Would you believe I might be able to see the larger picture?"

Rex thought the original question was now sufficiently loaded to bring down a bear. What did his dad think he was going to say, anyway? That his own son didn't trust him? What the hell was this all about?

I am way too tired for this shit, Rex thought. He shrugged. "Sure."

When his father looked unconvinced, Rex forced himself to add, "Absolutely!"

"All right, then. I hope to God you mean that."

"Dad!" He heard his own voice grating with weariness. "I told you. I do."

"Then listen to me. And this time, really listen. For five minutes, don't be a goddamned teenager who listens with half a brain to what his parents say. Are you listening?"

"Yes! Jesus, Dad . . ."

"This may be the most important thing I ever tell you. I'm serious now. I am trying to prepare you for something. You need to know that you're going to hear some things about that girl's death that you aren't expecting to hear."

Rex's body jerked involuntarily. His heart hammering, he blurted, "Like what?"

For the first time, his father's gaze slid away from him.

"You'll hear soon enough. All you need to know right now is that I'm telling you to keep your mouth shut about it, no matter what you hear. You are never . . . and I mean *never* . . . to talk to anybody about last night. Ever. Not Mitch, not Abby, not anybody. If you have anything to say about it, you'll say it to me."

"Fine with me," Rex said, but his father talked right over him.

"If anybody asks you about it, you tell them it's an active homicide investigation and your father won't allow you to discuss it. Period. End of story. Can I trust *you* to do that, Rex?"

Rex had looked off into the distance, but now there was a silence that brought his attention back to his father. He realized the old man was staring at him, waiting for something.

"What do you want me to say, Dad?"

"I told you. I asked if I can trust you."

Rex nodded his head solemnly, as he knew his father wanted him to do. He said, "Yes," in the serious voice he knew his father wanted to hear. But inside, he was thinking, *This is bullshit. Nobody has to shut me up, no matter what weird things I hear.* The last thing he ever wanted to do as long as he lived was to talk about it, to talk about her.

"What about Pat?" he asked.

"Pat's going back to college."

"How? He flunked out."

"There are other schools."

Not for this family, there has never been, Rex thought. He felt almost as shocked at this news as he was at everything else. His family was K-State from the git-go. It had been a major blowup when Patrick flunked out; it was taken for granted it was where Rex would go next year, just as he had taken it for granted that Patrick would, somehow, end up back there again.

"And that's something else," his father said to him.

"What is?"

"Patrick. Who knows he's been home?"

Rex started to shrug, but even that made his hand hurt, so he stopped. "I don't know."

"Well, who have you told?"

"Nobody."

"Nobody? Are you sure? What about Mitch?"

"No, I never told anybody. It's not like I want to brag about it."

His father's face darkened a little, and he seemed to wince. "I want you to forget he was here this week. You and I found that girl's body, just the two of us, nobody else. Patrick is still at K-State."

"Huh? Why?"

And then, suddenly, Rex didn't want to know why.

Which was just as well, since his father didn't give him any reasons.

The world was tilting, throwing everything off-kilter.

It shifted even further that morning when his mother got so sick that Quentin Reynolds told them they needed to get her to the hospital in Emporia, because it sounded like pneumonia. And it blew Rex clear out of the known universe when he got home hours later and picked up the phone. It was his friend Matt Nichols on the line, saying in an excited rush, "Man! Where have you *been*? Everybody's been trying to find you! We heard you found that murdered girl on your ranch last night, and she was beaten up so bad you can't even tell she has a face left! Is that true? Do you know who she is? And, hey, what do you know about Mitch Newquist leaving town all of a sudden like that, and supposedly never coming back?"

It all blew at him so fast, so unexpectedly, that it panicked and confused him, and he totally forgot the warning his father had given him. The pain medication they had shot into him at the hospital when they set a cast up to his elbow was making him dopey, too. So instead of saying, "It's an active homicide case," he blurted, "My mom's in the hospital, Matt. I can't talk now."

"Oh! Hey, I hope she's okay. Call me."

The next time he got asked, he was ready for it, even though every word of what he had to say hurt him like a stab in the gut: *It's an open homicide investigation, and my dad won't let me talk about it. I don't know who she was. And I don't know where the fuck Mitch is. He never said a word to me.*

•   •   •

A few weeks after Mitch left, on a day when Tom and Nadine had gone to Kansas City, Abby grabbed the keys to their house that Mitch had once given her, and sneaked into their home.

She ran upstairs to his room, and found it just the same as it had been.

Her photo wasn't on his dresser where it always was, but she figured that could mean anything. Maybe he had taken it with him, which would be a good sign, but maybe he didn't. Maybe Nadine got rid of it after he left.

Abby obsessively searched every drawer in his room.

She looked on every surface, checked under his mattress, and under his bed.

She went through the pockets of all the remaining clothes in his closet, looking for a secret note he might have left her, an explanation, a solution to the awful mystery of his absence. She didn't find that, but in the pocket of his best dress suit, she found a wrapped chocolate mint, which she unwrapped and ate. Then she buried her face in his clothing, breathing in his scent until she couldn't bear to smell it anymore. On the bed, she lay on her back, then her side, then her stomach, trying to feel where he had lain.

Abby didn't find any note to her. She hadn't had any mail from him, either.

All of his yearbooks were still there. He hadn't taken them, with their many photos of her in school activities, and of the two of them, caught in snapshots as a couple. In one, her favorite, they were in winter coats. Mitch had his arms around her in a bear hug, and they were both grinning at the camera, looking as if they could be happy forever.

She had gone there, to his home, hoping to find something, some clue to why he left, or some indication that he had taken his love for her with him when he went, and that he still treasured her.

She didn't find anything like that, but when she slowly descended the stairs to the first floor, she found Mitch's pet parrot, J. D. Salinger, in his cage. Mitch and Rex had named J.D. after the author of *Catcher in the Rye,* their favorite book their junior year, because they thought it was a hilarious name for a parrot. Abby was shocked to see that the poor bird had pecked half of its feathers out. She was shocked, but she understood it. If she'd had feathers, she'd have plucked them all out by now, too, out of her uncontrollable craving for the boy she couldn't have.

When she saw the awful state J.D. was in, Abby felt really angry at Mitch, so angry that she hated him. It felt really good to hate him. It felt good to see that there was another creature on earth who was suffering, as she was, and for the exact same reason. She didn't want J.D. to hurt, but seeing him like that made her feel a little less crazy. Maybe she was only as sane as a half-bald parrot, but at least she knew that another creature was taking it as hard as she was. From that moment, Abby swore to rescue the parrot and love him back to happiness. Three weeks later, she got her chance, and stole him off the Newquists' screened-in porch. It took a long time to bring J.D. around, but eventually his feathers began to grow back, his eyes lit up again, and his appetite came back. On a day when he nuzzled her hair and gently nibbled her earlobe without drawing blood, she knew it was going to be okay.

The only thing about the bird that changed permanently was that he never squawked again, as he had used to do when Mitch was around. The parrot had a squawk that could rouse roosters from their perches, the judge had always said, but now the big red bird only made quiet noises, as if he was afraid of offending.

"I don't know what I did wrong, either," Abby told him.

*   *   *

When Abby went back to high school after the blizzard, she felt like a frozen girl, barely able to remember how to smile back at people, or to pick up a tray in the cafeteria line, much less to eat the food on it. In class, it was too hard to raise her hand to ask a question, though she answered when she was called on. When somebody came up behind her and said her name—"Abby!"—she jumped. She walked in dread of hearing *his* name, and quietly walked away when there was talk of him. There was a gold heart necklace he had given her; she stuck it deep into a pocket of whatever she was wearing on any given day and rolled it around in her fingers where nobody could see.

When Ellen came home from KU, Abby hid in her room. When her girlfriends dropped by to try to see her, she fended them off, even her best friends Cerule and Randie. Now and then she picked up the phone to call Rex, or started to talk to him in the halls, but he seemed to be avoiding her, and she was mad at Rex anyway, because he hadn't called her. Every time she was tempted to try to talk to him, she got mad all over again, and hung up before anybody answered. She wondered if Rex was feeling bad, too. He had been Mitch's best friend forever. But then, maybe Rex *knew* why Mitch had left the way he did. Maybe Rex wasn't calling her, because he didn't want to tell her anything.

Well, the hell with him, then, she thought.

The hell with everybody.

They all thought Mitch had left town because of her, because his mother had made sure to tell them so.

*   *   *

Eventually, Abby caught on to how to do natural things again.

She began to be able to hear other people say his name.

One day she accidentally left the heart necklace in some shorts she was washing. When she heard it rattling around inside the clothes dryer she took it out and put it in the bottom drawer of her jewelry case.

A detached part of her understood how lucky she was: she was pretty, she was well-liked, there were boys who wanted to try to be with her now that Mitch was out of the picture, and there were girls who felt closer to her now that she had been dumped like anybody else could be. Slowly, lured out of her loneliness by other kids, she came to life again. But it wasn't the same. She wasn't the same. She was a girl who had lost the boy she loved for reasons she believed she would never understand, and she felt estranged from her other best male friend, Rex, and she'd been accused of things she hadn't done, and even her father seemed to be distancing himself from her, and now her best friend was a big red South American parrot.

The distance between her and Rex continued through the following lonely summer, and then he went off to college. Each time they saw each other after that, it was a little easier to be in each other's company. By the time they had both graduated from college, they were back on steady ground. A few times Abby tried to talk to him about Mitch, but Rex wouldn't do it. She finally gave up the effort. But Abby always suspected that Rex felt like she did, like a triangle with one side missing.

Chapter Seven

January 23, 2004

There had been a bad wreck east of Small Plains—a tractor-trailer had overturned in the blizzard—and then there were motorists for Rex Shellenberger and his deputies to help out of ditches. Now that the sun was up, more or less, he was tired from fighting the storm, and starving for a big breakfast in town. But before he could even begin to fantasize about bacon and eggs, his cell phone rang.

It was Judge Tom Newquist, transferred to Rex's cell phone in his SUV and sounding frantic because he couldn't locate Nadine.

"Where do you think she went, Judge?"

Rex felt all of his police senses go on high alert again.

No rest for the wicked, he thought. Or eggs or bacon, for that matter.

"If I knew where she went, I'd find her!" Tom Newquist sounded angry, like a desperate man. "In her condition, she could go any-where. There's no point looking for logic in it."

"But you think she's outside the house?"

Rex drove with one bare hand on the steering wheel, feeling the cold plastic under his fingers, the other holding the metallic phone to his ear. As slick as it was out, as thick as it was still coming down, he'd a whole lot rather have had both hands on the wheel.

"I know she's not *inside*." The judge's tone was sharp, unhappy. "I found the kitchen door open. Snow was blowing in."

Shit, Rex thought, but didn't say out loud. An Alzheimer's patient, out in this weather?

"Go look outside again, Judge. See if you see any footprints leading in some direction."

"I already did that." The judge was no fool. "There's nothing to see."

Double-dip shit, Rex thought. That meant she'd left some time ago, long enough for fresh snow to fill in any tracks she left. "I'm on my way," he promised the judge. "Please don't you go looking for her, all right? Nobody with any sense would go out on a day like this." He realized what he had just said, and regretted it. "I'm sorry, Judge. I didn't mean to say that."

"I thought she was doing better," the judge said, ignoring the tactless comment. "Enough so that I sent her nurse home last night. She was making sense when she talked. She was walking around okay, taking care of herself. She wasn't crying all the time like she has been. I thought it was safe to let her sleep in her room by herself."

On second thought, maybe the judge *was* a fool, Rex thought. Alzheimer's patients roamed at night, worse than they did in the daytime. Anybody who'd ever known one well knew that. If the judge couldn't handle that basic fact, he should have put her in a nursing home long ago.

"Is Jeff there?" Rex asked him.

Jeffrey was their other child, the one who had come along eighteen years after Mitch's birth, the adopted child whom some people called their substitute son. Ordinarily, Rex wouldn't have felt the need to inquire if a kid had stayed home on a school night while a blizzard raged, but Jeff was a high school senior, a breed that Rex didn't trust any farther than he could throw them. Mainly, because he remembered his own final year of high school. But either he had whitewashed his own memory, or Jeff was worse than he or any of his friends had been at that age, and more given to copping an attitude, too. It didn't help that his mother had gone mental, and that the judge was still the oblivious workaholic he'd always been. There had been too many times already when Rex had picked Jeff up someplace he wasn't supposed to be, and delivered him home to his parents, who hadn't even realized he was gone.

The judge assured him that Jeff was asleep in his room.

Rex refrained from asking, "Have you actually opened his door to make sure?" The judge didn't need one more family member to worry about this morning. If Jeff was out someplace he would likely survive, which was more than could be said of the chances for his mother.

"How soon can you be here?" the judge demanded.

"I'll cut through the cemetery."

"You're not coming here first?"

The judge sounded as if he was ready to argue about it.

"I'm taking the fastest route from where I am now," Rex said to calm him.

The Newquists' place backed up to the cemetery, so there was a good chance Nadine had gone that way.

Another call came through while he was on the phone with the judge, but Rex ignored it. By the time he hung up, his mind was focused on finding Nadine. Forgetting about the second call, he laid his cell phone back down on the seat beside him in order to concentrate on his driving. As bad as the conditions were, they weren't bad enough to take his mind off an awful irony that confronted him. He wondered if the judge was aware of it, too: It was January 23, and he was going out searching in a blizzard. It wasn't the first time he'd ever done that on this date. He could only hope that it ended better this time than it had the time before.

It took him more than twenty minutes to draw near to the cemetery.

"My God—"

He spotted a black Ford pickup truck, wedged deep and damaged in a drainage ditch across the highway. Scrawled across its passenger-side door was a logo written in white script letters: *Abby's Lawn & Landscape,* with a phone number and a website address.

"No!" Rex yelled the word as he slid to a stop as close as he could get to the truck. *No!*

To his horror, he saw a body slumped against the window on the driver's side.

Rex felt his heart begin to break, just as it had once before, a long time ago. He had never been in love with Abby, except for one brief time when he was seven and she was five. Even then she'd had long curly blond hair, just as she still did, and big blue eyes, and she'd been easy to love. And that was even before she had developed the figure that looked so good in tight jeans and snug shirts. But he had transferred his affection to a little red-haired girl who moved to town, and then to a series of other girls who mostly hadn't loved him back. And so it had fallen to Mitch to love Abby, a job at which he had proved himself to be piss-poor.

Rex tore out of his SUV, grabbing his gloves, and leaving the door hanging open behind him.

He half-slid, half-ran toward the wrecked pickup truck, yelling and praying all the way. He loved Abby like a sister, and he didn't think he could stand it if she was dead. Losing Mitch had been bad enough, but this would be so much worse. When he got to the truck he jerked the driver's-side door open.

"Abby!"

At the sound of Rex's voice, she started to come to. She saw a white sky through a windshield that was tilted, for some strange reason, upward. She saw that she was inside the cab of her own truck, held in place by her seat belt. The outside of her left arm and the left side of her head hurt. A lot. She was so cold she felt numb all over. When she turned to see who was saying her name, the view spun sickeningly for a moment. With effort, she recognized the handsome-homely face that was staring at her as if she was some kind of horrifying sight to see, as if he had just come across Godzilla in a pickup truck.

"Abby, talk to me! Your eyes are open . . . Tell me how many butt-ugly sheriffs you see standing in front of you."

"Three."

He looked even more horrified, until she smiled.

"Kidding. There could only be one of you, ever."

"Whew. Don't scare me like that. What happened to you?"

Abby put her left hand cautiously up to her forehead, and when she pulled it down to examine it, she saw blood on her glove. Feeling stiff as a corpse, she reached up her right hand to lower the visor and lift the cover of the mirror there. What she saw scared her, too—how pale she looked, how blood was trickling from underneath her black wool cap. Her pupils looked big and black, which must account for how much her eyes hurt, she thought. She grabbed sunglasses from the seat beside her, and gently eased them onto her face. Then she snatched the cap off to see her own smashed blond curls, now tinted red and pink.

"I look punk," she said weakly. "All I need is a safety pin through my eyebrow."

"Put your hat back on before you catch pneumonia."

"Yes, Dad." Despite her sarcasm, she did as he said, even though the pain when she lifted her left arm made her suck in her breath. When she saw that her coffee had all spilled out, she realized she couldn't smell it and wondered for a panicky moment if her nose had frozen. When Rex leaned in to examine her face, she was relieved to smell the leather of his jacket.

"You scared the shit of me, Abby," he said, accusingly. "When I saw your truck in the ditch . . ."

The window wasn't cracked, and neither was her head, she guessed, though the skin was definitely split up there. The pain of disturbing her own wounds woke her up some more. She remembered, in a rush, how she had landed there.

"What happened to my truck? Get me out of this seat belt. Have you got Nadine?"

"No. How do you know about Nadine?"

It was Abby's turn to look horrified. "Didn't you hear my message?"

"No, I just happened to be coming this way—"

"Oh, my God, Rex! Nadine is in the cemetery! I saw her walking there in her bathrobe—"

He straightened up and looked in that direction. "Jesus," he said in a low, urgent voice. Quickly, he shoved back the glove on his left wrist and checked his watch. "It's six thirty-two. Do you know when you crashed?"

Abby was already fighting her way out of the cab of her truck, using Rex's big, lanky body as leverage to propel herself safely down to the ground, into the deep snow where he stood. The snow was so deep that if he had on boots, she couldn't see them.

"It had to have been around six," she told him. "Oh, my God, Mitch, a whole half hour!"

"Mitch?" Rex had looked as if he was ready to leave her there, and go find Nadine. But now he turned back. "You called me Mitch, Abby."

She stared into the familiar brown eyes that now held a hint of anger.

"I did? I called you Mitch? Well, that's his mother out there. Who cares, Rex! Does it really matter if I call you Fred or Harvey? Come on, we've got to find her. Help me, I'm dizzy—"

"You're not going. You may have a concussion."

"Oh, shut up, Rex. I'm freezing, I need to move. I can show you where she was."

She felt her vision starting to black out, and quickly leaned into him until she could see again.

"Yeah, you'll be a big help," he said, still sounding angry.

"Nadine!" she snapped at him, and tugged at his coat to get him to hurry.

He grabbed her to steady her, and then kept tight hold of her as they hurried up out of the culvert and made their way through the snow to his SUV. Three times, one or the other of them slipped, nearly bringing both of them down, but his strength kept them upright, and she was determined not to let him go alone. Abby didn't trust a man to be able to find anything. Not even Rex, not even to find a sixty-three-year-old woman in a rose-colored bathrobe in the snow.

*   *   *

"She was near there, the first time I spotted her, Rex."

With a frantically waving finger, Abby pointed to a place about a hundred feet past the front gate.

"Hurry, hurry, hurry," she urged him, even though she knew he couldn't go any faster. "She wasn't much farther along the last time I saw her." Abby's voice choked on the words. Rex reached over to squeeze her hand, before he put his own back on the wheel. "She has on a bright pink bathrobe, Rex, so we ought to be able to find her." Hopefully, she said, "Maybe she doesn't know she's cold, you know? Maybe she thinks it's summer. Maybe she thinks she's just crossing the street to visit my mother."

"Maybe" was all Rex replied to that fantasy, but at least he didn't try to squelch it.

That was one of the things she loved best about Rex, Abby realized, that he was a realist, but not a squelcher. People could believe six crazy things to Sunday, and he'd just nod his head in a respectful sort of way, and say, "Interesting." Of course, he picked up a whole lot of information about people that way, too, which came in handy when he was investigating something or other. Rex wasn't like Mitch's mom, who had always been more likely to say something like, "That's the stupidest thing I've ever heard," and hurt somebody's feelings. Of all her parents' closest friends, Nadine had always been the only one she didn't like, and the only one she'd felt afraid of. Rex's sheriff father was gruff to his boys, and the judge could be intimidating, but both men had always been pussycats to Abby. Nadine was a different story. She had a sharp tongue on her, and strict ideas of how the world ought to be. Alzheimer's had only made her harder to get along with, as if it had eaten down to the core of her bitter character, revealing the heart of her Inner Bitch. When Abby had complained about Nadine to her own mother, Margie had usually said some version of, "Oh, Abby, I've known Nadine all my life, and besides, this town's not big enough that we can be all that picky about our friends."

The two of them, Nadine and Margie, would bicker and sometimes stop speaking to each other for a few days—it was weeks after Mitch left before they spoke again—but they had always wound up at the same card tables again. Nadine had been smart, with a sharp, gossipy wit, and Abby's mom had always said it was wiser to be friends with her than to be her enemy. It wasn't that Nadine couldn't ever be kind—she was, sometimes, especially if it boosted her reputation. It was that kindness wasn't her instinctive reaction, her default position, as it had been with Margie, and still was with Rex's mom, Verna.

"Rex?" Abby said, as they scanned the white landscape. She was still feeling dizzy, but the cold was bracing her awake. The front half of the cemetery she was searching with her eyes dated to the 1800s, with gravestones worn thin, slick, and plain with time. In the back half, over a high ridge, the elegant old tombstones gave way to flat modern markers. Abby hated the back half, even though it was so much easier for her guys to mow. Everybody hated the back half, but nobody knew how to stop the march of lawn-mowing progress, not even the owner of Abby's Lawn & Landscape. "She could die without ever seeing Mitch again."

"We'll all die without ever seeing Mitch again," Rex muttered.

Abby started to say, "Maybe she wouldn't even remember him," when she spotted a daub of color in the snow. "Rex, there!"

He pulled the SUV as close as he could get, his tires crunching over snow, and they hurried out of it. Holding on to each other again, they slogged through the deep snow to get to her. Nadine Newquist lay on her left side between two ragged lines of gravestones that were nearly up to their tops in white. Snow had already begun to cover her; in another few minutes of the heavy fall, they wouldn't have been able to see her at all.

Even though Abby was half-expecting this outcome, it was still a shock.

It was so cold, so lonely.

She smelled wood fire from somebody's chimney, and tasted it on her tongue. The contrast between cozy and comfortless seemed at that moment unbearably cruel.

Rex knelt, touched Nadine, gently turned her over so they could see her eyes were open, staring into the gray-and-white day. For form's sake, and not because he thought she lived, he bent his ear to her chest, placed fingers on her throat and wrist, checked for a pulse that wasn't there. She wore a thin white nightgown under the rose bathrobe, prompting Rex to shake his head and say, "Jeez, she was probably already half-frozen by the time she got here." Her long, thin, bony feet were as bare as the day she'd been born. Her auburn hair—which she had always gone to Kansas City to get fixed, because she hadn't trusted anybody local to do it—showed roots as white as the ground on which she lay.

"You know what people are going to say, don't you?" Abby asked, in a shaky voice.

He leaned back and stared up at her. She stood above him with her hands fisted down in her pockets and blood crusted onto the swollen side of her pretty face.

"No, what?"

Abby pointed beyond Nadine to the top of a particular tombstone that poked up over the drifts. The inscription on it was hidden by the snow. "They're going to say Nadine was trying to get to *that* grave," Abby told him, referring to the partly obscured tombstone. "They're going to say that if Nadine could only have stumbled a few more feet, it might have saved her."

Rex turned his head to stare at the gravestone that Abby meant.

He knew it well.

It was the burial marker of the girl that he, his father, and brother had found in another blizzard seventeen years ago. Back then, the people of the town of Small Plains had been horrified by her murder and saddened by the fact that nobody claimed her. They had pitched in to pay for her funeral expenses. They had turned out in their best clothes for her burial. And since that time a legend had grown up around her. People claimed that the unidentified murdered girl could heal the sick, that she interceded on behalf of people who needed help, all because she was grateful to the town for caring about her.

"Yeah?" Rex said in a voice that came out harder than he had intended, "Well, people frequently prove themselves to be idiots."

"Rex!"

He frowned at her. "You don't believe all that crap, do you?"

"I don't know—"

"Oh, for God's sake." He sounded disgusted. "Forget all that. Just come on. I'll carry her to the car, and we'll take her home."

"Okay." But then she said, "Nadine would hate this, Rex. It's . . . undignified."

"What else can we do?"

"Yeah."

He looked again at the other gravestone she had pointed out.

"What?" Abby asked, noticing his distraction.

"You know what today is?" Rex said.

"Monday?"

"No, I mean the date. It's the twenty-third of January." He looked at Abby, as if expecting something to dawn on her. After a moment, when it didn't, he said, "Just like on the day we found her."

Abby frowned, then understood what he was saying. "It is? Oh, God, Rex, I always forget that you found her."

"Not just me. My dad and . . . my dad was there, too."

Abby glanced at the almost-hidden gravestone. "I was barely aware of it, Rex. I know that sounds awful, but I had my mind on other things. You know how it is when you're sixteen, the whole world is only about you. A meteor could have hit and I wouldn't have noticed." She looked at him and he saw her brow furrow above her sunglasses, as if she was puzzled by something. "I don't remember seeing much of you."

He nodded. "I think I was hiding, like you."

"Hiding?" Abby was, at first, uncomprehending, but then in a rush, staring at his face, she got it; after seventeen years she finally understood something she had missed before. "Oh, God, Rex, it was awful for you, wasn't it? Finding her body. And then Mitch leaving . . ." Tears stung her eyes. "Rex, I'm sorry. I should have known, I should have said something a long time ago. I was thinking only of myself."

He waved it off. "Are you kidding? I wasn't exactly a great friend to you, either."

She sniffed in the cold air, and said, "Well, I'm sure glad we got over *that*."

"Yeah." He smiled at her, but then his smile faded. "Come on. I don't want to do this any more than you do, but we've got to."

"Déjà vu, for you."

"Not so much. I've picked up other frozen people in the snow since then."

"Lucky you. Strange coincidence, though."

Rex squatted down in the snow, and squinted at the body of his former best friend's mother. "Yes, it is," he agreed, in a voice gone suddenly thoughtful and quiet.

"Well, I hear life is strange."

"No kidding."

"Maybe my mother killed her," Abby said.

He jerked around and stared at her. "*What?*"

Abby touched the sore side of her face, winced, and said, "When Mitch left, Nadine was not very nice to me. My mother said she'd kill her for being so mean to me." She made an effort to smile a little, but it hurt, so she gave that up and just looked down at him. "Maybe my mother lured her out from the grave and got her revenge."

"Sometimes," he said, still staring at her, "you are pretty strange yourself."

"Yeah, and you're a fine one to talk."

"What do you mean by that?"

"Oh, nothing." Abby pointed at something. "What's that, Rex?"

"What?"

"That thing she has in her hand. What's she carrying?"

Carefully, Rex turned the thin hand over, revealing what Nadine Newquist had gripped in tight fingers. He could see just enough of it to be able to tell Abby what it was. "It's a picture of Jeff."

"Oh!" Abby grabbed the fabric of her coat above her heart. "That's so sad."

This one thing had finally brought her to tears. She had felt anxious and scared when they were searching for Nadine, but now, finally, she felt sorrow—even if she did suspect it was more for her mother and other people she had lost than for the woman in the snow before them. Still . . . Nadine may have had a serpent's tongue, but she had gone to her death clutching a photograph of her adopted child, her younger son.

Rex lifted the thin, light body, and carried it back like a baby to his car. Abby ran alongside, pulling at the robe and nightgown to make sure Mitch's mom had some modesty in death.

.   .   .

Rex carried Nadine into the Newquists' house, through the front door.

At the judge's suggestion, Rex laid the body down on a double bed in a guest room on the first floor.

"I thought you'd want me to bring her here," he told Tom Newquist. The judge stood in the bedroom doorway, blocking the view from Abby, who stood behind him. "I thought you'd want to call McLaughlin's and have them come and pick her up here, rather than have me carry her into the funeral home like this."

Tom Newquist nodded his head without speaking.

He hadn't said a word about his wife since they had arrived, except to ask, "Where'd you find her?" He had looked drawn and tired when he opened the door—admitting them into the immaculate, fragrant home his wife had kept for him for many years—but there wasn't any shock in his eyes. It had never been a situation that was going to end well, and they all knew it.

As Abby looked up at him—at all six feet four of him—from behind, outside the guest room, she saw that his back was stiff as always, his posture suggesting what it always did, that this was a big man capable of shouldering big responsibilities.

She had felt nervous at the front door, as if somehow he'd blame her.

Rex came out of the room, and the judge stepped aside to let him pass.

"You're famous for always locking your doors," Abby heard Rex say as the two men moved toward the kitchen at the back of the house. "How in the world did the door come to be open this time?"

She heard the judge say in his deep voice, "One of the damned nurses."

As she heard the men's footsteps moving away toward the kitchen at the back of the big house, Abby quietly walked into the bedroom and then over to the side of the bed where her late mother's friend lay. There was a silky white comforter folded at the foot of the bed. Abby reached for it, pulled it open, releasing its scent of potpourri, and she neatly covered Mitch's mom with it, up to her shoulders. She took a few moments to straighten and smooth Nadine's hair, which was still wet from the snow. Rex had closed the eyelids when he had knelt beside her in the cemetery.

The right hand still clutched the photo of her adopted son Jeff.

Abby stood for a moment staring down at the woman she had feared and disliked, but whom she had been raised to treat with courtesy and respect, no matter what. Then she leaned over and—dripping snow, herself—gently kissed the cold forehead. It wasn't a forgiving kiss, and she knew it. She did it for her own mother, and for Mitch. As she did it, she hated herself for the thought that had occurred to her the moment she knew for sure that Nadine was dead. It wasn't a thought for Nadine's final suffering. It wasn't for the judge. It was the absolutely last thing she ever wanted to think at this moment, but she was powerless over it, and so it came to her anyway . . .

Maybe he'll come back for her funeral.

Chapter Eight

He didn't come back for the funeral.

The day of the service for Nadine was one to stir up ghosts, Rex thought, as he stood at the back of the crowd gathered around her open grave, and all those ghosts seemed to be howling at once. He, himself, was feeling distinctly un-nostalgic, but he could tell by the somber, faraway looks on some faces that the day was bringing other days to mind for some people. The cottonwood trees and the tall, flat-topped hills didn't even begin to break the wind that snaked in between everybody standing around the grave. Rex thought he wouldn't have gone so far as to call them *mourners,* except maybe as mourners of their own losses, or maybe as mourners of life and death in general. One thing they all had in common, though, was they were cold. The wind was frigid from its slide down the front face of Colorado, fast from its skid across the plains. It was a wind with a serrated edge that cut under the raised coat collars of the men and chapped the thighs of any woman in a dress.

At graveside, the minister's lips were so cold he could barely move them to pray. He mumbled everything he said, fumbling all that he touched. Finally, he put his Bible on a metal folding chair, stuck his bare, chapped hands down into the pockets of his black overcoat, and left them there. Rex wished he would just mumble "Amen," and release everybody to go back to the heaters in their cars, vans, and trucks.

"Come *on*," Rex thought as the minister lingered overlong on a prayer.

There was a space, a body's width, between Judge Tom Newquist and seventeen-year-old Jeff Newquist, as if they had saved a place for someone who hadn't gotten there yet. Rex saw Abby staring at that space, and his heart felt bad for her. Her face was still bruised from her accident in the truck, and she kept her left arm close in to her side, as if it hurt her. She'd heal from those wounds, he knew. But some things, some heartaches, rejections, and surprises, you just never got over. Abby was probably never going to get over the feeling that she had done something wrong.

Me, too, Rex realized, with a start. He had his own reasons for feeling that way.

He glanced at the burial marker of the girl who had died on that other January 23. The girl's gravestone had no name on it, because she had never been identified. It held only the year of her death, and an epitaph: *Peace Be Unto You.*

When the minister finally let them go, Rex took note of the number of people who just happened to pass by the grave of the murdered girl, and touch it. Abby's prediction had been right—he'd heard more than one person say something like, "Well, you know why Nadine Newquist was out in the cemetery, don't you? She was trying to get cured of her Alzheimer's, poor thing. In her mind, she probably thought that if she could drag herself to the cemetery, she'd get a miracle."

Around town, they not only attributed healing powers to her, they called her the Virgin.

The first thing wrong with that theory, in Rex's opinion, was that she hadn't died a virgin. Rex would never forget his father's voice stating she had been raped. He would never forget the blood frozen on her legs. Of course, nobody outside of his family knew about that because his father had forbidden them to talk about it. But a cockamamie rumor had gone around that when Doc Reynolds examined her, he had pronounced that prior to the attack she was pure as the driven snow. Rex supposed that appealed to people's love of melodrama. She couldn't just be an unfortunate girl who got killed, she had to be a *virgin*, to boot.

The second thing wrong with that theory was that Doc couldn't necessarily have proved such a thing, even if he had wanted to. And a third thing wrong with it was that Quentin Reynolds would have sliced himself open with his own scalpel before he would have spoken a cliché like "pure as the driven snow."

I'll show you a miracle, Rex thought, as sunlight cut through the clouds and lit up the plains. He looked at his boots, which were standing in cold slush. *This snow is finally starting to melt.*

.   .   .

On his way out of the cemetery Rex made a point of walking up to a heavyset woman he recognized as one of Nadine Newquist's hired nurses.

"Mrs. Kolb," he said to her. "Have you got a minute?"

When she indicated she did, Rex drew her off to the side, away from other people leaving the service. "You've heard how Mrs. Newquist got outside that day?" he asked her, looking straight into her brown eyes.

"Somebody left the door open," she said, with a raised eyebrow and a judgmental air.

Rex could be blunt when it suited him. "The judge says one of you nurses did it."

"Well, then, he's a lying bastard!" the woman exclaimed in a voice loud enough to draw startled glances from the people closest to them. She saw the reaction and lowered her voice to a furious whisper. "I was the last one on duty, as I'm sure you know or you wouldn't be talking to me about it, and I will swear to you on any stack of Bibles, up to any height you want me to swear, that I never . . . *never* . . . left that door open. It was worth our jobs to leave that house unlocked! That was the first rule of the house—always make sure the outside doors are locked. If he said that, then he's just trying to make other people take the blame for what is surely, as Christ is my witness, his own damned fault."

Rex scratched his chin with the gloved forefinger of his left hand. "You think he left the door open?"

"Oh, not him, he'd never make a mistake like that," she said bitterly. "But if he wasn't watching her close enough . . ."

She let the implication hover between them.

Rex made sure he understood. "If the judge didn't watch over his wife closely enough she might have opened the door herself?"

"Could have. Or . . ."

Rex raised his eyebrows inquisitively.

"She wasn't the only one in that house without a sensible thought in her head," the nurse said, in the same tart tone in which she had spoken of the judge.

Rex looked over her head at the departing widower and his teenage son. Just as he did so, both of the Newquist men happened to look over to where Rex stood talking to their former nurse.

Jeff Newquist reminded Rex a little bit of Mitch around that age, although there wasn't any genetic reason he should. But he had picked up certain Newquist mannerisms just from living with them that gave the illusion that he actually looked like them. He had a confident—in Jeff's case, cocky—way of walking that mimicked Tom's, and an amused squint of the eyes that came straight from Nadine. His posture wasn't as good as Tom's, though; he slumped a bit about the shoulders. He wasn't as good looking as the "real" Newquist men. He was tall, but a lot skinnier, and nothing like the athlete that either Tom or Mitch had been. His eyes were a color that no

Newquist had ever had, and his complexion was paler, blotchier than theirs. That there were different genes at work in him was obvious, but only if you looked past the walk, the height, and the look in the eyes.

Rex looked back at Mrs. Kolb. "You think Jeff left it open?"

"Well, he left his clothes on the furniture and his towels on the floor and his dirty dishes any place he happened to be."

"What about doors, did he leave them open or unlocked, too?"

"Well," she said, sounding reluctant, "I never saw him do it."

Rex nodded, and released her with a smile. "Thanks."

As he watched her walk off, he wasn't sure why he was pursuing the matter. Somebody accidentally, or unthinkingly, left a door open and a mentally deranged woman had walked out of it to her death. It was a human, if unadmirable, thing to do. It could have been a nurse, despite what this one had claimed; it could have been the judge, or Jeffrey, or even Rex's own mother, who had visited her old friend Nadine the previous day. It could have been Rex's own father, who had stopped by to see Tom the night before, or any one of a number of people who might have visited, as people did in small towns every day, with gifts of flowers or food, or just to hold a senile woman's hand for a few minutes. What it wasn't was criminal, unless there had been some conscious intention to speed a suffering and inconvenient woman to her death.

She was dead. That seemed more of a blessing than not, to Rex.

She was dead and he was the sheriff. And he didn't know what, if anything, he was going to do about the uncomfortable juxtaposition of those two facts.

•   •   •

Mitch Newquist didn't come back for his mother's funeral, but an idealized ghost of him did, albeit a ghost who stirred up resentment on the day of Nadine's burial. Rex heard it in the whispers at the judge's house, at the reception afterward. When Rex walked in he noticed the house had a cigar smell, which Nadine would never have tolerated. He also wondered what she would have thought of the homemade catering by the church ladies. Too many casseroles, she might have sniffed. Rex headed straight for them, the macaroni and cheese, the green beans with fried onion rings on top, the apple pies.

"You'd think a son could come home for his own mother's funeral!" he overheard.

But then he also heard the turnaround to sympathy. "It's sad, really, when a man can't even come back to his own mother's funeral."

This last was said with a sidelong glance at Abby, a glance that burned Rex up.

Good grief, people, he wanted to snap at them, *it's ancient history! Let it go!*

And now, unfortunately, the idea that Abby might have saved Nadine, if only her truck hadn't wrecked, was feeding the lie of Abby's Fault. It was Abby's fault that Mitch left town. Abby's fault that nobody got to Nadine in time. "Did you have your seat belt on?" Rex's father asked her. "You sure that truck isn't too much for you, Abby?" her own father asked. "You can't just slam on the brakes, you have to turn into the skid," another old codger informed her, as if she'd grown up in Miami. "You'd better trade in that old truck-bucket for one with air bags," somebody else opined.

Rex remembered Abby's bloody forehead, and that she'd had to make a choice between saving herself and calling for help for Nadine, and he wanted to slug every one of them. As for causing Mitch to leave, Rex didn't know why their best friend had gone away, but he would have bet everything he owned that it wasn't Abby's fault. It infuriated him when people tried to blame her for it.

In the years since Mitch Newquist had packed up and left town overnight, he had turned into a Golden Boy for a lot of people who hadn't known him all that well—a Joe Montana on the football field, a Jim Ryan on the track, a born politician, entrepreneur, rancher, and general all-round Renaissance man. At first, when he'd left, there'd been some nasty speculation that maybe *he* had killed the girl, but that had quickly died away as more people came to find out he had an alibi in Abby. After that, his memory had taken on a glow. Some people even remembered him as playing the piano, an alteration of history that made Rex laugh rudely when he heard it. If Mitch had stayed, he would have benevolently run the town, was the underlying assumption, like a handsome, strapping, blond god with a grin that never aged. Nicer than his mother, less autocratic than his dad, he was Small Plains' star that got away . . .

The Mitch Myth, Rex called that one, though nobody liked it when he did.

How this image fit a man who didn't return for his own mother's funeral was a conundrum nobody seemed willing to address. Just like they had never figured out how to harmonize the dissonance between the Abby they all knew as a nice person, and the pushy broad who forced her boyfriend to leave his hometown forever to escape her clutches. Both paradoxes—the actual eighteen-year-old boy and the romanticized one, the actual Abby and the One to Blame—existed in many minds, like alternate realities held in opposite hands.

It all came down to one twenty-four-hour period:

Before January 23, 1987 . . .

After January 23, 1987.

You were seventeen years old and fell asleep over your homework one night, Rex thought, as he left the reception early. Memories he had fought all day to keep at bay came roaring in like the wind that had snaked around his ankles at the cemetery. *And when you woke up, everything was changed. For you, for your family, for your best friends, for your hometown, forever.*

Chapter Nine

January 23, 1987

By the time Mitch got home that night from Abby's house, his bare hands were so cold he could hardly get his house key out of his pants pocket and insert it in the door. When he finally got inside, he looked down and saw that his hands and feet were red from the cold. His coat and shoes were back in Abby's bedroom. Snow coated his clothes; he felt it dripping from his hair, he felt it on his eyelashes.

Nothing on the outside of him matched the freezing shock he felt within.

He lifted his head and slowly looked around, as if seeing his own home for the first time. There was Persian carpet at his feet and climbing the stairs to the second floor. Paintings lined the front hallway. His mother's favorite potpourri, scattered about the rooms in wide-mouthed Chinese porcelain bowls, permeated the air in a comforting, suffocating kind of way. He looked left into the living room, then right into the dining room. Everything was immaculate as both of his parents preferred for it to be. He felt glad to step back into an ordered universe, but it also felt unreal to him, as if he had stepped into a fantasy.

A door to his father's office at the back of the house opened, and suddenly his father stood in the doorway, dressed in pajamas, slippers, and a bathrobe, staring at him. Tom Newquist was a big man; at six feet four, he was four inches taller than his only child. With a jowly face and beefy physique, he cut an imposing figure, whether in the judicial robe of the Sixth Judicial District, or at home in his bathrobe. It wasn't unusual for him to be working late; he liked to work in the quiet and solitude of his home after his wife and son had gone to bed, and didn't like it whenever either one of them decided to stay up late for some reason.

"Mitchell! What in the world—"

"Dad." His lips trembled, his voice shook. "I have to tell you something."

"You're barefoot! Where have you been? Are you drunk?"

"No! Dad, listen to me, something's happened—"

His father stepped forward. "Were you in a car accident? Are you all right? What were you doing out driving in this storm?"

"Dad!" He raised his voice. "I was at Abby's! I wasn't in a car! Listen to me!"

His father frowned, unaccustomed to such a tone. "Put on some other clothes first. Get warm. Then come down to my office. And don't wake up your mother."

"Dad." Mitch took a pleading step forward. The single word hung in the air. His voice strained from what felt to him like a superhuman effort to speak in a calm, quiet tone that might compel his father to finally listen to him. Speaking slowly, trying to penetrate his father's infuriating assumptions, he said, "Do you remember . . . the girl who used to come and clean for us? Her name was Sarah? She wasn't from around here. I mean, she was from Franklin." It was another, much smaller town about twenty-five miles from Small Plains. "Dad, she's dead. I saw her . . . I saw . . ."

His mouth wouldn't form the words that should come next.

Staring at his father's face, a face that had gone blank and puzzled, Mitch was struck dumb with the enormity, the awfulness, the sheer weirdness of what he was going to have to say next. *Say it!* he told himself, screaming at himself inside his head. But he couldn't, his voice gave out on him, his brain refused to kick in the orders. He was filled with dread at the effect the news he had to give his father might have on the judge. These were his father's best friends he was going to . . . to what? *Betray* was the word that came to him. But that couldn't be right. He wasn't betraying anybody, he was only telling about the horrible thing that he had witnessed. It wasn't his fault that he had seen them do it. It wasn't something he could just witness and then never talk about to anybody. His father might be their friend, but he was also a *judge*. Mitch had to tell him, he knew he had to . . .

His father was frowning, as he might have over some ill-prepared legal briefs that an attorney had submitted to him.

"Who? Was this girl in an accident? What are you saying?"

"Sarah," Mitch repeated, but then he began to shiver uncontrollably. He couldn't remember her last name. How awful was that, he berated himself, that he couldn't even come up with her last name? Through chattering teeth, he managed to say, "I . . . can't . . . talk." Ten feet away, his father didn't move. Mitch said, "W-wait for me, okay? I'll ch-change clothes. I'll c-come back down . . ."

He fled to the stairs, and ran up to his room.

*   *   *

When he came back down, he was not only fully dressed in several layers of clothing, including wool socks, but he also had a blanket wrapped around him to try to still his inner, and outer, shivering. But when he sank down on a couch in his father's office and told the judge what he had witnessed, all he got for his pains, at first, was disbelief.

"First of all," his father said, sternly, "what were you doing in Quentin's office?"

"What?"

Mitch froze, taken by surprise by the question. *First of all?* What kind of stupid "first" question was that? What did it matter? Who cared? Hadn't his father heard anything he said? A girl was dead! Somebody they knew, somebody who used to work for them, was dead! When Mitch heard his father's all-too-parental question, he nearly laughed, but stopped himself in time. Caught off guard by a question that felt irrelevant to him, his mind went blank. He felt completely unable to think of a lie.

It seemed his father had a whole litany of questions/demands to spring on him. "Secondly, what were you doing in their house at all at this time of night on a school night? And third, you can't possibly have seen what you think you did. I think you were drinking, Mitchell. I suspect you may have been taking drugs."

Mitch threw his head back, and groaned.

"Mitchell!"

This was *crazy!* Mitch thought, feeling a kind of desperation deep inside. He had just witnessed a barbaric act committed on the dead body of a beautiful girl by one of his father's best friends, and all his father could do was act like a fucking robot *parent*!

But then, he thought again, trying to comprehend his father's strange reactions . . . *of course.* He was talking about his father's best friends, men who were as close to Tom Newquist as Abby and Rex were to him. If his father had come to him with such a story about Rex and Abby, he wouldn't have believed it, either. Not at first, anyway, and not without some pretty goddamned convincing proof.

Mitch was amazed he could even think so clearly.

He knew he was going to have to slow down again, as if his father was a slow learner, which God knew, he usually was not. But this was different. This wasn't a criminal case in his courtroom concerning people he didn't know. This was personal. Mitch felt as if he, himself, had nearly gone into shock when he saw it; he knew his own brain had wanted to reject it, so was it any wonder that his father was being obtuse?

With a sigh of resignation, Mitch realized he was going to have to tell the entire truth, condoms and all. There was a bowl of his mother's favorite buttermints beside him; he took one of the pale yellow candies and popped it in his mouth, buying a little time while he ate and swallowed it.

Then he started talking.

Twenty minutes later, when he had finished doing that, it was his father who seemed to be shivering. Staring at the judge, Mitch caught a glimpse of how his father would look as an old man.

"My God," his father said, in a near-whisper. "This is true, Mitch?"

"Gospel, Dad." He forced himself to ask, "What do we do now?"

His father's head jerked up. In an instant, the temporary aging fled from his face and body, and he was immediately himself again, straight-backed, intimidating, commanding. "I'll figure that out. You will go to bed, and you won't do anything until I tell you what it's going to be." His voice and face softened just a little. "Try to get some sleep."

Mitch felt immense relief to know his father had taken the awful burden from him.

He got to his feet, stumbling a little on the bottom edge of the blanket.

Without another word, suddenly far too exhausted to talk anymore, he did what his father had told him to do. When he was leaving the room, his father had a hand on the telephone.

.   .   .

His mother woke him before the sun was up.

When Mitch dragged his eyes open, he didn't understand what he saw: His mother had two large suitcases open on the floor of his room. She was pulling his belongings out of his dresser drawers, and putting them in the luggage.

"Mom? What are you doing?"

He was tired, with an exhaustion that made his eyes want to sink back into his skull, that made him feel like throwing up.

His vision cleared enough for him to realize she was upset.

"Mom? What's going on? What's the matter?"

"Your father's taking you out of town." Her voice sounded strange, as if it were clogged with tears or anger. Was she mad at him? What had he done? He heard her say, "Get up and get dressed, and help me pack your things. Take as much as you can. I'll pack everything else up and send it to you."

"Send it to me where? I don't understand. Are you mad at me?"

She finally turned around so he could see her better. His mom was also tall, also imposing in her way, though her way consisted of elegance of fashion and sharpness of tongue. Mitch was honest with himself—he'd never liked his mother very much, and he wasn't absolutely sure he even loved her. He knew he was supposed to, because didn't all sons love their mothers? But she wasn't any fun, she was a little scary, because nobody ever knew who she was going to cut to the quick next, and she was about the least huggable mom there could be. Not like Margie Reynolds, who he loved almost as much as he loved Abby. Not like Verna Shellenberger, who was practically a walking hug. On the other hand, it wasn't as if he liked his father better. If he could have picked a father, it wouldn't have been Nathan Shellenberger, though. It would have been Abby's dad . . .

His fuzzy brain stopped cold at the words, "Abby's dad."

A sickening memory of the previous night came back to him.

Awake now, and filled with foreboding, Mitch looked up at his mother.

"You have to go," she said, and turned back to emptying his drawers.

"Go where? Why?"

But he got no answer from her, just increasingly peremptory instructions to *move, move, move.* He tried to hurry, without understanding the reason for the haste. When he stepped outside of his room, he saw his father carrying a suitcase of his own down the hallway. When he saw that, Mitch sensed, with an ever-deepening feeling of sick dread, that all these strange goings-on had something to do with the awful thing he had accidentally seen the night before. He wished—for what would turn out to be the first of a million times in his lifetime—that he had never been at Abby's house the night before, that he had never sneaked down their stairs, never hidden and watched from the closet.

· · ·

He could hardly believe they were taking to the roads in such deep snow.

His father put chains on the tires, something Mitch had never seen him do before. The judge seemed as determined as Mitch's mother was to remove him from home as quickly as they could get him to budge.

Mitch took it as long as he could, until his father drove past the Shellenberger ranch, and then he burst out, "Tell me!"

Without taking his eyes from the road, his father said, "They're denying what you saw, son. Quentin and Nathan. They claim it never happened the way you said it did. They say she was already beaten when Nathan and Patrick took her in."

"Dad, no! I saw Quentin use the bat!"

"They say that if you tell that story to anyone, they will point out that she worked for us—"

"She worked for lots of people, Dad!"

The girl, Sarah—whose last name still escaped his memory—had only cleaned for his mother for a few months. He wasn't even sure how often she had done it. Maybe once a week? That seemed like the usual thing. He was pretty sure she had cleaned other people's houses on other days. She was older than Mitch, already out of high school, and earning her own money that way because there were probably zero jobs where she came from. He didn't know what she was earning it for, whether for living or for college, maybe. He didn't know anything about her family. He knew that all his friends practically swooned every time they caught a glimpse of her. And he knew that he hadn't paid any attention when she stopped working for his mom.

One day there was some other woman doing it, and she wasn't gorgeous like Sarah had been, that's all he knew.

"I *know* she worked for other people," his father answered him, sounding as deliberate and patient as Mitch had forced himself to be the night before. "Unfortunately, it wasn't those people who saw what you saw last night. They'll say that she was young, like you. They're claiming that everybody knew she had a crush on you—"

"What? She did *not*—"

He wasn't sure about that. He remembered her smiles when she had been in their house the times he had come home from school or from football practice. He remembered how his own body had reacted to her body when he saw that smile. He remembered feeling flustered, saying, "Hi," and then hurrying away again. And he had to admit to himself that a lot of girls supposedly had crushes on him through the years. *Shit.*

His father was saying, "They will put you under suspicion in her death."

Mitch was stunned. These were his mother's and father's *friends* they were talking about, these were men whose children were *his* best friends. This was a man—Quentin Reynolds—whom he had looked forward to having as his father-in-law some day. He had even dreamed that Quentin could be the funny, looser, more likeable dad that his own father could never be. Mitch had thought the men cared about him, the way they cared about Abby and Rex and Patrick. The feeling he had at that moment of stark betrayal carved a dividing line in his heart: *before* and *after.*

His father glanced over at him. "They are the sheriff and a doctor, Mitch. It would be your word against theirs."

"But you're a judge!"

"And your father, which is why no one will take my word for it, either."

"They're your friends!"

His father was silent.

"Why are they doing this, Dad? They know me!"

In a strangely cold tone that made Mitch stare at his father, the judge said, "I think they are no longer sure that they know you very well, Mitch."

Mitch laid his head back against the seat, feeling stunned and frozen all over again. Did his own father suspect him of something terrible? Was he believing them, instead of his son?

"Dad? You know I'm telling you the truth, right?"

"We'll get you out of here," his father said, "and then we'll find out the truth."

"What do you mean, find out?" Mitch was so upset he was yelling. "I told you the truth!"

"Stop yelling. I'm only saying, we don't know everything yet."

That was true. God knew, that was true. And yet the way his father had said it . . . did Mitch only imagine the doubt he thought he heard in his father's voice and saw in his face? Mitch wondered if this was what a defendant in his father's courtroom felt like when being accused of something terrible that he hadn't done. Did somebody like that feel as if his whole world was spinning out of control?

"Where are we going?" he asked, in a dull voice.

"Out of this storm track, first. Then we're going to Chicago, where we will stay until we have you enrolled in a college far away from here."

"What?" Mitch stared at his father across the car seat.

He wasn't going to be graduating with his class, his father told him. He wasn't going to be going to the University of Kansas with his friends. He was going to be sent where nobody could reach him to accuse him of anything he didn't do.

A great sadness and hopelessness came over Mitch as he heard these things.

He was too confused to be logical, except to follow one terrible train of thought that struck him harder than anything ever had, even harder than what he had seen. *I'll call Abby from our hotel room,* he thought at first. And then he realized that not only could he not call her, but that he might never be able to talk to her again.

When that realization struck Mitch, he lost it completely.

He turned his face to the window, and began to cry.

He did it silently, but his broad shoulders shook, and his father said nothing.

It was Abby's father who had done the terrible thing. It was Doc who was betraying him. It was Rex's dad who was doing it, too. Mitch couldn't tell his best friends what their fathers had done without having that horror hanging between them for the rest of their lives. And no matter how much Abby and Rex cared about him, who were they going to believe? Were they going to believe him, or their own fathers, whom they had never had any reason to doubt? Would anybody, even Mitch's own parents, ever believe him over the word of those two men? With a feeling of utter hopelessness, Mitch thought he knew the answer to that one: *No.*

I'm never going to marry Abby . . .

How could she ever choose between him and her own father? How could he ever marry into a family about which he knew such a terrible thing? Her father would never let him back in. Which didn't matter, because he would never trust Quentin Reynolds again.

It was at that moment that Mitch realized he was never coming home.

"Dad," he said, after a few miles had passed. "Maybe they killed her. Or . . . Patrick was there. Maybe Patrick killed her and they're covering up for him. Maybe she wasn't really dead when they brought her in. Maybe Doc killed her when he hit her."

"Mitch! They wouldn't have done something like that!"

"Right. They'd accuse me of it, but they're such nice guys, they'd never—"

"Be quiet, Mitch."

"What *happened* to her, Dad?"

"I don't know."

Later, after still more miles, Mitch said, "What are they covering up?"

His father shot him a glance. "You're going to have to forget about it."

"Forget!" He was young, he was overwhelmed by events, he was confused, he was frightened, he was in despair, but he was clear about one thing. *Forget?* He would never forget, and he would never, ever forgive.

*   *   *

In his second semester at Grinnell College in Iowa, after he hadn't gone home for Thanksgiving, hadn't gone home for Christmas, hadn't gone home at the semester break, he got a letter from his mother that led him to understand that she and his father had not broken off their friendships with the Reynolds and Shellenbergers.

Life in Small Plains was continuing as before, but without him.

Such bitterness began to grow in Mitch that he stopped writing to her, refused his parents' calls, took only their continuing checks for as long as they were willing to pay them. For most of his undergraduate years, he was more lonely and bitter than he had ever dreamed it was possible to be.

When his mother sent him photographs of the baby boy they had adopted—"Jeffrey Allen," she wrote—he knew whom they had chosen to believe. He didn't know exactly what they thought he had done, but he knew he had been replaced, as if he had never lived in their house as their son, as if he had never been.

Chapter Ten

May 31, 2004

On the Memorial Day after Nadine Newquist died, Verna Shellenberger went out early to visit the Virgin's grave.

Nadine had been dead four months by then, but that wasn't what
drew Rex's mother to the cemetery. At that hour of the morning, just
before 6:00 A.M., mist lay on the prairie like a beautiful, graceful, dangerous gift that the chilly night had left behind for the morning. In
the low places, the mist thickened to fog that swirled in her headlights
like smoke from the pipes of a Pawnee ghost. Or Shawnee. Or
Potawatomi. Verna could never remember which tribes had roamed
these hunting grounds. Over the years of their childhood, her boys
had collected a couple dozen arrowheads from high points in pastures, where warriors had lost them. But history wasn't Verna's strong
suit, as she was the first to confess when watching the television
show, *Jeopardy!* Her subjects were cooking, cleaning, raising boys, and
putting up with husbands. Or, rather, husband. "I majored in family," she liked to say when she felt inferior for her lack of a college degree. "You don't need a fancy degree to get dinner on the table every
night for forty years."

Privately, she wished she had somehow managed to take a few college courses.

Just because she didn't know any history didn't mean she couldn't learn it, she thought.

Or repeat it, she also thought, with a kind of gloomy optimism.

She had to drive with great care to remain safely on her side of the highway, which only added to her rising anxiety. It was worry that had pulled her out of a restless sleep and put her in her car so early in the morning.

There were long stretches where her headlights blinded her in the fog, and it was only the presence of the yellow line that pulled her along to the cemetery. She prayed no crazy rancher was trying to cross the highway with his cows in this weather. She'd known a few that crazy, but most of them had gone out of business—or died—by now. Still, cows and the men who herded them were unpredictable. She knew something about that, too, if she did say so. If a cowboy on a horse suddenly loomed in front of her in the fog, she wouldn't be surprised. She'd be horrified, because she'd be bound to hit them with her van, but not all that surprised.

With a feeling of relief for having survived the ride, Verna eventually pulled through the cemetery gate.

Normally, she would never have come on a Memorial Day when half the county would show up with their bouquets of real or plastic flowers. Verna lived close enough so that if she wanted to visit graves, she could drop by anytime. It was only because she was feeling desperate that she was here on this day, out of all the days in the year. She had come early, for privacy, and hoped nobody saw her.

Verna threaded her car halfway up the road that led to the top of the hill. There, she pulled over to the side, parked, and got out. She felt a little shaky and out of breath, and had to pause a moment, with her hand on the side of the car, to steady herself before going on.

If she were a kid, she thought, as she started walking onto the grass, she'd feel spooked at being in a cemetery in a fog like this, where she couldn't see three rows of tombstones ahead of her. But she figured she was too old to be scared by mere death. She had seen too much of it, between the animals and the friends.

The grass smelled newly mown; the air was damp against her skin.

Verna paused by a neat gravestone to say hello to one of them, her old friend Margie Reynolds.

"Hi, Margie." She cleared her throat and folded her hands together at her waist. "You'll be pleased to hear that Ellen is doing her usual great job as mayor. That girl is going to be governor some day, I swear. Quentin's okay, I guess, but we hardly see him anymore. He seems to keep busy with his medicine, and not much else, as far as I can tell. I wish I could tell you that Abby has fallen sensibly in love with my Rex, and that they are going to get married, and that they're planning to have grandbabies for you and me, but you'd never believe me, if I tried to put that one over on you." Verna sighed. Neither of her sons, not Patrick nor Rex, had married yet. "By the time I get grand-children, Margie, I'll be so old they'll think I'm already dead." She purposely avoided telling her late friend about certain recent activities between her *older* son and Margie's younger daughter, not wishing Margie to roll uncomfortably in her grave.

"Have you seen Nadine yet?" she inquired. "You know she's here, right?"

Verna looked around, aware that she'd sound like a nut to anybody who heard her.

If the fog had ears, or there was anybody over the hill, she couldn't see them.

"Well, I'll see you later, honey," she told Margie Reynolds. She started to walk away, but then turned back, and said, in a voice that suddenly trembled, "I still miss you. You oughtn't to have gone so soon."

Ellen and Abby's mom had been only fifty-eight when the cancer took her.

Next, Verna paid her respects to the more recently buried Nadine Newquist.

"I hope you're back in your right mind again, Nadine," she said, rather more sharply than she had intended to speak. She told herself it was only because she was trying to pull herself together and get the shakiness out of her voice. "I'm glad you're out of your suffering, but I'm sorry you had to go that way." Reluctantly, she dredged up an insincere sentiment, just so she wouldn't hurt anybody's feelings. "I miss you, too." *Like hell,* she thought, giving up all pretense of feeling the same about Nadine as she had felt about Margie. It was almost shocking what a relief it was not to have to endure Nadine's barbed wit anymore. If anybody in the world missed that, then Verna was a monkey's uncle. "Tom seemed kind of lost for a while without you," she lied. The judge seemed like a man with a heavy burden lifted, as did many relatives of Alzheimer's victims after their loved ones died. She and Nathan had Tom over for dinner once a week, and it was good to hear the big man laugh again.

"It's a good thing that he's got Jeff to take care of."

As if he ever does, Verna thought, but also didn't say. No use worrying dead people.

Briskly enough to be almost rude, Verna walked on toward the real goal of her morning.

On this day, with the snow long gone, the simple gravestone stood fully revealed: *Peace Be Unto You, 1987.* While Verna was in the hospital in Emporia, Nadine and Margie had led the community drive to raise money for the girl's burial and stone. Then Nadine had topped off the donations with enough extra funds to give her bragging rights to the available virtue. But it was a nice stone, with a hint of pink in its color. The McLaughlins, who owned the funeral parlor and the cemetery, had donated one of the very last plots in the picturesque old part, so there could be a real headstone, and not just a nondescript marker. That's what everybody had wanted—something that stood tall and substantial, as if to verify that even an unidentified girl had once been real. Everybody had cared, was how Verna remembered it. Everybody had felt awful about what had happened to the girl, and even worse about the idea that nobody had claimed her. The girl had died a stranger among strangers, and so the kindhearted strangers had buried her. That's how Verna was determined to remember it. History wasn't her strong suit, which meant she could write it any way she chose.

"Good morning," she said, formally, to the gravestone.

"I'm Verna Shellenberger, in case you don't remember me." Verna had made a few previous trips to the grave, in years past. "It was my husband and boys who found you. I'm awfully sorry about what happened to you, though I expect that's long gone from your mind by now. Probably even forgiven, too," she added, hopefully.

"The reason I'm here is to ask you to help my Nathan. I know he doesn't deserve it. I know all about that. But he's in constant pain now, from the arthritis. It's got him so crippled up he can barely leave his bed some days, and it just kills me to see him like that. The only pleasure he ever gets is when he goes to town to have lunch with Quentin and Tom. I know that Harmony Watson said you cured her baby's colic, and Frank Allison is convinced you made his shingles go away. He was in awful pain, too. And now he's just fine."

Verna wondered if she should kneel and fold her hands, as in prayer.

She decided that wasn't necessary, and besides, the ground was damp.

"If you can find it in your heart to help Nathan, I'd be so grateful. I know this probably doesn't work tit for tat. Nobody's ever said you require payment of any kind." Too late, Verna realized she probably should have brought flowers, just out of respect. "But I'd be glad to help out somebody else, if you let me know if there's anything you want me to do. Not as payment. I don't mean to insult you. Just as, well, a kindness in return for what you might do."

Tears sprang to Verna's eyes. Her husband was only sixty-five, but he moved like a ninety-year-old man. It wasn't only that she felt sorry for him, but also that it was hard to live with somebody who was in as much pain as Nathan was, and who was as bad-tempered as he could get when the pain got the worst. The doctors had said he could live a normal life span with this misery, which meant that she could live another thirty years of keeping company with his miserable self, too. The thought of it made her envy her departed friends.

The night before Nathan had actually cried from pain, and she had cried with him.

It had frightened Verna, and sent her out early on this morning to beg.

"Please," she said to the silent grave. *Please, please, please.*

Maybe it was just the fact of saying it out loud to somebody, or maybe it was something else, but Verna was suddenly swept by a wave of peace such as she hadn't felt in years. Her muscles, her internal organs, her very bones relaxed. It was wonderful, a feeling Verna wished she could keep forever. Even if her wish for Nathan never came true, at least she'd had this moment of unexpected, blissful peace of mind and heart.

"Thank you," she whispered to the Virgin.

When Verna turned to leave, she discovered that while she had been concentrating on her errand, the mist had lifted, revealing a bit of sunshine, stretches of green grass, rows of gravestones . . . and the fact that she wasn't alone, after all.

●   ●   ●

"Oh!" Verna exclaimed as a young woman in blue jeans and a green T-shirt stepped out of the fog. Her hands went to her heart, in shock. "Abby!"

"Verna, I'm sorry! I didn't mean to scare you."

"What are you *doing* here so early?"

"Memorial Day," Abby explained. Her T-shirt had white letters above her left breast: *Abby's Lawn & Landscape.* "Gotta have it looking its best. What are *you* doing here so early?"

"Paying my respects," Verna hedged, without admitting to whom. "I didn't see your truck."

"I parked behind the maintenance shed."

It was only then that Verna noticed there were clippers dangling from Abby's gloved hands, and now the fog also revealed a black plastic yard waste bag behind her. "How long have you been here? Did you hear me talking to myself like an idiot?"

"I've been here awhile." Abby gave her an apologetic smile. "I came to get some last-minute work done, but then I couldn't see a damned thing in the fog. So I was just sitting on a gravestone, waiting for the fog to go away, when you came up. I couldn't see it was you, and I didn't want to scare whoever it was, so I just kept quiet. By the time I realized it was you it was too late to say anything." She made an embarrassed grimace and laughed a little. "I was kind of hoping you'd leave and never know I was here."

"What did you hear me say?"

"Oh, nothing! Really. Not much. But . . . I'm so sorry that Nathan is having such a hard time." Abby had taken to calling her parents' friends by their first names when they encouraged it, which Verna Shellenberger did. Quickly, as if she just wanted to be tactful and change the subject, Abby said, "Verna, who do you think she is?"

It was impossible for Verna to pretend that she didn't know who Abby was talking about. Abby had pointed the tips of her grass clippers straight at the tombstone.

Verna shook her head, afraid to say anything.

"What was it like, that night they found her, Verna?"

"What was it like?" The older woman looked at the grave rather than into Abby's frank blue eyes. She had always loved Abby like a daughter, but at this moment she wished the earth would open up and swallow one of them so she didn't have to answer questions like that from a girl she didn't want to lie to. "What do you mean, what was it like?"

"I mean . . . what do you remember about that night? Did Nathan tell you about finding her, or did Rex? Was it awful for Rex? I mean, he was so young . . ."

"It was pretty bad," Verna admitted. "I was sick that night . . . you wouldn't remember this, but I had pneumonia and even went to the hospital the next day . . . and Rex came in and sat on the edge of my bed and told me they'd found . . . a girl's body in the snow."

"I thought I heard you tell . . . her . . . just now that your 'boys' found her."

Verna's breath stopped when she heard those words come out of Abby's mouth.

"No, not both of them. Patrick wasn't even home," she stammered. "It was just the one of them, it was just Rex and his dad, that was enough, believe me."

"Why did you say that Nathan doesn't deserve her help?"

A chill of fear swept through Verna, so that when she breathed again, her body shivered.

It was obvious that Abby had heard every word she'd said, and now the girl was unnervingly curious about it. *Just like her mother,* Verna thought. Margie Reynolds had been bright and curious about the world, and so were her daughters. The Reynolds women liked to collect facts, even from people who were chary with them.

She fought to keep eye contact with Abby, to let nothing of the sick dread she was feeling on the inside show on her face. "Just that he's an ornery old cuss," Verna said, with a laugh that she hoped didn't sound as forced as it felt coming up from inside of her. "You know Nathan, Abby. If he even knew I had come out here to ask for help from a ghost, he'd disown me. That's all I meant, that he wouldn't even be grateful if she helped him."

Abby smiled and seemed to accept it. They were both quiet for a moment, and then Abby said, "Do you really think she cures people?"

Verna felt suddenly exhausted. "I don't know."

"I guess it doesn't hurt to ask."

"No," Verna said, in a near-whisper. "I hope it doesn't."

"I wonder if I knew her."

Verna's head jerked up and she stared at Abby. "What?"

Abby wasn't looking at her, but was frowning toward the grave. "I wasn't paying attention, Verna. I was all swept up in Mitch leaving. But I've been thinking about that night, and how she . . ." Abby nodded toward the grave. ". . . was in my *house* that night." She shivered visibly enough for Verna to see it. "My own father saw her all beat up like that. It must have been terrible for Dad, too, but we've never even talked about it."

"Abby, I don't think you ought to talk to your dad about that."

Abby looked up at her, with a puzzled expression. "Why not? Verna, sometimes it seems like everything in the world changed that night, or at least everything in my world. It wasn't just that Mitch left the next day. It was that my dad was never the same, either. It was like he withdrew and never came back to us again."

"Well, it was . . . upsetting, Abby. Why would you want to make him remember?"

"But I've never even asked him about it. I've never told him I care about how it affected him. Maybe if I did, he'd open up and . . ."

"People don't need to open up," Verna said, with a feeling of desperation that went even deeper than what she'd felt in coming to the grave. "That's just psychology stuff. People need to get over things and go on with their lives . . ."

Abby smiled at her, a sweet smile that told Verna that she was being humored.

"Okay," Abby said in a pacifying kind of way. "Maybe I'd better get on with trimming around the headstones."

"And I've got to get back to fix breakfast for Nathan." Verna paused before turning to go. After a moment's hesitation, a moment in which she told herself it would probably be better if she didn't say anything else, she said, "Why are you so interested in the Virgin *now,* Abby? I've never heard you ask about her before. What's different now from any time during the past seventeen years?"

She watched Abby take a deep breath and let it out like a sigh.

"When Rex and I found Nadine? It was like something inside of me woke up, Verna. It's like I've been asleep all these years, not even realizing how much other people were affected by . . . her death. It just seems like it's way past time for me to think about somebody besides myself. I never even thought much about *her.*" Abby nodded toward the Virgin's grave. "She was young. She could have been somebody I'd seen, or maybe I'd even met her. And I never even thought much about her, I was so wrapped up in myself."

"I'm sure you didn't know her. Nobody around here knew her."

"How can you be sure, Verna, if we don't know who she was?"

Verna thought Abby Reynolds was one of the least selfish girls she'd ever known, so she didn't understand at all what Abby meant about thinking of people other than herself. Verna only understood that if Abby was waking up to that crime, the way she had just said she was, then Verna needed to persuade her to go right back to sleep.

"The best thing you can do for her is to let her rest in peace."

Abby gave her a funny look. "But nobody lets her rest in peace, Verna. Not even you. Everybody wants something from her. And it just seems to me that it's about time we all gave something back to her."

"What?" Verna's heart was pounding. "We gave her a funeral, Abby. And this grave, and that headstone. People cared, they really did. We still do. But what can we possibly give her now?"

"We can give her her name back," Abby said, in a firm voice that frightened Verna more than any specter walking out of the fog ever could. When either of the Reynolds sisters made up their minds to do something, it tended to get done, come hell or high water. Ellen had wanted to become mayor, and it happened. Abby had decided to run a landscaping business, and she did it. Verna forced herself to pay attention to Abby's next words, over the deafening pounding of her own blood in her ears. "We can find out who she was, or at least we can try again. There's new technology. Rex will know. There have to be things he can do now that Nathan couldn't do back then."

"Abby, *don't* . . ."

But Abby had bent down to clip a handful of grass that her mowers had missed. She didn't give any indication of having heard Verna's words, or of recognizing them as the warning they were. Suddenly the smell of the new-mown grass threatened to rise up and suffocate Verna; her chest felt tight, as if she was having an allergic reaction, or even a heart attack. She grabbed the front of her dress with her right hand, but dropped it hastily when Abby stood back up and looked at her again.

"Don't what?"

"Don't . . ." Desperately, Verna searched her mind for a substitute to what she was really thinking. ". . . forget to come by soon. I'm making blueberry pie today."

Abby grinned. "I would never forget such a thing."

After a few moments, Verna slipped away with a quiet "Bye," and a repeat of her invitation to drop by soon. When she reached her car, she turned to look back and saw that Abby was staring at her.

Abby waved. After a moment's hesitation Verna waved back.

•　•　•

Abby knelt on the damp grass, clippers in hand, as her old friend's mother, and her current boyfriend's mother, drove away. People could be so resistant to change, she thought with both fondness and irritation, even to good changes. What possible harm could it do to finally put a name on a grave? She looked up in time to see Verna turn onto the highway. Rex's mom looked small behind the wheel of her car, and plump in a way that reminded Abby of a dozen other local women. On this morning, Verna was wearing one of the A-line, cotton shirtwaists she favored, a short-sleeved, print dress belted at her waist that made her plumpness blossom below the belt and above it. It was a style that made her upper arms look full and fleshy, and gave her a pale appearance that belied her actual physical strength. Abby knew that Verna Shellenberger could lift a calf or toss a hay bale across a fence, if she wanted to.

When Abby couldn't see Verna's car anymore, she stood up and scanned the horizon.

She could never look out over such a span of prairie without thinking about the Indians who used to live there. Her mother, who had loved facts and dates and history, had made her aware of them from the time she was old enough to look for arrowheads in the dirt. And now Abby found herself thinking about another time and another crime that nobody talked about, just like Verna Shellenberger didn't seem to want to talk to her about the murder of the Virgin.

Once, the Osage and Kansa tribes had roamed forty-five million acres, including the patch of ground on which she stood. They had shared it with thirty to seventy-five million bison. If she used her imagination, she could almost hear the pounding hooves and see the dark flood of animals pouring over the fields. But the Indians had been chased and cheated down to Oklahoma, including a forced exodus in 1873. The bison had been killed. Abby had friends who owned a bison ranch, and she had toured it, had stared into the fierce eyes of an old bison bull. In search of native grasses to plant and sell, she had also walked onto the land of Potawatomi, Iowa, and Kickapoo reservations that remained in the state. She had a natural affinity for underdogs, and she thought she had at least some small sense of what it must be like to feel helpless in the path of history. She couldn't solve those million crimes, but she thought that maybe she could help solve one crime.

On her way out of the cemetery, Abby whispered a few words to her mother, and then she touched the Virgin's gravestone.

"If you'll tell me who you are," she promised the dead girl, "I'll make sure that everybody knows your name."

Chapter Eleven

After finishing her touch-up work for the cemetery, Abby drove home again, feeling satisfied with her work there and full of resolve about renewing the search for the Virgin's identity.

Even though it was a holiday, there was still plenty of work for her to do on her own if she wanted to. Flowers to transplant from ground to pots. Beds to dig and fertilize. Orders to process and advertising to plan. But first she walked back into her bedroom, just in time to find Patrick Shellenberger sitting on the edge of her bed pulling one of his socks on. He had on his jeans, but no shirt. The sight of his broad cowboy shoulders and biceps gave her a flutter she wished they didn't.

"Where'd you go?" he asked her, looking up.

"Cemetery."

"You'd rather go to a cemetery than wake up with me?"

She smiled at him. "Not a whole lot of difference between the two. You were sleeping like the dead."

Patrick laughed.

"I saw your mother," she said, picking up his other sock and handing it to him.

He took the sock but then tossed it over his shoulder and reached for her. With his arms around her waist, Abby sat down, straddling his legs, facing him so their noses were mere inches apart.

"Where?" Patrick asked her, as his hands began to move toward her chest.

"Umm. At the cemetery. She was visiting graves."

Patrick made a face and faked a shudder. "Whatever turns you on."

"Nice way to talk about your own mother."

He leaned forward to kiss her, and murmured into her lips, "I know what would make my mother happy."

"Hmm? What?"

"Marry me."

"*Marry* you?" Abby reared back and nearly tumbled off his knees. He grabbed her to keep her from falling, and she stared at him. "I barely even let you sleep here! Why in the world would I want to marry you?"

"Because it makes sense for both of us."

"It only makes sense for *you*, Patrick." She got off his knees, batting his hands away when he tried to hold her there, stepped a safe distance away, and wagged a finger at him. "I know what you're up to. You want to rehabilitate yourself, and you think I'm step two in your plan."

Patrick grinned at her. "Not really. I'd say, more like step six. No offense."

"Oh, believe me"—Abby rolled her eyes at him for effect—"when I say, none taken."

She turned and walked out of the room.

"Hey, where are you going? I just proposed to you!"

Patrick got up, grabbed the sock he'd tossed aside, and his shirt and his cowboy boots, and followed her into her kitchen.

"I'm serious, Abby!"

"You're seriously crazy," she retorted, without even turning around.

It was still early, not quite 7:30, and the sun was only gently coming in through her white cotton curtains. She and Patrick were both at the start of the busiest seasons in their respective jobs. For Patrick, on most mornings when he woke up at her house, it meant riding back out to his family's ranch to round up cattle for weaning, vaccinations, spraying, or whatever other spring work needed doing. For Abby, it meant strolling a few yards from her house to her plant nursery. Usually, some of her employees would be driving out to do yard work or plantings for the city, for businesses, or for private residences. A couple of others would stay at the nursery with Abby, to sell the annuals, perennials, seed, fertilizers, pots, saplings, shrubs, and other assorted gardening supplies she stocked there and even sold online.

But this day, a holiday, Patrick was hanging around.

"Okay, let's back up a minute," he said. "You said I've got a plan to rehabilitate myself and you're supposedly one of the steps in this grand plan of mine. So if that's true, then what was step one?"

Abby turned to study him.

Patrick Shellenberger, older brother of her friend Rex, teasing bane of her childhood and now an unexpected swain, had set his boots down, tossed his shirt and sock onto a chair, and leaned his back against the kitchen doorsill, so that he was suddenly all tousled hair, bare chest, and blue eyes.

"Just out of curiosity," he added, raising his eyebrows, which gave him an innocent appearance that didn't fool her for a moment.

"Well," she said, after giving it a bit of thought, "I'd say that step one must have been coming home and taking over the ranch so your dad could quit working."

When he nodded to indicate she'd guessed right, Abby said, "If step two isn't me, what is it?"

"Working hard," he told her, promptly. "Making a go of it."

"Uh." Abby voice took on a grudging tone that suggested she had to admit he had succeeded in both of those steps, thus far. "Step three?"

"Not drinking, and making sure everybody knows I'm not."

"And step four?"

"Not getting arrested for anything."

Abby shook her head in wonder. "I can't believe I am actually having a conversation with a man with such a plan. Have I really come to this?"

Patrick laughed as he pushed himself off the doorsill and stood up straight. Suddenly the room seemed much smaller, and Abby instinctively stepped back a little. Patrick reached for the ceiling, stretching luxuriously from his bare toes to his long, tanned fingers, while she watched him.

His jeans slipped down on his hips, revealing the lighter skin where the sun didn't shine.

He had a great laugh, Abby had to admit, and a sexy, husky voice, and broad shoulders and those blue eyes and in spite of her defenses against him, now and then her body responded to that laugh and those hands in a way that suggested it had a mind of its own. Standing in front of him, Abby concentrated hard on giving none of those feelings away to him. Patrick had taken her to supper in Council Grove the night before, and then he had driven her around his family's ranch to show her the new cattle pens and other improvements he had been installing there. It had been a beautiful spring night and he'd been sweet to her, especially when he'd nicely asked if he could stay, rather than go home to his childhood bedroom at his parents' house.

Patrick shook off his stretch and stuck his thumbs in the belt loops at the sides of his jeans. Staring straight at her, he continued his recitation, saying, "Step five was that I would completely foil everybody's expectations, and *not* date a skank."

"Not drink, not get arrested, not date a skank." Abby ticked the points off on the fingers of her right hand. "Gee, how can any woman resist you?" She gave him a prim look. "I hate the word skank."

"Why?" Patrick looked honestly baffled.

"Why?" She boggled at him, which made him grin again. "If you have to ask, you'll never understand, so just stop using it, okay? You could try being nice, you know."

"I'm nice to *you,* aren't I?"

"Yeah, but you want something from me."

"I certainly do," he leered at her.

Before she could move out of his way, Patrick darted forward, grabbed her, and started tugging her backward with him.

"Let me go! I've got to feed the birds, Patrick."

She not only had a business to run, but also a porch full of pet birds to tend.

Instead of releasing her, Patrick pulled her closer, and leaned down to kiss her again.

"See, Abby?" He nibbled around her eyebrows, kissed her down her nose, and landed softly on her lips. "We have fun together. We're good together. We need each other. I need you to make me look good. You need me, because, frankly"—Patrick smirked right into her mouth—"with your history, who the hell else will have you?"

"My *history?*" Abby pulled away from him. "What do you mean, my *history?*"

He shrugged, all innocence again. "You chase your first love clear out of town so he never comes back. You never date anybody longer than a few months. You can't find another man . . ."

"You're a fine one to talk about somebody's history!"

Abby placed her palms against his bare chest and shoved him away.

"Exactly!" he said, as she stomped away from him. "My point exactly! We're made for each other. Hey, Abs, you got a clean towel for me? I'm going to take a shower."

"Linen closet," she said, "where they always are if you weren't too lazy to look for them yourself." And then on nothing but a wild impulse, and seemingly out of the blue, Abby blurted, "Patrick, what was it like that night you found the dead girl?"

He blinked, frowned, and then he said, casually, and over his shoulder as he walked to the shower, as if it was no big deal, "What, did Rex tell you I was home that night? Nobody was supposed to know that. What do you *think* it was like? It sucked. I'd just as soon not do it again, thanks."

. . .

Abby stared after him, at the space he had occupied, with her mouth open.

She had expected him to ask her where she'd gotten such a crazy idea. She had never expected him to confirm it! Her question had been all bluff. She had only asked it because she had been confused by what she had overheard in the cemetery that morning. Especially because she remembered something that Rex had said the day they found Nadine Newquist. Or rather, something he had seemed about to say, but then didn't. *"My dad and . . . my dad was there, too."*

She didn't know why that had stuck in her mind, but it had resurfaced because of Verna's . . . Verna's *what?* Slip of the tongue? Verna's senior moment of forgetfulness? Verna's lie?

But Abby had never expected Patrick to essentially confirm that Verna really *had* said "boys," plural. And now that Abby had that information, she didn't know what to think about it. Why did everybody think it was only Rex and Nathan who had found the girl, when Patrick had actually been there, too? And why, for heaven's sake, had Verna lied to her about it?

Abby realized she was fuzzier on the facts than she had ever known.

She hadn't paid much attention at the time. Even later, through all the years, she had tended to avoid listening to any discussions about it, because it brought up her own unhappy memories.

Maybe everybody else didn't have some facts wrong; maybe just she did.

That made more sense to her, and yet . . .

She felt uneasy, without even knowing precisely why.

Feeling as if the fog had followed her home, Abby walked over to her coffeepot to pour out the dregs of her first pot of the morning and make a fresh one so that Patrick wouldn't have to drink sludge when he got out of his shower.

She and Patrick had been seeing each other for three months. It had taken him almost that long to get her to go out with him at all, and she thought that if there had been one other available man to date in town, she never would have. His own brother didn't approve. Her friends didn't like it. But what was she supposed to do? Move to a city where there were more men? Sit home all her life?

As Patrick took his shower, Abby put the other matter out of her mind for the time being. And anyway, it was all too easy to find another subject, such as Patrick, to obsess about. She berated herself for having given in to the unfair torture of being thirty-three years old, unmarried, with no good prospects, living in an impossibly small town, and horny.

On the other hand, he could make her laugh.

Suddenly she ran back into her bedroom and then over to the door of her bathroom. She opened it and called in to him in the shower.

"Patrick! You say you want to marry me. Do you love me?"

"I could!" he yelled back at her, over the sound of the water running.

There, she thought. It was things he said—like that—that made her smile and shake her head over him, regardless of everything else. At least he was honest in his way. Or maybe "blunt" was a better word for it. Infuriating and blunt. He was also really good looking, if you liked them a little tough. Good in the sack. There was that, there was definitely that. And, yes, sometimes he was fun to be with, in an adolescent kind of way. But marry Patrick Shellenberger, a man who had a hell of a wild reputation to rehabilitate, if he could ever do it at all?

Rex would kill her if she ever did such a stupid thing. She'd have to be really desperate to ever think of marrying Patrick.

One more time, she yelled at him. "*Why* do you want to rehabilitate yourself, Patrick? What's in it for you?"

From the shower, he started singing, "Mandy" at the top of his lungs.

•　•　•

When he came back into the kitchen, smelling fresh and clean even though he'd had to put on yesterday's clothes, he accepted a mug of black coffee from her and said, "That thing about me being home that night? When we found the girl? How long have you known about that?"

"I don't know," she equivocated, with a little shrug.

"Who else knows?"

"Beats me."

"Well, keep it quiet, okay?"

"Why isn't anybody supposed to know, Patrick?"

He gave her a crooked, charming smile. "Because yours truly had just flunked out of K-State, that's why I was home."

"I didn't know you flunked out of K-State!"

"Exactly." He grinned. "My parents were ashamed of me. My dad was ready to kill me. Hell, I wasn't all that proud of it myself. Everybody was supposed to think I left because I didn't like it."

"Okay. My lips are sealed," she told him.

He pressed his mouth against hers. "Now they are," he murmured, and then he backed away and sat down in a kitchen chair to finish dressing.

He reached for one of his boots and started to pull it on.

"Goddammit!"

Abby whirled around from where she had begun to chop fresh fruit at the sink. "What?"

One of his brown boots dangled from his right hand. "They did it again! Your goddamn birds shit in my boots again!" He looked furious enough to wring somebody's neck, either hers or her birds. "Look at this!"

He turned the boot so she could see a river of white down the inside of it.

Somebody had obviously perched on the edge of it and then let loose.

"Oh, Patrick, I'm sorry," she said, and tried hard not to laugh.

"It's not funny, goddammit! Your birds hate me, Abby."

She would have tried to deny it, but it was so obviously true. Her gray conure, her peach-faced South African lovebird, and her South American parrot all hated Patrick with a loathing that in another species might have been called venom. They screamed whenever he appeared, unless they were in their cages covered by sheets. They bit him if he got close enough to nip. And they shit on his belongings every chance they got.

"That's it," he said, staring grimly at her. "I can't take it anymore."

"Oh, come on, Patrick. Those boots have seen more cow shit than the inside of a barn. Give it to me. I'll clean it up."

He handed her the boot and she washed it out with paper towels. But when she gave it back to him, he said, "Those birds have got to go."

"What?"

"I mean it, Abby. It's them or me."

"Oh, really?" She narrowed her eyes at him, and matched his ominous tone. "Well, then, don't let their cage doors hit you on your way out, Patrick!"

"I'm going to kill those birds one of these days."

He wasn't joking and she didn't laugh. This was the other Patrick, the Patrick she didn't like, and never had, the one she remembered from when he was Rex's hateful, sarcastic, older brother who had often teased her until she cried. Every now and then, that Patrick surfaced again, and she couldn't stand him. Not only that, but she felt afraid of him, the way she had when she was six and he was ten, and for a lot of years after that. He had gone away *that* Patrick, and returned a nicer guy. But not always. And she knew that he hated the birds every bit as much as they hated him. "You ever touch them," she said in a low, warning tone, "and I'll have *your* ass in a cage."

He glared at her, then grabbed his boots and stomped heavily out of the kitchen and onto the porch at the side of it, hurrying past the big covered cage where the three birds spent their nights. Before she heard the screen door slam, she heard him mutter hatefully to her covered pets, "Fried chicken! Chicken cacciatore! Duck l'orange!"

She couldn't help it, she had to laugh again. It was the duck l'orange that did it.

Abby realized full well that there was a not-very-hidden violence in Patrick. The couple of nights he'd spent in jail when he was younger had been because of fighting, after too many beers. If he hadn't had a sheriff for a father there might even have been more than those couple of nights behind bars. That streak of his had always been there, as long as she could remember. But it was hard to take seriously when he said things like "chicken cacciatore"—things he knew would make her laugh.

Abby ran after him, her bare feet picking up birdseed from the floor of the porch as she hurried to fling open the screen door. "Patrick!" she yelled at his departing back. "Don't forget to bring me those bales of hay you promised me!"

Patrick didn't turn around, but he did raise an arm to indicate he'd heard her.

When he didn't also raise a third finger, Abby grinned, and took it to mean, "Okay."

*　　*　　*

From under the cover, harsh squawks grabbed her attention.

With coos of greeting she lifted the covers off the spacious cage where her birds, J.D., Lovey, and Gracie spent their nights. When Abby had added two more birds to her menagerie, long after she stole J.D. from the Newquists, she found that it helped people to remember which was which if she called them something that sounded like the kind of bird they were. So the little gray conure was Gracie and the multicolored little lovebird was Lovey. Her customers got a kick out of seeing the birds on her porch in warm weather and often ran over to tap on the screens and chat with them.

"So which one of you guys shit in Patrick's boot, huh?"

"Hello!" said Gracie, offering her only word.

The three of them hitched rides on her arms and shoulders for the trip back into the kitchen for breakfast. On the way, she noticed something Patrick had missed in his rush to leave her house. "Hey, he forgot his sunglasses, guys." The shades sat on the kitchen table where he had left them. She knew he was going to be pissed as soon as he turned east into the rising sun and had to squint to see the highway.

"Serves him right," she told the birds, "for talking mean about you."

As she distributed fruits and nuts into their bowls—while eating almost as much as she gave them—Abby complained, "Do you know what that big jerk said to me? He said I should marry him because nobody else would want me, can you believe that?"

She carried the birds and bowls out to her screened-in porch so they could eat atop their perches. Every spring, she brought over tropical plants from her nursery, hung mirrors and toys from the rafters, and turned the porch into an aviary for them.

"Next time?" she told the birds, feeling angry at him all over again. "Aim for both boots."

Chapter Twelve

Memorial Day. All sorts of people went home for Memorial Day.

That's what Mitch Newquist told himself as he stood with one hand on the gas pump and his other hand propped on the side of his Saab. As gasoline poured into the tank, he stared at a highway marker at the entrance to an interstate only a few dozen yards away, and tried to make up his mind. Go? Not go?

"Your mother passed away yesterday, Mitch," was how the phone call from his father had begun. That had been way back at the end of January. It was now Memorial Day, the last day of May. *"She got confused and wandered out into the blizzard last night. Rex Shellenberger and Abby Reynolds found her in the cemetery behind our house. She froze to death. I thought you'd want to know."*

Mitch hadn't known whether to laugh or cry. His mother was dead, which ought to produce tears, he supposed. His father had "thought you'd want to know." Which was almost as "funny" as his dad using Rex and Abby's last names, as if Mitch wouldn't have recognized them otherwise.

He had supposed, as he had stood in his house holding his telephone and not saying anything, that "funny" was the wrong word to use to describe his father's approach to him, but he was damned if he could think of the right one. Ironic? Gratuitous? Finally, he landed on "cruel," which seemed—and felt—accurate.

"What was she doing out in the snow?" he asked his father.

"One of the damned nurses left the back door unlocked."

"I'm sorry. When is the funeral?"

"Tuesday. You think you'll come?"

"I don't know, Dad. I'll think about it."

"If you have to think about it," his father said, sounding suddenly cold and furious, "then don't bother coming. She was your mother, for heaven's sake."

Mitch stood alone in his house and shook his head over the old man's words to him. It was unbelievable. Feeling the old bitter resentment and fury rise, he retorted with all the heat that had been missing from his father's tone. "You don't think there's anything to think about, Dad? Nothing at all to consider before I come back? Doc will be at her funeral, won't he? And Nathan. You seriously think there's no good reason to think about anything before I just show up there?"

"Bygones," his father shot back at him.

"*Bygones?*" Mitch laughed, a loud, bitter bark of laughter. "You've got to be kidding me. Those two sons a bitches lied about me. They were going to accuse me of murder. They ruined my life, or would have if I had let them do it, and neither you nor my mother raised a hand to help me defend myself against them."

"What are you talking about? We got you out of town!"

"*Ran* me out of town, you mean."

"We put you in a good school, we saw to your every need . . ."

"Stop. Just stop. Do you really think I can just sail back into town and let bygones be *bygones*?"

"Do as you please, Mitch," his father said, and hung up on him.

When he called his father back to say he wasn't going, Mitch had not felt any need to explain his decision. He didn't tell the old man that he had realized that if he went back after all these years he would become the center of attention instead of the woman whose funeral it was. Mitch had given his mother the only measure of respect he knew she would appreciate: He had allowed her funeral to be all about her. And he had decided he would drive down on the next Memorial Day to see the grave, when nobody was expecting him, and he would stay out of everybody's way, and there wouldn't be any fuss.

At least, that was the plan.

He was halfway to fulfilling it. More than halfway, actually, since he stood at the intersection of I-70 and Highway 177. To the north was Manhattan, to the west lay Denver, and toward the east was Kansas City, where he had lived for the past seven years. Small Plains was straight south from where he stood. If he remembered correctly, the cemetery was on 177 north of town. He could run in, take a look, and then get right back in his car and head home without even having to drive through Small Plains. There were only a few more miles to go to get there, and then he'd be done with it. But what was the point of this trip, he asked himself for the hundredth time? Hell, he wasn't even taking flowers, because he didn't want to leave any sign he'd been there. Whether or not he visited made no difference to his mother now, and maybe had never made any difference to her. And nobody else, including his father, would ever know, so why go at all?

"You're being ridiculous," he told himself.

He was going because something inside of himself demanded it.

Some hole in him needed to be filled by the basic act of standing at his mother's grave, that was all.

The pump clicked, telling him the tank was full. He replaced it in the holder, took his receipt, shook his head over the price, and then got back behind the wheel, his hands smelling of gasoline. But as he drove toward the ramp with four choices of directions he still didn't know which one he would take—until the Saab seemed to point itself straight south.

Within minutes, he was driving deep into the Flint Hills, where he was born.

•   •   •

It wasn't the only time that day that events seemed to take him over.

At no point on the drive from Kansas City did Mitch ever once entertain the idea that Abby's face might be the first he'd see upon arriving back "home." If anything, he hoped to avoid her, altogether. But when he happened to notice a green-and-white sign with an arrow that said ABBY'S LAWN & LANDSCAPE, and it was only two miles from town on Highway 177, his turn signal seemed to go on by itself. Again, his car seemed to have a mind of its own, turning off the highway and then maneuvering onto a narrow, paved street, which quickly turned into a dirt and gravel road.

And suddenly, there he was, kicking up dust behind him, like a farmer.

Just because the sign had her first name on it didn't mean it was her business.

Or any business of his, he reminded himself.

But still his car kept going down the road that was lined on either side by brown fence posts strung with barbed wire. He remembered what it felt like to dig holes for posts like those, and to drive them in all day. He remembered the feel of the thick leather gloves the men wore to handle the wire, and the cuts and blisters he used to get in spite of the gloves. He recalled the huge, greasy, delicious noontime meals the "hands" ate, all stopping work at the same time to troop into a ranch woman's kitchen or into the café in town.

The grassy fields were full of wildflowers he couldn't identify—purple, yellow, pink, and white ones. Red-and-white Hereford cattle dotted the fields on one side of him; black-and-white cattle, a Hereford and Angus mix, grazed on the other side. Every now and then his wheels scared birds out of the grass on the shoulder. The birds—meadowlarks? Mitch almost remembered what they were—fluttered up and away from him.

He found himself regretting his urge to come now, when the Flint

Hills were at their most stunning, especially now in the fresh light of a spring morning. He'd forgotten how gorgeous this area could be at certain times of year, in certain light, in pleasant weather. Maybe he hadn't even noticed the beauty when he was a kid. Maybe it had been something he had taken for granted, like fresh eggs, rodeos, and dogs that were allowed to run loose. But now, seeing it so many years later, and through adult eyes, it struck him that he had lived his childhood in the heart of an impressionist painting. It galled him to have to admire it. He wished he had come, instead, in the midst of harsh winter or searing summer, when only a diehard Kansan could have loved the daunting landscape.

Mitch rolled his car windows down to let the fresh air flow through.

His ears ate up the sounds of his wheels moving over gravel, of wind through grass, of birds and insects singing. He stopped the car in the middle of the road and turned off the engine, craving to hear more.

After a few moments, he started the car again.

In the few hundred yards since he had turned off the highway, he had learned that the trip was going to be painful in ways he hadn't expected. He had forgotten how much he had loved a lot of his own childhood, how good it had felt to live in the heart of a huge country, with land spreading out in every direction. He had forgotten what it was like to climb to the top of one of the high flat hills and be able to see into four counties, what it was like to be able to walk or ride anywhere for miles around, and always run into people who knew him. He had forgotten what it was like to feel safe. He had forgotten what it was like to feel loved, if not convincingly by his own parents, then by an entire community.

It was too painful. He nearly turned the car around to go back to the city.

But then he saw a second small green-and-white sign with an arrow pointing north.

* * *

He already had on dark sunglasses. Now he reached across his car seat to grab his Kansas City Royals baseball cap and put it on. He felt slightly idiotic, like a spy in disguise. But the last thing he wanted was a sudden meeting with the girl he'd left behind. If "Abby's Lawn & Landscape" was *that* Abby, and she happened to be driving down this road going the other way, he wanted to be able to sail past her without being recognized.

The girl he'd left behind . . . *in bed.*

Cut that shit out, he told himself. But not before an image of a naked sixteen-year-old girl flashed through his inner vision, making him feel like a dirty old man.

Mitch tugged the brim of his cap down tighter over his forehead.

He realized he was there. Just ahead on his left, there was a fenced property on which he saw a small white house with green shutters, a screened-in porch to one side, and a front porch with a white swing on it. He also spotted a barn that had been converted into a plant nursery. He saw an entire field of young trees and shrubs, and what looked like a field of wildflowers that had been planted on purpose.

It was attractive, in a rural, struggling kind of way.

The house and barn could have used a coat of paint. A black truck parked at the side of the house looked the worse for wear, though there was a shinier, bigger, newer red truck parked beside it. It looked like the kind of place where the owners had to work their tails off to keep it going.

He had slowed down as he approached it, and now he stopped.

Just as he was about to speed up and move on past quickly so that he could turn around and leave, the door of the side porch flew open and a man came barreling out of it, and let the screen door slam behind him. He had the look of a cowboy, down to the boots in his hands. He was a good-looking guy, tall and muscular. He looked like he had some miles on him, as Mitch remembered his father used to say of men who drank too hard and traveled too fast. He was walking in his stocking feet over the gravel in the driveway as if he was too pissed off to feel the rocks. Suddenly, Mitch recognized him. Jesus Christ, it was Patrick Shellenberger, Rex's asshole of an older brother.

Abby had married *Patrick?*

Before Mitch could even consider what that might mean, the screen door opened again and there she was. The sun had come up just enough to illuminate her face.

Mitch's heart stopped in his chest.

It was Abby, almost exactly as he remembered her.

She yelled something after the departing Patrick, who raised an arm in reply.

Mitch saw her grin behind Patrick's back, and pain shot through him.

She was still as pretty as she had ever been. And judging from the way his heart was pounding, it seemed to think it still belonged to her.

Damned, stupid, foolish heart, he thought.

Quickly, he stepped on the gas so he could glide as unobtrusively as possible past the entrance to their property, before Patrick had time to steer the red truck down the drive.

Mitch drove for several miles, not paying attention to where he was going, or how long it took him to get there. As his wheels bumped over the rough roads, all he could think of as they turned was what he had *lost, lost, lost.* Everything, he had lost it all. His dreams, his expectations, his hopes, his illusions. He had lost his home and family, his friends, his high school, his college, his girl. He had lost his innocence and his childhood. He had lost faith. He had lost trust. He had lost hope. Over time, through the years, he had regrouped, tried to rebuild a life, to make it all up to himself by gathering around himself the things and people who might do, instead. But here he was, after all of that, and the only thing he felt was the bitter loss of it all. Maybe he would never have married Abby. Maybe he wouldn't have stayed in Small Plains anyway. Maybe he and his parents would have ended up estranged from each other over something else. But he would have had some choice in those possibilities, he would have had some power over them.

Finally, he stopped, turned around, and drove back the way he had come.

When he passed the green-and-white house again, there was nobody in sight.

Mitch drove through the dust that Patrick's truck had raised.

Back at the highway, he looked northeast toward Kansas City and then south toward Small Plains. Again, he thought about turning back. What difference would it make for him to see his mother's grave? What was a five-minute visit going to satisfy in him that still needed satisfying?

"You can't know until you get there," he reminded himself.

He had not grown up to be the man he had thought he would be. Events had changed him, or he had allowed them to change him. It hadn't even occurred to him before this morning that the same thing might have happened to Abby. She, too, must have hardened and coarsened over the years. The girl he had loved could never have grown up to marry someone like Patrick Shellenberger. It just couldn't have happened, not the way their lives had been going back then, not as the people they were growing up to be, back then. *The old Abby might not even like the present me,* Mitch realized, as his hand hovered over his turn signal. The Abby he remembered might not want anything to do with the ambitious, driven man he had become. But then, she wouldn't have wanted anything to do with Patrick, either, and yet there he was. *So, okay, she wouldn't like me now . . . but why would I want anything to do with that disappointing woman in the doorway?*

Mitch signaled a right turn, toward the Small Plains Memorial Cemetery.

Chapter Thirteen

At the Stagecoach Inn on the east side of Small Plains, the day man-ager stared helplessly at a young woman in a wheelchair, and apolo-gized for having no room for her.

"I'm real sorry," he said, and meant it, because he hated losing any chance at a $37-a-night room rate. "I just don't have any more handicap-accessible rooms left. I swear, we can go months without needing a one of them, and here all of a sudden, it seems like that's all anybody wants. It's because of Memorial Day. Some family re-unions going on. I do have a few rooms left, but there's no elevator, and somebody would have to carry you up there, and I don't know who'd do that. I can't, not with my back, although I sure would, if I could," he said, sincerely. "I'm awful sorry. Last I heard, the Econo Lodge was all full up, too, and I mean, completely full up, but I could call there for you, if you'd like."

"Would you please?" she asked him.

She was really sick. He could tell that by how gray she looked, and bent over, like it was all she could do to sit upright, even with the help of the chair. Plus, the dead giveaway to him was the scarf she wore all around her head, which probably meant she was bald underneath there, and most likely on chemo for cancer, or something. She was traveling alone, which the other people who'd come in this week needing handicapped rooms had not been. They had relatives or friends with them. This poor young thing had driven up in a brown van and had to honk to get somebody to finally come and help her out of it. She must be really desperate, he thought. He imagined he smelled something medicinal. He thought she looked at death's door, so while he would have liked to help her, and would have really liked to get the room rate, he was just as glad to send her elsewhere. He didn't want to have to worry about what his maids might find when they walked into her room in the morning. Not meaning to be offensive, he assured himself, but he hadn't gotten into the motel business to run a morgue.

"I'll just call over to the Econo right now," he assured her. "If they can't take you, there's a bed-and-breakfast that might be able to, but I got to warn you, it's more expensive, although why it should be, since all the furniture's so old it creaks, I don't know—"

"I'll take anything," she whispered. "Thank you."

"They only serve breakfast."

"That's okay."

He guessed that meant she didn't eat much and probably couldn't taste it anyway.

As he waited for a desk clerk to pick up the phone at the other motel, he asked conversationally, "So, do you have family around here?"

"No," she said. "I don't know anybody."

That surprised him. Usually, they knew somebody.

"Well, then, what brings you out here in the middle of nowhere?"

He was pretty sure he knew what she was going to say, if she was honest enough to say it. When strangers showed up out of no-where . . . sick strangers . . . it could only mean one thing, which was they'd somehow heard about the Virgin and they were here to see if they could get healed. It was amazing, he thought, how word could spread until his own little hometown got a reputation like it was some kind of one-stop shop for miracles.

"I'm going to the cemetery," she said in her faint voice.

"To see the Virgin?" he asked, with a sympathetic and knowing glance.

She looked embarrassed and even turned a little pink, but she nodded.

"How'd you hear about her?"

"The Internet."

"Really!" This was a new one to him.

Again, she nodded. "There are chat rooms about . . . miracles."

"I'll be darned."

"Is it true . . . about the miracles?"

"Well, I've heard some stories, that's for sure."

He was careful to be vague. On the one hand, he didn't want to make any promises and get sued. But on the other hand, the Virgin, in her small way, was good for business. And in a small town in the heart of Kansas, they could use any commerce that came their way.

When the Econo Lodge reported full, he called the bed-and-breakfast.

"They've got a first-floor room for you!" He beamed down at her, happy to be of service to the suffering. "What's your name?"

"Caitlin Washington."

He was so busy giving that information to the owner of the B&B that he didn't hear her whisper, "Or, Catie. My friends call me Catie."

"They'll fix you up just fine," the manager told her when he got off the phone. "Want some help getting back out to your van?"

She nodded, tears of gratitude appearing in her blue eyes.

As he pushed her chair from behind, she turned her head so she could ask him, "Can you please tell me how to find her grave?"

Chapter Fourteen

Mid-morning, Abby walked into her parents' house and yelled, "Dad?"

"I'm in the kitchen," her father yelled back.

She walked into the cheerful, spacious room where her mother had once ruled with a magic spatula and a frying pan, and found him seated at the table in his bathrobe, staring at the screen of the laptop computer he had set up there.

"Whatcha doing?" she asked him.

It being a holiday, this was one of the few times in the year when he wasn't working. Unless an emergency called, of course, in which case his holiday would be over.

"Reading *The New York Times* online," he said.

"Oh, sure," she teased him. "You can't fool me. I know what you're really reading. *TV Guide.* Checkin' up on your soaps."

Her father never watched TV. She would have been willing to bet that he hadn't had any of their sets on for anything but the weather since her mother died. Before computers, he had amused himself by reading books and medical journals. Now he was as addicted to the Internet as any teenager could be.

"Aren't we having dinner at your sister's tonight?" he asked her, with a brief glance up.

"Yeah, but I thought I'd stop by." She walked over to his coffeepot and touched the side of it. "Is this coffee old enough to vote yet?"

"It was fresh yesterday."

Abby poured a bit of it into a cup, looked at it, sniffed it, and said, "Yes, it was."

She turned her back on the coffee, leaned against the counter, and said, "Dad? Remember the night the Virgin died?"

"Mm," he said, through closed lips, and without looking up from his screen.

"You know Mitch was here that night, right?"

"Mm. Your mother told me."

Abby looked at him, feeling irritated that he wasn't looking at her. "Dad? Do you mind? Could you pay attention to me for a minute?"

It had come out sounding harsher . . . and more full of latent meaning . . . than she had meant it to, but her dad didn't appear to have heard anything amiss in it. He merely responded by finally looking directly at her.

"Yes, Abby," he said. "What is it?"

She stared at her stout, gray-haired father, her very smart, very hardworking, very respected doctor-father, and felt so much love for him in that instant that she nearly burst into tears. However remote he had become over the years, it didn't erase the sixteen years of love that had come before, when he had been a funny, affectionate dad to both of his girls, and perhaps especially to his younger one. The words, "I miss you, Dad," almost burst out of her mouth at that moment, but she clamped down on them, not yet ready to deal with whatever might come after them.

"Why are you asking me about that girl, Abby?"

She shrugged a little. "Because I never have before?"

He smiled a little. "Are you asking me?"

"No." Abby smiled a little, too. "That's why I'm bringing it up, I guess. Because we've never talked about it, and now I want to."

"All right."

He sounded cautious, but Abby didn't feel like being cautious. "That night. I want to tell you what I remember." When he didn't say anything, she went on. "Mitch and I were in my room. You and mom were in yours. At some point, Mitch went downstairs in the dark to get something." She had a feeling her father knew what that was, so she hurried over that part. "After he left my room I heard your emergency phone ring in your bedroom and right after that I heard you walk down the hall."

She paused, and he nodded as if to say, *Okay, go on.*

"I ran out and asked you what was going on, but you just told me to go on back to bed, and you went on downstairs."

He nodded again. "I think I remember that."

"Dad, that was the last time I ever saw Mitch."

He looked down and for a moment she thought she had lost him to the computer screen again. But he shifted his gaze toward the window and stared out of it at the beautiful Memorial Day weather.

"Did you see him, Dad? In the house that night? Or afterward?"

"No, Abby, the last time I saw Mitch must have been earlier on that day."

"Oh, and there's something else I remember," Abby said. "After I went back into my room, I saw headlights coming up our driveway and I heard a car, or a truck. Was that her, Dad? I mean, was that Nathan bringing her up to your office?"

"I imagine it was."

"What happened then, Dad? Did he carry her in by himself? Was it Nathan who called you on the phone? Did you know he was coming and did you know they'd found a dead girl in their pasture?"

"The answer to all of that is yes, Abby." Her father cleared his throat. "If you want to know what happened next, I'll tell you what I remember. I had him put her in one of my examining rooms, but we both already knew she was dead. He had already established that, of course. So all I could do was have him lay her down and then leave her there until morning, when we could get McLaughlin's to pick her up."

Her father stopped speaking.

"That's all?" she asked him. "That's all that happened?"

"That's all that happened, Abby. Why, do you think there was something else?"

For the second time, she felt tears backing up in her throat and behind her eyes and she fought them back. "I don't know, Dad, I guess I just wondered if maybe Mitch might have seen it, and it upset him, and I don't know . . ."

Her father looked puzzled.

"I guess I'm still looking for a reason for why he left," she admitted. "It sounds crazy when I say it to you, though. I mean, it would be terrible to see a murdered person, of course, but that wouldn't make somebody leave their home and never come back."

"I wouldn't think so," her father said, sounding cautious again.

"Dad, you know I didn't drive him away, don't you? Whatever Nadine said about me, you know it wasn't ever true?"

"Abby." He looked pained, embarrassed. "Of course I know that."

She turned around and started making a fresh pot of coffee to hide her face from him. It was ridiculous, she told herself, that she should still feel so emotional about the whole thing after so much time. When she had the pot washed out and a fresh filter and new grounds inserted and the pot turned on, she turned around to face him again.

"Do you remember anything about her, Dad?"

"Like what?"

"She was young . . ."

"Yes, probably not much older than you."

"What color was her hair, was it long or short?"

"Abby, I don't remember that."

"You don't? Was she thin or fat? Do you think she was pretty?"

He took a deep breath, thought for a moment, and then said, "My memory of her is that she was rather tall for a girl, and she had long dark hair, and she wasn't thin, but she wasn't fat, either. I'm afraid it was impossible to tell if she was pretty."

The horror of that sentence hung between them.

"Was it hard for you, Dad?"

Something in her father's eyes at that moment frightened her. It was something that sharpened his gaze, something hard, like pain or anger. For a moment she feared she had tread too far.

But his answer was mild. "I'm a doctor, Abby."

She supposed he meant that to explain everything, as if a doctor would never be upset by any condition of any patient, but Abby knew that was far from the truth, and that he got very involved with his patients—angry at them when they didn't follow his advice, angry at diseases he couldn't defeat, sad when he lost somebody, delighted with recoveries and babies. Doc Reynolds may have drawn away from his family, but he had, if possible, drawn even closer to his patients over the years.

The coffee finished perking and Abby stayed to drink a cup of it.

When she said good-bye to him and let herself out, her father barely looked up to say, "I guess I'll see you tonight," before returning his gaze to his computer again. She was surprised, then, to look up from inside her car and see the edge of the living room curtains fall. It seemed that her father had actually gotten up from his computer, walked to the window, and watched her leave.

Chapter Fifteen

He didn't know where his mother was buried, a fact that left him feeling strangely unmoored. Even if he hadn't seen her in years, he had always known where she was. Now he could only make an educated guess. He parked on the cemetery road halfway between her family's plots and his father's family, or at least where he thought he remembered they were. Assuming his father would have put her in the Newquist section, Mitch got out of the Saab and was starting to hike over the grass in that direction when he looked a little way up the hill and saw something disturbing. A young woman was attempting to get out of a van, but it looked to Mitch as if she was having some kind of difficulty doing it.

He watched her, until he was positive she was in trouble.

Then he jogged the few yards up the hill to where she clung with one hand to the door handle on the driver's side of her van and the other hand on the car seat. As he got close he could see the handles of a wheelchair folded behind the driver's seat. But she looked as if she was attempting to walk without it.

"Can I help you?" Mitch called out to her.

"No," she said in a breathless voice. "I can do it."

No, you can't, was Mitch's thought as he saw her take her hand off the door handle, then sway and grab for it again. She didn't look even thirty years old, more like twenty-five, and she wore the telltale head scarf of the chemo patient. When she looked at him her eyes were big and dark in her face. He read both fear and determination in them.

"I'm walking that way, myself," he said, drawing close enough to see how her muscles looked like strained and trembling ropes in her forearms as she tried to stand and balance. "Grab hold of my arm and I'll take you where you want to go."

"No thanks, really, I can make it."

She took, or tried to take, a step, but immediately stumbled and had to reach for support again. This time when she looked at him he saw that she was close to bursting into tears. And this time, when he put out his right arm to her, she didn't argue, but instead grabbed onto him as to a life preserver.

"I thought . . ."she started to say apologetically.

"I know." He grinned down at her. "I'm stubborn, too."

That forced a little smile from her and a little warmth into her eyes.

She was so light he barely felt her pressure on his right arm. He started to walk her away from her van but then discovered that that wasn't going to work, either. She could barely shuffle one foot in front of the other.

"You really need to get over there?" he asked her.

"I have to. I *have* to."

"Okay. Here's what we're going to do. I'm going to pick you up and carry you."

Her eyes widened even more. "Oh, no. You'll hurt yourself."

He smiled. "I doubt it."

She didn't object as he reached down, put one arm under her knees and the other under her back, and gently hoisted her up to a level at which he could carry her.

"You okay?" he checked with her.

She bit her bottom lip and nodded.

"Okay, then just point me to where we're going."

She lifted one thin arm and pointed to an old-fashioned upright tombstone that had a pinkish tint. Mitch shut her van door with one foot and then he carried her where she wanted to go.

"Put me on the grass," she told him.

"On your feet?" he asked, doubtfully.

"No," she whispered. "So I can sit."

With her in his arms, he bent his knees until he could gently transfer her to the ground. She propped herself up with her own arms then, reminding him of the spindly woman in a famous old Andrew Wyeth painting called "Christina's World."

"I could prop you against the stone," he suggested.

For a moment she looked taken aback, but then she seemed to accept that she was going to need some support in order to sit upright. She nodded and he picked her up again and put her down again, this time with her thin back against the solid comfort of the pink granite.

"I'll be over there," he said, pointing vaguely toward the Newquist plots.

"Okay," she said, gazing up at him. "Thank you."

"When you're ready to go, give me a wave."

"I will."

It wasn't until he walked away and then turned around to check on her that Mitch looked at the stone above the grave she was so determined to visit. She had managed to adjust her position so that she was leaning her right side against one edge, with her right arm pressed up against it, her left hand splayed against the bottom of it, and a single line of engraving visible above that hand.

Peace Be Unto You, the engraving said, but there wasn't any name, only a year: 1987.

●   ●   ●

Mitch hadn't known what he would feel when he finally stood at his mother's grave, but he hadn't expected it to be restlessness. He found he couldn't stand there at all, he had to move, and so he began strolling around the cemetery, periodically glancing back to see if the sick girl needed him.

It was only when he happened upon Margie Reynolds's grave that he actually felt the emotions he had wondered if he would feel for his mother. First of all, he was shocked. *Mrs. Reynolds died?* Then came anger that he hadn't been told about her, and then sadness for a woman he had liked a whole lot better than he had liked his own mother. He checked the dates of her birth and death and figured out that Abby had been twenty-eight when Margie had died. They'd had a close and loving relationship.

It must have nearly killed you, he thought, of Abby.

Before he even consciously realized what he was doing he was pulling his wallet out of his back pocket and opening it to a small photograph inside. His six-year-old son grinned up at him, and Mitch smiled back down at the picture, feeling a sudden sharp pang of missing the boy, who was with his mother for the week.

Mitch held his wallet out to Margie Reynolds's grave.

"This is Jimmy," he said softly. "My son."

He found himself telling her more. "We have joint custody. I guess it works okay. Better than only getting him on weekends. You'd probably like my ex-wife. I know she'd like you. I probably could have tried harder, but it just didn't work out for us. I thought I loved her enough to marry her, but then I've thought a lot of things that didn't turn out to be true . . ."

Mitch folded the wallet closed and slipped it back into his pocket.

"Anyway. That's Jimmy. I'm sorry you won't get to see him."

It killed him to think that Jimmy was born a whole year before Margie Reynolds died. If there had been some way to bring his son down to meet her . . .

Hers was a funeral he might have come to, Mitch thought, but then he realized, no, there was no way he could have done that and faced Abby. And no way he could have walked into the Reynolds's home for the first time with a son that he'd had with another woman. With that thought, and the memory of seeing Abby together with Patrick, Mitch felt a rise of grief that nearly staggered him. For a moment, he thought he was going to need somebody to hold him up, like he had supported the sick girl. But there wasn't anybody who could do that. He forced himself to tamp down the sorrow and the devastating disappointment.

There'd been a place inside him where he had still held out hope.

Suddenly Mitch felt the rise of the old anger again, a red, vicious, pulsating fury, accompanied by the cry that had echoed in his skull for seventeen years: *I didn't do anything wrong. I don't deserve this. This was my town, too.*

Something in his peripheral vision caught his attention.

He looked up the hill. The young woman was waving at him, a limp, slight wave, but it got her message across.

Fueled by the energy of his anger, Mitch walked quickly up the hillside to her.

"Ready to go?"

She nodded and even held up her arms to him, like a child, to be picked up. This time when he did it, she smelled of grass.

As he did it, he asked, "Who's buried here?"

"The Virgin," she said.

"Excuse me? Who?"

"The Virgin." When she didn't see comprehension in his face, she said, "Don't you know who the Virgin is?"

"Never heard of her." He thought she felt even lighter in his arms, if that was possible.

"She's a girl who was murdered a long time ago. A horrible murder, and nobody knew who she was. She had been beaten so badly that they couldn't even identify her. Her face was all beaten in."

Mitch stumbled on a clod of dirt, causing her to shift in his arms.

"I'm sorry," he said, barely able to get the words out.

He thought he was going to be sick.

"That's okay," she said, though she had gone even paler and there was sweat beading her upper lip now. Still, she kept on telling him the story. "So, what happened was, the people of this town gave her a funeral and they buried her in that grave. And they say that out of gratitude she heals people and helps them."

He suddenly felt so ill that he thought he was going to have to put her down and turn away and actually throw up in the bushes.

"Are you all right?" she asked him.

He swallowed. "I'm okay. Do you live around here?"

"Me? Oh, no, I'm from Wichita."

"Then how did you ever hear about . . . the Virgin?"

"She's kind of famous, like that place in France . . ."

"Lourdes?"

"Yeah, that's the one, where they say the water cures you."

He felt bile rising in his chest again, and fought it back.

"I asked her to help me," the girl told him in a reverent whisper.

"Did you?" They had returned to her van. "Here we are again."

Mitch gently set her on her feet long enough to allow him to open her van door for her, and then he helped her back into it.

"Is it cancer?" he asked bluntly, looking into her wide eyes in her thin face.

She nodded, and then stuck out one thin hand. "I'm Catie."

"Mitch," he said, and took the hand. "How far do you have to go? Are you sure you can drive?"

"Not far. I'm staying in town. And really, I'm okay when I'm driving."

Mitch stood by the side of the road and watched her leave the cemetery. There had been a kind of happy glow to her face as she gave one last look out her side window at him. If nothing else, the visit to the grave seemed to have made her happier for a little while.

When she was gone, he walked slowly back to the grave of the girl that Catie had called the Virgin. Mitch stood staring down at it for a long time, until enough other people began to enter the cemetery with their memorial flowers that he began to worry about getting spotted by somebody he knew.

One last time, he looked at the gravestone.

"So they couldn't identify you," he said with a cynical, bitter twist to his tone. "But there's one person who still knows who you are, isn't there . . . Sarah?"

On his way out of the cemetery in his own car, he looked to the side, right into the face of a woman who looked vaguely familiar to him, as if she might have been someone with whom he had gone to school. Mitch didn't allow any expression to enter his eyes, but he thought he saw a startled spark of recognition in hers.

"Screw it," he thought angrily, as he found himself turning left toward town instead of right toward the interstate up north. "If I didn't have a good reason to stay longer before, I do now."

His heart was pounding hard as he crossed the town limits.

As he slowly drove around the once-familiar streets of Small Plains he put on his sunglasses again, and his Royals baseball cap, and he propped his left arm on the doorsill to hide the side of his face. He took in the surprising fact that downtown looked better than he remembered it, but he also noticed a number of FOR SALE signs placed in storefront windows.

His father, Abby's father, and Rex's father had considered Small Plains to be their territory, their fiefdom, theirs by right of inheritance by their own fathers and grandfathers before that. As Mitch drove around, an idea began to grow in him of how he might get a measure of revenge, and possibly even justice.

He recalled his own vow to himself: *I'll never forget. I'll never forgive.*

He thought of a beautiful girl with her face beaten, her identity erased as if she had never existed, and he thought of how too many years had gone by without him doing anything about it.

Feeling a turbulent mix of fear, anger, and resolve, Mitch turned his car toward a bit of acreage and a small ranch house that his family had owned. He was betting it was still there and that his father still owned it. If the ranch house was still there, if they hadn't sold it or rented it to somebody else, if the keys were still hidden where they had been for all the early years of his life, if it was still habitable, then that's where he would spend the night.

Chapter Sixteen

"Because I say so."

At 11:30 that morning in his office in the sheriff's department in downtown Small Plains, Rex gave two of his deputies an exasperated look that did not even begin to hint at the indigestion they were giving him. Unfortunately, when they heard him say that, instead of taking him seriously, they both laughed at him.

So did his other visitor, the fourth person in the room.

"Yeah, right, Dad," the male half of the deputies scoffed.

"And go to our rooms?" chimed in his female counterpart, with a grin.

"You tell him," Abby said, egging them on.

That earned her a darkly repressive glance from her old friend and their boss. *This is all your fault,* his expression said. And, of course, it was. She had driven here straight from her father's house and solely to encourage Rex to reopen the Virgin's homicide case, having decided to keep moving while the impulse was still strong in her, and while the holiday gave her time on a Monday that she didn't usually have.

By happy chance, she had run into a couple of eager deputies in the hallway outside his office and promptly enlisted them in the cause.

Abby knew them both, having gone to high school with one of them and having sold a lot of garden supplies to the other. The female deputy and gardener was Edyth Flournoy, thirty years old, only the fourth woman ever to serve in the sheriff's department of Muncie County. The male deputy was John Marvel, a ten-year-veteran whose last name provoked eternal ribbing from the good guys and the bad guys alike. Now he leaned forward, looking as eager and excited as a rookie cop, instead of the jaded thirty-three-year-old he really was. "Listen, boss, when's the last time we even had a homicide to investigate? Seventeen years ago, when she was killed, that's when! And there wasn't another murder for five years before that, and it got solved. We can't leave this one homicide hanging over our department!"

"Hell, no," Flournoy weighed in. "It makes us look bad."

"How come it didn't make us look bad until now?" their sheriff asked.

But they all knew that that was merely a rhetorical question.

"Think of how many new technologies have been invented since the Virgin was killed," Flournoy said.

"Dozens, probably," Abby chimed in, helpfully.

"Don't call her the Virgin," Rex griped.

"Why not?" Deputy Flournoy shot back at him. "Everybody else does. If we call her Jane Doe, nobody will know who we're talking about."

"They'll know."

"But listen," Flournoy persisted. "There's so much we could do now that your dad couldn't do back then. We could use CODIS, we could try AFIS . . ."

"What's Codis?" Abby asked her.

"Combined DNA Indexing System," Deputy Flournoy said, rather proudly. "And AFIS stands for Automated Fingerprint Identification System."

"Uh huh," Rex interrupted, "and do any of you happen to have the two thousand bucks we'll need for a DNA comparison with the DNA of missing people?"

"I might," Abby offered.

"Oh, shut up," he snapped at her, and then turned back to his deputies. "And where do you think you're going to find fingerprints when there wasn't any weapon and she wasn't wearing any clothes—"

"There was a blizzard, right?" Flournoy asked him. "Was your dad able to collect any evidence at the scene?"

"No, not until the snow melted, which took a few weeks."

"And?"

He shrugged. "Nothing."

"Why didn't he go out with a generator and heating fans and melt the damned stuff?" Marvel said.

"I don't know. I could be wrong about some of this. Maybe he did."

"We could go back out and search all over again," Flournoy offered.

Rex gave her a deeply skeptical look. "In a pasture? Seventeen years later?"

"Hey, boss, what do you think archeologists do?" she retorted. "What difference does it make how many years have gone by? Something could have gotten buried, or even just overlooked—"

"Definitely," Abby agreed, with a vigorous nod of her head.

"Or eaten by coyotes, or trampled by cows, or picked up by a tornado," Rex shot back. He sat forward to try to impress them all with his earnestness. "Listen, I know you're eager to delve back into this. I understand that. Or, at least I understand why the two of you are. You're being good cops. And it's quite the thing these days to solve old crimes. You—" He glared at his dear friend. "You, I don't know what you're up to. You, I suspect of just being a pain in the ass. But hey." He forced a smile at his deputies. "I watch *Cold Case,* too."

His deputies grinned back at him, both of them looking a little shamefaced to be caught getting their inspiration from a TV show about investigating unsolved crimes.

"And I am happy you want to get into this, truly, I am," Rex continued. "But here's the thing. You've got to face some facts that aren't cold. One of them is that we have the same limited resources we've always had. No county crime lab. Not enough money. Not enough people like you."

Rex inclined his head, his way of pointing out the window of his office.

"We may not have much crime in this county, but hell, we don't even have the budget or personnel to handle what little we do have, much less remove any of you from those duties in order to investigate a seventeen-year-old crime."

He held up a hand when all three started to speak at once.

"Do you know how much work is involved in cold cases?"

Flournoy's face brightened again. "There's a seminar down in Miami . . ."

"Yeah, right," Rex said, and had to laugh. "That's gonna happen. I'm going to send both of you to Miami about the same time I buy Hummers for everybody." He got serious again. "It is incredibly tedious and time-consuming. The paperwork alone is enough to kill you. And I know how much you guys love paperwork."

Their eager looks faltered a bit, as he had hoped they would.

"And speaking of paperwork that needs doing," Rex said ominously.

His deputies took the hint. They picked up their coffee cups and departed the office together, leaving Abby alone to face the bad mood their boss was in this morning.

·　·　·

Rex swiveled his chair so he could stare at his old friend Abby.

"What's up with this?" he asked her.

"I'm not sure," she admitted. "Or maybe I am. It started when we found Nadine, Rex. I started to think more about that girl who was killed, and how maybe now we could find out who she was—with all the new technology, like Edyth said."

"And find out who killed her?"

Abby shrugged. "I don't know about that. I just want to put a name on her grave."

"Why?"

"Why?" Abby blinked. "Don't you want to identify her? Wouldn't everybody like to know who she was?"

"Of course. That's not what I meant. I guess I mean, why you?"

Abby took her time answering and stared over his shoulder, out the window, while she thought about her answer. "Maybe I'm just curious."

"There must be more to it than that."

Abby could only shrug again. "I really don't know."

He took a breath and sat up straight in his chair. "Okay. Well, here's the deal. I'm sorry, but it's not going to happen, not unless we get some kind of lucky break like we've always been depending on. We'd have to exhume her to get DNA, Abby. And we can't afford to do that, and we can't afford to do any of the rest of it, either, and don't give me any baloney about you paying for it. I've seen how bad your house needs paint and I know how old your truck is. So just forget about anything like that, all right?"

"All right," she said, so quickly and meekly that he was immediately suspicious.

"Abby . . . ?"

"No, really, all right, Rex. I mean, what could I do by myself? Nothing."

"That's right," he said firmly. "Nothing. Please do exactly that."

Abby got up from the chair, gave him a warm smile, and started toward his doorway. When she got there, she turned around and said, "Your mother didn't want me to do anything, either."

"My mother?"

But Abby had already gone, leaving his doorway empty but his office filled with the musky scent of her perfume. Or maybe that was John Marvel's cologne, Rex thought, and smiled in spite of himself.

He got up, walked over to his office door, and shut it.

Then he went back to his desk, picked up his pile of keys that lay on top of it, and rifled through them until he found the one he sought: a tiny silver key that fit into the bottom drawer of his desk. Once unlocked, the drawer revealed only papers . . . until he lifted the papers and then the false bottom beneath them. Below it, there was a box about four inches square.

He reached down and lifted the lid of the box.

Inside, there was a red circlet of fabric and elastic. The girls he had gone to high school with had called them "scrunchies." This one had a dark stain on one side of it. It also had several long dark hairs curled within its wrinkles. When his father, Patrick, and he had lifted the dead girl into their truck and laid her down on the cold metal floor of it and covered her with burlap feed sacks, Rex had been the last to climb back down to the ground.

His father and brother had walked on toward the doors of the truck.

It was he who had sighted something dark lying in the snow.

He had reached down to pick it up, and found that he was holding a red elastic band that had tied back her hair.

*　　*　　*

The sound of someone clearing her throat made Rex look up toward his doorway.

He closed his fist over the red hair band, quickly hiding it.

Rex was shocked to see that a half hour had passed while he had just sat there.

Edyth Flournoy stood in the doorway with a grin on her face. Upon getting the boss's attention, she said, "Hey, boss, I forgot to tell you . . . saw your brother doing something interesting this morning."

Rex heaved a big sigh. "What? Robbing a bank? Driving under the influence?"

"Nah." She laughed, assuming he was joking. "Shacked up with Abby, from the looks of it. I passed him coming from her place early this morning."

Sensing a sudden change in the atmosphere, the deputy said, "Guess it's none of my business," and quickly walked away.

Rex felt the flash of intense anger he experienced almost every time his brother crossed his mind. It didn't improve his temper to think that Abby had sat right there across from him and never said a word about being with Patrick last night. Not that she was likely to tell him, he had to admit, knowing how he felt about it, as she did. If he ever thought it was getting serious between Abby and Pat, he thought he might have to arrest her for something just to keep her from making the biggest mistake of her life. Or maybe he'd just shoot Patrick. He had to admit, though, that if he could have shot his older brother and gotten away with it, he probably would have already done it by now.

Rex opened his fist and stared down at the object in it.

It had slid off her hair when they handled her. When he had found the red "scrunchie" lying in the snow, he had hesitated for a moment, staring at it. Then he had quickly stuffed it down into his coat pocket, meaning to give it to his father. Or maybe he never had really meant to do that, he thought now, alone in his office. Maybe he had always meant to keep it as a private memento, since he was the one who had given it to her.

Chapter Seventeen

August, 1986

Maybe it was the heat—110 degrees on the thermometer that was screwed to an outside corner of the barn—that propelled him into following Patrick that summer day. Or maybe it was the fact that for three days out of the last five, Patrick had vanished from the fields where they were both supposed to be baling hay, leaving Rex to sweat through the work alone.

Despite the fact that he felt resentful enough to stick Patrick's face in a water trough and drown him, Rex hadn't complained about it to his parents. That wouldn't do anything except bring parental wrath down on his own head. They had never allowed the brothers to come running to them to settle fights; from an early age, the boys were instructed to settle it themselves or to stew over it privately, their choice. So even when his father yelled at them that they weren't getting enough work done fast enough to please him, Rex's eyes had shot pitchforks at his older brother, but he'd kept his mouth shut while his parents were around. He figured his father wasn't stupid. Nathan could read the signs. He knew he had one hardworking, sporadically dutiful son and one lazy-ass, rebellious one. Even if Nathan didn't know the precise nature of the disagreement this time, he surely knew Patrick was the cause of it. But he still expected Rex to handle his complaints on his own. He also expected the hay to get put up while the weather held, whether both brothers did their shares or one brother did it alone. It was one of the prices the brothers paid for having a father who also held a full-time job as the county sheriff. Without two strong sons to work in his place, Nathan could never have pulled it off.

When the mechanism of the baler got clogged up for the second damn time in the past hour, Rex stopped the big machine. When he opened the door of it he realized that all the fields were quiet except for the buzzing of insects. There should have been the low roar of another baler. He looked over at the next field for the dust his brother should have been raising. All he saw was heat rising from the field. That was the last straw for him.

Furious, he flung himself out of the cab, down to the prickly ground, and stalked off to where his old secondhand beat-up truck was parked at the far end at the gate.

He got in his truck, peeled off toward the next field, and found that Patrick's old truck was gone again. *Where the hell does he go?* Rex fumed. Probably off to one of his equally worthless friends' houses to hide out in air-conditioning and drink beer for a couple of hours. Or off to visit one of the infinite number of girls who always seemed willing to put up with his good-looking, no-good self.

And how do I think I'm going to find him?

It dawned on Rex that if he didn't know where his brother had disappeared to, then he probably couldn't find him, at least not without taking a couple of hours to do nothing but drive from one possible place to another. And it wasn't like Patrick was stupid enough to park his truck out in front of somebody's house, or a bar, where their father or one of his deputies would be likely to see it.

With a string of curses, Rex turned his truck around and returned to the field where he was supposed to be working. Maybe he couldn't find Patrick today, but he thought he knew how to find him the next time he did this.

. . .

For two days in a row, Patrick worked the way he was supposed to, as if he had calibrated exactly how much slack he had before their father might come roaring home to check on them. But then on the third day, he vanished mid-afternoon again.

This time, Rex was ready for him.

He had watched his brother's work like a hawk since the last time, throwing constant beady-eyed glances in that direction, on alert for the moment when the dust in that field stopped rising and moving.

When he saw it happen, he immediately shut down his own machine.

He ran to his truck and was on the road, following Patrick's dust before his brother could get so far ahead that he was impossible to follow.

. . .

Mitch's parents owned a place that bordered the far western edge of the Shellenbergers' much bigger spread, in the section across the highway. Rex was totally surprised when his brother drove in the back way to the Newquists' small ranch. The main entrance—with a wrought-iron gate—was around a bend in the road to the west. This back way was the one that he and Mitch always used on the rare times they spent any time at the place. Mostly, the Newquists' ranch was only used by Mitch's parents for entertaining out-of-town judges and lawyers who were easily impressed by a cattle ranch of any size, even if it only had a few dozen head of cows on it. To people from the city, five hundred acres sounded huge. The Shellenberger spread was closer to ten thousand acres. But then, the Shellenbergers ran a real, operating ranch, not just a showplace.

Rex had no idea in the world what his brother could be doing there.

It couldn't be good, though. He had a sudden, awful vision of his brother and friends using the elegant little ranch house for parties.

Patrick would know it was empty most of the time. They could break in and trash the place without the Newquists ever knowing it until it was too late to stop them. Rex doubted that it would bother Patrick's alleged conscience in the least to think of using property, even of family friends, in such a shabby way.

His truck bounced over the rough terrain, while anxiety ate at his stomach . . . anxiety and glee, because this might turn out to be the one offense his parents couldn't forgive. Could a sheriff overlook a serious act of vandalism by his own son? Could he overlook breaking and entering? Patrick might have to be charged with a crime. Patrick might have to go to jail. Rex stepped harder on the gas in anticipation of that exhilarating possibility.

* * *

He didn't remember a time when he didn't hate Patrick.

Rex felt as if he had hated his older brother on sight. His earliest memories were of Patrick tormenting him in some way or other, and of feeling furious and helpless to do anything about it. He figured Pat must have hated him on sight, too—the younger brother coming along to take his place.

So maybe it was understandable, in a way.

But that didn't make it forgivable, not when you were the younger, smaller, vulnerable brunt of it, and not when your parents never did anything stronger to protect you from it than to snap, "Patrick, stop it."

Patrick never stopped it. Rex hoped he went to fucking prison.

* * *

When Rex finally came around a bend and saw the Newquists' ranch house, he was surprised to see only Patrick's truck there, instead of a whole slew of his friends.

Instead of barreling onto the scene, he backed up, and parked among some trees.

After looking around to make sure that Patrick wasn't anywhere in sight, Rex began to work his way down and around to the house, keeping to the shade of the trees and the outbuildings to hide his presence there.

When he got closer, he heard music coming through the open windows.

Party, he thought, hoping it was true, after all.

It wasn't that he wished damage on his best friend's property, it was that he wished damage on his brother. If Mitch was with him, he'd be thinking the same thing. Patrick had never been any nicer to Rex's friends than he was to his brother. When Abby was little, Patrick could make her cry in about ten seconds flat, and that, alone, had made Rex and Mitch want to kill him.

With murder very much on his mind, Rex sneaked up to the window where the loudest sound of music seemed to be coming from. He flattened himself against the side of the house and peered around to see in. It was a bedroom, but there was no person in it, so he kept going from window to window until he finally saw his brother's broad, bare, tanned, muscular back, the back that made otherwise sensible girls go all swoony when they saw him at the county swimming pool.

Bare chested, in jeans and cowboy boots, Patrick was talking to someone else in the room.

When his brother took a step to the side, Rex saw who it was, and he couldn't have been more surprised. Or disappointed. Really disappointed to the point of feeling stabbed and betrayed, even if he didn't have a right to be. It was a girl named Sarah who used to work as a housecleaner in a lot of homes in Small Plains. She was Patrick's age, Rex knew, and she was from another town about twenty-five miles away.

Rex understood why she used to drive all that way to work.

Or at least he understood it after Abby explained it to him one time.

"There's nothing wrong with cleaning people's houses," Abby had said, looking earnest, "but I wouldn't want to do it in my own hometown, not if I didn't have to. Or, like, if I lived in a city, I wouldn't want to do it in my own neighborhood. If that's what I had to do to make money, I'd go someplace else, too."

"That's stupid," he'd declared.

"No, it's not! If some girl we know did that, you think that kids wouldn't be mean to her about it?"

Rex had thought at the time, but didn't say to Abby, that if any girl they knew was as beautiful as Sarah was, she could do practically anything she wanted to do, and it wouldn't matter what anybody said about it. Abby was pretty, really pretty, but Sarah was from a whole different planet of beauty, in Rex's opinion. With her dark hair and pale, perfect skin, with her kind of weird but beautiful light blue eyes that slanted up a little, and her big boobs and flat stomach and long legs, he thought she was just about the sexiest, most incredible-looking girl he'd ever seen outside of a movie screen. But maybe he didn't know about how kids in her own hometown would treat her. He wasn't a teenage girl. Maybe Abby was right. Plus, he'd heard that there was trouble with Sarah's family, so maybe she had other reasons for traveling twenty-five miles to work.

As Rex stood, feeling dumbfounded, at the window, she saw him.

Because of the look on her face, Patrick turned around, and saw him, too.

"You little bastard," he yelled, "you sneaking little bastard!"

Patrick moved fast, running toward the front door, then onto the porch, then around to where Rex stood rooted to the ground.

He stood like a cement statue when Patrick grabbed him by the shoulders, and half pulled, half pushed him. "What the fuck are you doing here? Did you follow me? Listen to me, you stupid kid, if you tell Dad about this, I'll kill you!"

"Tell him about what?" Rex said, starting to come to life again.

He pushed his brother away, which made Patrick push him again.

"I'm warning you, don't say one word about seeing me here. You don't know I was here, you don't know anything about Sarah being here, you were never here!"

"Okay, I was never here," Rex said, ducking out of the way.

He backed up until he was out of reach. Although he was no longer a "little" brother, although he was within an inch of Patrick's height, he was still a string bean compared to his brother's more filled-out body. At nineteen, only a week away from heading off to college, Patrick looked like a man. At seventeen, soon to be eighteen, Rex still looked like a teenage boy. But he felt man enough to say, in a low, taunting voice he hardly recognized as his own, "I was never here—if you never come back here."

"What the hell are you talking about?"

Patrick moved threateningly forward.

"Just what I said." Rex stood his ground. "If I ever see you leave the fields again and come over here, I won't keep quiet about it. You stay there doing the work you're supposed to do, and I'll keep my mouth shut about this forever."

"You wouldn't tell them, you little fucker."

"Try me, asshole."

Patrick hesitated, and Rex knew he'd won. At last, he'd won a battle with his brother! He knew he'd probably have to pay for it someplace down the line, but for right now, it felt terrific.

Then he glanced in through the screened window and saw her.

She had moved back into shadows inside the house, but he could see her eyes staring out at him. He couldn't read them. There weren't any answers or explanations in them, not that she owed him any.

He was suddenly painfully aware of how filthy he was, how smelly and sweaty.

He turned back to look at his brother.

"Well," he said, a little cockier than was safe for him, but he couldn't help but swagger anyway. "You coming? We've got extra work to do today, thanks to you screwing around over here."

Patrick looked as if he felt as murderous as Rex had felt when he drove over.

"Yeah, I'm coming. I've got to get my shirt."

Rex walked back to his truck, feeling so victorious it was all he could do not to pump his fist. But just to be sure, he didn't leave the property until he saw that his brother was right behind him. They finished their separate baling jobs, went home, ate supper, and went their ways that night, without speaking to each other.

Their parents noticed only the relative peace, and not the animosity.

When Patrick left for K-State, Rex drove back to the Newquists' ranch.

He didn't expect to find her there. He hadn't told Mitch or anybody else about seeing her there. So he was shocked, yet again, when he drove up and she opened the front door.

She was living there, she told him that day.

It was a secret from certain people, and she asked him to swear not to tell anyone.

Eventually, he went out to see her so often that she presented him with periodic lists of supplies for things she needed or wanted, which was how Rex happened to purchase a red scrunchie for her long dark hair.

Chapter Eighteen

May 31, 2004

Abby knew something was up that evening the minute she spotted certain familiar cars parked around her house. She'd been out in a distant wildflower field gathering blossoms to hang from the rafters so they'd be dry for making wreaths for Christmas, and the time had gotten away from her. She had hurried back in her truck, expecting to jump in the shower and rush to her sister's house for dinner.

But her sister was *here,* instead.

There was her sister Ellen's Volvo station wagon, and there was Cerule Youngblood's red convertible, there was Susan McLaughlin's black Caddy, and there was Randie Anderson's white pickup truck.

It wasn't her birthday, so it couldn't be a surprise party.

And it was suppertime, on a holiday, when they all should have been home cooking, or over at their relatives' houses . . .

Was something wrong? Was that why they were here?

Heart thumping with worry, she hurried into her own house.

Four female faces turned to look at her, all of them smiling in various stages of welcome, but their smiles looked tense to Abby. Between them, they represented a goodly chunk of the movers and shakers of Small Plains: there was her own trim, efficient older sister, the mayor, dressed in her trademark Western shirt, tan trousers, and brown leather cowboy boots. There was Ellen's best friend Susan, who owned her family's funeral and cemetery business. There was Randie, married into the Anderson grocery clan, and Cerule, who worked at the courthouse, both of whom had been friends of Abby's since high school.

They had the three birds in the kitchen with them, which pleased Abby.

Ellen was at the sink mixing drinks of some kind—margaritas from the look of the tub of mix on the counter. Susan, in her black funeral director's suit, was pulling glasses down from the cupboard. Randie was seated at the kitchen table trying to keep Gracie away from the salt she had poured into a dinner plate in preparation for dipping the rims of the glasses in it. Cerule was on her cell phone, saying a quick good-bye and flipping it closed as soon as she saw Abby in the doorway.

"We heard you turn in the drive," Ellen said, by way of explaining their drink-making organization, and then she turned back to measuring out alcohol.

"I thought I was having dinner at your house," Abby said to her.

"You need a drink," Cerule announced.

"I do?" Abby saw that Gracie, stymied from eating salt, was now going after Patrick's expensive sunglasses. She darted toward the kitchen table to rescue them. "Why do I? Why are you guys here? What's up?"

"There's something we have to tell you," Susan said, without quite looking at her.

It was then that Abby realized that Susan wasn't the only one avoiding her eyes. Ellen was, too. And although Randie and Cerule were staring at her, they were observing her like a specimen under glass.

"What's *up*?" she repeated, with more urgency. "You're making me nervous!"

The others looked toward the sink, expecting Abby's sister to take charge. In the silence, Ellen turned around. She exchanged glances with the other women, and then finally looked straight at her sister. It made Abby's heart beat faster to read worry and concern in Ellen's eyes.

"*What?*" she demanded. "Is it Dad? I just saw him this morning . . ."

"No, no," Ellen assured her. "Dad's fine. It's nothing like that. It's . . . he's back, Abby. Mitch is in town. He was at the cemetery, at Nadine's grave this morning. Susan saw him."

Abby looked at Susan, who nodded to confirm it.

"I don't think he recognized me," she said. "But I'm positive it was him."

For half a second, Abby thought she might get away with saying, "So what? It's not like I care." But in the next half of that second, she felt herself slipping down to sit on the kitchen floor, and she heard her own voice whisper, "Shit."

Almost before she knew it, they were all down on the floor with her, sprawled out on the linoleum, or sitting cross-legged, passing around glasses, with the pitcher of iced margaritas in the middle of their circle.

Even the birds joined them, taking up perches on the friends.

"Why?" Abby asked them. "He didn't even come back for his own mother's funeral, so why would he come back now?"

They all shrugged and looked helpless.

"Guilty conscience," Cerule suggested tartly.

"Better late than never," Randie sneered.

"I don't want to see him!" Abby wailed at them.

"Hell, nobody wants to see him," Randie said. "Fuck him and the horse he rode *out* on."

"I want to see him," Cerule admitted, but then added hastily, "but only from a distance. I just want to know what he looks like after all these years. I hope he's blotchy, bald, and a hundred pounds overweight." She looked over at Susan. "Is he, Susan? Is he fat and blotchy and ugly?"

The funeral director looked down at her drink. "Well. Not exactly."

"Well, shoot," Cerule said. "It's not bad enough that he's back, but he has to still be gorgeous, too?"

" 'Fraid so," Susan said, with a sigh.

"Why should I care?" Abby said, her voice rising on the last word. "It's been *years!*"

"You don't care," Randie said stoutly. "You're just surprised, that's all."

Abby gave her a weak smile. "Nice try."

Suddenly Ellen got to her feet and made an announcement. "I think this calls for a large pizza with everything on it."

"But what about dinner with the family?" Abby asked her.

"This is family, too," Ellen informed her. "And this is a family emergency if I ever saw one. Emergencies call for pizza."

Cerule joined her in standing up. "And chocolate ice cream."

"Gross," said Randie, also getting up, "but delicious."

"Can't we just stay here and drink?" Abby whined, but they wouldn't let her sit still. Having emptied one pitcher of margaritas between them, they cleaned up her kitchen, secured the birds in the big cage, and then piled into Ellen's car, because she'd taken only a couple of sips of the alcohol.

At a sedate pace befitting the mayor of Small Plains, they drove into town for supper.

To the west, towering white cumulus clouds were building higher and higher in the muggy air of the early evening. Behind the white clouds, there were other clouds that were turning to gray tinged with black. Even as the friends traveled down the highway, the atmosphere around them seemed to thicken, to get hotter and stickier, as if it were August instead of May.

But the friends weren't paying any attention to the weather.

As they drew closer to town, Abby realized what they were all trying to hide from one another and especially from her. Every one of them, including herself, was sneaking peeks at the cars and people they passed on the streets, looking for *him*. She wanted to say, "Stop it!" She wanted to roll down a window and scream, "Go back the hell where you came from!" She wanted to whisper, *Why did you leave me?*

When they drove by the cemetery Cerule suddenly said, "Hey, Susan, is the Virgin only supposed to cure people? Do you think she ever gives people *bad* luck?"

From the front seat, Susan said, "I don't know. Why ask me?"

Cerule raised a sardonic eyebrow. " 'Cause, next time you're at the cemetery? See if you can get the Virgin to give Mitch Newquist the plague."

Chapter Nineteen

"You ever seen the jails in Douglas or Johnson County, Sheriff?"

"I have," Rex answered Deputy Marvel, who walked in front of him down a short row of traditional cells with bars. The air was so heavy that the ancient central air conditioning was laboring like some kind of mechanical behemoth, noisy and distracting. Rex said, "Are you telling me you're jealous?"

"Man, they're like state-of-the-art, sir."

"Not like this, you're saying?"

They stopped in front of a particular cell, where an inmate in an orange jumpsuit sat on a single bed attached to a wall, looking out at them. Rex detected curiosity, but no fear in the eyes, a fact that suggested to him that his deputies were not abusing their positions. Or, at least this deputy didn't do that, and he, himself, had no reputation for it. He wondered how much tougher he would have to act if he reigned over a more populated, more violent kind of county. It was something he was probably never going to have to find out. In the meantime, he and his few deputies and their few "guests," would continue to co-exist in their dim, confined, separated world.

"At the Douglas County Jail," Marvel said, conversationally including the inmate by making eye contact with him as well as with

Rex, "this kind of section looks like a hospital emergency room, instead of a jail, you know? The central command post looks like a nurses' station, every inmate's got a private room with a door with a window in it, and it's all clean enough to eat off the floor."

They all looked instinctively at the ancient cement floor of the cell, with a drain in the center of it.

"We could use more taxpayers," Marvel observed.

"Yeah, but then we'd get more crime," Rex countered.

"And a worse class of criminals," the man in the cell contributed, with a grin that revealed a lifetime of inadequate dental care.

"I wouldn't say that," the deputy joked, opening the cell door.

He stood aside, wiping his sweating forehead with the back of one arm.

Rex stepped inside, allowing Marvel to lock it behind him and then hand him the keys.

"Did Abby Reynolds convince you?" the deputy asked him.

"Of what?" Rex said.

"To reopen that—"

"No!" Rex thundered, before the man could say anything more.

Marvel raised his eyebrows, exchanged a glance with the prisoner, and said, "Okey-dokey."

He walked off, whistling, down the long corridor.

"Nothing scarier than a cranky lawman," said the man in the cell.

"Best not to annoy us then," Rex snapped, before taking a breath to calm himself.

Careful to keep his own shirt and trousers clean, he picked a spot to stand that was close to, but not touching, the dampish cement wall opposite the jailed man. On hot humid evenings like this, the place smelled like a cellar.

Rex would have been tempted to think of the inmate's presence here, at this time, as a remarkable coincidence, if it were not for the fact that the man had been a fairly frequent "guest" over the years.

"I'm gonna stop drinking," the man announced, seemingly out of the blue.

"Worth considering," Rex agreed, poker-faced. "When did you start?"

"Drinking?" The man raised his face toward the ceiling and squinted at the lightbulb in it. "I dunno. I was maybe ten, could have been younger."

"How long is it since you've had a driver's license, Marty?" Rex inquired.

"Oh, God, three years, going on four. At this rate, I'll never get it back."

"That's certainly possible."

"How the hell's a man supposed to make a living when he can't even drive a truck, and the nearest employment is miles away?"

"I don't know," Rex said.

"The court takes away a man's driver's license, but if the only way he's got to make a buck is to drive to it, he's going to drive a car anyway, you know he is, right?"

Rex nodded, knowing that that was the truth of it.

"Were either of your parents alcoholics, Marty?"

The other man laughed. "Them and every other cousin."

"You've got a couple of brothers, right? How do they do with it?"

"One's an AA fanatic, the other got killed in a bar fight a few years back."

"What about sisters, you have any sisters?"

Rex kept his own breathing slow and even, to control his pulse rate as he neared the questions that were the reason for this visit.

The inmate quirked a corner of his mouth in a disgusted kind of way. "A couple. Worthless bitches."

"Yeah, why so?"

"Well, one of them, younger than me, she married a worse asshole than me, and he beat her to death, but it was hard to blame him. She was a complaining kind of girl, if you know what I mean."

Rex kept still, listening to the man reveal himself.

"The other one, she was the oldest of all of us. Ran away from home when she was, I dunno, seventeen, maybe—"

Nineteen, Rex thought, remembering this man's sister, Sarah.

"She was a looker, believe it or not."

"Is that right? Where'd she end up, Marty?"

The man shrugged and then finally seemed to grasp that the sheriff of Muncie County was displaying an unusual degree of interest in a drunk-driving offender. "Why you asking me all these questions about my family?"

Rex shrugged, and began to move toward the cell door. "Thinking about instituting a new program for drug and alcohol offenders," he said, making it up as he went along. "Get a feel for their families, look for root causes, that kind of thing."

"Fucking social work?"

Rex smiled a little. "Exactly."

"Would it get me my license back any sooner?"

"Not a chance."

"Well, fuck it then."

Rex took the keys the deputy had handed him, reached his hands through the spaces between the bars, and released himself from the cell. Before he departed, he turned to ask one more question.

"Your family ever look for that runaway sister, Marty?"

"My family?" He sounded amazed the question would even occur to the sheriff. The man showed his teeth again. "Nah. We all split for other places, all except me. I'm the only one left around here. Most everybody else is dead, anyway. But I'll sure as hell look for her—"

Rex's chest muscles clenched. He thought, *I have made a mistake in raising this.*

"—if I find out she married a rich man."

Sarah's brother boomed out a laugh that bounced off the cement walls.

Rex relaxed again, and nodded a good-bye to the man in the cell.

He walked alone back down the corridor.

Nobody in her family had bothered to look for her in all these years. Apparently, they hadn't even questioned her existence. And there was no reason, ever, for them to connect that girl—whose own brother couldn't even correctly remember her age when she "left"—with a battered body in a grave.

.   .   .

His relieved feeling didn't last long.

When he emerged into the light of the central office, Edyth Flournoy trotted up to him and said, "You know that rain we might get tonight, Sheriff? Looks like it's going to get nasty. Funnel clouds sighted in Marion County fifteen minutes ago."

Marion was one county over from Muncie.

"Any on the ground?"

"None reported."

"What's the weather service saying?"

"So far, just a tornado watch for us, warnings out for them."

"Are we in the path?"

"Yes."

"How long have we got?"

"Storm's moving at forty miles an hour. The front edge of it is about ninety miles out from us."

"A little over two hours then." Rex thought of something. "Damn."

"What?"

"It's Memorial Day. Get out to the cemetery. Clear it, and close it."

His locals knew what to do in the case of tornado warnings, but visitors might not. Plus, what was he going to do with them if a bad one did strike? In a flash, Rex mentally reviewed all the basements he could remember in town, from churches to schools, the courthouse, and downtown businesses.

Small Plains hadn't had a really bad hit from any kind of storm for several years. The snowstorm that killed Nadine Newquist last winter had caused a lot of traffic accidents and killed some animals, and an ice storm five years previously had taken down many trees and a lot of roofs with them. But it had been longer than that since a tornado had done any more damage than to lift a few outbuildings off their foundations on outlying farms and ranches. When that happened, it wasn't unusual to find cattle in the wrong pastures after the storm passed, it having picked them up and deposited them to graze on a neighbor's grass. But they hadn't had a tornado go through town in Rex's lifetime; he couldn't even remember the last human injury from one. An optimist might have considered that a good sign of the night to come, but Rex thought, as he always did, that they had probably been pushing their luck.

"When you get to the cemetery?" he called out to Deputy Flournoy. She turned around to hear the rest of it. "Get the Virgin to give us a pass on the tornadoes, okay?"

The deputy grinned. "Will do, Sheriff."

Only after he'd said it did Rex feel the cringe inside, and taste the guilty bitterness, that came from joking about her. She deserved better than that from him.

Chapter Twenty

August, 1986

The summer before his senior year, Rex couldn't stop thinking about the girl he knew only as Sarah. It wasn't as if she had never entered his mind previously. She had already played a starring role in his fantasies, back when he used to catch glimpses of her cleaning houses in town. But then she had stopped coming to Small Plains, and he had mostly forgotten about her. Actresses, or girls he knew, took her place in his imaginings. Now, though, after seeing her in the shadows of the Newquists' ranch house, where Patrick had stood talking to her with his damned bare chest sticking out, now all of Rex's other fantasies were swept clean off the movie screen of his mind. Now there was only Sarah, hot and sexy, beautiful and willing Sarah. Or, at least that's how she was in his dreams.

In your dreams! he scoffed at himself, but that didn't stop him.

He didn't tell anybody about seeing her at the Newquists' place—not because he was keeping his word to his brother, but because he wanted to keep her his secret. If he didn't tell anybody about that day, not even Mitch, then they couldn't take it for granted that she was Patrick's girl, instead of his. In his fantasies, he could erase Patrick altogether, or fight him to the death for her. If Rex could have spent the next month in his room, on his bed, with the door locked, he would have spent it doing nothing but making up erotic fantasies about her.

He had to go back to school a few weeks before Patrick left for K-State in Manhattan. What with football practice every day, and the ranch work that never stopped for anything or anybody, and what with also getting started with his senior year, he managed to distract himself enough to keep from driving out there until the day Patrick officially left.

It had killed him to be in school all day, leaving Patrick back home, free to do what Rex didn't want him to do—find Sarah, be with Sarah, make Sarah fall for him. Or, just "make" Sarah. That was the nightmare scenario, the extremely likely possibility of his brother in bed with the girl of Rex's dreams.

She was way too good for Patrick. Rex hoped she realized that.

Not that he actually knew her, or anything about her.

But, on general principles, any girl was too good for Patrick, in Rex's view. And, anyway, he could tell just by looking at her.

Though he hadn't done so yet, one day he planned to casually inquire of Mitch if he knew what Sarah's last name was, and what town she was from. If Mitch didn't know, Rex planned to casually ask one of the women Sarah had cleaned for, if he could remember—or find out—who they were. He could ask Mrs. Newquist, but he'd rather not. Mitch's mom had a way of turning any question back on whoever asked it, in a way almost guaranteed to make them feel stupid or embarrassed. Rex already felt stupid and embarrassed; he didn't need Nadine Newquist to make it worse.

He planned that once he had Sarah's last name and knew her town, then maybe he'd just happen to have some reason to drive to that town. And maybe he'd just happen to run into Sarah, and the two of them would start talking, and then you just never knew what might happen after a remarkable coincidence like that . . .

He didn't let himself really ever admit it was impossible. These were his fantasies. He could make them star any woman he wanted, and he could make them turn out any way he wished them to.

One of his fantasies was that after Pat left for K-State, Rex would drive up to the Newquists' ranch house and she would still be there, for some reason. He didn't care why. Maybe they had hired her to clean it, that was a good enough reason for his fantasies. Maybe she had left something there from the day he had seen her with Pat. Or, and this was his favorite, maybe *something,* some inexplicable inner urge, whispered Rex's name to her and made her drive out into the country, without knowing exactly why. Maybe she'd have a feeling that her fate, her *destiny,* her own true love awaited her somewhere just off Highway 177 . . .

It could happen, he told himself.

In your dreams, he told himself, as he actually drove out there.

No one could have felt more shocked than he did when he drove onto the Newquists' ranch, pulled up to the house in his truck, and saw her.

·　·　·

She was standing in the front doorway, staring at him with an expression of alarm on her beautiful face.

"Who are you?" she called to him, sounding defensive and nervous.

He got out of his truck and quickly identified himself. "I'm Rex. I didn't know you were here. I mean, I didn't know anybody would be here. I'm sorry. I don't mean to bother you—"

She seemed to relax a little, and she interrupted him by saying, "Okay."

He was so surprised to find her there, as surprised as she looked at the sight of him. She looked a little younger than he remembered, and just as beautiful. She was wearing white shorts that showed off her long, tanned legs, and a loose, orange T-shirt that gave him the impression she didn't have a bra on. She had her long straight hair tied low on the back of her neck, and she was wearing dangly earrings that sparkled in the sunshine when she moved. Rex felt his body responding. He wanted to whip off his cap and hold it over his crotch to hide what was happening to him. Instead, he stared fiercely at her face, keeping his eyes above her collarbone.

She shaded her eyes with one hand, suggesting, to his immense relief, that she couldn't see him all that well in the bright sun. "Oh! You're Pat's brother, aren't you?"

Apparently she saw him well enough to recognize him. Rex felt a confusing mixture of worry and pleasure. On the one hand, he was surprised she had ever really seen him. On the other hand, he wasn't sure he wanted her to remember him from that day.

"Yeah," he confirmed for her. "Pat left for college."

"Right. K-State."

He hated it that she knew.

"You were here before," she said.

He nodded, wondering if she thought he was an idiot.

"You made Patrick leave."

He thought he saw her smile, just a little.

Rex was tongue-tied. All he could do was nod again.

"Why'd you come out here?" she asked him.

He thought fast. "I'm looking for Mitch."

She looked alarmed again. "Mitch Newquist? He's coming here?"

"No. I mean, I don't know. I'm just looking for him." Feeling as fake as a dimestore cowboy, Rex asked her, "You haven't seen him?"

When she shook her head no, he didn't know what to do next. After an awkward moment, Rex turned around to leave. But she called out to him, with a tone of urgency in her voice that made him turn around in a hurry. "Hey! Don't tell anybody you saw me here, okay?"

He took a couple of steps toward her. "Why not? Aren't you supposed to be here? Why *are* you here, anyway? Are you, like, cleaning the house for them?" He didn't see a car that she could have driven here. Come to think of it, he didn't recall seeing any vehicle but Patrick's the last time he was here. A wild idea came to him out of nowhere. "You're not, like, *living* here, are you?"

Once again, he was totally surprised when she said, "Yes," and then, "Would you like a beer?"

Would he ever.

She invited him onto the porch that first time, but not into the house, and brought a cool bottle out to him. "You're not having one?" he asked her, feeling awkward if he was going to be the only one to drink. She shook her head. Rex quickly got over his hesitation and sucked down a swig, reveling in the beer, the forbiddenness of it, and being on a porch alone with a gorgeous girl.

"I'm living here," she said.

He sat on the porch railing while she leaned against the frame of the screen door, and explained it to him, or part of it, anyway. "You don't know my family," she began, a statement with which Rex could only agree. "If you did, you'd know why I have to get away from them. My dad—" She stopped, shook her head, then started in with another sentence entirely. "I can't tell you the reasons. They're personal. But Judge and Mrs. Newquist know about it, and they told me I could stay here, until I figure out somewhere else to go."

"You're hiding from your family?" he asked her.

She nodded her head. "Please, please don't give me away."

"I wouldn't!" he promised her, feeling terribly protective. He felt horrified for her. For a girl to have to hide out from her own family like this—from her father—it could only be something horrible, like beatings, or . . . worse. Rex thought, *incest,* but couldn't bear to hold the word in his head for longer than an instant. He didn't know who her father was, but whoever he was, Rex already hated the man and would have gladly killed him for her.

"Does Mitch know?" he asked her. Rex could hardly believe that his best friend could know something like this, and never spill the beans. He hastened to assure her, "If he does, he never told me, and he tells me everything."

"Mitch doesn't know I'm here, at least, I don't think he does."

"Really? I guess that's possible. We don't use this place. Him and his friends, I mean. His folks would kill us if we ever did any damage to it."

It amazed him that the Newquists had given their party house to anybody, much less to a girl who only cleaned for them. Rex had never thought of Mitch's folks as being that generous, or sensitive to other people's troubles, but he could see that he had badly misjudged them. When push came to shove, as it maybe literally had with Sarah, unfortunately, it seemed that the judge and his wife were okay.

It was funny. Now he was going to be the one to keep this secret from Mitch, and it was Mitch's own house, so to speak. Rex kind of liked having a secret that Mitch ought to have known, but didn't. But he also thought he was going to have a hell of a hard time keeping it. Or at least he thought so until Sarah looked at him with her strange, beautiful, pleading eyes, and said in a near whisper, "If you tell any-body I'm here, you could get me killed. I'm not kidding. They'll come after me, and I don't know what they'll do. Please, please, you've got to promise me never to tell Mitch, or anybody else."

Of course, he swore on his life that he would never do that.

It was only when he was on his way home, just moments later, that Rex realized that his brother must know. She trusted Patrick not to tell anybody? Obviously, she didn't know his brother very well, or she'd know that Patrick drunk was an even bigger blowhard than Patrick sober.

At first, it really worried him to think of Patrick entrusted with such a secret.

It was only later, a couple of days later after the glow had worn off a little, that Rex began to feel the first tug of doubt. How secret could something be if Patrick knew it? And how likely was it, really, that Mitch's mom, who wouldn't give a spare sandwich to a bum if he was starving to death on her doorstep, would turn her precious ranch house over to a "mere" cleaning girl? But if all of that was unlikely, then so was Sarah's story, and if that wasn't true, then what the hell was she doing out there?

Still, he said nothing to Mitch, or to anyone else, just in case it was true.

He started going out there every few days to check on her, to see if she needed anything, to try to figure out the truth of the mystery of her being there. And he tried a few other gambits that wouldn't give anything away.

Chapter Twenty-one

"Mom," Rex asked Verna, in his first foray into checking out the truth of Sarah's story. "How come you guys don't party at the Newquists' place in the country anymore?"

His mother looked over from the counter where she was mashing potatoes for supper, with a surprised expression on her plump, pleasant face. "What in the world made you think of that, Rex?"

"I don't know." He shrugged, walked closer, stuck a finger down into the potatoes, dangerously close to the whirring blades, and got his hand slapped for his trouble. He still managed to emerge with a grin and a fingertip-full of potato, which he sucked off. After he swallowed, he said, "I just got to thinking about it the other day, how much fun we used to have when we'd all hang out there. You and Dad, Doc and Abby's mom, the judge and Mrs. Newquist, and all of us kids. I thought that was almost like your favorite place to be with your friends."

"I'm sure we'll do it again sometime."

"Why did you stop?"

"Stop? We didn't stop, Rex, it's just . . . you know how Nadine is, if she can't have something perfect, then she doesn't want to have it at all."

"What's not perfect?"

"According to her," his mother said, with a comically sarcastic twist to the pronoun, a twist that made him think of her other friend, Margie Reynolds, "the house isn't fit for company anymore. She says she's not having anybody out there ever again until Tom lets loose with enough money to fix it up the way she wants it done. And you know what that means."

Rex laughed, thinking of Tom the tightwad and Nadine the perfectionist. "Never gonna happen?"

"Probably not in my lifetime," his mother said, grinning. "Maybe in yours."

*   *   *

"Hey, Mrs. Newquist," he said the next time he was in their house. "How come you guys don't use the ranch house anymore?"

Mitch's mother took her time answering him. Finally, she looked up from the newspaper she was reading in the den, and said, in her cool, precise way, "I'm having it redone, Rex."

"Redone? Like, how?"

"I am having a new foundation put in, new roof, painting inside and out, new furnishings, and we're putting a gazebo in the backyard."

"Sweet," he said. "So it's all torn up right now?"

He watched her hesitate, though he wouldn't have called it that if he hadn't been watching for it. He would have just thought it was one of her controlling moments, when Nadine answered people when she, and only she, damn well pleased. "Yes. I don't want anyone out there while the work is in progress."

It almost jibed with what his mother had told him, except for one thing—from what he had seen at the ranch house, there wasn't any work going on at all. It appeared to him that Mrs. Newquist had told his mother one story and now was telling him a slightly different one, but they both added up to the same thing: hiding the fact that the Newquists were giving shelter to a girl who didn't want to be found.

Mitch's mom went up in his estimation in that moment.

Not only was she a pretty damned good liar, much better than he had ever given her credit for being, but she was doing a good deed without getting any credit for it from her friends and neighbors. His mother and Abby's mom would be amazed if they knew about it. Which they weren't going to, because he wasn't going to tell them.

• • •

"Hey," he said to Mitch while they waited for Abby and his own date to come back from the bathroom at the movies. "Remember that hot chick who used to work for your mom? Sarah, I think her name was? What the hell was her last name, can you remember? And where was she from, anyway?"

"Sarah?" Mitch turned toward him, with a lascivious grin. "Ah, Sarah."

Annoyed, Rex thwacked his friend's sack of popcorn so kernels flew out.

"Hey!" Mitch objected. "Why'd you do that?"

"Do you remember her last name, or don't you? I was trying to think of it the other day, and I can't remember it, and it's driving me crazy."

Mitch picked popcorn off his lap and dropped it onto the floor. "Um, I dunno. Oh, wait. Yeah, I do know." He reached over and grabbed a huge handful of Rex's popcorn and put it in his own sack.

"Hey!" Rex objected.

"Francis," Mitch said. "I remember it was two first names, and her last name was like the town she was from. Sarah Francis from Franklin. That's how I remember it."

Rex moved his feet so Abby could walk by him. His own date sat down on his right.

"Why do you want to know her name?" Mitch asked him, too loudly.

"Whose name?" Rex's date immediately wanted to know.

"Our second-grade teacher," Rex said.

"You're kidding!" His date gave him a disbelieving look. "You for-got Miss Plant's name? How could you forget Miss Plant's name? She looked just like a rhododendron."

All four of them started to laugh.

"I don't even know what that means," Mitch said, almost choking on the popcorn he had been swallowing when she said it, "but you're right, she did."

"Not nice," Abby reproved them, but her giggles undercut her dis-approval.

After the movie started, Mitch leaned in close and said in a lower voice, "So. You gonna look her up?"

"Who?"

"Don't give me who. You know who. You going to look her up?"

"No way. I just couldn't remember her last name, that's all."

Even in the dark he could sense his best friend's suspicious grin. "Yeah? As I recall, Sarah Francis doesn't look like a rhododendron."

"No," Rex had to admit, "she does not. Did not. Now shut up."

"She looks like a rose, a beauteous, blossoming, ripe and luscious, fragrant—"

"Shut the *fuck* up."

Mitch subsided, chuckling to himself, which made Abby turn her face to look at him quizzically. He answered her by darting toward her and planting a quick kiss on her lips, which made her smile over at Rex, and then subside back into her seat.

●　　●　　●

On the pretext of needing some shaving cream, Rex stopped by the Rexall Drug Store where one of his high school history teachers worked behind the counter between school sessions.

"Rex," she said, "what are you up to this summer? Helping your dad at the ranch?"

"Mostly." He passed the shaving cream over to her, adding a pack of chewing gum to it at the last minute. "Hey, Mrs. Aldrich, aren't you originally from over near Franklin?"

"I am," she said, looking surprised and pleased. "How did you ever remember that?"

He grinned at her. "Every time we played your old high school, you'd tell us about your mixed feelings."

"Oh, dear," she laughed. "I'll bet that got old fast."

"No, no, it was okay. But I wondered, did you ever know a family named Francis over there?"

"Francis?" She nearly rolled her eyes at him. "I'll say I knew them. Everybody knows that family. I'll tell you a secret, Rex. All by themselves, the Francis family is a good reason to teach school in this county instead of that one."

"No kidding. They're that bad?"

She shuddered. "Rex, I have opinions about those children that teachers aren't supposed to have about their students." She smiled at him again, passing over his change and his items in a sack. Then she winked at him. "Don't tell anybody."

He grinned back at her. "I won't. Are they all like that?"

She squinted, in thought. "Almost. There's an older sister who's a nice girl, or at least she was the last I knew of her, which is some years ago. I substitute taught in their grade school the year I was pregnant, and she was in my class. Pretty child, maybe not an Einstein, but she tried hard, and she was very sweet. I never had to deal with her parents, thank goodness, because they never came to school to check on their kids, but her younger siblings were already raising hell. Even the sister was a mess. How that girl came out of that bunch, I'll never know. I remember thinking at the time, if she's smart, she'll get as far away from them as she possibly can." She leaned over the counter and said in a whisper, "I don't say this easily about anybody, Rex, but they're trash, nothing but trash, from their worthless parents on down to the littlest child, God help him."

"Except that one daughter."

Mrs. Aldrich shrugged, a little sadly. "I don't know how she turned out." Then it finally occurred to her ask the obvious question. "Why'd you ask me about them, Rex?"

He shrugged right back at her, and made a face as if it was no big deal. "I heard a couple of boys from that family might be looking for part-time ranch work, and—"

"Don't even think about hiring them, Rex."

"Thanks, Mrs. Aldrich. I won't. I'll tell my dad."

"I doubt you'll be telling your father anything he doesn't already know," she said, looking cynical. "I'll bet sheriffs all over the state know the name Francis by heart."

•   •   •

One last stop, and he was finished pursuing the story she'd told him.

The next Saturday, after morning football practice, and on a day when his father had released him from work at home, Rex fended off his friends who wanted him to drive around with them, and he drove alone to Franklin, twenty-five miles away.

He hadn't had a reason to be there in years, and he was a little shocked to see how much the tiny town had declined since then. There never had been more than a handful of jobs there, and a scattering of houses. It was barely even a town. But it was in even worse condition now, with hardly a sign of life on the bedraggled-looking, two-block Main Street. Immediately, he understood why Sarah Francis had regularly driven all the way to Small Plains to find work cleaning houses, and it didn't have anything to do with status in her hometown. It had to do with survival, from what he could see.

He hadn't been able to find out where her family lived, not without drawing attention to the question, so he hadn't asked. Now he realized it didn't really matter. There wasn't a decent house in the town. It appeared that every resident lived on the edge of poverty, or deep down in it. Add that to a bad family, and a girl wouldn't need any other reasons to want to run away. So maybe Sarah hadn't sounded totally convincing to him when she had explained her presence at the Newquists' place, but then maybe that was only because she was ashamed of where she'd come from and what she was going through.

I should have believed her, he thought, feeling bad about it.

He turned around and drove back home. Two days later, he worked up the nerve to go back out to see her again.

"I just wondered, is there anything you need that I could bring you?"

"Well, Mrs. Newquist makes sure I have groceries, but . . . yeah, there's some stuff I don't really want to ask her for."

She gave him a short list, mostly expensive snack foods, which he happily filled at a grocery store in yet another town, where nobody would know him, and where nobody would ask why the sheriff's son was buying women's magazines and frozen diet dinners, among other things. Doing it made him feel happy and needed, and the nature of the things she asked him to get gave him the feeling of intimacy with her. When he handed them over to her, and she forgot to ask him how much they cost, he didn't mind. After what he had seen in Franklin that day, he was happy to help her in any way she might need help. After that, he began to think of his trips to stores for her as favors that she was doing *him,* by allowing him to be of service.

Chapter Twenty-two

May 31, 2004

Randie raised her head, and looked around Sam's Pizza, where the friends sat at a big round wooden table. "Am I going blind, or did it suddenly get dark in here?"

"It's not you," Abby told her. "Look outside, guys."

Obediently, they turned to stare out the picture windows facing the main street. Cars were driving with their headlights on, even though the sun hadn't gone down yet. Right at that moment, pings against the glass told them that rain had started falling.

"Looks like we got in just before the downpour," Ellen observed.

One large pizza sat on the table in front of them—loaded with everything, thin crust, double cheese, sprinkled with hot pepper by Cerule's liberal hand. The three women who weren't either a mayor or a funeral director had beers in front of them. For Ellen and Susan, who might get called out by emergencies at any time, there was iced tea. The women were halfway finished eating when the lights in the restaurant suddenly seemed to glow a whole lot brighter than before.

"Ooo," Susan said, "I just love the weather when it gets like this."

"You would," Cerule said, with a derisive snort. "You love morgues, too."

"No, seriously," Susan insisted. "Don't you just love it when the air gets all dark and spooky like this? I think it's exciting, like anything could happen."

"Yeah, like we could all get blown away at any moment," Cerule retorted.

With perfect timing, the manager of the restaurant stopped by their table. "We're under a tornado watch, ladies. If it turns into a warning, we can head to the basement." She smiled at them. "If you don't mind sitting on cases of tomato sauce."

When she moved on to the next table, Randie said, "If a tornado hits us and breaks all that tomato sauce, they'll think there's been a massacre." After a laugh went around the table she returned them to their prior hot topic of conversation. "What do you think he's been doing with himself all these years?"

"I heard he's a lawyer," Cerule said.

"You did?" Abby stared across the table at her. "I never heard that."

"I heard real estate," Susan offered.

"Well," Ellen said, "we know he got married and had a kid, right Abby?" Nadine had made sure their mother knew that much. "A son, the year before Mom died. And we know he settled in Kansas City at some point. And we know he still looks better than he has any right to."

It was the consensus of the women that any man who wouldn't come back for his mother's funeral was an unfeeling, selfish, no-good son of a bitch, no offense intended to Nadine. They were so busy dissecting him that none of them paid any attention to the worsening weather.

•   •   •

At 7:10, the sheriff's department got word from an amateur storm spotter of a funnel cloud sighted half a mile west of U.S. 177, near state road 12. Five minutes later, it was reported "on the ground." It was timed moving on the ground for sixteen seconds before it lifted back up into the air.

The spotter followed it in his van, keeping in touch by cell and short-wave radio.

At 7:22, he reported it moving, "in the air, over the cemetery, heading southeast at about fifteen miles an hour."

When Rex got the first report, he realized the twister had touched down in the approximate location of Abby's home and greenhouse. When he couldn't raise her by land or cell phone, he ran to his car and rocketed out of town to check on her. Partway there, he got a report that the tornado had taken a sudden veer in his direction. It was now moving southeast along the same general route where he was going northwest. *Southeast?* Rex thought incredulously. Tornadoes didn't go southeast, they went northeast. He saw it when it emerged from clouds that looked about a mile and a half away from him. What the hell was this one doing?

At least it wasn't on the ground anymore.

It was high up in the air, but to his eyes it looked as if it was dipping lower by the second, and then it split in two, forming twin funnels.

Oh shit, Rex thought.

It might come back together again, or one or both of them might touch ground or they could both vanish harmlessly into the clouds again.

If they were still moving at fifteen miles an hour . . .

And they were only a mile and a half away . . .

Less than that now . . .

There were no highway overpasses handy. There were no side roads going in a safer direction. If he were to drive off into the fields, he was going to have to plow through fences to do it, and there'd be budgetary hell to pay for the damage later. If, on the other hand, the tornado picked up his car and hurled it, not even the county's insurance agent could argue with that. A human body inside in a car during a tornado was a bad idea, however.

Rex drove his SUV onto the shoulder of the highway.

Just as the first small hail arrived, he flung himself out of his vehicle and down into a culvert at the side of the road, pulling his jacket up over his head to protect himself from the hail, rain, and flying debris.

•   •   •

"This is the real thing, ladies," the Sam's Pizza manager told them, and then she raised her voice for all of her customers to hear. "Tornado sighted, coming this way! Everybody follow me! Everybody into the basement, now!"

"Sure, sure," Randie scoffed, even as a customer said, "Tornado?" in a loud, scared voice. But Randie said only to her friends, dismissively, "How many times have we heard that?" She sliced into a triangle of pizza as casually as if the restaurant manager hadn't said anything. "You know what I think, I think Rex runs that siren too damned much. Do you guys even take it seriously anymore? I swear, the thing goes off if somebody so much as breathes heavy! Did you all hear it when it went off the other night? It finally woke me up, but all I did was turn over and go back to sleep."

"I know!" Susan reached for the hot pepper flakes while some customers around them hurried to follow the manager. At a couple of other tables, people just kept eating, like the five friends. "It's like crying wolf. Someday, we'll have a real one, and we won't pay any attention to it, and we'll all die."

"Good for business, though," Cerule teased her.

Susan gave her a repressive look, which earned a wink.

"Rex wouldn't run the siren," Abby defended him, "unless there's a good reason—"

"Whoa," Cerule interrupted.

They saw that she was staring out one of the big windows near their table, and they all turned to look, too.

"Jeez," Randie breathed. "Could be a real wolf this time."

With glances at one another, but without much talk, they put down their food and drinks and started getting up from the table.

Abby hurried over to the window to get a closer look at the conditions outside. They saw her crane her neck to look up, and then look from side to side down the street. In front of her, on the other side of the glass, the evening air had taken on a strange yellow-greenish tint. When she turned around and said, "You ought to see these clouds," the other four women went over to join her. They saw the oily, boiling look of the black clouds above them. Hail began to *ping* against the glass.

"Okay, I believe it," Randie said, and turned to seek shelter.

Abby, Ellen, Susan, and Cerule followed her over to where the restaurant manager stood, waving stragglers like them down the stairs. As they joined the people moving toward the open door, Cerule poked Abby in the ribs. When Abby looked at her, Cerule nodded her head to point to somebody.

Over by the cash register, Abby saw Jeff Newquist, the judge's teenager, the adopted boy known cruelly around town as "the substitute son." He was a sharp-featured kid, taller than average, husky, with dark eyes and long dark hair that he wore caught back at the nape of his neck in the kind of ponytail that was sure to get yanked on by every cowboy who walked past it. As the two friends watched him, Abby suddenly drew in her breath in a little gasp, and whispered, "Did he just do what I thought I saw him do?"

Cerule gave her a startled glance, and nodded.

Jeff Newquist, seventeen years old, out for pizza with a couple of his buddies, and heading for the basement along with everybody else, had just lifted several candy bars from a display on top of the cash register counter and slipped them into a pocket of his jacket. He fumbled one of them, which fell to the floor at the feet of his friends. One of them laughed. Jeff looked around the restaurant, and stared straight into Abby's face. And then suddenly, the three of them turned around and trotted toward the restaurant door.

"Hey!" Cerule yelled to them.

Behind them, the manager yelled, "Boys! Don't go out there!"

But the kids just laughed, rolled their collars up on their necks, and continued running out of the restaurant and into the street, where the first drops of rain were starting to fall, and the wind was picking up.

At the basement door, Ellen said to the manager, "Do you know those boys stole some candy bars from you?"

The manager sighed and just said, "It wouldn't be the first time. Must be nice to be a judge's kid."

The friends vanished down the staircase, hurrying behind everybody else. There was a rising chatter from the underground shelter, where it seemed as if everybody was reaching for their cell phones at the same time. The women heard snatches of concern, of people trying to check on children, husbands, wives, homes, businesses, and some expressions of scared worry when their calls didn't go through. In the dim light, they saw they were surrounded by anxious faces. They were all the way to the bottom, and seated on packing cartons, pulling out their own cell phones to try to call their families, when they realized that Abby hadn't followed them down.

"Abby?" Her sister Ellen stood up just as several things seemed to happen all at once. Thunder rolled so loud it sounded as if it was right above their heads, lightning cracked almost instantly afterward, and the electricity went out, throwing them into total darkness. A crashing noise above their heads made them all jump, and a few women screamed. In the darkness, a child began to cry.

•   •   •

Abby had hurried back to the windows to check on the storm one more time before going to the basement, but then she found that she couldn't pull herself away from the sight of her town's main street. There was something magical to her about the moments right before, and then immediately after, a thunderstorm. There was something uncanny and beautiful about the quality of the light and the way everything looked in it.

As she stared, mesmerized, she saw the three boys run to a pickup truck, hop in it, do a U-turn in the middle of the street, and then drive off into the direction of the storm. Her heart pounded when she saw what they were doing; she wanted to grab their rear bumper and haul them back to safety.

A few other cars were still plying the road, and there were even a couple of people out on foot. The rain hadn't started to pour yet, though it felt to her as if it could at any moment. Then this odd, suspended moment of beauty would be gone.

How could Mitch have stayed away so long?

Abby had thought he loved their hometown as much as she did. She thought they had talked about it, how they wanted to stay here, where their families had roots going back a long, long time.

She was scared to see him again. The very thought of it dried up her mouth and made her feel shaky. She didn't know what she'd say; she didn't know how she'd act. Paralyzed, probably. Maybe she should be combative: Why the *hell* did you do that? Where the *hell* have you been? But what if she burst into tears, as she was prone to do when she was angry? That would be humiliating.

Maybe she should play it cool.

Yeah, that's gonna happen, Abby thought, echoing the sarcastic tone that Rex had used with his deputies that morning. Yeah, right, she was going to be cool when she saw Mitch for the first time in seventeen years like Rex was going to send his deputies to Miami for a forensics conference.

Maybe she could avoid him altogether. It was just a visit, her friends had guessed. Visits didn't last long; people left again, after visits.

Abby looked at how the asphalt glistened on the street outside, she looked through the store windows into the strange clarity of their interiors, able to see shelves and merchandise, colors and forms.

And still she didn't move, even when she heard the basement door close behind her.

The air darkened even more, changing the feeling of the scene at which she was staring. Now, in the eerie, ominous cast of the greenish light, everything looked hyper-accentuated, as if an artist had outlined every building with a black line, making all of them pop out from the air around them. Abby thought it still looked beautiful in a strange way, like a painting by a demented artist. There were odd angles she had never noticed before, juxtapositions of signs she could swear she had never seen before. The gargoyles on the nineteenth-century bank building on the corner seemed to shift on their pedestals, to flash their bulging eyes.

Her hometown looked vulnerable in the strange light.

Because it is *vulnerable,* Abby thought, with an inner shudder.

No matter how much better it was doing than a thousand other towns, Small Plains was always just one disaster away from their fate. Most of the stores along this main street were occupied, but that didn't mean there were no empty storefronts at all. There were, in fact, three of them in a five-block area, counting both sides of the street. Their empty interiors were hidden behind the civic advertisements that Ellen, as mayor, had persuaded the owners to let her put up, so nobody could see the dirt and bleakness within. Their FOR SALE signs were discreetly posted in a lower corner of their front windows.

Three wasn't much, as such things went, in old towns of this size, but it only counted the vacant ones. For every one of those three that had already failed, Abby knew of a dozen others that were struggling. They were making it, still making it, but barely. She was a small-business owner herself; she knew about struggling to make a go of it. She doubted those particular store owners had sufficient insurance, or any at all. If a tornado swept straight down Main Street, in minutes there would be changes they might not be able to rise above.

One disaster away from disaster . . .

Something outside caught Abby's eye.

An old man was coming out of the Wagon Wheel Café, or trying to.

She watched, appalled, as he was struck by a sudden blast of wind, and pushed back against the brick wall of the building. Abby stepped away from the big window and ran toward the door to go help him, just as the hair on the backs of her arms rose and her scalp tingled. In the instant afterward, a lightning bolt hit the electrical transformer half a block away, turning the sky bright green, and throwing downtown into darkness. The bolt ricocheted off the transformer, shot horizontally above Sam's Pizza, and struck the light pole in front of it. The pole cracked in two, sending the top half through the plate glass window where Abby had just been standing. The power of the lightning blew her against a table, which fell over, taking her to the floor with it. Glass flew like shrapnel behind her. The top half of the pole missed her by less than two feet; splinters from it landed all around her. The crossbars of the pole lay several feet beyond her head. Electrical wire draped the tables. Abby had already accidentally brushed against an exposed end of it before she realized it was dead. She felt astonished to realize *she* wasn't dead, or even injured. There was a burned smell all around her, but no fire. When she realized she had just touched an electrical wire of who knew how many thousands of volts, she nearly lost her pizza. Just to be sure it was *all* dead, she grabbed pieces of pizza and crust from the floor and tossed them onto the wires at various places. When nothing happened, no sparks or crackling, she decided it was safe to move the wires. Using the legs of a wooden chair, she pushed at the wires and moved them out of the way so that they wouldn't scare people to death when they came back upstairs, and so that nobody would trip over them. Plus, there was no telling if they might suddenly come to life again, and pose a deadly risk.

She ran to the basement door, but a chunk of the light pole had tightly wedged between the door and a permanent counter, and she couldn't budge it.

At least they're safe down there, she hoped. For now, anyway.

She tried yelling down to them, but the noise of the storm covered up her voice.

She tried calling Rex to get help, but her call wouldn't connect.

Abby pushed against the wind to open the front door so she could run to the assistance of the old man down the street.

Chapter Twenty-three

The name, "Cotton Creek Ranch," was still above the front gate, the ranch house was still down in a hollow at the end of the dirt road, and the keys to it were where they had always been, but when Mitch walked in he discovered that the house looked like nothing his mother would have allowed. There were beer cans everywhere—most empty, some partly full. The furniture that his mother had been so insistent on keeping clean was in disarray, with dining room chairs in the living room, a couple of them overturned, and the sofa and armchair cushions scattered on the floors.

What with the stale beer and being closed up, the place stank like a tavern.

He walked into the back of the small house and found the two bedrooms in much the same condition: sheets and blankets tossed about on the beds, stains on the carpets, rings on the tops of the furniture.

He didn't even want to see the bathrooms.

Mitch suspected for a moment that his father had sold the place, lock, stock, and love seats, following his mother's death, and he nearly walked back out again to put the keys back where he'd found them. But then he saw some family photographs, even one of him as a small boy, and an old file cabinet containing ancient legal documents. His father would never have let strangers get their hands on the photos or papers.

Mitch opened all the windows and propped open the front and back doors.

Had kids broken in and used it as a party house?

If that was true, they had known where to find the keys, because no door locks or windows showed signs of a break-in.

He located a roll of plastic trash bags and started picking up beer cans.

*   *   *

It didn't take him long to discover there were many more things he had forgotten about living in the country than he remembered. Well water, for one thing. He'd forgotten that his parents' small ranch house wasn't on a city water line, and so his first glass of water surprised him with its mineral flavor.

He used many gallons of it to mop, wash, scrub.

It made him feel better to work hard, sweat, get results.

After two hours of nonstop cleaning that left nine full trash bags propped outside against the house, he closed the windows and doors again, turned on the air conditioner, put one last load of towels in the washing machine, and then—feeling suddenly starved—went through all the cupboards to see if there was any food. The refrigerator was empty except for one lone beer can and a container of rotten salsa. On the cupboard shelves he found cans of gourmet stuff: little cans of sardines that might be a decade old, mustards in brands that local grocery stores would never sell, cocktail onions, and several different versions of liver pâté.

There had been cocktail parties here, he recalled, with the Old Friends.

The Shellenbergers, the Newquists, the Reynoldses.

While the six adults had drunk themselves silly, with a lot of laughter and card playing, he, Rex, Abby, and Patrick had chased one another around in the grass. The memory of that made him think again of the grown-up Abby and Patrick he had seen that morning, which made his stomach clench and drove him restlessly outside again.

Mitch stepped onto the front porch and then into the middle of the front yard, where he stopped and turned in every direction, looking around. That's when he saw another thing he couldn't believe he had ever forgotten—the drama of an approaching thunderstorm.

"Wow," he breathed, unable to keep from saying it out loud.

He was facing southwest, looking straight into the leading edge of the blackest, biggest, baddest storm he had seen since he left his hometown. *My God,* he thought, *did I ever take these for granted? Did I used to think this was no big deal?* The line of black was huge, rolling for miles horizontally, and also up, up, up until he had to bend his neck back to see the top of it. He'd seen dramatic clouds in the city sky, but nothing had the overwhelming drama of this panorama in which he could view the whole front edge, and watch it marching toward him.

It was close, he realized with an inner start.

The wind was kicking up in front of it.

He could see the lightning now, hear the rumble of the thunder.

It was spectacular. He didn't know how he had lived without seeing this for so many years. He felt as if it was made of sheer energy—which, he supposed, it was—and that all of it was starting to infuse him with something that felt exciting. Ions of excitement. He glanced to the south and saw that part of the countryside had gone stark black, hiding everything that stood there. Then there was a ferocious crack of thunder followed by a lightning bolt that flew from sky to ground, lighting up the southern scene with false daylight. In that incredible instant, he saw cattle standing in the pastures. Then, just as quickly, they were gone, disappeared into the blackness of the storm again.

Once, but only once, he had seen a tornado when he was a boy.

He and Rex would have chased it if they'd been old enough to drive.

Ever after that, they had eagerly scanned the bottoms of every storm cloud, hoping for that characteristic roiling action, that spooky special color that looked like car oil, praying for the storm to work itself up into the full boiling fury of a funnel. They'd never lucked out. Friends of theirs claimed to have seen plenty of twisters, but Rex and Mitch had never witnessed another one.

Mitch almost didn't believe it when he saw one start to form to the southwest of him.

A bit of black cloud dipped down, went back up, dipped farther down.

He saw the unmistakable shape of it.

Jesus! he thought, and wondered what to do. Call 911? Call the weather bureau? Get himself the hell out of the middle of the yard and down into the storm cellar at the back of the house?

He knew he wasn't going to do that.

He remembered the storm cellar more vividly than he wanted to. His mother had been a bit claustrophobic. She'd made his father get it dug bigger than average. She had insisted on cement-lined walls, instead of just dirt, and a ceiling high enough to make it feel like a room, instead of a grave. She had even put in plumbing for a toilet and sink, and electricity. It had seemed silly, until you had to race into it when storms like this one roared across the prairie.

All of the kids he knew had hated storm cellars; there was something so creepy about the lightbulb-lit underground refuges with their old splintery wooden doors. Everybody had always been afraid of getting imprisoned in one of them. And now, even as an adult, everything in him rebelled at the idea of closing himself into such a dank, dark, anonymous space where it might be that nobody would ever come to look for him. Which they never would, since nobody even knew he was there.

While he stood there, awed, indecisive, the cloud with the funnel moved away from him, and around to the southeast. When he saw he was out of its path, he kept staring at it. It was amazing to see it veer off suddenly yet again, this time to the northeast, in a straight, fast, and deadly path.

It dawned on him that its path led straight toward Abby's place.

With his mind screaming at him not to be a fool, his body ran to his car, hopped in, started up the engine, and tore off toward the way the storm was heading.

· · ·

The deputy didn't mean to leave anybody locked inside the cemetery before the storm hit. The girl with the wheelchair in her van didn't intend to get left behind. On this, her second visit of the day, she had stayed in her car without trying to reach the grave. When the deputy drove through the graveyard, stopping every time he saw people and pointing to the clouds and ordering everybody out, they all had to drive in single-file down and around, winding through the cemetery in order to get to the gate again. When Catie Washington got near the point in the road where there was a large equipment shed, she began to feel nauseated. She knew she had only a few seconds before she'd be too sick to drive. And so she jerked her van out of line, drove up a short gravel byway toward the shed, and scooted back around it, not wanting anybody to see her getting sick.

She was behind the shed, helpless and miserable, for a long time.

When she finally felt well enough to steer the van again, her hands were trembling, her body was soaked with perspiration, her mouth was sour with vomit, but she felt the gratitude that came when the worst was over.

It was starting to rain very hard now.

Catie turned her windshield wipers on, and then her headlights.

It grew darker by the instant, it seemed, but not so dark that she couldn't detect the oily green-black roiling of the bottom edge of the clouds directly above her. The deputy had rousted them because of tornado warnings, and now she saw the accuracy of them. There wasn't a funnel, not yet, but she looked up into the clouds, and knew the signs of what might come. Disoriented by her sickness and the worsening weather, she got back out to the one-lane road and made the mistake of turning left instead of right.

That way took her back to the top of the hill where the Virgin lay.

The air had gone a greenish-yellow; even in the darkness, she could detect the change in color, the coming vacuum, the impending stillness in the center. Under the darkest part of the storm, there was enough light to be able to watch the cloud formations. They curled, they stabbed the air beneath them, they began to rotate, and then she saw the tornado a few hundred yards away.

She put her van in park at the top of the hill.

Without thinking, hardly knowing what she was doing, and even less why she was doing it, the girl flung open her door against the rain. It was hailing now, small, hard, rough balls that pelted her weakened body, and would have hurt if she had been capable of feeling anything at that moment except the overwhelming desire to run to the top of the hill to meet the storm. She stumbled, and fell to her hands and knees on the dirt road that was turning to mud. With the rain and hail pelting her back, and the wind pushing at her like abusive hands, she crawled toward the Virgin's grave.

When she reached it, she turned over and lay spread-eagle, her face to the clouds.

All around her, the branches of the trees danced and the trees themselves leaned one way and then the other. There was a howling all around her, and then there was a roaring like a train coming closer to her. She felt like a damsel tied to the tracks, but that's how she had felt for months in the path of the cancer that was killing her. This was no different: No one could rescue her.

No strong, handsome man would come along to pick her up this time.

This was her third go-round with chemotherapy for her brain tumors. Each of the first two times, she had "known" she would lick it. When the third diagnosis came in, she lost the will to fight. She would endure one more round of chemo, she told her doctors, but that would be it. In the other two rounds, she had fought to control the nausea, using acupuncture and medicine, using whatever worked, and for a while, it had seemed to work.

It wasn't working anymore, nothing was working anymore.

She was in pain a lot of the time, and so very ill.

Now, from under the black, black oily layer of clouds, she watched the funnel form high in the air, watched it dip down once, watched it rise back up again, always moving in her direction.

When it traveled directly over her, it was one hundred feet wide at the tip.

She gazed up directly into the mouth of it, where she could see the revolution of the air and things—objects—whirling around inside of it. The roar was deafening and terrifying. She felt her whole body being picked up as if she were levitating, and then being laid back down. And then some of the things inside of the funnel began to fall on her. She closed her eyes, expecting to be killed by them. But they fell lightly atop her and all around her.

When she opened her eyes, she discovered she was covered with flowers.

     •   •   •

The three teenage boys following the twister parked across the road from the cemetery. One of them hopped out of their pickup truck and ran around to the front of it while his friends stayed inside where it was dry.

"Are you *crazy*?" was the last thing he heard them say before he slammed the door.

As the twister roared safely above him, Jeff Newquist realized he could get the video of a lifetime: actual footage up inside a tornado. Although he was getting pelted by rain and hail, pushed and pulled by wind, he took an educated guess that he'd live through it. The 'nado was just high enough not to kill him, just low enough to reveal its black heart to him.

People always claimed a tornado sounded like a freight train.

He felt as if he were chasing it down the tracks.

Jeff propped himself against the grille of his friend's truck and started filming. First, he panned the sky for context, then he focused on the eye of the storm and hit "zoom." Feeling an illusion of safety behind the lens, he began to follow the twister—across the highway, over to the opposite shoulder. He stopped beside the fence, propping himself against it to steady himself, still filming as the tornado moved on.

While he was looking in the viewfinder he couldn't tell what the hell he was seeing; it was all black and wet to him. There was a moment, though, when an odd bright greenish light filled the sky, illuminating the scene as if a director had shone spotlights on it. Even so, it was only when he hopped back in his truck, and took a look at what he had filmed, that he and his friends saw that his zoom had caught a shower of stuff falling from the funnel. Excited to find out what it was—litter from somebody's house? fence posts? arms and legs? dogs and cats?—he hopped out of the truck again, and then climbed over the cemetery fence toward where his camera had been pointed.

What he found there, at the top of the hill, scared the hell out of him.

At first, he thought it was a body dropped out of the center of the storm.

Then he thought maybe it was a corpse tossed out of a new grave, because if it wasn't, then what in God's name were all those *flowers* doing on top of her, and all around her?

He raised his camera and started shooting again.

When the "body" moved, he yelped in fright, but never put the camera down.

Jeff watched the "corpse" rise to her feet, shedding petals as she got up.

When he realized she was definitely alive, he ran toward her, yelling, "What happened?"

Smiling in a dazed way, the young woman looked at him, and then pointed up.

Toward the sky.

It finally registered with him that she was bald. And very thin. She would have looked mortally ill except for the expression of wonder and bliss on her face.

"Where'd you come from?" Jeff called to her.

"Wichita," she called back, and laughed.

"What's your name?"

"Catie!" She threw her arms wide in a gesture of pure joy. "My name is Catie Washington and I'm alive!"

She walked away from him, moving like a zombie in a trance, albeit an ecstatic zombie. Jeff filmed her getting into her van and then driving away.

When he raced back to the truck to show his friends, they watched with amazement at video proof of a "miracle": flowers falling from a deadly storm, a young woman rising from a grave, and walking away with a look of bliss on her gaunt face.

"You going to sell this to the local news?" one of his pals asked him.

"Local news, hell," Jeff Newquist scoffed. He could already feel the cash in his hands. "What do those big tabloids pay?"

Chapter Twenty-four

Mitch was pretty sure he was acting crazy. This was not a good precedent, he thought wryly, as he barreled toward the entrance to the highway on the north edge of town. With the rain coming down on his car, and the worst of the storm ahead of him, he felt like a storm chaser trying to catch up to a twister. *This is nuts,* he told himself, but how could he just stand by and watch a tornado fly toward her home, and not do anything about it? Was he supposed to just stand in his yard and hope for the best for her? What if she was there alone, what if she got hurt, what if she needed help, and he was the only one who could get there in time? He had to make sure, it was the only decent thing to do. If he got there and saw that everything was okay, he could just quietly drive away, with nobody the wiser.

Nuts. This place is already driving you crazy.

He was on his way to see if Abby had survived the tornado, and he hadn't even tried to see his father yet. Or, his brother, Jeff, whom he had not laid eyes on since his college graduation, when the boy was only four. *I have a brother . . .*

It was how he used to think of Rex, like a brother.

Rex. Mitch tried to think out ahead of time what he would do if he encountered the principals in what he thought of as his own little melodrama, now that he had decided to stick around for a while. What would . . . could . . . he say, not only to Abby, but also to Rex, or any of the other people who'd known him years ago? What was his attitude going to be if—more likely, when—he ran into Quentin Reynolds and Nathan Shellenberger? What about Verna, for that matter? And now he had Patrick to consider in his scenarios, as well. What was he going to say to people about why he had left, much less so suddenly, and why he had never returned until now?

He tried imagining it with Rex, albeit a fantasy Rex who had a grown man's body with a familiar teenager's face. He tried saying, "Hey, I'm sorry I left like that," but that wasn't going to work. If he said he was sorry for anything, he was going to have to explain why. "I'm sorry I left like that, but the thing is, I had just seen your father carry a dead girl into Abby's house, and then I saw her father . . ."

Yeah, right. He tried imagining what it might be like to run into the older men.

Immediately, rage welled up inside of him, so that all he could see himself saying was something like, "You goddamned sonsabitches . . ."

He couldn't apologize. He couldn't explain. He couldn't defend.

He was damned if he was going to employ the defense his mother had used on his behalf. "When people ask why you left like that," she had written him, "I tell them things were becoming too intense between you and Abby. I tell them we didn't want you to feel pressured to get married so young, or, God forbid, start a family at your age. I say, we thought it best for you to go away where there are greater opportunities, and different girls to date."

Upon reading that letter, he had scorched the telephone lines with a call to her, telling her to stop it, telling her not to do that to Abby, who was completely innocent in all this. "How could you?" he had yelled at his mother. "How can you say things that make people think of her like that?"

To which she had cooly replied, "Well, I have to tell them *something*, Mitch."

There had been a time, nearly nineteen years of time, when he would never have talked to his mother like that. Out of respect, and because he wouldn't have dared; he would never have dreamed of raising his voice to her, much less speaking to her in such a harsh tone, with such peremptory, accusatory words. In his family, politeness had reigned. By the time of this phone call, he had lost the respect, if not entirely the fear.

"Not that!" he had yelled at her. "You don't have to tell them anything. It's none of their business. But don't tell them *that*."

He had no idea if she paid any attention to him.

Now he was going into a situation where he didn't know what people thought, what lies had been spread, what stories had been made up to compensate for the truths that had never been told. He decided to take his cues from others, at least while he was still testing the waters, timing his moves. If they were friendly to him, that's how he would be to them, up to a point that stopped short of reactivating friendships. That wasn't going to happen. It couldn't happen. If they were cool, he would be, too. He decided his best bet was to be courteous but distant pleasant but unapproachable. That way, nobody could get hurt, or at least not as badly as the truth could hurt them.

He preferred not to think about how his other plans might hurt some of them.

As Mitch turned north on the highway, he had a feeling he had already lost his grip on all that rational planning. Where was it that morning when he had impulsively followed little green arrows to Abby's place? And where was it now when he was following a tornado, for God's sake, straight back to her?

"Courteous, aloof, neutrally pleasant," he reminded himself, out loud. "I'll be so goddamned pleasant my own ex-wife wouldn't recognize me."

He was more than halfway there when he saw something that made him pull over to the side of the road and park. Just ahead of him, there was a Muncie County sheriff's car that was parked crooked on the shoulder, as if its driver had pulled over in a hurry and left it there. And off in the nearby culvert, a tall man in a uniform was getting to his feet and appearing to dust himself off, a sheriff's deputy, maybe.

The storm had gone through here in a big way.

Mitch got out of his car, to make sure the deputy was all right.

.   .   .

Rex endured small hailstones pounding on his back, and drenching rain. Wind howled around him, picking up gravel and hurling it at him. He thought he even heard the metal in his car rattle. He wanted to raise his head and look, but didn't want to take the chance of being blinded by debris.

It seemed to last forever, but when the worst of it was over, he realized he had only been a victim of the more ordinary part of the storm, and not the twister itself. When he did look up and scan the sky for it, he couldn't even see it, but only spotted the dire black clouds from which it had emerged, receding toward the northeast. Where twisters were supposed to go. Rex looked due north, checking for damage and people and not seeing any. Then he turned to look south and spied one car, a black late-model Saab, parked on the same shoulder where he was.

He watched a tall man get out of the car, and walk toward him.

There was something about the way the man moved that struck a vaguely familiar chord in Rex. It was the aggressive tilt of the broad shoulders, the straightforward carriage of the head that made him think it might be somebody he knew. It brought back memories, for some reason, of playing in football games when he played left tackle, running ahead, making big blocks for their talented tight end . . .

I'll be damned . . .

When the big man got close enough, Rex found himself looking into Mitch's eyes.

.   .   .

Mitch saw it in Rex's face, the exact same immediate impulse he felt in the first second when they recognized each other: a natural, almost irresistible impulse to grin. In that instant, the years between them didn't exist. There was only the same old close friendship, the same chemistry and rapport. There was a flash of amnesia, a wiping out of old sins, a memory only of affection and great times. In that moment, there was only the day before yesterday; yesterday, itself, disappeared. In that moment, they could have slapped each other's shoulders, they could have shouted, "Goddamn!" and laughed out loud. They could have said, "Where you been?" and laughed about it. They could have taken up right where they had left off.

And in the next instant, Mitch saw Rex cut it off, so he did, too.

Mitch had a sense of being in a twilight zone where he and Rex had seen an open door that they could have stepped through to a different, happier conclusion. Instead, given the choice, they both slammed that door shut. It left them standing in the rain on the shoulder of the highway, staring at each other in wary disbelief at what they couldn't believe they were seeing with their own eyes, after all these years.

"Mitch," Rex said, in a neutral tone.

"Yeah. I didn't know it was you when I pulled up—"

"Or you might not have stopped?" Rex cracked a grin, after all, but a cynical one.

"No, I mean—" He stopped trying. "You okay?"

"I'm fine." Rex made a show of knocking mud off his clothes. Mitch sensed he was doing it just so he didn't have to look him in the eye. "No harm done." When Rex straightened up again, he said, in the same careful, neutral tone, "I never heard you were coming back—"

"Just for a visit—"

"Sure. Wouldn't want to stick around."

"Jesus." It slipped out of Mitch. He hadn't meant to react angrily to anything any of them said, but Rex's sarcasm had poked him into a response. "It's not that."

"Whatever. Looks like you're already heading back the way you came."

"What?" Mitch realized that Rex meant, *you're driving north*. Away. "No, I just . . . came out to see the storm."

"Yeah, well, I'm on my way to check on . . . people in that direction."

He isn't even going to say her name to me, Mitch thought.

"Okay, well, I better not keep you from it."

"You're not. I guess, if you're going to be around for a while, I'll probably see you."

"I don't know how long I'll be here." Mitch paused, then added reluctantly, "My dad doesn't know I'm here, so I'd appreciate it if you wouldn't say anything."

Rex raised his eyebrows. "You going to tell him?"

"Pretty soon. So . . . are you a deputy to your dad now?"

"No." Rex smiled slightly. "He's retired. I'm it."

"*You're* the sheriff?"

There was another moment then, following Mitch's incredulous question when they might have laughed together about it, about the idea of either one of them growing up to be a lawman, but again they kept it from happening.

"Yeah, I'm the sheriff."

"I'll be damned."

Rex restrained himself from commenting on that.

"What about you? he asked Mitch.

"What do you mean?"

"What do you do?"

"Some law, some real estate."

"Sounds lucrative." Rex looked over Mitch's shoulder at the black Saab.

"It's all right," Mitch said. "You married?"

"No, you?"

"Divorced. I have a son. Any kids?"

"Not so I've heard."

Mitch smiled, but Rex didn't return it.

And that was that. There was an instant when they might have shaken hands in parting, but they didn't.

"Good to see you," Mitch said awkwardly.

"Yeah. Take care."

Each man turned and went toward his car without looking back.

Mitch got into his vehicle and sat and watched Rex drive off. If Rex was going to check on Abby, then he didn't have to. He felt shaken by the encounter. He felt angry, sad, a jumble of emotions he realized he had not anticipated fully, and did not know how to absorb in a way that might make them go away. He just wanted them to go away. For a moment, he again considered just going away, himself.

Not yet. Not until he had done what he needed to do for himself . . . and Sarah.

It occurred to him that the aftermath of a storm might be a good time to start.

Mitch waited until the sheriff's car was out of sight. Then he turned the Saab around on the highway, and headed back toward Small Plains to see if the high winds and rain had produced any damage that might be of benefit to him.

Chapter Twenty-five

The rain had washed the air clean, giving everything a bright, sharp edge.

Mitch drove into town, noting tree limbs and wet leaves in the streets, and gutters backed up so high that water stood in pools at the intersections. He spotted minor property damage in some places—a shutter torn here, a large tree branch fallen on a roof there.

The only place Mitch saw serious damage was at Sam's Pizza.

It looked dark, but then so did everyplace else. It appeared the electricity was out all over town. There didn't seem to be anybody inside the restaurant with the light pole sticking out of it. Maybe they had all gotten out in time, he thought as he drove slowly past it. But what if they hadn't?

He pulled over and parked, and hurried to find out if anybody inside needed help.

It struck him as ironic that he couldn't recall ever having gone to the rescue of anybody in all the years he'd lived in Kansas City. Yet, here he was helping out for the third time that day, counting the girl at the cemetery and stopping to check on the man who had turned out to be Rex Shellenberger.

•
•   •
•

Across the street, in the shadow of a store's doorway, Abby crouched beside the elderly man, who had fallen during the storm. She had one hand gently on his shoulder and in her other hand she held her cell phone, on which she was in the middle of a conversation with her doctor-father. Once the storm had passed, she had been able to make calls again. Still unable to raise Rex, she'd finally connected with the sheriff's department to tell them about the trapped people in the basement of Sam's Pizza. She tried not to think about how scared her sister and her friends must be right now, and to focus instead of the immediate needs of the old man in front of her.

"He says his arm hurts, Dad, and he can't seem to get up—"

She heard a car door slam, and turned to see if help had arrived.

But instead of seeing Rex or his deputies, she saw a tall man get out of a black Saab. He glanced around the street without noticing Abby and the old man, and then hurried toward Sam's Pizza.

Abby's voice faltered; her breath stopped in her chest.

"Abby?" she heard her dad say. "Are you there?"

"Hold on, Dad," she said into the phone.

Abby watched, disbelieving, as Mitch Newquist crossed the street in front of her.

She crouched deeper into the shadows, trying to keep him from seeing her. In spite of everything, and whether it was stupid vanity or not, she couldn't bear the thought that he might see her for the first time in seventeen years like this—looking like a drenched rat from running in the wind and rain. She felt suddenly as unsteady, as wounded and dazed, as the old man beside her. When Mitch never turned around, she relaxed a little bit. Before he vanished into the restaurant, however, she saw how broad his back was across his shoulders, and how it tapered to his waist, and how his legs looked long and lean in his jeans, and how his blond hair had darkened, but not thinned, over the years. When he disappeared inside Sam's Pizza, she said helplessly, "Oh, dammit!"

"What's the matter?" her father demanded.

"Just drive on over here Dad, and check on this guy, will you?"

She hung up, still staring at the darkened restaurant across the street. And suddenly she no longer felt helpless, she just felt furious.

"You rotten lousy no-good runaway son of a damned bitch!"

The old man stared at her in alarm.

"Not you," she soothed him. "I didn't mean you."

* * *

When Mitch walked into Sam's Pizza, he whistled at the damage the top half of the light pole had done, the way it had shattered plate glass and broken tables and scattered silverware, food, napkins, and plastic glasses. There was room to walk without running into the danger of any wires that might come to life. It almost looked as if somebody had moved the wires out of the way. A part of the pole had lodged in a way that held shut a door that he decided must lead to the basement. When he heard pounding and yelling voices coming from behind it, he hurried to apply muscle to the broken pole.

"The door's stuck!" he called to the voices behind the door. "Hold on."

Their calls for help subsided, but he could still hear talking on the other side.

It took him several minutes, but Mitch finally managed to dislodge the splintery wood, and when he did the door popped open on its own. He saw a couple of people he didn't recognize standing toward the middle of the stairs, but couldn't see anybody else in the dimness beyond them.

"Thank you!" the woman closest to him said, and was echoed by other voices.

"No problem. Everybody all right down there?"

"We're fine. Just scared, with no lights."

"I'll bet. There's a lot of broken glass up here. And watch out for electrical wires when you come up."

Having ascertained that they were okay, Mitch turned and walked out.

Down at the bottom of the stairs, four women stood, dumbfounded, staring up at the open doorway where the tall, baritone-voiced man who rescued all of them had stood just an instant before. He hadn't been able to see any of them, but they had been able to see him clearly, framed as he was in the new clear light of the evening.

"Uh oh," Cerule Youngblood whispered to her friends.

•   •   •

In the time it took Mitch Newquist to free the trapped people in the basement, Quentin Reynolds had pulled up in his car and taken over the care of the tourist from Abby. She was just getting ready to tell him about seeing Mitch when her cell phone rang and she answered it, glad of a distraction from the way her heart was pounding and her knees were trembling. When she said hello and then heard Rex's voice, she asked, "What did the storm do?"

"Come home, Abby," Rex told her, in a somber tone of his own. "The tornado only landed in one place, but it just happened to be your greenhouse."

"Oh, no!" she cried, and then blurted the first concern that came to her mind, and it wasn't about her flower and landscaping business. "Rex, my birds!"

•   •   •

Mitch walked down the Sam's Pizza side of the street, looking at storm damage.

When he came to a small business with a discreet FOR SALE sign and a front display full of broken glass, he walked in, and said to the woman who was sweeping up her mess, "Need some help?"

Without even waiting for an answer, he grabbed a second broom that was propped against a wall near him. *Why, I'm just a Boy Scout,* Mitch thought, feeling nearly amused enough to laugh out loud, though he managed to restrain himself. This wasn't exactly the way he had planned to ingratiate himself with the marginal property owners of Small Plains, but if this was the opportunity that fate was laying across his path, then he would grab the broom end of it, and see what he could sweep into his grasp.

When he finished that task successfully, stepped back outside, and looked down the street toward his car, he saw a stocky, gray-haired man helping an older man into a vehicle. At first, Mitch didn't recognize Abby's father. It wasn't until Doc Reynolds stepped away from the vehicle and stood by himself on the sidewalk that recognition kicked in—and with it, a resurgence of rage so overwhelming that for a minute Mitch thought he might black out from the power of it. He stared, clenching and unclenching his fists, not trying to hide himself, inwardly daring Quentin Reynolds to turn and look him in the face.

But the doctor turned the other way and got into his own car.

He drove past Mitch without looking his way, but Mitch got a good look at how dramatically the man had aged in the past seventeen years. If the devil left telltale marks, Mitch thought, then Quentin Reynolds deserved every line on his face, and then some. Any doubts Mitch had been feeling about his purpose in Small Plains were swept away by the sight of his enemy.

●　　●　　●

Abby bolted out of her sister's car even before it stopped in her yard.

Ignoring her leveled greenhouse, she raced for her screened-in porch.

"The door's open!" she screamed, panic and despair in her voice.

When her friends came hurrying up behind her, she was already on the porch, on her knees, cradling a trembling little gray bird in her hands. "Gracie!" The conure was alive, but the body of Lovey, the lovebird, lay against the door leading into the house, where it had fallen, as if the wind had hurled it into the glass.

Randie tiptoed over to where the colorful little body lay. She knelt down and stroked Lovey's feathers. When there was no response from the beautiful peach-faced lovebird, she whispered, "Oh, no."

There was no big red parrot anywhere to be seen.

"Look for J.D.!" Abby begged them, sobbing over her lone remaining bird.

Carrying Gracie, Abby made a frantic tour of the inside of her house, hoping against hope that somehow she'd find the parrot there. In keeping with the sometimes bizarre path of tornadoes, her greenhouse had been destroyed, but her house was undisturbed—except for one thing.

The only thing she noticed missing was Patrick's sunglasses.

Abby had put them back on the kitchen table before leaving for supper with her friends, and now they were gone. She stood for a long time, cradling Gracie and staring at the empty space where they had been.

The other women ran off the porch and scattered around the property. They called out over and over for the twenty-year-old South American parrot. They stared helplessly up into every tree, searched all around the bushes, lifted fallen boards, and ignored every other need while they fruitlessly searched for him.

Chapter Twenty-six

By the time she got back to the bed-and-breakfast where she was staying, Catie Washington felt exhausted again, or at least her body was. Her mind was still racing, and her emotions were still in a rising, swirling white tornado of their own. Her thoughts were floating, her feelings were sailing, they were riding out ahead of her body's ability to keep up with them. She felt *alive*. Emotionally, she couldn't wait to get back to her bedroom in the B&B and open her laptop computer and log on to write her story down as fast as she could, in the hope of remembering every detail of the miracle while it was still incredibly vivid in her mind. But physically, she felt terrible again, ill, worn down to the marrow, drained of the tiny bit of remaining energy that had driven her to Small Plains in desperation.

Was it a miracle? she wondered, though she didn't really feel any doubt that it was. But other people might question her, so she needed to be able to answer them. Was it still a miracle if your body didn't feel healed, but you felt happier than you ever had in all your life, and you felt lifted up onto a higher plane of existence where amazing things could happen, like fresh flowers raining directly onto you, only onto you, from out of a terrifying sky?

A few of the flowers lay around her on the floor of the van.

When she had risen from the grave, she had gathered into her hands some of the flower heads and stalks, leaves, and buds that had fallen on her. When she got to the car, she let them fall into her lap, from where most of them had tumbled around her as she drove the van. Now she bent, painfully, to pick up as many of them as she could carry again.

But she couldn't force her body to move after that, and finally she gave up the effort, and simply pressed the horn until the proprietor of the inn came running out to help her.

* * *

In her room, seated in a straight-backed chair in front of a scarred old wooden desk, Catie logged onto thevirgin.org, which was the most popular of the small number of websites that had sprung up about the Virgin of Small Plains. Without even stopping to read through the entries from that day, she opened a new window to type up her own account of the astonishing thing that had truly happened to her.

"I have a miracle to report," she typed. "Some of you know me, because I have participated in this blog before today. If you recognize my blog name, then you know that I have advanced breast cancer that has spread to my lymph nodes, my lungs, and most recently, my brain. I drove down here to Small Plains two days ago after my doctors told me I was going to have to go through another round of surgery, chemo, and radiation, and that there wasn't much chance left that any of those miserable things would do any good for me. Like you guys, I had heard about the Virgin, and how she had helped lots of people in this town over many years. So here I came, and here I am."

After that preface, she typed what had happened to her that day, ending her story with, "I survived a tornado that flew directly above me! I actually looked up into the cone of it! And it released flowers on me! I have never felt so protected, so blessed. I know now that no matter what happens in regard to my cancer—even if I die tomorrow, or today—I will be all right. Something in the universe is watching out for me, keeping me safe from the most terrifying harm there could possibly be. Until today, I thought that was cancer. But I have looked up into a deadly tornado, and it has sprinkled flowers onto me, and I have lived to tell you my story. If that's not a miracle, then I don't know what is.

"I wish blessings on all of you, as I have been blessed today. May the storms of life fly safely over you and may the flowers of the Virgin bring you beauty and peace as they have done for me today. I don't know if you will ever hear from me again, but when the storm clouds gather around you, think of me, and know there are flowers in the storm."

She signed it with the only name by which they knew her, "Love, Catie."

Slowly, feeling ill but calm, she closed out the blog window.

Then she turned off her computer and lowered the lid of it.

Too ill to get back into her wheelchair, or even to crawl to the bed, she slid as carefully as she could out of the chair, and slipped to the worn, flowered carpet. There, she lay on her side, curling up against the pain she felt, closed her eyes, and grasped some flowers in her hands. Breathing in a shallow, careful way to keep her chest from hurting, Catie lay on the carpet wondering if she could sleep, wondering if she would ever wake again. She felt so transcendent, so peaceful to the depths of her soul, that she wasn't sure she cared.

Chapter Twenty-seven

By the time he got back to the ranch house, Mitch felt both wired and tired, exhilarated by the storm and by his own anger, and also exhausted by them. He'd been up since before dawn. He'd traveled a long way in both the literal and the figurative senses. He'd had a few surprises, none entirely pleasant, and he had even managed to launch the business end of his plan of attack. Practically the only thing he had not managed to do in the long day was see his father. He hadn't stopped by the old man's house, had even driven out of his way to avoid that street. He hadn't gone to the courthouse to look for his father there, hadn't even been able to bring himself to look up at the tall, wide windows where the courtroom used to be, and most likely still was.

Now he felt exhausted one minute, and too keyed up the next.

He knew he'd probably feel better if he could go running, but the idea of running over rough, unfamiliar dirt roads in the dark didn't appeal to him, so he left his running shoes in his suitcase for now.

It seemed incredible to him that among all the things he had managed to do on his first day back, one of them was to avoid getting killed by a tornado. But it had also occurred to him that if it had dropped its deadly tail on the ranch, he'd have had to head for the storm cellar.

He'd better make sure he could actually get the damned thing open.

* * *

It was full nighttime when he approached the old storm cellar with a flashlight in his right hand. He suspected that he had picked this time of night on purpose, just to test his courage. Mitch was damned if he was going to allow a stupid hole in the ground to spook him anymore, as if he were still a boy. He might allow himself to feel frightened of a tornado, but not of a hole in the dirt.

The grass that he walked through to reach it, behind the house, was still wet.

His flashlight picked up gleamings in the brush a few yards to either side of him—small creatures, doing their nocturnal things. He stopped for a long moment to listen to one coyote call from the east, and another one reply from the west. There were no bears in Kansas. A few wildcats, yes, but no bears, panthers, crocodiles, or other predators that a grown man had to fear. There were rattlers, but he had found a pair of his father's old cowboy boots in a closet, and put them on to protect his feet and legs against snake strikes in the uncut grass.

He felt like an idiot to even be considering such things.

When he'd been a boy, he'd never thought about predators, except to hope to get to see them, to have great stories to tell his friends.

At the entrance to the storm cellar, he saw that it was badly overgrown with vines.

Daring himself not to think about spiders, and cursing himself for having turned into a city boy, he ripped the leaves and tough green cords away with his bare hands, after setting his flashlight on the ground.

When he had cleared enough away to see the door, he picked up the light again.

It was a wooden door, dark and splintery now, aged like a cask of wine.

The metal handle looked so rusted he was loath to touch it.

"What the fuck's wrong with you?" he muttered to himself. "You'd think I'd never rehabbed an old house or apartment building. You'd think I'd never seen a rat, or cleaned up filthy properties."

But it felt different to be standing alone, with only a flashlight, in the country, in the deep darkness. He was a lone human in a million acres of solitude, the last man on Mars, the first man on the moon, that's how it felt to him. All around him there was a profound silence such as he hadn't heard in seventeen years. He glanced overhead to see the stars again, just to remind himself they were still there. The Milky Way had been invisible in Kansas City for decades, since even before he had moved there. But here, it still curved and stretched across an endless sky that wasn't hidden by city lights.

It was both frightening and deeply satisfying.

He let out a breath that seemed to come up from his soul, a breath he felt he had been holding onto for almost two decades of his life, a breath that gave him a shuddering release so deep it shocked him.

"I missed you," he murmured to the stars.

And then he laughed out loud, glad there was no one to overhear him.

"Don't get attached to anything," he warned himself. "Remember, there's no decent cup of coffee for a hundred and fifty miles, or a movie any closer than Emporia. There's no Krispy Kreme. There's no—"

He finally realized there was a padlock on the handle, a big sucker, so rusted and crusted it was invisible until his flashlight shone full on it. How was he going to get in to save himself from a tornado if there was a padlock on the storm cellar door, and he didn't have the key?

"Maybe it's in the house," he said, out loud. He was beginning to enjoy the luxury of talking to himself out loud, inside or out. Nobody to see him do it. Nobody to hear what he had to say. "Dad probably still has a key, but since I'm not going to ask him for it, that's not helpful."

Then he noticed that the plate that held the hasp through which the lock was looped was loose in the wood. It was all so old, so weather-beaten, that the screws that held all the pieces in place had come loose.

Mitch couldn't get his fingers under the plate to give it a pull.

He flipped his light over and gave the loose screws a few expert knocks with the flashlight handle. It put a few dents in the aluminum, but it did the trick of knocking the plate completely loose.

The padlock held, but now it held on to a hasp that dangled in air.

Mitch pulled at the door handle, and was unsurprised to find it didn't open easily.

He planted his feet and put his weight and strength into pulling on it.

When the old door finally gave way, it opened so suddenly it knocked him back.

Mitch shone his light through the black opening, but that revealed nothing to him.

He stepped through the doorway, bending over to protect his head from getting bumped on the low doorsill. And then an instinct moved his left hand to brush the wall beside it. Old knowledge had kicked in, causing his fingers to move before his brain knew it was telling them to do it.

He touched cool plastic. His fingers brushed up.

To his utter astonishment, electric lights went on in the storm cellar.

The fact that the wiring still worked—and that it hadn't been used enough in recent years even to wear out the lightbulbs—didn't surprise him nearly as much as what he saw in the illumination.

He thought he remembered only a single light fixture hanging from the ceiling. He thought he remembered only cement floor, walls, ceilings, and the plumbing his mother had put in. And he was pretty sure there used to be a few shelves where his mother had stored fruits and vegetables that friends of hers had canned and given to her.

But now . . . there was a single bed, rumpled with sheets as if somebody had gotten out of it that very morning. There was a table with two chairs. There was even a toilet and a sink. There was a small refrigerator. There was a tall wastebasket with a brown paper sack lining it. There was a chest of drawers. There was a rack with hangers, and there were clothes on them, women's clothes that didn't look like anything his mother would have worn: short cotton blouses, T-shirts, and summer shorts.

Mitch stood staring at the furnished storm cellar, trying to make sense of it.

He moved around inside of it, and found there was even more than he had first noticed. There was a pile of what looked like rags near the bed, and when he got to the bed, he saw the sheets were deeply stained with some dark color. It could have been anything—a water stain, anything, but Mitch felt he knew what it was: very old, dried blood.

A noise outside, some animal noise, made him jump nearly out of his skin.

With one last look around, one sweep of the light, he hurried out.

He pushed the storm cellar door closed again, leaving the lock to dangle against the rotten wood, and all he could think as he made his way back up to the house was—what the *hell*?

Had his claustrophobic mother furnished it like that so she could fool herself into thinking it wasn't really a storm cellar if they had to use it? Was she scared of getting caught in it, and so she made sure there was even running water? But that didn't explain the clothes, or the bed that somebody had actually slept in, much less the blood.

Maybe it wasn't blood, he told himself.

He had no way of really knowing it was blood. Probably he was wrong. Probably it wasn't.

It had looked like a goddamned *apartment*.

The idea of somebody, anybody, actually staying in the storm cellar for any longer than it took a tornado to pass over gave him the shuddering creeps.

Having earlier stocked the kitchen with food and drink, Mitch had one beer before he went to bed. As he lay between the clean sheets, he allowed himself to think of Abby for just a moment and to remember how pretty she'd looked that morning on her screened-in porch. Her hair was just as blond and curly as it had ever been, her grin was as open-hearted and infectious as he remembered it, and her voice, calling to Patrick, had sounded just like the girl who used to yell across their lawns at him. *Enough,* he told himself. He had to tell himself a few more times. *The woman is not the girl,* he told himself.

Mitch fell asleep and dreamed of dark and secret places where he didn't want to go. Because of his dreams, he didn't sleep long. In the middle of the night, Mitch got up and got dressed again.

He walked to his car and went for a drive.

Chapter Twenty-eight

September, 1986

On Rex's third trip out to see the girl, Sarah Francis, she invited him into the house.

Once in, he didn't know what to do with himself. She made it easier by calling to him to come into the kitchen and offering him a can of beer that she pulled from the refrigerator. He was still underage, but then so was she.

"Did Pat get some beer for you?" he asked her, attempting to hide his resentment.

His brother was also too young to buy beer legally, but those sorts of things never seemed to operate in Patrick's world the way they did in most people's.

She nodded. "He left me enough to party for a year, but I can't drink, and nobody ever comes to see me anyway." She glanced over, looking surprised, and smiled a little. "Except you."

"Why can't you drink?"

She shrugged, but didn't answer him.

Rex and his friends usually had to struggle to a) find somebody old enough who was also willing to take the chance of getting booze for them, or b) find somebody with a fake ID to do it, and even then there wasn't anybody local who'd sell it to them if there was a whiff of suspicion that they were the ones who wanted it. Usually it required trips out of town to stock up on cases they could hide where parents would never find them. Pat, on the other hand, seemed to have never-ending supplies of anything he desired, especially girls and alcohol, and he was never inclined to share with his younger brother unless there were serious bribes involved. Once, out of desperation before a field party, Mitch had paid Pat a hundred dollars on *top* of the price of the keg of beer he obtained for them.

Rex didn't know much about alcoholism, but he guessed that considering the family that Sarah came from, that might have something to do with her reluctance to drink alcohol. He decided to be tactful for once in his life and not push her about it.

"What *can* you do out here?" he asked her.

He pulled up a kitchen chair and sat down in it with his cold, sweating beer. He could hardly believe he was there with her, and with a beer in his hand on top of it. He sat back and just enjoyed being able to look at her without having to come up with some kind of excuse for staring.

She wore the same T-shirt he'd seen her in before, a plain orange cotton one, and again he would have sworn she wasn't wearing anything underneath it. Her shorts were different this time—black ones instead of white. But her legs were just as long and tan, her feet just as bare, her face just as beautiful, her hair just as long and black. It was hot in the house—there was air conditioning, but she didn't have it on—and she kept lifting her hair up off the back of her neck in an irritated kind of way and draping it over one shoulder. Then when it fell back on her neck again, she'd lift it up again. Rex wanted to go over and lift it for her, hold it on top of her head for her like an Egyptian slave, fan her until she sighed with pleasure, bend over and kiss that sweet, sweaty place on the back of her neck . . .

"What?" he asked, having missed whatever it was she had said to him.

She smiled a little, as if she could read his mind, and then she leaned against the kitchen counter. "I said, I don't do *anything* out here. Thank God there's a TV, and I've got some magazines and music. Hey, do you think you could get some books for me?"

He sat up straighter. "Sure!"

Then he slouched again, feeling foolish for being so eager.

"I like romances," she said, "and mysteries." She added wistfully, "I wish I *could* go someplace. I get so bored!"

"Don't you get lonely all by yourself out here?"

She shrugged, but he thought he saw her eyes glisten and her lower lip tremble a little before she heaved a big sigh and said, fervently, "I'd give *any*thing to get out of here for a few hours."

"You don't ever leave? Like, never?"

Solemnly she shook her head so that her hair swung again and she lifted it again. "Nope. I haven't left this place at all in a whole month."

"How long you gonna have to stay here?"

She turned, and shaded her eyes and looked out into the sunshine. "A while. 'Til I have enough to make it out there."

"Have enough what? Money? How are you going to do that?"

She turned her head quickly, and looked flustered. "I just meant . . . I just meant, since I don't have any expenses, I'm not spending anything. So I get to save a lot. That's what I meant."

He didn't understand much about it, and didn't quite have the courage to ask the questions that were piling up inside his head. She couldn't just stay here forever avoiding her family, could she? Was she waiting until she could get a way out of here, find a job, get some transportation, a job someplace else? But how was any of that going to happen if she never left this house?

"I could take you someplace," he blurted.

"No you can't. I can't go anyplace they might see me."

He would have asked who "they" were, but he was sure he already knew: her family.

"I don't mean a place, exactly," Rex said. "I just mean, I could take you for a drive."

"A drive?" She looked at him as if he'd spoken a foreign word she didn't comprehend. "You mean, like—"

He grinned. "Like a drive. In my truck. Just drive around, you know?"

"Drive around . . . where?"

"I don't know, out of town, maybe, where nobody knows you."

"No." She shook her head violently. "No, no. I can't. I can't be seen."

"I don't mean in the daytime. At night. And not early in the night, either. I mean, like, really late?" He laughed a little, because it sounded like fun. "We could do it, like, after midnight. And we could just drive around with the windows open so you could feel the breeze and, I don't know, just get out of here for a little while."

When she looked at him then, he saw a hopeful, mischievous glint in her eyes.

"It would have to be *really* late," she said slowly.

He liked that idea. In fact, he loved that idea. "Sure!"

In an instant, a whole fantasy ran through Rex's mind. He saw himself making an excuse to his parents to be somewhere else that night, hiding his car, maybe even sleeping in it until it was time to pick her up. He imagined himself driving to pick her up under a romantic full moon. No, on second thought, that would reveal too much. It should be dark and cloudy. He saw her waiting eagerly for him to arrive, running out of the house to hop into the car with him. He could feel how the bench seat on his truck would sink down a little with her weight, though just a little. He could sense the presence of her body next to him, smell the clean soapy fragrance that trailed behind her when she moved. He could see her eyes shining in the dark cab of the truck, see her teeth when she grinned like a conspirator at him, see her eyes widen when she looked at him in that dim light and realized that he was sexier than she had ever realized, that he was more mature than his older brother . . .

"I don't know," she said, looking suddenly doubtful and frightened.

He didn't want to frighten her. He didn't want to make her unhappy at all, about anything, ever.

"Okay," he said, temporarily giving up. "Whatever you think."

She looked both disappointed and grateful that he was dropping it. But he wasn't, not really. Rex figured this was an argument he was bound to win eventually, because nobody sane, not even somebody with a good reason for hiding, could possibly stand being cooped up in one place for very long. Eventually she was going to go so stir-crazy that she'd practically beg him to take her for that drive.

He was surprised how long she held out.

It took another three weeks of irregular visits—and magazines and beauty stuff and feminine products and groceries—before she finally greeted him at the door one night with, "I can't take this anymore! You've got to get me out of here. Let's go for that drive you talked about! Do you promise me that nobody I know will see us? Do you swear?"

As if I have control over her universe, he thought, pleased that she was giving him that much power. He felt so turned on that he could barely walk into the house to put down the sack of goodies he had brought to her.

•   •   •

They took their drive the next night.

"I brought you something else," Rex said, before he started the car.

"What?" Sarah looked beautiful in the darkness, just as he had fantasized she would. He prayed that he looked better in the dark, too.

He reached into a little paper sack at his side, brought something up out of it, and handed it to her. "Here. So your hair won't blow in your face and drive you crazy."

"A scrunchie? What color is it?"

She held it up, but it was impossible to tell its color in the darkness. "Red."

"Good." She raised her arms, smoothed her hair into a ponytail, and slipped the elasticized band around it. Then she sighed, a nice long *ahhh* that suggested it felt really good to get her hair held back like that. She turned and smiled at him. "I don't know how in the world you thought of this, but thanks."

He wanted to reach over and touch it, but restrained himself.

⁕　⁕　⁕

They drove and drove for two and a half hours, from a quarter to two in the morning until he dropped her off at a quarter after four, while it was still dark even in the east, where the sun would be coming up.

But instead of driving away with his heart soaring, Rex drove away with his heart aching.

She had loved the drive. She had talked and laughed, joked, and even made teasing affectionate fun of him now and then. But what she had talked about was another boy. Sarah was in love with somebody else.

"He's sooo good looking!" she exclaimed. "Don't you think so?"

"I don't really think about guys that way."

"Well, he is. And he's so nice—"

"Nice?"

"Oh, yeah, really nice, and smart. Does he ever talk about me?"

"Um, I think he mentioned you—"

"Really? Oh, God, what did he *say*?"

"I guess he thinks you're pretty cool."

Again, she sighed, but even more happily this time.

It bugged him that she sounded just like any ordinary, average teenage girl he had ever known. But it killed him much more to hear her saying the same damned things he'd heard most of those same girls say to him at one time or another over the course of his lifetime. Ol' Rex, the Cute Girl's Best Bud, never the boyfriend. Good ol' Rex, always the bridesmaid, never the bride. He was used to swallowing his pride and his own desire. He was accustomed to being the confidant, the good sport. He was used to telling himself it didn't matter if a million girls didn't want him, because all a man really needed was one true love, and even he was surely going to get to have that someday.

Of course, Mitch always laughed, and claimed that the trouble with Rex was that he wanted the girls who didn't want him, and ignored the ones who did. And, okay, maybe that had been true once, or twice, but it wasn't the point. He *wasn't* a handsome guy, not like some of his friends were, and he *was* the one that other guys' girls always sought out to tell their secrets to, instead of wanting him as much as he wanted some of them. It always hurt to be placed so far down on the Choice List, but this time it ripped at him like he was a goddamned fish being filleted.

The only comfort to Rex was that it wasn't Patrick that Sarah loved.

No, there was one other comfort . . . when Patrick came home from college, Rex would make sure he knew that Sarah cared only for Mitch.

*　　*　　*

He felt so hurt, so disappointed and ego-flayed that he didn't go out to see her for three long weeks. Let Nadine Newquist supply her with what she needed, he thought bitterly. He'd practically gone broke buying her stuff anyway. She had never paid him back for any of it. Not that he had minded at the time, figuring that she couldn't possibly have much money to spend. But now it pissed him off and made him feel used. Hell, he couldn't afford to be her errand boy any longer. He wasn't gonna do it anymore. And why should he, when it wasn't even him she wanted to see?

He hadn't asked her if Mitch ever went out to see her. Maybe he didn't want to know. It would be awful if he found out that not only did Mitch own her heart, but that his best friend was also cheating on Abby, his other best friend. And then what would Rex do? He didn't think he trusted himself not to be so pissed and jealous that he wouldn't spill the whole thing to Abs.

Rex didn't spend much time with Mitch during those three weeks, either.

He made excuses about ranch work and homework, he joked

about needing to fill out college applications for Harvard and Yale, he hinted there was a new girl in another town that maybe he was driving off to see.

Mitch didn't seem to sense anything was wrong, except to begin to look annoyed and say, "Where the hell you been, man?"

Abby was starting to give him funny, appraising glances, and starting to sidle up to Rex and whisper, "What's her name, hmm?"

When he finally did drive out, just to make sure Sarah was okay (he told himself), she wasn't there. Not only was she not present at the house, but it was locked up tight the way the Newquists liked everything to be, down to a shiny new padlock on the storm cellar door. When Rex tried to look in through the windows of the house, he didn't see any sign that Sarah had ever been there.

He never saw her again, not until he saw her in the blizzard five months later.

Chapter Twenty-nine

In the aftermath of the tornado, Abby sat in the dark, in a chair backed into a corner of her screened-in porch. She had a small bird on one shoulder, pressed up against her neck, and a shotgun on her lap. Her electricity was out. Her business was destroyed. One of her birds was dead, another was missing, and the third was still too terrified to be moved into its cage. Gracie had crawled into a tent of Abby's hair, moved into its shelter, and would not be budged, on pain of biting. Abby could feel the little beak pressed against her skin, and Gracie's feathers, soft and trembling.

"Baby, baby," Abby whispered, over and over, as tears ran down her face.

The bird made tiny sounds, then went still, then made the little sounds again. They broke Abby's heart. She felt horrible guilt every time she thought about how terrified and helpless her birds had been. She was heartsick imagining J.D. out in the countryside with no idea how to feed himself or protect himself from predators. If he was still alive, he was a target for hawks and eagles.

Just like her remaining pet, Abby was trembling, in fits of shakes and sobs that came and went like tornadoes inside of her. She wasn't crying for her business. It was only wood and nails and glass she'd lost.

Nurseries could be rebuilt, and that's what insurance was for. Flowers would grow again. That's what flowers did. She wasn't crying for her business, and she wasn't shaking from fear. People had warned her about the possibilities of looters, but she had scoffed at the idea of anyone who would come all the way out here to pick through shattered pieces of clay pots and slivers of rotten barn wood. Her sister and her friends had offered to stay with her, but she had shooed them back to their own homes to check for storm damage. Rex had said he'd post a deputy to discourage evildoers, but she had declined that offer, too.

"Mitch is in town," he'd told her.

"I know. I saw him."

"Me, too."

"Did you . . . talk?"

"Said hello, that's all," Rex told her. "Did you?"

"No, I don't think he even saw me."

That was all they'd said about it; they had more pressing problems on their minds.

And now, sitting on her porch, Abby wasn't afraid, and she wasn't waiting for looters.

She was waiting in the darkness with a shotgun for Patrick.

He had come back to her house while she was gone. But not during the day. The sunglasses had still been on the kitchen table when she had arrived home and found her friends in her kitchen. The sunglasses were gone the next time she saw the table. She had figured out that he had to have come by between the time they all went into town and when they all rushed back after the tornado hit, probably to deliver the hay she had requested that morning, and maybe to check on her. She hadn't heard from him.

Patrick hated her birds.

Patrick had said only that morning, "It's them, or me, Abby."

He had threatened to kill them, a threat she hadn't taken as a joke even when he had said it.

And tornadoes, no matter how strange their paths of destruction, did not unlatch bird-proof locks from the inside.

• • •

When he finally showed up, he didn't drive up to the house.

Abby heard the vehicle coming up the road, heard him park it on the verge, heard the door close quietly, and then barely heard his footsteps as he came up her driveway. He was trying not to wake her, she thought. He was trying to sneak up and into her house and then into her bed. He would think he had nothing to fear from her birds anymore—he had probably expected Gracie to fly away in a panic, too. But he would know that he needed to arrive in the way he had in the past—opening her front door so that the hinges didn't squeak, removing his boots and tiptoeing past the cage as if he didn't know how empty it was now.

Finally, she heard gravel under his feet, and knew he was close by.

"I'm out here," she called to him. "On the porch."

She knew she'd scared the hell out of him by doing that. He had probably jumped a foot from sheer surprise and guilt. If Patrick ever felt any guilt. Abby doubted it. How could any man do what he had done that night and also be a human being who felt the agonies of guilt, such as she was feeling for having ever allowed him into her life, her house, not to mention her bed and her body!

She saw the outline of a tall, broad-shouldered man in the darkness.

Quietly, she put both of her hands on the shotgun, moved it until it was pointed at the door, and slowly, carefully, almost silently, pulled the safety back. Her right index finger crooked around the trigger. She wasn't actually going to shoot him, she was only going to scare the holy hell out of him and run him off her property.

The tall, dark figure stepped silently onto her porch steps.

He fumbled for the door handle, then slowly pulled it open, and stepped in.

Abby raised the gun until it was aimed at the figure's chest.

"Hold it right there, Patrick!"

"Abby?" he asked, in a shocked tone.

When she heard his voice, she nearly pulled the trigger from shock, herself, and only just in time lowered her gun before she killed him. When the man took two more steps forward, Abby's breath caught in her throat, and she went dead silent.

It wasn't Patrick standing in front of her looking nervously at her gun.

"Mitch," she said, and it wasn't a question.

.   .   .

Mitch stood in front of Abby on the dark porch and said, "I didn't expect to see you. I was—I was just—"

"Yeah, everybody drives down my road at two in the morning," Abby said coldly.

"I heard you got hit by the tornado—"

"So you just showed up after seventeen years to, what? Help?"

She was shocked at how calmly she was able to talk to him, how frigid she could keep her tone, and how well she was managing not to shoot him, in lieu of Patrick. They both deserved it. But she was also furious at herself for rolling the number "seventeen" off her tongue so quickly, giving him the idea she knew or cared how long he had been gone.

"What the hell *are* you doing here, Mitch?"

He gestured toward her gun. "Taking my life in my hands?"

Abby said nothing, but she did put the safety back on.

"Were you really going to shoot your husband?"

"My *what*? Patrick's not my husband," she said scornfully. Let him think she had some *other* husband if he wanted to. "Where'd you get that idea, anyway?"

"I don't know, I just—"

He lapsed into silence. Stubbornly, she vowed not to be the one to break it.

.   .   .

I never meant for this to happen was Mitch's thought as he stood on the dark porch trying to figure out what to say next to Abby Reynolds, who didn't appear inclined to speak to him.

He had thought he was only going to meander around on the country roads until he got tired enough to sleep again. But somehow the roads all seemed to direct him toward the north and east. He had turned onto the highway, where he was alone with the big tractor-trailer trucks ferrying goods between Kansas City and Wichita and beyond. Quickly tiring of that, he had taken one of the first turnoffs he came to, which had just happened to be the road with the small green arrow pointing down the lane.

Strictly coincidence, he was sure of it.

Then curiosity had gotten the best of him, and he had decided that he needed to know if Abby's place really had been hit by the tornado he had seen. He decided he would drive by it in the dark, that was all, just drive past, check it out, and then drive home again. When he heard himself apply the word "home" to the ranch house, he quickly amended it.

But when he had pulled within sight of her property, there was something wrong.

Because he had seen it only twice before—driving past it—he couldn't figure out at first what was wrong, or missing. And then, *Jesus!*, he realized her whole barn/greenhouse was down. There was . . . nothing . . . where a dark profile of a good-sized building should have been. His heart began to hammer with fear as he looked toward her house. Thank God, it was still standing. That was all he could think over the pounding of his pulse.

There were no lights on, but he saw one truck parked there.

Mitch remembered it as being the "other" truck he had seen that morning, which now seemed ages ago. One truck, the one that Patrick Shellenberger had torn out of the driveway in, was new, red. This one was battered, older, black. Abby's truck?

Was she all right? Was she home when the twister hit?

Either Abby was asleep in that dark house—without Patrick, apparently—or she had gone to stay with somebody, or . . .

He couldn't just drive by. He couldn't do it. He had to know . . . something.

Mitch got out of his car as if invisible hands, ghost hands, were tugging at him.

They bade him leave his door ajar so he wouldn't make a noise by slamming it, then pushed him along her gravel driveway, pointing him in the direction of her home.

This, he thought, remembering Patrick, *is a good way to get myself shot.*

Nevertheless, he kept walking, and the invisible hands kept tugging.

When her voice called out, "I'm out here. I'm on the porch," Mitch felt shock and then relief. *Abby!* And it wasn't just any relief—it was enormous, surprising, overwhelming relief. She was all right. She was alive. He realized he would have recognized that voice anywhere, even if he hadn't already heard it once that day, even if he had never heard it again until the last day of his life on earth. He realized that if he had been lying on his deathbed and the telephone had rung, and he had picked it up and she had said, "Hi," from that single syllable, he would have known her.

He didn't want to think about what his feeling of relief might mean.

If he could, he was going to refuse to allow it to mean anything.

This, after all, was the disappointing woman who had married Patrick Shellenberger.

His own feelings just now meant nothing, Mitch informed himself. He moved to do her bidding—her shout had an implied order in it, *come here!* His strong emotional reaction, he told himself, meant only that he wasn't an entirely hard-hearted bastard, after all. It suggested that even *he* could be glad that a fellow human being had survived a storm.

Yeah, Mitch mocked himself as he opened the porch door. *Sure. That's what it means, all right. And if you believe that, I've got a piece of real estate on a dry lake to sell you.*

*   *   *

Abby had two clear thoughts as she looked up at the man who stood before her on her porch. One was, *God, he's gorgeous.* The other was, *I look like hell.*

Mitch cleared his throat. "You said Patrick's not your husband. Is somebody else?"

She almost laughed. "No. You're married, aren't you?"

"Divorced."

"Oh."

"I have a son."

"I heard."

"He's six."

"That's nice."

It *was* nice, she thought. And it made her throat close up with grief for her own loss of the children she had once dreamed she'd have with him.

"What about you?" he asked.

"What about me *what?*" she asked, purposely obtuse.

"Do you—" He seemed to have something stuck in his throat, too. He cleared his throat. "You have kids?"

Abby thought, *This is ridiculous, and I'm not going to play.*

She sat with the bird hidden on her shoulder and the shotgun not hidden on her lap, and recommenced being silent.

But, after a moment she relented and said, "No."

After another moment, he shifted from one leg to the other, and turned his head to look toward where her barn used to be.

"I guess you got hit by the tornado."

"I guess I did," she said dryly.

He turned back around to look in her face. "Abby—"

"What?"

This time, he was the one who lapsed into silence.

"This is the part where you say you're sorry," she blurted, surprising herself and, judging by the expression on his face, him. "This is the part where you tell me why you left, Mitch."

It had been a ferocious day, dramatic things had happened to her, somebody she trusted, sort of, had done a terrible thing to her. Her emotions were as raw as a fresh wound, and his appearance was pouring salt by the bucketfuls into it. The dam she'd try to place before her words broke loose and all hell with it. "What are you doing here, Mitch? Why are you in town, after all these years? And why . . . why in the *hell* . . . are you here, at my *home,* at two o'clock in the *morning!*"

It came out sounding anguished. It *was* anguished, as was the look he gave her.

Abby set the shotgun aside, and rose urgently to her feet.

"How could you?" she asked, helplessly. "Why *did* you?"

Hating herself, she started to cry in noisy, gulping sobs.

Mitch crossed the space between them in under a second, and reached for her.

Just before he kissed her, after he had wiped her tears with his hands, and stroked her wild, flyaway hair, and whispered, "I'm sorry, I'm so sorry, you'll never know how sorry I am," a million times, Abby said, just as urgently, "Wait!"

She pulled away from him.

Gently, she grasped the small creature on her shoulder. Holding him wrapped in her right hand, she brought him out from under her hair. Mitch's eyes widened, but even in the darkness she saw a smile in them. Abby wrapped her other hand around Gracie so that the bird was safely cradled in a cocoon of her hands that did not allow the bird to bite anybody. Then she looked up into Mitch's face, allowed him to wrap his arms around her again, bird and all, and let him bend his face down to kiss her, at last.

Mitch thought, *This is a mistake,* even as he kissed her with a passionate longing, with a passionate sorrow that he hadn't allowed himself to know he still felt. Abby thought, *Tornadoes can come and wipe you off the earth, people you love can disappear overnight, you never know what's going to happen in the next moment, and if you don't take this one, it will never come again.*

"Wait!" she said, but only so she could put Gracie in a cage.

"I'm not a virgin anymore," she whispered, as he backed her toward her house.

"Neither am I," Mitch whispered back, as he followed her into her home.

●　●　●

Seventeen years before, they might have been deliberate, careful, gentle.

Seventeen years later, they were in a rush, for fear of whatever might still come between them. Neither of them was going to let that happen. This time, nothing was going to stop them. By the time they reached the edge of her bed, a powerfulness of emotion took them over, a furiousness. They pushed and pulled at each other as if they were angry—at life, at fate, at each other. They made love as if they were arguing, as if they were battling over who was to blame, and who would pay, and whether anything could ever make up for what they had lost, and whether terrible, soul-crushing debts could ever be paid in full.

He pulled her T-shirt up over her breasts. She worked her hands between their two bodies, until she could find his belt buckle. He ripped at the button and zipper on her shorts until he got them loose. She got his belt off, got the button and zipper of his jeans open, and pushed her hands up his bare skin under his shirt, onto his chest.

He rolled her roughly onto her back.

She grabbed the back of his head and pulled his face down to make him kiss her.

He pushed her legs apart with his knee. He pushed his hands down under her panties, down onto her thighs, between her legs.

He pushed into her, she pulled him into her.

They were violent with each other, and wild. Abby felt a great pressure build up in her chest and then it burst out in a great cry that felt as if it scraped the bottom of her soul. Her tears started flowing halfway through their passion and then wouldn't stop, but just kept coming out of her in painful sobs. When she cried, he held her tighter, so tight it hurt her, but instead of fighting against the pain she welcomed it and let it hurt without telling him to stop. She heard him say her name over and over, but was afraid she was only imagining that he sounded as if he was pleading. When it was over, when they were panting and exhausted, they still clung together as if their sweat were adhesive. Finally, they relaxed their grip, and let each other go.

Mitch rolled over, onto his back, and stared at the ceiling.

Abby moved a few inches away from him, turning her face to the wall.

After a few minutes, she said, "Why did you leave?"

He didn't answer.

Both of them thought, *This was a huge mistake.*

* * *

"I take the pill," she told him, after their silence had gone on way too long.

It would be all right if you didn't, Mitch almost said, shocking himself.

He didn't say it. Instead he turned toward her in the bed and started to reach for her.

She stopped him. Pushing her hands against his bare chest, she worked herself up into a sitting position above him. "You have to go."

"What?"

"People are coming early, to help me clean up and rebuild. You have to go."

"You don't want them to know I was here?"

"No," Abby said, turning to face him. "I don't want anyone ever to know." She swallowed, ignored the renewed pain in her heart, made her voice go firm and confident, made herself remember the pain he had caused her. And still refused to explain. "It was just one time, Mitch. That's all. We were just making up for something we didn't get to do a long time ago. That's all it was. There won't be any more."

He felt as if she had stabbed him.

"You're right," he told her, his struggle for words making it come out harsh.

"I know I am," she said, her fight for control making it come out cold. "We'll pretend we haven't even talked to each other, okay?"

"Sure." He rolled away from her, to start grabbing his clothes. "Fine."

"Good," she said, as she stared at his naked back, and fought her tears.

You're not going to do it to me again, she thought. *I won't let you.*

Mitch turned at her bedroom door to look back at her in the bed. He felt as if he'd been struck by lightning, blinded by its light so that everything looked dark now. It reminded him painfully of when he had taken his last look up at her bedroom window on the night everything had changed for them. All the light was going out. For a little while on this one night, the world had lit up again for him, and now it was all going out again. He couldn't love her without hurting her in terrible ways, and so it was better to try not to love her at all. And, obviously, she didn't care anything about him after all these years. In allowing him to make love to her—have sex with her—she had only been scratching an itch that had lingered from a long time ago.

He couldn't figure out a way to say good-bye that didn't diminish what had just happened between them, any more than it was already demeaned, so he didn't say anything at all. He just walked out of her bedroom, and then out of her house.

•   •   •

Patrick stood in the shadows of the cottonwood tree outside Abby's front fence line, and watched a tall man exit from her side door. It was four o'clock in the morning, and the sun wasn't up yet. Patrick had arrived two hours earlier, had seen the unfamiliar and expensive car parked on her road. He had driven past, turned into the first cutoff, parked his truck out of sight, and walked back to wait and watch. Abby didn't know anybody with a late-model Saab. Hell, she didn't know anybody with a Saab. It wasn't the kind of car that anybody in Small Plains drove, not because they didn't want to, but because it would have been impossible to get repairs done locally.

The tall man had to get a lot closer before Patrick recognized him.

Mitch Newquist. In a way, Patrick wasn't even surprised. He had heard that Mitch was back. He wasn't even surprised that Abby had let him back in, only that it had happened so fast. Mitch couldn't have been back more than a day or two, and he was already sleeping with her?

Patrick stood by the side of the road, fighting the urge to kill somebody.

He hadn't felt this kind of cold/hot anger in years, not since his younger brother had told him, with a snide, satisfied, smirking air, that Sarah Francis wanted Mitch Newquist, instead of him. Patrick wasn't going to let that happen again. There was too much at stake to lose it to a bastard who thought he could just waltz back into town and take over again.

* * *

When Abby walked into her kitchen at five A.M., Patrick was already there.

Startled to see him, and way beyond anything called "angry," she said, in a hostile, shaking voice, "What are *you* doing here?"

He turned around quickly at the sound of her voice.

"You mad, Abs? You mean, what am I doing here now, instead of last night, when you could have used some help? I'm really sorry I didn't come over. We had some storm damage on the ranch, and I was stuck taking care of that. I tried calling but our lines were down. I didn't even know you'd had trouble, or I would have dropped everything and come over." His face was a mix of expressions—apology, sympathy, surprise at the way she was speaking to him, and also something that looked like frustration. "Listen, I hate to mention something so petty when you've got a whole barn down in your backyard, but while we're standing here—have you seen my sunglasses?"

"What?"

"My shades. Damn things cost fifty bucks. I don't want to lose them."

While Abby stared at him, Patrick bent down and peered under the kitchen table.

"I left them here yesterday when I—aha!" Patrick hurried over to her refrigerator, reached into the space between it and a counter, and pulled out his sunglasses. He stood up, put them on, turned to face her, and grinned. "How the hell did they get down there? I think your damned birds must have done it. They hid them on purpose, Abby. I told you, those birds hate me."

She stared at his teasing grin.

"Abby? What's the matter? You know I'm only kidding, right? I don't really think your birds hid my shades." When he grinned at her again, but she just kept staring at him, he said, "Are you okay?"

"My birds," she whispered, and sank onto the floor, and burst into tears.

Patrick pushed his sunglasses up into his hair and hurried to comfort her. "What happened?"

"Lovey's dead."

"Dead?"

"In the storm. And J.D. flew away and hasn't come back. And Gracie is traumatized. And I thought you did it, Patrick! I was positive . . . I was *sure* you left those glasses on the table this morning. I just knew you did. And they were there when I got home the first time this evening, but then they were gone the next time, and I thought that meant you'd come out here, and you hated my birds, and you took the opportunity to . . ."

"Hurt them?" He sounded horrified. "I may hate them, but I wouldn't *hurt* them."

"My sister and Cerule and Randie and Susan were here. I must have seen some sunglasses belonging to one of them and I thought they were yours. I was upset about . . . something else. I guess I wasn't seeing things correctly."

"What were you upset about?"

"Never mind," she said, and began to sob again.

He let her cry in his arms, waiting a bit before he said, "Hey, you know who's back in town? Your old boyfriend, Mitch Newquist. Have you seen him?"

Abby buried her face in his shoulder for a moment before whispering, "No."

He tensed, but hid it by gently tightening his embrace of her. "You'd better marry me, Abs."

She pulled away enough to look into his face. "Why?"

He nodded toward the devastation outside her house. "Because this is a lot for one person to handle. I know you can do it, but why should you have to? When things happen, don't you want somebody here to help you? And you wouldn't just be getting me, you'd get my whole family that already loves you." One side of his mouth crooked up in a half grin. "Better than they like me."

Patrick gently kissed her damp face. "You can't stay single forever."

"Why can't I?"

"Because you're not built for it, Abby."

"I always thought you *were*."

"That was before I fell for you." He kissed her again, and as he did he smelled fresh soap on her, felt how damp she was from the shower, a shower taken sometime between four and five in the morning. "Poor Abs," Patrick said as he stroked her hair. "I know you loved those birds."

•   •   •

After Patrick left, Abby got into her truck and drove aimlessly around for a while, looking for a flash of red in the skies. She made posters with J.D.'s photo on them and tacked them up all over town. She begged Rex to tell his deputies to keep a watch out for the parrot, and she went door-to-door downtown to ask everybody she saw to do the same for her. On an impulse, she even stopped by the cemetery to touch the Virgin's grave and ask her help in finding him, or at least to keep him safe from harm.

Finally, feeling stunned by loss and by the enormity of what she had done a few hours before, she drove back out to her property to join her employees as they began the work of cleaning up after the storm.

Chapter Thirty

Mitch spent the day distracting himself in every way he could think of to take his mind off Abby. He finished cleaning the ranch house and drove to another town to do more shopping that would make it possible to stay awhile. He spent the hours planning what he was going to do next, and considering the consequences of those plans. He drove into Small Plains only once, toward the close of the business day, to conduct some business of his own, parking on backstreets, wearing his baseball cap, lying low, avoiding eye contact on the streets.

Everywhere he went, people were sweeping up after the storm.

Storm . . .

He heard the word in his brain, and felt a wry, unhappy laugh rising inside of him at the sound of it. He'd been inside of a storm, all right. He'd been swept up in a tornado of sex and memory, naked regret and short-lived ecstasy. Now he felt tossed out of it onto the hard, prickly ground. He felt bruised and used. It was, he decided, as the rueful, bitter feelings rose higher, an altogether appropriate way to feel as he worked up to the moment when he would walk back into his parents' home for the first time in seventeen years.

And then he thought, as he had many times over the preceding years, "Nobody loves a martyr. You lost. Get over it." And *then* he thought, with a certain hard, delicious energy that wiped out everything else, "Get even."

●   ●   ●

It felt like history repeating itself.

Early that evening, as twilight turned the prairie lavender, Mitch used his old keys to let himself into the big house at the top of the long driveway. He stepped inside, without knocking or ringing the bell, because . . . *the hell with it, I'm his son, I won't fucking knock first.* Then, just like the last time, he closed the front door behind him and before he could take another step, there was the judge emerging from his office.

"Hello, Dad."

"My God! Mitch!"

His father looked him up and down, while Mitch stared back. He had expected to feel shocked at how his father had shrunk over time, but now he found it had not happened. The old man was still taller than he was. The hair was thinner, but not much, and still more brown than gray. His father had the same ramrod-straight posture that had always intimidated some defense attorneys in his courtroom. Reading glasses were perched halfway down his nose, as he stared over the tops of them. Mitch realized he had been picturing his father as aged, as if he were ninety-three, instead of merely sixty-seven, which was relatively young as such things went these days.

It wasn't true that Mitch had never seen his parents since he left. They had come to his college graduation. But they had not attended his wedding, because Mitch had not invited them. They had not seen his son, their only grandchild, though Mitch's former wife had softened and sneaked some photos to them. He'd been furious at her for doing that, but then she had never really understood the depth of his feelings of betrayal and abandonment. Mitch had always had the feeling that she'd secretly believed he must have done something to deserve it, that there must be another side to the story, because he wasn't always easy for her to live with, and because surely no parents would ever treat their son like that. But then, as Mitch had reminded her more than once, she had never met his parents. If she had, she might have understood how rigid and unforgiving they could be. Although—what was there for them to forgive? That was the question that Mitch always came back to, the point he kept trying to make to his wife—that he hadn't done anything wrong and yet they had behaved as if he had committed some kind of awful crime, as if they were ashamed of him, as if they were doing him a favor by spiriting him away from everything he knew and loved. They had never visited any of the places he had lived in Kansas City. He wasn't sure his father knew what he did for a living. There had come a point at which they had all stopped trying.

After his wife sent the photos of their grandchild, there was no response.

That, at last, had convinced her that maybe he was telling the truth.

"I'm here," Mitch said evenly. "You may as well invite me in."

The judge shook his head, as if chasing away cobwebs.

"*Why* are you here?"

"I came to see Mother's grave."

"A little late, aren't you?"

Mitch felt his face twitch with anger before he could control it.

"There's coffee," his father said, abruptly. He turned his back and led the way into the kitchen as if expecting Mitch to follow after him.

After a moment of inner debate in which he seriously considered stalking out and slamming the door, Mitch took a step forward and then kept going into the kitchen.

•　　•　　•

"House looks mostly the same," Mitch observed, over a cup of the atrocious instant coffee that his father still seemed to prefer. "So do you."

"Yes. It was your mother who changed."

Mitch's hackles started to rise, he started to snap out something argumentative, but then he realized his father had said it in a neutral tone and that he was only talking about her illness. If the old man so much as hinted it was Mitch's fault, that she had got sick because of him, Mitch was going to tell him to go to hell. But so far, everything was diplomatic, safe. Instead of cursing his father, Mitch reached for a sugar bowl in a futile attempt to improve the coffee. When he had left home, he wasn't a coffee drinker. Now he was. Now he was many things that were different from the way he'd been before. Being a coffee addict was probably one of the more benign of them, he thought.

"Was it Alzheimer's, for sure?"

"Don't know. I wouldn't let them do an autopsy on her."

Mitch didn't know much about the disease, but he did know that it took a brain dissection to find the telltale plaques that screamed "Alzheimer's!"

"Why not?"

"What would be the point?"

"I guess." Mitch stirred his coffee. Seated across from him at the kitchen table, his dad wiped an invisible spill with a napkin. "Was it hard? Her illness?"

"What do you think? It wasn't easy."

"How bad did she get in the end?"

"Some days she knew me, some days she didn't."

"What was it like for her?"

His father frowned slightly, as if Mitch had thrown him a curve, a question whose answer he had not previously considered. "How would *I* know?"

Mitch supposed it was a fair answer. But he thought there were other ways his father might have answered it. He could have said she didn't suffer. He could have said she suffered all the time. He could have found a million different ways to describe the daily life of a sharp-witted woman who was losing her mind. But Mitch noted, like a doctor picking up clues to a diagnosis, that his father's first answer to the question, "How bad did she get in the end?" had been purely solipsistic. It was all about him, not about her. As would his mother's answer have been, Mitch thought, if their roles had been reversed. Two more self-absorbed people he did not think he had ever met. He suspected they had been perfect for each other, existing in one intimate world on parallel tracks.

"She lived in hallucinations and the past," his father said, in the same neutral tone, "but at least she always knew who Jeff was."

For a second, Mitch didn't know who he was talking about. Then he remembered, with a start of rueful realization that left him feeling stupid and foolish and even jealous: his brother, the adopted son who had come to take his place in the strange scheme of things in his so-called family. They had brought four-year-old Jeff to Mitch's graduation. His own son had an uncle, Mitch thought, whom he might never meet. For a moment, it rushed over him that an entire family life that he didn't know anything about had unfolded in this kitchen in his absence.

"I'd like to see him," he said, though he wasn't sure that was true.

For the first time, his father looked unsure, too. "He's not here right now."

"Okay. Some other time. Can he drive?"

"He's seventeen."

"That's a yes?" Mitch regretted his sarcasm the minute it appeared. He wanted information, and getting the old man's back up too far wasn't going to accomplish that aim. "The reason I asked is, I thought he might drive out to see me if he wants to. I'm staying at the ranch, Dad."

"What do you mean?"

"I mean I let myself into the ranch house and I'm staying there."

His father's eyes narrowed as he took this in. "You might have asked permission first."

"I might have, yes, but I didn't, and now I'm there."

"For how long?"

Mitch bit back the bitter retort on the tip of his tongue. "As long as it takes to straighten some things out, Dad."

His father reared back in his seat, instantly getting the point. "You leave it alone."

"Leave what alone?" Mitch asked with a softness that only barely hid the venom beneath it, and with every subsequent sentence he spoke, his voice rose and the poison leaked out. "Leave her name off her grave? Leave people thinking nobody around here has any idea what happened to her or who she was? Leave people wondering why the hell I left like that and never came back until now? Is that what you think I should leave alone, Dad?"

His fury didn't move his father, who was accustomed to passion—both real and phony—in the courtroom. "You've intelligently left it alone for all these years."

"So why mess with success?" Mitch's laugh was bitter.

"That's one way to put it, yes."

"Jesus, you're a cold bastard!"

"And you're an ungrateful son," his father shot back at him.

"Ungrateful?" Mitch stared at him.

"I protected you!" his father roared, suddenly as furious and animated as his son.

"You never believed me!"

"Don't you get it, son? All these years and you still don't understand it?"

"What? What don't I understand?"

"Of course I believed you! Your mother and I both believed you. She did to the day she stopped remembering anything, and I still do. My God, of course I do. But *that doesn't make any difference,* because nobody else will believe you. It was a teenager's word against two of the most respected men in this state and it still is. *It still is,* Mitch."

"You've never heard of lie detector tests?"

"Inadmissible in court," his father said, with a dismissive wave of one hand. "Good God, Mitch, you're a lawyer, you know that. And just what other evidence do you think you would have anyway? If Quentin and Nathan did what you said they did, there is no way in hell you will ever prove it. Nathan was the sheriff! Do you think he hung on to evidence? Quentin was the doctor, do you think *he* did? And even if you had evidence that they covered up her identity, what would you have then? No evidence about how she died or who killed her. You don't have *anything* except your own wounded ego, Mitchell, and it is seventeen years past the time for you to force yourself to get over that, because there is absolutely nothing that you, or even I, can do to change things."

Mitch stared at him and for a long time his father stared back at him.

Finally, Mitch said, "You chose them over me."

"We had to live here," his father said in the cold blunt way he had always used when stating what he believed to be unalterable facts. "You didn't. And besides, I trust them."

"What?"

"They are my best friends, just like Abby and Rex were your best friends. I have always believed that even if they did what you saw them do, then they must have had a good and decent reason for it, and I trust them enough to leave it alone."

"Good and *decent*?"

"I believe you," his father said, "and I believe in them."

"My God." Mitch turned away, and stared unseeing out a kitchen window. He was appalled by most of what his father had said, the parts that involved the hiding of a young girl's identity so that she had to be buried in an unmarked grave, the parts that seemed to suggest nobody cared who killed her, the parts that let two grown men get away with threatening him if he told the truth about them. But even though he hated himself for it, he was helplessly gratified to finally hear seven words he felt he had been waiting a lifetime to hear and which he had never, not once, dreamed his father would actually ever say to him: *Your mother and I both believed you.*

But still, he couldn't quite believe it.

"If you believed me, why have you never told me so until now?"

For the first time in Mitch's life, he thought he saw his father's eyes get moist. "We wanted you to stay away. It was safer for you that way.

And if that meant encouraging you to hate us, well then, that's what we had to do."

Mitch felt stunned, momentarily unable to process the information.

Finally, slowly, he said, "How can you possibly believe in men who made it unsafe for me to return?"

And again, Mitch saw something in his father's eyes that he had never seen before, only this time it wasn't tears, it was confusion. "You just don't understand," his father said. "You never will. But there's one thing you have to understand and that is that you've got to leave it alone. *Leave it alone.*"

Mitch sat back in his chair and said nothing.

* * *

It was several minutes before either of them spoke again.

"You want more coffee?"

"No." *God no,* Mitch thought. It was awful stuff.

His father suddenly blinked, and sat up even straighter. "There he is again."

"Who? Jeff?" Mitch turned to look where his father's gaze was directed, but all he saw was an oak tree in the backyard, and a flash of red in it.

"No." His father stood up, walked to the window to look out. "A damn bird."

"You into birding?"

"Of course not. Come here. Look at him. See what you think it is."

Mitch followed his father to the window, and stood searching the landscape for whatever it was his father wanted him to see. The flash of red caught his eye again. He stared, and then stared harder.

"No way," Mitch breathed, and he turned to stare at his dad. "He's still alive? You still have J.D.?"

"Who? What are you talking about?"

Instead of answering, Mitch hurried to the kitchen door and stepped outside onto their back porch. The flash of red darted out of the tree. It flew through the early morning air, and swooped down onto Mitch's outstretched right arm. Then the big bird walked up the arm until it was close enough to stare Mitch in the eye.

"J.D.? Is it really you?"

The bird let out a squawk that could have raised the dead.

Then the parrot screamed and screamed, as if everything that he had not said for years, everything pent up inside his red breast, had come pouring out in one unstoppable deafening burst of parrot squawk.

* * *

They dug up an old cage out of the basement. There had been one cage for J.D. in Mitch's bedroom, where they both slept. That was the one they found tucked away in a corner of the basement that, even two years after his mother's slow demise, still had the exquisitely organized and tidy appearance she had left it in before she forgot it existed. There had been a second cage they kept for the bird on the porch, but that larger one was the one that had disappeared when, Mitch's father told him, the bird was stolen.

"Stolen!" Mitch said, as he encouraged the parrot into the smaller cage. "I'll bet Mom just forgot and left the door open and he flew away."

"Your mother wouldn't do anything like that."

That was probably true, Mitch had to admit. Even though she hadn't been fond of the noisy parrot, Nadine Newquist wasn't a woman to leave doors open behind her, nor was his dad likely to do it. Neither one of them would have wanted to own up to other people that they had been careless enough to let an expensive pet escape. But none of this made sense, Mitch thought. A bird didn't get stolen seventeen years before, and then mysteriously turn up on a tree branch as if it had never been gone. And yet, unless this wasn't really J.D., unless this was some amazing kind of parrot-coincidence, that was exactly what had happened.

"Who would steal him?" he asked his father.

"I have no idea. I can't believe this is the same bird, Mitch."

"It is, Dad. Wouldn't you know that ear-splitting squawk any-where?"

"All parrots are noisy."

"Yeah, well, they don't all have a notch on their beaks where they got bit by another bird when they were babies. Don't you remember that notch? I got him cheaper because they said he was flawed."

"You're going to have to find its owner."

Mitch stared at him. "Like hell I will. I *am* his owner, Dad. This is J.D. My bird. *My* bird. If you think I'm going to go looking for the asshole who stole him, you're out of your mind."

"What are you going to do with a bird?" his father said, as dismissively as if Mitch had found a squirrel in the woods and brought it home.

"I'm going to feed him some fruit from your refrigerator, if you've got some. And then I'm going to town to buy him some seed. He's probably starving. And then I'll drive him back out to the farm with me."

His father was silent as Mitch searched the refrigerator for fruit, found some strawberries and blueberries, and then began to chop them up on a cutting board. "You have any nuts of any kind that I could give him?"

Still without saying anything, the judge walked over to a cabinet, reached in, and brought out a large tin of mixed nuts, which he handed to Mitch. Mitch mixed it all up in a small bowl and started to go back onto the porch to give it to the bird, when his father said, "You're not going to cause any trouble while you're here, are you?"

"Trouble?"

"Yes. Now that we've talked about it. Now that you understand better."

"Trouble," Mitch repeated, as if tasting the word. "You mean, like, asking Quentin Reynolds why he beat her to a bloody pulp, or asking Nathan Shellenberger why he let him do it? You mean, like asking them why they threatened to blame her death on me if I ever told anyone what I saw them do?"

His father stared at him with an unblinking gaze.

"No," Mitch assured him. "I'm not going to cause trouble like that."

It was an honest answer. The operative phrase, Mitch thought, was *like that.*

He put the food inside the cage, along with a small bowl of water. For a few moments, he stood and watched the big parrot attack the fruits and nuts as if he really was starved.

"Then what *are* you going to do next?" his father asked him.

Mitch returned the level gaze with one of his own.

"Pick up my boy, J.D.," he said, as he smoothly lifted the cage with the parrot in it, "and take him home with me."

Chapter Thirty-one

It had been a long day for Abby. Insurance agents. The hard physical work of pickup and cleanup. Dump trucks and hauling. The pain of seeing at close range exactly what she'd lost and the worry of thinking what it was going to take to replace it. All that in one day, plus trying to keep her landscape services going as her customers needed her to, and it was all a long way from over. Her property still looked as if a tornado had hit it and it was going to be awhile before it looked any different.

By the time she sent everybody home, she was too tired to cook for herself.

Patrick had called, saying he had to drive to Emporia to see his accountant.

It occurred to Abby as she stood exhausted under a hot shower with her stomach growling, that with Patrick away, there might be a way for her to kill two birds with one stone that evening. When she realized what metaphor she had unthinkingly used, her eyes welled up again.

•   •   •

Half an hour later, she rolled down her window and let the cool air whip her face and blow over her hands on the steering wheel. She loved driving on country roads at night when the only lights were the stars and the moon and the spotlights of single bulbs above barn doors, and animal eyes flashing in her headlights, and the glow of lights inside the farm and ranch houses she passed along the way.

As she approached the cemetery on Highway 177, she whispered, "Hi, Mom."

At that moment she would have given anything to be able to talk to her mother. Since she couldn't, she was going to do the next best thing.

•　　•　　•

Abby turned in to the gravel driveway of the Shellenbergers' ranch house just after somebody in a pickup truck pulled out of it. She waved a hello, but no answering arm stuck out the truck window. The truck peeled off down the highway with a squeal of tires as if somebody wanted to get away fast.

"Abby!" Verna Shellenberger, standing in the cheerful light of her kitchen, beamed a welcome through the screen in the door. "I'm so glad to see you! Get on in here right this minute. Patrick told me what that storm did to you and I was just so sorry to hear it. Have you eaten? I've got leftover meatloaf and mashed potatoes and gravy. I'll bet you haven't had a thing to eat today, have you? You single girls never feed yourselves right. And guess what . . . I've got your favorite pie."

"Sometimes I really do have impeccable timing," Abby bragged as she stepped inside. Her exhaustion slipped away in the bright, fragrant, familiar welcome of Verna's kitchen. "Who was that in the truck?"

"Jeff Newquist," Verna said. "Since his mom died . . ."

"You have him over for supper? That's nice."

"I'm not so sure he thinks so." Verna held open the door for Abby and smiled at her. "I think his father makes him come, just so Tom doesn't have to deal with him. He's a handful, that boy."

• • •

"Guess what, Verna? Your son asked me to marry him."

Verna stopped in the act of passing over a plateful of strawberry-rhubarb pie to Abby and froze for a moment, a startled, happy look in her eyes. But then her expression changed. Her hand moved its way over to Abby, who grabbed hold of the green glass dessert plate.

"Oh, God, I'm sorry," Abby said contritely. "I meant Pat. For a minute there, you thought I meant Rex, didn't you?"

Verna Shellenberger shook her head and smiled as she sat down in a chair on the other side of the kitchen table. "I should have known better." She picked up a fork, but didn't stab down into her own piece of pie. "Of course you don't mean Rex."

"What if I did it, Verna? What if I married Patrick?"

Patrick's mother lowered her gaze to her pie. "You know I love my son."

"Everybody knows that."

Verna finally looked up at her. "If Patrick married you, it would be a good thing for him, probably the best thing ever. He would be lucky to have you, Abby. The rest of us would be lucky to have you in our family, too."

"Aw, shucks," Abby teased. "What about *me*, Verna? Would I be lucky?"

Abby had listened to Verna complain about Patrick's behavior often enough to feel it was safe to kid about him. So she was shocked to see Verna's kind brown eyes suddenly fill with tears.

"Oh, Verna, I'm sorry, I shouldn't have said that. I was just teasing . . ."

"Oh, honey, it's not that, it's just that 'lucky' is not a word I would ever use with you." While Abby was still getting over the shock of hearing her say that, Verna really set her back by asking, "Does this have anything to do with Mitch Newquist coming home, Abby?"

"Of course not! You heard he's back?"

Verna nodded. She picked up a fork and poked gently at the piece of pie she hadn't eaten. "Are you going to see him?"

Abby blurted, "I already have, Verna."

The older woman looked up at her and seemed to read something in the flush of Abby's complexion and the embarrassed lowering of her eyes. "Does Patrick know Mitch is back?"

"Yeah."

"Does he know you've been with him?"

"No." Abby wondered if Verna actually meant what it sounded like she meant, and if so, how she'd guessed. And she was puzzled by the anxious look on Verna's face. "Why?"

Patrick and Rex's mother stood up and started busily picking up plates and silverware. "Because I say it's none of his business," she said with uncharacteristic sharpness, "even if I am his mother."

"Verna, Patrick told me he was there the night Nathan and Rex found the Virgin."

Dishes clattered into the sink as if they had slipped out of Verna's hands.

"Why did you tell everybody he wasn't there?" Abby asked her.

By "you," she meant Verna, Nathan, and Rex.

Verna took her time filling the sink with water before she turned around, with a dish towel in her hands. "We shouldn't have done that, Abby, and I hope you won't ever tell anybody we did. But there was Patrick, always in trouble of one kind or another. And he had just flunked out of school. And there was that poor murdered girl, and she was found on our property. And we were just afraid people might suspect him."

"Suspect Patrick? Why would anybody do that, Verna?"

But Patrick's mother turned around to begin washing dishes as if she had to get every last bit of invisible bacteria off of them. "Because people are just that way, Abby. Because they need somebody to blame."

"Verna?"

"Yes?"

"Did Nadine ever tell you why Mitch left the way he did?"

Finally, Verna turned around again, but this time she had a bit of a smile for Abby. "Let me put it this way, Abby. Nadine never told me a reason I ever believed. Not for one minute. That boy was crazy in love with you, just like you were with him. I don't think he wanted to get away from you, I think she wanted to *get* him away from you, and not because it was you. She had bigger ambitions for him." Verna's voice turned a little tart. "And from what I hear, he has pretty much fulfilled them."

"But why did they make him go *then*, Verna? Why then, of all times?"

Verna's kind voice clouded over again. "You mean, not just because he'd come in late from your house that night? Well, they had a teenage boy, too, Abby. And Mitch was over here nearly as much as Rex and Patrick were. Maybe they were worried people might suspect him. I think a lot of us with teenage boys were a little worried that winter. Like I said, people need somebody to blame."

"But nobody would have blamed *Mitch*. He didn't even know her, Verna."

"You don't know that, Abby."

"What do you mean, I don't know that?"

"You don't know who she was," Verna reminded her.

"I know Mitch wouldn't have killed anybody!" Suddenly Abby felt a little shocked. "Verna? Don't you know the same thing about Patrick?"

"Of course I do!" Verna turned to drain the sink. "Of course I do."

●　●　●

After their visit, Verna walked her outside to her truck.

"How's Nathan?" Abby asked her. He hadn't come downstairs

while Abby was there; Verna had told her that he was upstairs talking on the phone to cattle buyers; now and then Abby had heard the rumble of his bass voice through the floorboards.

"He's better," was the surprising answer. "Quentin found a new drug for him, and he has felt a lot of relief since then."

"That's so great, Verna."

The older woman laughed wryly. "You don't even know."

Abby teased, "Must have come from seeing the Virgin."

But Verna took it seriously. "Yes, I guess it did."

"Really?" Abby didn't know what to think of this, even though she herself had made a special trip to ask for help in finding J.D. But somehow asking was one thing; actually receiving was something else entirely. "You believe that?"

"Well, it was right after that that Quentin gave us the new medicine."

"Hmm. I guess we never know, do we?"

Abby turned and looked in the direction of the highway going south.

"Maybe you'll see Patrick coming back from Franklin," Verna said.

"Franklin?" Abby frowned in surprise. "Patrick went to Franklin?"

"That's where he said he was going. I can't imagine why. There's nothing in Franklin except a few falling-down buildings."

"I can't imagine why, either, especially since he told *me* he was going to Emporia."

Verna matched her surprised frown. "That boy," she said, as if he were still nineteen years old and keeping her up at night from worry.

"Verna?" Abby suddenly reached out and touched the other woman's arm. "Is everything okay?"

"What? Of course it is! Why do you say that, Abby?"

"I don't know. You seem a little . . ."

"Tense?" Verna's laugh sounded forced. "Have you seen cattle prices lately? Believe me, they've got everybody tense."

"Okay." Abby gave her a hug. "Thanks for the pie and the company."

"Any time." Verna tightened the embrace. "You know that. And Abby? You won't say anything to anybody about Patrick being home that night, will you? We let it go too long without setting people straight. They'd just think it was strange now."

"I won't say anything, Verna."

When Abby got out on the road and looked back, she saw that Verna was still standing in the driveway watching her leave. For some reason, it reminded her of the curtain that had dropped in her father's living room the day before, when he, too, had stood and watched her depart.

Chapter Thirty-two

Verna walked back into her house a lot more slowly than her heart was beating. She figured that to anybody passing by on the highway, or to Nathan happening to peer down from their bedroom, she would have looked just like she always looked, which was to say, like an ordinary ranch woman walking calmly back into her house as if she had nothing to worry about except whether to wash the supper dishes now or later.

The truth was, when Abby had driven off in her truck, the sight of her red rear lights disappearing down the highway had filled Verna with an awful, almost unbearable anxiety.

Was she *tense,* as she had said to Abby? *Tense* didn't even begin to describe it.

She'd been feeling anxious ever since hearing from Rex that Mitch was back.

And now Abby said that Patrick wanted her to marry him.

Verna loved both of Margie's girls, but she held a special place in her heart for Abby, which was no reflection on Ellen, it was just a fact. There was just something about Abby that hadn't changed in all these years, a quality of natural goodness she had possessed since the day she was born to Margie and Quentin. Partly it was Abby's appearance that made people love her, no matter what she did. She was irresistible, with her flyaway hair and her big open smile and the way she stood in front of you with her blue-jeaned legs apart and her hands on her hips and smiling that sweet smile and looking you right in the eye. Partly it was also her way of being mischievous now and then, in ways that startled people, but tended to make them smile, instead of condemn, things that probably nobody but Abby Reynolds could have gotten away with, and maybe not in any place except Small Plains. Like stealing Mitch Newquist's parrot all those years ago, an act that Margie Reynolds had confided to Verna and that had made them both laugh until they cried at the thought of Nadine overhearing a muffled squawk sometime when she was visiting at the Reynolds's house.

But it was also more than any of that, it was also how there was a continuing kind of innocence to Abby that time and loss and heartache had not altered very much. It was the look in her blue eyes that told you she could still be shocked, still be hurt, still be trusting, still love somebody wholly with all her heart. It wasn't right that a girl like that didn't have anybody better than Patrick to love her . . .

Oh God. Verna brought her hand to her mouth. She had just thought a terrible thing about her own son . . .

But it was true. And Patrick could be relentless . . . ruthless . . . when he wanted something. Usually he didn't stop until he got it. It could happen that he would wear Abby down, persuade her at some vulnerable moment when she was feeling lonely, or even play on her desire to have children.

Having Mitch back in town, rubbing salt in those wounds, didn't help.

It couldn't happen. Verna couldn't allow Patrick to have Abby.

What kind of person would she be, Verna was forced to ask herself, if she allowed Margie's girl, a girl like that, to marry a boy whose own mother couldn't swear he hadn't killed somebody?

. . .

Until the night the girl's body was found in their field, Verna had never allowed herself to give serious credence to her greatest fear about her firstborn, which was that Patrick might be capable of anything, might even be one of those people on whom a terrible label is hung, like sociopath. She preferred to think that the very worst that could be said about him was that he was conceited, cocky, thoughtless. Ever since he was a child she had watched him use people, manipulate them, even torment them with his teasing. She had tried her best to instill feeling for other people in Patrick, but over the years Verna had seen precious little evidence that he had a conscience, not like Rex, who was afflicted with almost too much conscience than was good for him. But Verna had also seen that *both* of her boys were popular, not just Rex; both of them always had friends, had fun, laughed easily . . .

Her fears had blossomed on the night when she had uttered what she now thought of as fateful words: "What happened, Rex?"

Her youngest had sat on the side of her bed, holding his own poor broken fist, and the words had burst out of him, words she'd had to hear even though she had desperately wanted to put her hands over her ears to block them out. First, he told her that they had come upon the frozen body of a dead girl in a pasture.

"I know her, Mom! I didn't tell Dad, but I know her. And Pat knows her."

Then he had told Verna about being mad because Patrick was running away from his work that summer, about getting in his truck and following his older brother, and about finding him in the Newquists' country house, bare-chested, barefoot, and in the presence of a girl who used to clean houses for families in town. He told her about how he had blackmailed Patrick into staying away, though he couldn't swear that Patrick did. He told her about how he, himself, had fallen in love with Sarah Francis, about his visits to see her, to take her things, to help her, to keep her company. He told her about their drive in the darkness, and about finding out that the one she really loved was Mitch. And he told her about how he had thrown that fact in Patrick's face, knowing it would make Pat furious and jealous.

It had been obvious to her that Rex was heartbroken over the girl's death and that his greatest fear was that in making his brother jealous he had contributed to her death. Rex, stunned, guilty, grief-stricken, and only eighteen years old, thought his brother had killed her in a jealous, possessive rage.

"Pat didn't tell Dad he knew her, Mom!" Rex had burst out to her.

"Neither did you, honey," she managed to point out, as she fought to stay calm even in the fog of her fear and her illness.

"That's different!"

"He's your *brother*, Rex."

"He's *Patrick*, Mom," Rex had shot back at her.

Rex's self-recriminations and his accusations against Patrick had raised submerged and hideous anxieties in Verna's heart. She didn't, she *couldn't* believe that any son of hers could hurt a girl, no matter how jealous he might be.

But she didn't know, she didn't know . . .

·   ·   ·

Verna stared at what was left of the pie on the plate in front of her.

She felt as if she might never have an appetite again.

"Rex," she had told him all those years ago, "your brother could not have done such a horrible thing to that girl. You must stop thinking such a thing! Put these thoughts away forever, Rex. And don't ever, ever share them with anybody else. Not even with your father."

"If such thoughts bother you again," she had told him, "come to me."

Rex never had. The subject was never again raised between them.

Verna had never told Nathan about what Rex had said to her. She had let him come into their bedroom much later that night, let him crawl wearily into bed, and whisper to her about finding a body in the field, about taking it to Quentin's office. And then Nathan had said to her, "She was beaten so bad, Verna, that you could hardly even tell she had a face."

Verna had felt an electric jolt when he said that, because Rex hadn't mentioned anything about her being too disfigured to recognize. In fact, he *had* recognized her, and he seemed to be positive that Patrick had, too. So how did her sons, her teenage sons, recognize a naked dead girl if they couldn't see her face?

Verna had lain awake until dawn, getting sicker by the second, for many reasons.

There were things she didn't know. There were things she did not want to know. It had come as a relief when she had been forced to go into the hospital in Emporia, where she could be given drugs that made her sleep, sleep through an investigation that did not include her sons, sleep through the quiet departure of her older boy to another town, another college, and sleep through the funeral and burial of a beautiful girl who'd had a name, who'd had a family, who'd had a life.

At the kitchen table, Verna put her face in her hands.

She thought of the dead girl, realizing that's who she should have been thinking of first, all along. "Thank you for helping my husband with his pain," Verna prayed silently. "Please forgive us and help us, Sarah."

Chapter Thirty-three

It was dark by the time Mitch pulled up in front of the ranch house and parked his car for the last time that day. He pulled out the over-sized birdcage he had finally located after driving back into Kansas City, as well as the bags of seed, and the grocery bags of fresh fruit and vegetables to feed J.D. He hadn't even tried the stores in Small Plains, knowing it was too small a town in which to find a cage this big. "You better appreciate all this, J.D.," he said as he walked in and turned on the lights. "I've driven about two hundred miles today to get it for you."

The bird let out a gentle squawk of hello.

Mitch returned to his car for more packages, and that was when he spotted something that made him pause in mid-step.

The door to the storm cellar was wide open.

      •   •   •

He thought about just walking over and looking in, but the hair standing up on the back of his neck suggested otherwise. Upon leaving the storm cellar yesterday, he had made sure its only door was closed tight. It had still been shut like that when he had driven away from the house this morning. It was a heavy wooden door that he'd had to work hard to open. No stiff breeze had just happened to blow it ajar.

Quietly, hurrying, Mitch walked into the house and straight into his parents' bedroom. Once there, he opened the drawer in the table between his parents' single beds, to see if his father still kept a firearm there.

Yes . . . there it was, small and deadly, and just what he wanted to see.

He remembered this gun, this specific gun. It had a distinctive black handle and silver barrel, and if he recalled correctly, it had been a birthday gift to his father from Quentin Reynolds and Nathan Shellenberger.

God only knew how recently the gun had been oiled, or whether the barrel was clean enough to fire a bullet without backfiring into his own chest. It could be that the gun—which was more like an old-West pistol, a collector's item, than a modern gun—had not been fired in twenty years, or more. There were bullets in the chamber, he discovered. Even if it couldn't shoot straight, it still had the potential for scaring the hell out of somebody, even if it couldn't kill them.

There were certain things a person never forgot about the country, Mitch thought.

One was how to shoot. Another was the stories of strangers who holed up in empty farm and ranch houses, people for whom any port in a storm would do, especially if it was somebody else's port. By and large, they were people you didn't want to mess with. They were, occasionally, escaped convicts passing through. It was a wide, empty, lonely countryside. Help could take hours to arrive.

Mitch quietly walked back outdoors, the pistol at his side.

Though he had shut the storm cellar door, he supposed that its broken lock hanging loose was as good as a "vacancy" sign on a motel. He imagined how pleased and surprised a visitor might be to find the cellar all fixed up like a small apartment. If somebody was in there now, however, they had been sloppy to leave the door open.

Or claustrophobic.

Or it might only mean they had been there and were gone.

Mitch fervently prayed for that to be the case.

The grass beneath his shoes was damp, muffling the sound of his approach.

When he reached the doorway, Mitch took a breath, raised the gun with his right hand, and flipped on the light switch with his left.

The light revealed the room as he remembered it, with one exception.

A teenage boy lay asleep in a bedroll on the floor.

"Up!" Mitch commanded.

The boy stirred, then shot up until he was sitting up. He was tall and skinny, dark-haired, with a thin face and a sour expression on it. "Wha' the fuck!"

"Get up," Mitch told him. "Slowly."

The kid looked more angry than scared. He glared at the gun in Mitch's hand, then up at Mitch's face. "Who the fuck are you, and what the fuck you doin' with my father's gun?"

•　•　•

Even though they were only standing against counters in the kitchen, it felt as if they were warily circling each other, Mitch thought. They were both getting used to the idea that they were brothers.

The kid was almost scarily blunt, it turned out.

"You're Jeff?" Mitch had asked him in the storm cellar.

"Yeah, who the fuck are you?"

"I guess I'm your brother," Mitch told him. "I'm Mitch."

"No shit" was the kid's response, accompanied by an unreadable look. "Got any beer?"

Now, in the kitchen, each of them with a can in their hands, Jeff Newquist said to Mitch Newquist, "Where the hell you been for seventeen years?"

"College," Mitch answered, deciding a literal answer was the safest one for the moment, "then Chicago. Denver. I've been in Kansas City the rest of the time."

"So why didn't you ever come back?"

Mitch detected no pain in the question, or at least he didn't think he did. He would have sworn that he saw and heard only a kind of hard curiosity. Nevertheless, he deflected it with his own question. "What have they told you about me?"

"Ma and Pa?"

Mitch started. "Ma and Pa?" Incredulously, he said, "You call them Ma and Pa?"

A glimmer of what looked like hateful humor suddenly appeared on the boy's sharp-featured face. "When I was little, she wanted me to call her Mama." He put the accent flutingly on the last syllable, making it sound French. "I changed it to Ma just to piss her off."

"That would do it," Mitch said, and started to laugh.

The boy looked surprised, and then he looked secretly pleased.

"So what did they say about why I left?" Mitch asked him.

Jeff shrugged. "You got in some trouble. It was best that you leave town." Again, he spoke in a flutingly false tone, clearly imitating the elevated way their mother and father spoke. "It was best that you not return."

Mitch snorted. "I got into some trouble?"

The boy raised his eyebrows. "You saying you didn't?"

"I'm saying it wasn't my fault."

That elicited a snort from the boy. "Yeah, well, good luck with that."

Mitch felt a warming to this boy.

"Did they tell you what kind of trouble I was supposed to have gotten into?"

"They never did, but everybody else has. Some people thought you might have killed somebody, that girl in the cemetery . . ."

"Jesus," Mitch breathed. "People really thought that?"

"Not really. I don't know. Nobody really knows. You know what they call me?"

Mitch blinked at the sudden change of tack. "Who?"

"People."

"No. What do they call you?"

"The Substitute Son. How you like that?"

Mitch was appalled for the boy's sake. "That's shitty, Jeff. It sucks."

Again, the boy looked pleased. Again, he seemed not to take very personally any part of what he was saying or hearing.

"What's it been like for you," Mitch asked, "growing up with them?"

That produced another shrug. "Livin' with old folks. They're old, all their friends are old. It's like this huge generation gap."

It was true, Mitch thought. His parents had been in their thirties, as their best friends had been, when they'd raised him. But they'd been in their forties when they'd adopted this boy. That might not have seemed such a large gap, but Nadine and the judge had always seemed older than their age anyway.

"You feel like you were raised by grandparents?" Mitch asked him.

"I guess." For the first time, the kid seemed to hesitate. "So what was it like for you? Being their kid. Back in the day."

Mitch didn't hesitate. "They weren't much fun," he said with wry understatement. "But I liked their friends . . ." He smiled a little. ". . . who weren't so old back then. I was close to the Reynoldses and the Shellenbergers . . ." He paused, to see if the kid would take up that subject in any way.

Jeff didn't show any interest. Maybe he wasn't close to those families, Mitch thought, since they didn't have kids his age.

"Where'd you get the bird?"

"Brought him with me," Mitch lied.

The boy gave him an amused squinty glance that slightly unnerved Mitch. The look suggested that Jeff knew he was lying, but how could he?

"Looks like Abby Reynolds's bird to me."

"Abby's? She has a . . . doesn't she have a smaller bird?"

"Well, yeah, she had two smaller ones and also a big parrot like this one, only it got lost in that storm. She's got notices up all over town, didn't you see them?"

"No." Mitch stared over at J.D., who had cocked his red head and was giving them the eye. His father had claimed that somebody had stolen the bird, but Mitch hadn't believed it. He thought that one of his parents had left the door open and allowed the bird to fly away because they didn't want to be bothered. Was it possible that somebody *had* stolen J.D. and that that somebody was Abby? He looked back at Jeff and said firmly, "This is my bird."

"Whatever."

It was strange, but now and then an expression crossed the boy's face that reminded Mitch of either Nadine or the judge. He knew that people who lived together for a long time could end up looking like each other, but it was still kind of amazing to see the right side of the kid's mouth quirk down in a disparaging fashion, like the judge's did, or to see him raise those eyebrows as Nadine used to do when she was confronted by information she could scarcely credit.

"Why'd you come back?" he asked Mitch.

There was a definite challenge in the question. For the first time Mitch thought he heard something personal in it. Maybe it was only his imagination, but he thought he was hearing, beneath the actual words, *How come you couldn't come back to see your brother for seventeen fucking years, but you come back now?* Or maybe, Mitch thought wryly, it was more like, *Who the hell you think you are to come fuck with my inheritance after all these years?*

In that moment, Mitch realized something, and decided to tell the truth about it.

"I don't think I ever got it," he said.

"Got what?"

"That I have a brother."

Something passed through the boy's eyes, some flicker of surprise and emotion that could have been anything, but that Mitch read as resentment and hurt. He knew he was right when Jeff said, "How the fuck could you not understand you had a brother?" The cold and angry tone reminded Mitch, creepily, of their late mother, though the language did not. Evidently, Jeff had picked up from Nadine and the judge their kind of cold anger, as opposed to the kind of hot anger that Mitch had always considered to be more honest. Whenever he heard that same kind of cold tone coming out of his own mouth, he hated it, even when he couldn't stop it.

Mitch took a long moment to answer, not wanting to bullshit the kid.

"I was . . . jealous," he finally said. "I was young. I'd been kicked out. I'd lost my home, my family, all my friends. I didn't even get to graduate with my class. I was a mess. I was alone, I felt falsely accused of something, my parents seemed cold as ice. And then they introduced you into the scene. You were total news to me. I didn't even know they had ever wanted to adopt. I didn't know they wanted any more kids. I couldn't have been more shocked if they had told me they had adopted an alien baby. If you were the substitute son, then I guess I felt like the forgotten son." He stopped, to think it through some more. "I didn't blame you. I blamed them. They were so fucking cold the way they did everything. I felt like they had decided I was too much trouble to bother with anymore. I felt like they threw me out and cut me off, so I cut them off."

The kid looked down at the kitchen floor. When he raised his face it was devoid of any expression that might give away any of his feelings. "Got any more beer?"

"No." He did have more—and if Jeff had seen the inside of the refrigerator he knew it—but Mitch wasn't going to encourage the seventeen-year-old to drink more. He suspected the kid already did plenty of that. "You want to stay here? You want the other bed?"

The kid shrugged, without saying yes or no.

"What's with the fancy storm cellar?" Mitch asked him.

"What do you mean?"

"Why is it all fixed up like an apartment?"

Jeff shrugged. "Dunno. First time I ever saw the inside of it."

"Really? How'd you get here, Jeff? I didn't see a car."

"I parked behind the house."

"*Why'd* you come out here?"

The boy hesitated, then shrugged again. "I was curious. Dad told me you were here so I came out to see what you look like. But you weren't here. So I saw the lock on the storm cellar was broken and I went over and that's when I saw it was, like, furnished. I decided to sack out until you got back."

"Why'd you leave the door open?"

"Are you kidding me? You think I want to get shut in there?"

"Yeah." Mitch knew what he meant. The storm cellar raised all kinds of primitive fears in him, too. It was the kind of place that made imaginations run wild . . . what if a person couldn't get out, what if nobody ever found them, what if . . .

"You have school tomorrow?"

Jeff shook his head. "I'm done."

"Graduated?"

"Next year."

"You got a job?"

A self-satisfied smirk appeared on the kid's face. "I did. Until this afternoon."

"What happened?" Mitch decided to give him the benefit of the doubt and then was surprised by the answer. "You quit?"

"Yeah, told them to shove it."

"What are you going to do for money? Unless the judge has changed a lot since I was your age, you're not getting any cash that you can't earn."

"I sold something," Jeff said, looking down and smiling to himself.

"Come on," Mitch said, when there was no further information coming. "We'll find you some sheets."

"No, I'm going back to sleep in that other place."

"In the cellar? You are? But you could stay here—"

"I like it there," he claimed.

Mitch let it go. He even felt relieved. This was new to both of them. Maybe they both required some separation. Feeling a wave of guilt, Mitch thought, *After all, it's what we're both used to.* The thought of separation made him think of his own son, and he felt a sudden deep longing to see Jimmy. Having his own child and experiencing powerful love for him had made Mitch even more incredulous that a father could ever abandon his son the way Mitch felt his own father had abandoned him, no matter what the excuse.

He would never do such a thing to Jimmy.

"Take some food with you," Mitch suggested to his brother.

He left the kitchen to do some things for J.D.—and so the kid wouldn't feel self-conscious about taking what he wanted.

After Jeff had gone to the storm cellar with a full grocery sack, Mitch returned to the kitchen to see what had appealed to the teenager. A loaf of bread was gone, along with a package of sliced turkey, a bottle of mayo, one of the six-packs of beer . . . and their father's black-and-silver pistol.

Chapter Thirty-four

At the edge of the town of Franklin, Kansas, Patrick Shellenberger slowed his truck down to call to a couple of teenage boys standing in a yard. One of them was holding a cigarette down by his right knee. They weren't doing anything, just standing there. Patrick remembered that stance, that frustrating bored feeling of standing around with nothing to do. At that age, he'd had about five minutes' tolerance for it before he split and found something, anything, to do instead—the "anything" usually involving girls, beer, or a game of pool, or all three. These two would have to drive many miles to find a pool table, and they'd be lucky to get any beer. If there were any girls left in Franklin, Patrick would be surprised, and even if there were, those girls would have to be desperate to give these two a chance.

"Hey!" he called to them. "Does the Francis family still live around here?"

The boys, tall, skinny, looked at each other before staring back at him.

They didn't move, or walk over to where he had his truck in idle.

"They're gone," one of the boys called back to him.

"Except the one brother that's in jail," the other one drawled.

Patrick doubted they had a two-digit IQ between them. He asked them, "There's a brother in jail?"

"Yeah," they both said.

"Which one?"

The shorter boy shrugged. "One of 'em."

"What'd he go to jail for?"

They looked at each other, laughed, and the second one said, "Drunk, I 'spect."

"What jail's he in?"

"County," the first one said.

"*This* county?" Patrick asked, with exaggerated patience.

"Naw, he's in jail over in Small Plains."

Apparently, it either didn't occur to them to ask why he wanted to know, or else they didn't care.

"Cool truck," one of them observed.

"Bitchin'," the other one echoed.

Patrick thought he had not heard the word "bitchin' " since he was in high school, and even then it had been several decades past its prime. He turned and raised himself up in the seat so he could reach over and get something from the floor behind him. Then, looking back at them, he said, "Come here."

They wandered over until they got close enough to see what he was holding out the window and offering to them.

"You givin' that to us?" the taller one asked him, looking astonished.

Now that they were within a few feet of him, he saw they were younger than he'd originally thought, maybe fourteen or fifteen.

"Take the whole thing," Patrick said.

The other one grabbed the six pack, and muttered, "Cool. Thanks, mister."

Patrick left them as he had found them, standing like scrawny statues in the dark, only now they had something to do. They could pop open beer cans. Whoopee. He would have bet any amount of money that they'd find a corner under some dark bushes and drain all the beers, one after another. Tomorrow morning, they might not remember what he had asked them or what they had told him. Even if they claimed to remember, nobody would trust the word of underage boys who got themselves drunk.

Patrick turned his truck around to head back toward Small Plains.

Maybe it wasn't too late to knock on Abby's door.

And there were two fewer birds to shit in his boots now.

Patrick smiled as he lifted a cup of coffee from a cup holder to his lips. The sunglasses had been a close call, but he had covered it well, judging by Abby's reaction. She seemed to have bought it hook, line, and sinker, just as she had believed his story about going to Emporia tonight.

What's in it for you, Patrick?

That's what she had asked him the day of the tornado. What was in it for him to marry her? *Everything.* His future. The rest of his life, although she wasn't the only part of the equation he was putting together.

Someday his dad would die. Maybe not all that long from now, even though he seemed to be feeling better at the moment. If his mom is still living, she'll need to turn the ranch over to her sons to run, and Patrick wanted to be in a position where anybody—even Rex—could see that it deserved to be him, because he was the one who'd been running it. If his dad went last, after his mom, Patrick wanted the old man to stipulate that he was to run the ranch.

He had no other future, he knew that.

There was nothing else he could do that would give him anything like the access to land and cash the ranch could give him. He needed to look—he needed to *be*—respectable, acceptable, for as long as it took to get firmly in control so that then he could do what he wanted to do with the land. Sell it to wind farms, maybe. Lease it to other ranchers. Open it up to oil and gas exploration. Whatever allowed him to take the money and run.

Abby was a necessary ingredient.

His parents already loved her; to them, she'd be the perfect daughter-in-law. His brother would have to come around, for Abby's sake. The town would figure that any man Abby Reynolds married must, at heart, be all right.

Patrick needed to be that man.

And he didn't need or want the complication of her fucking long-lost love.

Having satisfactorily completed step one in his plan to get rid of Mitch Newquist without actually having to kill the son of a bitch, Patrick was ready to move on to step two.

. . .

Rex made his last calls of the night to check on his department before getting ready to fix his late supper alone in his small house out in the country near his parents' place: one call to the dispatcher, one to each of his deputies on duty, and a last one to the county jail. It was a lightly staffed department in a lightly populated county. He could be as hands-on as he pleased, even when it didn't always please them.

There was nothing particularly interesting to hear until he reached the jail.

"Had a visitor just now, Sheriff," the night deputy informed him.

"This late? Who the hell was it and who did they want to see?"

"Well, it was your brother. And he wanted to see Marty Francis."

Sarah's brother. Once he got over the initial instant of shock, Rex felt a slow burn start to rise up his esophagus. "He say why?"

"Nope, but I told him he was too late, 'cause Marty got out today, but that if he waited long enough he'd probably catch him on the re-bound." The deputy's laugh was a deep, fruity, cynical sound.

"Your prisoner say where he was going when he left?"

"Get a drink he said, damn fool."

"Does he still live in Franklin?"

"Dunno, Sheriff. Want me to find out for you?"

"Yeah. Call me back. Wait! What did my brother say when you told him that Marty was gone?"

"What'd he say?" the deputy repeated, clearly stalling for time while he tried to remember. "I think he said, well, you can't say I didn't try, or something like that. I didn't know what he was talking about."

"You wouldn't be the first person to feel that way."

"Uh, Sheriff, doesn't your brother know we got visiting hours?"

"Rules have never stopped my brother, Deputy."

The deputy laughed again. "Stopped him this time."

Rex soon clicked the phone dead and then got up to put frozen shredded potatoes in a skillet of bacon grease to fry along with a thick slice of ham. As he moved the ham around while he waited for his deputy to call back, he poked at it viciously with a two-pronged cooking fork as if he were taking vicious pokes at his brother's gut.

*　*　*

Shortly before midnight, Abby heard Patrick's truck pull up in her driveway.

A few moments later she heard her front doorknob rattle softly, and then again, a little more noisily.

He was accustomed to finding her doors unlocked, but they weren't tonight. Would he knock, she wondered?

The doorbell rang, making her jump a foot.

When Patrick wanted something, he wanted it, she thought, as she got out of bed and pulled a light blanket around her shoulders. She padded barefoot to the front door and opened it to find him standing with his cowboy hat in his hands on her front stoop.

"A little late," she observed.

"But better than never," he said, and grinned down at her.

"How was Emporia?" she asked him.

"Empty without you."

"Get all your work done with your accountant?"

"Pretty much. Took a lot longer than I expected. You going to let me in?"

Abby smiled at him. They were not married. They were not even engaged. She had no formal commitment to him, nor he to her. He could do whatever he wanted to do, including lying to her about where he was going and why. But she didn't have to like it. And she was no longer sure she believed him about the sunglasses. "I don't think so, Patrick."

"Why not?" He looked surprised enough to nearly make her laugh.

"Because I don't have to," Abby said, and closed the door in his face.

She didn't remain on the other side of the front door to hear if he stood there for a while or if he walked away immediately, but it must have taken him a few moments of thinking it over, because it was a good five minutes by her clock before she heard his truck backing down her driveway toward the road.

Chapter Thirty-five

On the Wednesday morning following Memorial Day, Randie Anderson signed for that day's delivery of newspapers and magazines to Anderson's Grocery from the distributor's truck driver. Rather than calling for a stock boy to open the see-through wrapped packages, she picked up a pair of scissors and cut through the white plastic cords herself. She was eager to get hold of the daily newspaper from Kansas City to see if there were any sales at the big box stores to make it worth her while to grab Cerule and drive all the way up there this weekend. Maybe, she thought, they could even persuade Abby to take a break from the storm cleanup and go with them.

Randie lifted a stack of *The Kansas City Star* and set a paper aside for herself.

Then she looked straight down into the far-more-garish front page of a tabloid, and grinned at what she saw. The aliens were pregnant again. Brad Pitt was in love with somebody new. Big Foot was alive and well in Indiana. And a tornado had rained miracle flowers on a sick woman in . . .

"Small Plains?!"

Randie grabbed a copy and stared at the fuzzy dark picture on the cover.

It was impossible to tell if it was a picture of what it said it was, though it was sure dark enough to be a tornado. There was light in the middle and little dots of something. Quickly, Randie turned to the rest of the story inside.

There'd been a miracle cure of somebody with cancer, she read. It had occurred in the middle of a tornado at the grave of a young woman who was mysteriously murdered many years ago. Nobody knew her name or anything about her, except that she could cure anything that ailed you, including, it was suggested, bad credit, warts, and, as proven by the miracle, cancer. And when there was a cure, the heavens released an angelic sign, like flowers mysteriously dumped out of a twister.

"Small Plains?" Randie exclaimed again.

My God, they were talking about the Virgin!

And where did that photo come from, and who got cured, and how'd they ever hear about her hometown? She checked again, looking for local names, and finally found one: *Photo and story tip from Jeffrey M. Newquist of Small Plains, KS.* Randie'd sneaked peeks at enough tabloids in her time to know they paid actual money for tips on stories.

"That little twerp got paid for a photo that you can't even see!"

Tabloid in one hand and cell phone in the other, Randie started making calls.

She quickly found out she wasn't always the first with the news. Several people had already heard the story about the Virgin and the miracles and the flowers that fell out of a tornado from radio talk shows that featured story tips from listeners.

It appeared that Jeffrey M. Newquist had been one very busy teenager.

"And I'll bet he got paid for every single one of them," Randie said to Susan McLaughlin when she got her on the phone. "Sam's Pizza ought to send him a bill for all those candy bars he stole."

●　　●　　●

"Patrick asked me to marry him, Ellen."

Abby and her older sister were crouched beside a large flowerpot on Main Street, where Ellen was giving Abby a hand with repairing the damage done to the downtown flowerpots by the storm. They had bags of potting soil and new plants beside them and a garden hose running out from a spigot in the bathroom of the store just behind them.

"He didn't!" Ellen stared over the pot, wide-eyed. "You wouldn't!"

"Might keep me out of trouble," Abby said, trying to keep it light.

"Oh, sure. Any woman who'd marry Patrick Shellenberger is going to stay out of trouble, all right," Ellen retorted. "She'll never have a day's worry in her life." Then, getting serious, she said, "You're not even considering it, are you?"

"I told him I'd think about it."

"Are you out of your *mind*?"

"I'm not getting any younger, Ellen."

Her sister snorted. "And not any smarter, either, from the sound of it."

"What's so wrong with Patrick Shellenberger *now*, Ellen?"

Grudgingly, her sister said, "Well, I guess he has improved some. He seems pretty stable, at least compared to how he always was. But, Abby, he's still Patrick, and he'll always be Patrick." Shrewdly, she asked, "What does Rex think of this?"

"Rex doesn't know," Abby admitted.

"Aha. And if he knew . . ."

"He'd kill me."

"No, more likely he'd kill Patrick, but it amounts to the same thing. His own brother doesn't want you to marry him."

"Yeah, well, it's easy for all of you to say! It's not like I have any choices! This town is not exactly crawling with other men I can date."

"There are some perfectly nice men here! You just won't look at them."

Abby shot her sister an evil glare.

"Well, you won't! You never have, not since . . ."

Abby glared at her again, daring her to say the name.

The sisters' argument was interrupted by another woman's voice.

"Mayor! Abby! Good morning!"

Both of them looked up in the direction of the chirping voice. It was the middle-aged owner of a local fabric store, and she was beaming down on them as if she had invented sunshine. "Isn't this the most beautiful day?"

"I guess," Abby said sourly, as she punched a petunia down into the dirt.

"Hi, Terianne," Ellen said, with a quick smile. "you get through the storm okay?"

"I got through it just *great*," the woman said. "Pretty flowers."

Ellen gave her a closer look. "What's up?" The fabric store owner was not normally known for having a bubbling personality. "You look as if you just inherited a million dollars. Did you win the lottery?"

The woman looked startled, and blushed. "Me? No, no."

"Come on, you can tell us." Ellen rested her wrists on the edge of the big flowerpot and squatted back on her cowboy boots, squinting up into the other woman's round, happy face. "You won it, right?"

The woman laughed and looked even more flustered. But then she burst forth in an excited whisper. "Can you girls keep a secret?"

"Of course!" Ellen promised her, crossing her heart over her cowboy shirt.

"I just have to tell somebody, but I swore I wouldn't, so you both have to promise you won't." She looked around, checking for eavesdroppers, and then sidled closer to them. "You really won't tell?"

"Come *on*, Terianne, *give*," Ellen urged.

"After the storm?" the woman said in a dramatic near-whisper. "You know how my front window got busted? And there was glass all over my front displays? I swear, Ellen, it was the last straw, it really was. I just wanted to give up. I thought I'd just sit down on the floor and cry."

Ellen murmured something sympathetic, which Abby echoed.

The woman's fabric store had been for sale for months now.

"Well, I was feeling so bad," Terianne told them, "and I had a broom in my hand, and I was just standing there, sweeping up a little bit, and not feeling like doing even that much, when this *man* walks in the front door! He just walked in and volunteered to help me clean up! It was the nicest thing. A total stranger like that, just walking in and picking up a broom and offering to help. How often does *that* happen?"

"Uh huh," the mayor encouraged her. "And then what happened?"

"Well, we got to talking while we worked, and I told him I was going to give up, just close the door, and lock it, and never come back. And do you know what he said, Ellen? He said, 'Don't do that. I'll buy it.' "

Abby exclaimed, "He said *what*?"

"He said he'd buy my store!"

Abby's mouth dropped open, but her sister's eyes narrowed a bit.

The shop owner's eyes gleamed with tears.

"And that's what he did! I told him the sale price, and I warned him that it's 'As Is,' because I can't afford to fix anything, and he said that was fine, and he wrote me a check on the spot!"

Abby's mouth dropped open a little more.

"My God, Terianne, that's wonderful," she said.

Ellen's eyes only narrowed even more. She pursed her lips and said nothing.

"Ellen, didn't you hear what I said? I sold my store! Somebody bought my store! Now I can start over!"

"Who?" Ellen demanded. "Who bought it, Terianne?"

That simple question produced the deepest blush yet in the other woman. "Well, I don't exactly know his name."

"You don't know his *name*?" Using the big flowerpot, Ellen pushed and pulled herself to a standing position until she was eye to eye with the shop owner. "He bought your store and you don't know his name? What's the name on his check?"

Abby stared up at her sister, whose tone was uncharacteristically sharp. Ellen spoke bluntly to her own family, as Abby well knew, but when it came to the voters, she was usually as tactful as a politician had to be.

"It's for a corporation, and I can't read his signature."

"Didn't he introduce himself? Didn't you ask?"

The other woman appeared embarrassed, but defensive.

"You don't understand, it all happened so fast! The storm came and my store got damaged and I was just ready to give up. And then a miracle happened! A man walked in my door with a miracle. You just don't question miracles, Ellen. He even bought my fixtures and everything in the store! All I have to do is sign over the title and then I can cash the check."

"You don't even know if his check is any good!"

"It will be, Ellen. I'm telling you, he's a really nice man. I *know* it will be."

"What does this guy look like?" Abby asked, suddenly very curious herself.

"Oh, he's handsome! Tall, dark blond hair. And really nice eyes."

A nauseating feeling of unease, a low dull feeling of dread, hit Abby's chest when she realized the woman might have accurately described Mitch Newquist, the adult, all-grown-up Mitch Newquist.

Her own mouth clamped shut, but her sister snapped, "How old is this hero?"

"Maybe thirty-five, maybe forty."

Abby forced herself to say something. "Do you remember what he was wearing?"

"Remember! I'll never forget. He's so good-looking." The former fabric store owner smiled happily. "Or maybe he just seemed beautiful because he saved me."

"What was he *wearing*, Terianne?" This time it was Abby who snapped at her and Ellen who glanced over at her sister.

"Wearing? He had on jeans, I think, and a white dress shirt with the sleeves rolled up."

Mitch.

"You know why this has happened, don't you?" the woman asked them.

"Because you hung on until it could?" Ellen replied sensibly.

"No." The triumphant whisper turned reverential. "I was out at *the grave* over the weekend. I told the Virgin I was desperate for money. I told her I couldn't survive if somebody didn't buy my store. I asked her to help me. She brought that man to me. It's a miracle."

The sisters, one standing and the other still kneeling, on either side of the pot, went silent.

Finally, Ellen said, "Why is all this a secret, Terianne?"

"Because! He told me he wants to buy a lot of properties, Ellen! Isn't that great? For the town, I mean. He said if word got around the prices would go up and he didn't want other people to get more money for their property than I got for mine. Isn't that wonderful of him? It's going to be a miracle for the whole town, I can feel it, can't you?"

"Yeah," Ellen said in the same dark tone in which she had earlier referred to Patrick Shellenberger. "It's unbelievable, all right."

Chapter Thirty-six

After the owner of the fabric store walked away, still beaming with wonder and joy, Ellen crouched down by the pot again and took up her trowel to dig. But Abby stopped her from getting back to work again by saying, "You think it was Mitch, don't you?"

Ellen looked over at her. "Who bought her store? Yeah. Don't you?"

"Well, the way she described him," Abby said, "that's what he was wearing when I saw him."

Ellen looked startled. "You saw Mitch?"

Quickly, and without quite lying, Abby said, "You know! Before you all came out of Sam's. When I was across the street with that old man. I saw Mitch get out of his car and go inside."

"Oh." Ellen laughed a little, as if in relief. It was a reaction that told Abby a lot about her family and friends' concern for a reunion nobody thought was any good for her. If she had felt even slightly tempted to confide in Ellen, Abby squelched it then.

"Right," her sister said. "I forgot. And you don't think he saw you?"

"Nope."

They both glanced over to where the pizza restaurant was still in the dark. It had been the most heavily damaged of any building save Abby's barn/greenhouse.

"You knew something was up even before she described him, though," Abby said, a little accusingly. "What else do you know, Ellen?"

Her sister drew her upper lip in between her teeth and worried it, a habit she'd had since childhood, which Abby translated to mean that Ellen knew something and wasn't sure whether to tell her.

"What?" Abby demanded. "It's about Mitch, isn't it?"

Ellen shrugged a little. "I'm not sure. But Terianne isn't the only person who has been telling me about somebody poking around town inquiring about properties for sale. When we were in the Wagon Wheel this morning?" The sisters had met there for coffee. "I heard a rumor that Joe Mason sold that little shacky office of his—just like that, on the spot—to some unnamed buyer who also sounded a lot like Mitch."

"Why didn't you tell me?"

"It was just a rumor, Abby."

"You've got to *tell* me what you hear about him!"

Ellen looked surprised at her sister's sudden vehemence, but she said appeasingly, soothingly, "Okay."

Abby backed off a little, not wanting her sister to suspect that something irrevocable had already happened. She wasn't going to tell anybody, not her sister, not any of her friends, ever, that she had already fallen into bed with Mitch. Like the tornado that had blown through her life, in Abby's view that night had been a one-time, extraordinary occurrence that was totally over and that would never happen again.

"What do you think he's *doing*?" Abby asked in a fretful tone.

"I don't know." When she saw Abby's skeptical look, Ellen protested, "I don't!"

"He's only supposed to be *visiting*. He's not supposed to be doing anything that means he has to come *back*. So why is he buying properties all over town?"

"Well, so far it's not all over town, it's just downtown."

"I didn't mean it literally, Ellen! I just meant it—"

"Okay."

Abby gave her sister a shamefaced look. "I'm sorry, it's just—"

"It's okay, Abs, really."

With a struggle, Abby managed to ask more calmly, "So what *do* we think he's up to?"

"There's only one way I know to find out," Ellen said. "What the hell, I'm the mayor, I'll just ask him."

"No!" Abby panicked at the idea of her sister talking to Mitch, because what if he gave away their awful secret, that they had slept together? She didn't think he'd actually tell Ellen, but her sister might read undercurrents. "I'll do it! I'll ask him."

"You will? Abby, you don't have to do this. I can do it."

"No! I want to. I mean, I don't *want* to . . . but I *should* do it so I can get it over with. I mean, if he's going to be in town, then I'm probably going to have to see him eventually, right? So let me do it on purpose, let me plan it and do it my way, so he doesn't take me by surprise again."

"Again?"

Abby's face flushed. "Monday night . . . seeing him on the street . . ." Desperately, she looked around for a conversational diversion. "Speaking of streets, what's with all the traffic? I haven't seen this many cars downtown since the Founder's Day parade."

"It's that tabloid article." Ellen smiled down at the dirt.

"You're kidding. People *believe* that stuff? They'd actually drive here to see?"

"Believe it? You heard Terianne, didn't you? She thinks the Virgin sent Mitch to buy her store." Ellen laughed a little. "You notice how many handicapped stickers there are on those cars?"

"My God, they're coming here to get cured by the Virgin?"

Ellen looked at a vanload of senior citizens driving past and waved back when one of them waved at her. "I think so."

"Well, you're the mayor, can't you tell them to go home?"

"Go home? And drive all this business away? Abby, they'll eat at the Wagon Wheel. They'll buy groceries at Anderson's. They'll stay at the motels. They'll buy gas. This is the best thing that's happened to Small Plains since barbed wire."

"But it's not right." Frowning, Abby stared back at her sister.

"Why not? If it gives them hope and a little happiness?"

"And then disappoints them and wastes their money—"

"But Abby," Ellen said, reasonably. "You've heard the stories, too."

"Yeah, but—"

"And you can't prove they aren't true."

"You can't prove they *are* true."

"I don't have to."

"Ellen, that's a terrible attitude!" Abby stood up. She threw her own trowel down onto the pavement and it landed with a clatter that made her sister jump. "This is *wrong*. It's wrong to lead desperate people on! It's wrong to give them hope when there isn't any hope. It's criminal. It's . . . wrong." Tears came to her eyes, and her voice began to shake. "People get lonely and they get desperate and they'll cling to anything that gives them hope, and they just want to feel better, they just want to make all the misery go away, and it's just not *right* to take advantage of them when they're feeling that way, it's just not right, Ellen!"

As her sister stared up at her, Abby's voice broke on a sob.

Without another word, she turned on her heel and ran away, before Ellen could figure out that she wasn't really talking about sick people and the Virgin, she was crying about herself and Mitch. Down the sidewalk she raced, through the pedestrians, who turned to look after her, wondering what in the world would make such a pretty young woman so unhappy on such a lovely day.

* * *

As luck would have it, when Abby had run almost three full blocks, she spied a new black foreign-looking automobile signaling for a left turn that would take it right in front of her when she crossed the next street.

Seeing who was behind the wheel, Abby ran faster.

The driver, not seeing her, began his turn onto Main Street.

His brakes squealed when she stepped out in front of his car.

Mitch stopped midway in his turn and stared at Abby as she ran up to his window.

He didn't get to say a word before she started screaming at him.

"What do you think you're doing, Mitch? Why did you buy Teri-anne's store? Why did you buy Joe Mason's building? What are you doing, buying up properties? What do you *want*? Why did you come back?" Tears rolled down Abby's furious face. "And why don't you just *leave* again? Just go away and don't ever come back, just like you meant to do seventeen years ago. Why are you coming back and shaking everything up again? I want you to *leave*! This is *my* town! I want you to go away and never come back! Nobody wants you here! I don't want you! You don't belong here anymore!"

He had his hand on the door handle, and was starting to get out.

And then she was gone, walking away quickly against the traffic.

Abby wasn't finished screaming at people.

Now that she'd started, she felt as if she had been holding in a lot of screaming and a lot of tears for a lot of years.

She was running again, slowing down now because she was out of breath, but still fueled by the most bewildering set of emotions she had ever felt in all the years since Mitch left. But she had one more stop to make, now that she was on a roll, one more person to scream at, and he was going to listen to her, because it was long past time that somebody ought to, and it wasn't *right, none of it was right, it had always been so wrong,* and she was going to make it right if it killed her.

●   ●   ●

Mitch saw that he was holding up cars from four directions.

A couple of people started honking. Many others were staring.

He thought about chasing her down the street, grabbing her, holding her until she heard him out, until she let him explain, until she understood . . .

And then he got back into the Saab, finished his left turn, and drove on with his hands shaking, his heart pounding, his gut in an uproar, and all of his carefully laid plans in splinters. He had spent much of the last few days calmly and coolly figuring out his own legal vulnerabilities if he went public with what he knew. He had witnessed a crime and had not reported it. Normally, the Kansas statute of limitations would have run out a mere two years afterward, and he'd be safe from prosecution. But that rule didn't apply when an accused person was absent from the state, and he had been gone for the entire time from then to now. In that case, the statute of limitations only began to run again the moment he set foot back in Kansas, and here he was. The awful irony was that Doc Reynolds and Nathan Shellenberger *were* safe from prosecution because they'd been in-state the whole time and so the statute of limitations applied to them, at least in regard to the only crime that Mitch knew for sure they had committed, which was covering up the identity of a murder victim.

But being prosecuted for failing to report a crime would be the least of his problems if Doc and Nathan decided to play rough with him. There was no statute of limitations on murder. They were smart men. Between the two of them they could cook up a story and manufacture evidence to trap him. At the very least, it would be his word against theirs, as his father had always said it would be. And who was he but the boy who'd run away, which could also be used against him.

Mitch felt so filled with pain and anger that he thought he would explode if he couldn't release it, and he knew just who his first target was going to be. There was only one way for him to know what they had planned and that was to confront one or both of them and see exactly what they threatened him with.

Then he would decide what to do about them.

He pulled onto his father's street, but not into the old man's driveway.

Instead, Mitch parked in front of the big house across the street, the house where Abby had grown up. He got out of his car. It was Wednesday and apparently the clinic at the back was open for business. There were three cars parked in the wide driveway toward the rear of the house. Doc was seeing patients.

Mitch strode up the front walk, counting on the fact that, except for his own parents, nobody in Small Plains ever locked their doors.

*   *   *

Jeffrey Newquist stood outside the side door of his father's house and stared across the street at the foreign car parked there. Black Saab. It could only be his brother's cool car. *Brother.* It felt weird in his mind, even weirder to say, but he tried it out loud: "Brother." Didn't feel right yet, felt weird, but he thought he could get used to it.

Growing up, there hadn't been much talk of the brother who left, but the house had felt haunted by him. By how smart he was supposed to have been, how good looking, what a sports star, how popular, how everybody loved him. Every time Jeff failed at something he saw the comparison in people's eyes.

Substitute son.

Well, he was no failure now. After his success at selling his video and the story of the girl in the tornado, he felt the equal of anybody in town, even of his brother.

Sometimes he'd hated Mitch for going away and for abandoning him to Nadine and the judge. At those times, Jeff fantasized about how someday everybody would hear how Mitch Newquist was a serial killer or bank robber or something and they'd all realize how wrong they'd always been about him. Other times, Jeff imagined the perfect older brother—successful, rich, secretly devoted to his kid bro, who he would give anything to see but who he was prevented from seeing for some mysterious but totally understandable reason. And this cool older brother would come back to Small Plains and see how miserable Jeff was there and take him away to live in, like, New York City, where he'd buy him a cool car of his own and clothes and introduce him to gorgeous women.

And damned if it wasn't that version that was coming true!

Jeff stepped forward. His brother. He had a right to go see him.

The night they'd met, Mitch had seemed okay to Jeff.

They'd gotten along okay, he thought, even down to the beer.

He didn't know how Mitch felt about him taking the gun and the extra beer, because Jeff had left early so there wouldn't be the opportunity for any confrontation about it, but he figured Mitch was probably cool with it.

From that first meeting he had begun spinning subsequent scenarios. He saw the two of them getting in that black car and driving together back to Kansas City. Okay, it wasn't New York City, but it also wasn't Small Plains. He saw Mitch putting him up in his own house, giving him the run of the place, maybe giving him a job or getting him into college somewhere cool. He imagined how Mitch was probably ready to trade in that Saab for the new model and how he'd pass the keys to the "old" one over to Jeff.

He tried the driver's door and discovered it was not locked.

But instead of getting in to see how it felt to sit behind the wheel, Jeff looked up at Doc Reynolds's house. It was his childhood doctor up there. And his own brother. He had a right to go in there, too. Just like he had as much right to have their father's old silver pistol as Mitch did. He had it with him even now, tucked into his waistband, below an overhanging shirt, where he liked the weight of it and all it meant to own a gun. Or at least to have possession of one. On the other hand, he didn't really have a place to keep it where the judge wouldn't find it, so maybe he'd give it back so Mitch could return it to the bedside table, or maybe he wouldn't. Maybe that would depend on whether Mitch was glad to see him again. A lot of things might depend on that. With his right hand resting on the handle of the gun sticking out from his waistband, Jeff started up the front walk, taking long, loping strides.

Chapter Thirty-seven

It had very briefly passed through Marty Francis's mind to avoid drinking for a while after he got out of jail this time. Sitting on a stool at the bar of the Cottonwood Inn in the middle of the day, surrounded and jostled by a lunch crowd of strangers, he was on his sixth bottle of beer, thinking it over, pro and con, when somebody shoved a napkin under his nose.

The arm that shoved it was gone as quick as it had appeared and Marty's reaction time wasn't good enough to look around for the rest of the body that went with it, but he could see that the napkin in front of his nose had writing on it.

"Go to the Small Plains Cemetery," it said in plain block printing, in ink. "There's $ in it for you." He read it three times before he could focus on the important part: "$." Below the words was a roughly drawn map. It took him a while longer, but eventually he deciphered it: Cottonwood Inn to Highway 177 to Small Plains Cemetery, turn left inside the cemetery, go 100 yards, find the grave circled and marked with an X on the napkin.

"Johnny," he said to the bartender, who was wiping down the counter next to him.

"No," the bartender said without even looking up. "Six is enough, Marty. Seven is a car wreck."

"I don't want another beer, dammit. I want to know something. If somebody told you to go to the cemetery, because there was money in it, would you go?"

"What do you mean, money in it? Like in a grave, or something?"

"I don't know. It just says there's money in it."

"For you?" The bartender sounded skeptical.

Marty held up the napkin and the bartender bent over to look at it.

"This is a joke," he pronounced. "Or a scam."

"But it says there's money in it for me."

"Where does it say it's for you?"

Marty stared down at the napkin and noticed for the first time that his initials were there: *M.F.* "Here," he said, and pointed.

"Hmm," the barkeep said, after examining it again. Unable to refute the presence of the initials, he said, "And you want to know should you go? Well, do you owe anybody any money, Marty?"

"No, why?"

"Just checking to see if it could be a trick to lure you in to get you beat up. You got anything on you that anybody might want?"

"Not if I leave you a tip."

"Who gave this to you?"

"I don't know. It just got put in front of me."

The bartender smiled a little. "Like an act of God, or something?"

"Why not?"

"Well, me, I wouldn't trust this any farther than I could throw it, but I guess if you're telling the truth that nobody's out to get you, and even if there is—" He paused. "You got a gun, Marty?"

"Isn't that what glove compartments are for?"

They both smiled a little this time.

"Well, then, if nobody was out to get me, and there wasn't anything I had that anybody wanted, and I had a gun on me, then I'd go to the cemetery and lie down in a fucking coffin if I thought there might be money in it."

•   •   •

When Marty got to the cemetery, he discovered that he wasn't the only one looking for that particular grave. It gave him pause, because what if the mysterious stranger had dropped off similar napkins in other people's laps?

It took him a while to figure out how to apply the map to the cemetery, but finally he walked up to the right stone.

Peace Be Unto You were the only words engraved on it, along with *1987.*

But somebody had affixed another white bar napkin to the stone, below the words:

Sarah Francis
Born, Franklin, Kansas, 1968
Murdered, Small Plains, Kansas 1987

It took him a moment to put the name and places and dates together and realize it seemed to be describing one of his own sisters.

Feeling confused, he ripped the paper off the stone.

"Hey!" a man standing nearby objected. "What are you doing?"

"Fuck off," Marty told him and walked back toward his car.

When he got back to it, he found a tall man wearing a Western shirt, blue jeans, and cowboy boots leaning up against it smoking a cigarette. The man pointed to the crumpled paper in Marty's hand.

"You know her?"

"I dunno," Marty mumbled, feeling more confused than ever. "My sister, maybe."

"Really. That could be worth a lot of money to you."

"How so?" Marty perked up.

"Don't you know about this grave?"

Marty shook his head.

"It's famous," the man told him. "*She's* famous, although nobody has ever known who she really is. If that"—he pointed to the napkin with the name on it—"is your sister, there are a lot of people who would pay for her story."

"What people? What story?"

"Media." The man gave Marty a puzzled look. "They'd pay for you to tell them who she is, where she grew up, all about her, anything you know."

"Why the hell would they do that?"

Again, the man gave him a puzzled look. "Don't you live around here?"

"What do you mean?"

"The girl in this grave is supposed to be able to cure people of diseases—"

"No way!"

"Really. She's kind of a local saint, you might say."

"That's crazy."

"Maybe, maybe not, people claim some pretty amazing things about her." The man reached for the napkin, but Marty jerked it away. "Sorry. I just wanted to see her name again. I saw it on the gravestone before you came up here."

Marty covered the napkin with his hand.

"Who wants to know about her?" he asked the man. "How do I get this story out and get paid for it?"

The man smiled. "Just go into town and start telling people you know who the girl in the grave is. Say it's your sister. Start demanding they dig her up so she can be identified. Believe me, the people who want the story will come to you."

Marty, who was feeling more eager and more sober by the moment, listened up.

"And while you're at it," the man advised him, "you might want to be sure to ask people why Mitch Newquist left town when she died."

"Who?"

"Mitch. Newquist."

"Newquist . . . I had a judge who—"

"That's the one. Mitch Newquist is the judge's son."

"You're saying maybe a judge's son killed my sister?" Marty pulled himself up, feeling indignant. "This Mitch Newquist, he killed my sister?"

"I'm saying there's a reward for the person who identifies her and another reward for the person who fingers her killer."

"Reward? From who? Not *my* family."

Marty laughed a little at the very idea.

"The town, that's who," the man said. "For seventeen years, there has been a reward fund just sitting in the bank gathering interest."

Marty's eyes shone. "What's that guy's name again? The bastard who murdered my poor sister?"

"Mitchell Newquist, the judge's son."

It was only when they parted that Marty thought to ask, "Who are you? How come you know so much about my sister?"

"I don't know anything," Patrick Shellenberger told him. "I've just heard the rumors over the years. All I know is that somebody killed her and nobody has known who she is and there was some suspicion at the time because the judge's son left town all of a sudden right after they found her body."

"Did you put her name up there?" Marty asked, suddenly suspicious.

"Me? I was just here visiting my grandparents' graves."

"Then who put it up there?"

"Maybe your sister did it."

"Huh?"

"I told you. They say she works miracles."

.   .   .

Patrick walked away, leaving Marty standing in the cemetery holding the clue to the identity of the young woman in the grave. Now all Patrick had to do was stay out of town so that Marty couldn't spot him as the one who had talked to him in the cemetery. All he had to do was lie low, stay out at the ranch, and just wait for Sarah's greedy brother to do the rest of the work.

If Mitch Newquist wasn't long gone from Small Plains within twenty-four hours, Patrick would eat his hat.

      •   •   •

Marty forgot about the miracles as soon as the stranger walked away from him. His attention was focused on the paper in his hand. He fumbled for a pen in his shirt pocket and wrote down the other name he'd heard, using the top of his car as a table. *Mitch Neukwist.*

The judge's son.

Judges were rich, everybody knew that.

The hell with taking Sarah's story to a million different people. It wasn't like he remembered anything about her anyway. In a moment of clarity Marty had a brilliant thought: To make some money, he only needed to talk to one person.

Chapter Thirty-eight

"Sheriff? You've got a call."

"I'll take it in my office," Rex told the deputy.

"Shellenberger," he barked into the phone, feeling out of sorts. He needed to talk to Patrick, but he hadn't been able to find his brother either last night or this morning. Nor had he located Sarah's brother, Marty Francis, now that Marty was out of jail. At least Patrick hadn't spent the night at Abby's house, Rex had learned when he had called her to ask if his brother was there. In fact, she hadn't sounded all that pleased with his brother, so at least that was good news.

"Good morning, Sheriff," a young male voice said on the other end of the phone connection. "This is Bernie Simmons. I'm a reporter with *The Wichita Herald.*"

"All right," Rex said cautiously. It was rare for a journalist to call.

"I guess you had quite a storm up there?"

"That we did. Nobody hurt, though. Some property damage."

"Well, that's good. I mean . . ."

"I know what you mean."

"I'm calling about something else."

"And that would be?"

"That unidentified murdered girl they call the Virgin."

Indigestion rose in Rex's esophagus again. "You read the tabloids?"

The reporter laughed. "When the story's about miracles in Kansas, we do."

"Not much I can tell you. I wasn't the sheriff then."

"Who was?"

Rex silently cursed himself for having begged the obvious question. "That would have been my father."

"No kidding. That's interesting, a father-son sheriff's department. Maybe I'll do a story on how that happened—"

"It happened," Rex said dryly, "because he won elections and so do I."

"I wasn't suggesting nepotism, Sheriff."

"No? Most people do, until they hear it's an elected position."

"Let's get back to the girl in the grave."

Rex realized, too late, that he would have preferred to discuss nepotism. "What can I tell you?"

"Now that there's been this publicity, will you reopen her case?"

"Cases like that are never really closed," Rex said, stepping carefully.

"Too bad this isn't California," the young reporter said.

"That's probably true in many ways," Rex allowed, "but why in this case?"

"Because California has that law that requires coroners to submit DNA samples of all unidentified bodies. So they can run them past samples submitted by the families of missing people."

"Yeah?" Rex said.

"Too bad we don't have that law."

"Yeah, but even California didn't have that back when she was killed."

"Can't you still get her DNA and run it through the federal clearinghouse?"

"Maybe, if our county had the money."

"I'll bet people would contribute to a fund like that. Our paper could set one up. I could put it in the article I'm writing about her—"

Rex had a sudden vision of worlds colliding, of previously stable systems spinning out of control, of messes he wasn't going to be able to clean up. "Can I call you back, Mr. Simmons? I've got a deputy standing in my door"—Rex eyed his empty doorway—"needing my attention. What you should do is e-mail your questions to me." Without giving the reporter a chance to object, Rex reeled off his e-mail address at the sheriff's department, just happening to get one letter of it wrong.

By the time he hung up he was sweating.

But that was only the first of several calls he received that morning, some from other journalists, some from citizens wanting to give tips about the crime. Midway through one of them, Rex started making hash marks on a pad of paper, one mark for every lie he told. By the time he left for lunch at the Wagon Wheel, he had a little row of straight black lines with diagonal slashes through them.

Rex stood up, tore the paper off the pad.

Feeling disgusted with himself, he wadded it up and threw it in the trash.

He didn't realize there was a storm of a different kind chasing him.

•   •   •

Abby, still on her tear of furious emotion, reached the sheriff's department after Rex had left for lunch, they told her.

"Where'd he go?"

"Wagon Wheel."

So she went there, pushing her way through the front door, then winding through the little crowd of people who stood waiting for lunch tables, giving quick tense nods to those who said her name, avoiding eye contact and conversation, pulling away from hands that clutched her arm in an attempt to get her to stop and talk, keeping intent on her purpose, so that when she spied Rex eating at a table in the back with four other men from Small Plains, she charged forward as if they were the only two people in the room.

"Hi, Abby," Rex said, being the first to see her. "Want to join us?"

"I need you to come with me," she told him, over the heads of the other men.

Immediately he was alert, and getting to his feet. "What's the problem?"

"You," she said fiercely, while his lunch companions stared up at her, their forks and knives halted in mid-bite or slice. "You're the problem! And me. And everybody else."

Abby turned on her heels and fought her way back out of the café the same way she'd come, leaving in her trail a hurrying sheriff and a lot of people who wondered what kind of burr the younger Reynolds girl had got under her saddle today.

"We're taking your car," she informed him when he finally reached her side.

Knowing better than to argue, Rex said, "Where are we going?"

"To the cemetery."

*   *   *

"Look at them!" Abby said, pointing at a handful of strangers at the Virgin's grave.

"Okay," Rex said. He had pulled onto a shoulder of the highway next to the cemetery and parked there at Abby's command. It was a beautiful day without a cloud to suggest there could ever be any other sort of weather. He looked where she was pointing and saw cars parked along the cemetery road and he also saw that there were more people standing around one particular grave than any other. "I'm looking. What am I supposed to be seeing?"

"People being taken advantage of!"

"Who's doing the taking?"

"We are! This town is, by letting sick people believe those stupid stories, by letting them come here and make things worse for themselves!"

"There's no law against people believing everything they read, Abby."

"There are laws against defrauding people!"

"Who's doing the defrauding?"

"You've got to go up there and tell them to go home."

"Or what? I'm going to arrest them and throw them in jail for wanting a miracle?"

Abby turned to him. "You think this is all *right*, what's happening?"

"I think it's going to blow over pretty fast, Abby, without anybody having to do anything about it. And anyway, most of this county has believed in the Virgin for a long time. I didn't hear you raising a fuss about it before now. This is just a few more people, and they don't happen to live here. So what's the big difference? Why are you so upset about this? I left a pretty good chicken-fried steak and mashed potatoes, you know."

He tried to get her to smile, but it didn't work.

It not only didn't work, but it seemed to provoke her to come at him from another, even angrier angle. "If you or your father had ever solved her murder, if either of you ever so much as found out who she is, this wouldn't even be happening. She'd just be another poor murder victim in another grave, she wouldn't be some mysterious *saint* who can supposedly cure things and work miracles—"

"So you're saying those people up there, that's *my* fault?"

Rex did not like the direction their argument was taking.

"Well, what *have* you ever done to find out who she is?" Abby yelled at him in the small space of the interior of his SUV. "You won't send out her DNA, you won't let anybody else pay for it, you don't want your deputies to do any investigating, so yeah, maybe it is your fault, wouldn't you say so?"

"What is *wrong* with you?" Rex yelled back at her.

Abby burst into tears.

"I'm sorry. I'm sorry," she sobbed.

Furious and defensive, and not at all swayed by the water show,

Rex sat and glared across the seat at her, waiting for a better answer. But when it came, he wasn't prepared for it.

"I slept with him," Abby mumbled through her tears.

"With who? With my brother? I already knew that, and that just makes you a bigger fool than those people up there at the grave, and so what?"

"With Mitch. The night of the tornado. He came over. I slept with him, Rex."

Abby flung herself over the seat and up against Rex's chest.

"That *son* of a bitch!" he said, putting his arms around her. "That son of a *bitch*!"

He held her while she sobbed, which didn't keep him from also muttering, "Expecting some kind of miracle, were you?" And then he said, when she was finally quiet enough to hear him, "Abby, I did send out her DNA."

"What?" She pulled herself away so she could look at him.

Rex nodded. "On my own, with my own money, a long time ago. But I already knew who she was. Abby, I've always known who she was. I also think I know why she got killed. And I'm pretty sure I know who killed her. And since I've never been able to figure out what to do about any of it, and I've never talked to anybody else about it, maybe I ought to tell you, and then we can figure something out together."

*   *   *

He refused to tell her anything more until they got into his office.

Rex barked at his deputies to leave them alone, and then he closed his door and pushed the lock on it. While Abby took a chair on the other side of his desk he went around it and sat down. He reached toward the lower drawer that held the box with the red scrunchie in it and pulled it out, but he also pulled out what was below it: four thin folders. He opened the box first, took out the elastic red hair accessory, and placed it on his desk close to where Abby sat. "This belonged to her," he said. "She wore this." Then he picked up the top folder, opened it, and pushed its contents toward her, too. "Here's the DNA lab report on some hairs that were in it." He hadn't given the lab all of them. Even now, there were a few stray dark hairs in it, as if the beautiful girl who had worn it had only just taken it off.

Abby sat with her hands in her lap, not touching anything.

"Her name is Sarah Francis," Rex said, and waited to see if Abby reacted. When she didn't, he said, "You might remember her if I tell you she used to clean houses in town. She worked for Nadine for a while."

Abby frowned, and he could tell she still didn't quite recall.

"She was beautiful," Rex said. "A little older than us, long dark hair, really pretty. She lived over in Franklin."

Finally he saw recognition . . . and then horror . . . in Abby's blue eyes. Her hands flew to her mouth as she gasped, "Oh my God! Oh, Rex. I do remember her. I liked her. She was nice. And she was . . . gorgeous." Abby's eyes, which had only recently stopped leaking tears, filled up again. "That's *her*, in the grave, that's her?"

He nodded. "It's Sarah."

"And you've known this ever since you got the DNA report . . ." Abby leaned forward to look for a date on the papers in the folder. ". . . five *years* ago?"

"No," Rex told her. "I've known it since the night she died."

"What? You've known since *then*?"

He nodded. "I'm not the only one. My dad has known it, and my mom, and Patrick. I think your father has always known it, too."

"My dad? My father knows who she is?"

Rex thought Abby looked as if she couldn't absorb any additional shocking revelations, but he had many more to give her. For the next half hour, he told her the same story he had told his mother on the night that he, his brother, and father had found Sarah.

Abby didn't say a word through his telling of it until toward the end, when she said, "Wait a minute. She was supposed to be so beaten up that nobody could identify her. Wasn't that true?"

"She wasn't beaten," he said. "I think my dad and your dad just made that up."

"But why, Rex? Why would they do that?"

"To protect somebody," he said, and then held up a hand to stop her obvious next question. "Wait. Please, Abby. Let me finish telling this my way."

When he did finish—without telling her who he thought the fathers were protecting—Abby stared at him accusingly and said, "You've all *known*, all this time you've known, and nobody said anything? Rex, why haven't any of you identified her? Why have you let people think that nobody knows her name?"

"Like I said, they were trying to protect somebody."

"Who?"

"My brother," Rex said, and watched Abby's hands go to her mouth in horror again. "I'm pretty sure Patrick killed Sarah, Abby."

"Why? Oh, my God, *why*?"

Her old friend put a hand flat on each of the other three file folders.

"Because of these," he said.

Abby started to reach for the folders, but he pulled them back out of her grasp. Then he spread them out in a line, one, two, three, and commenced to open them one at a time. "These are the results of other DNA tests, Abby. Do you remember that I told you that my father said she had been raped?"

Wide-eyed, out of words, Abby nodded.

"She wasn't raped. She had blood down her legs because she had given birth."

"How do you know that?" Abby whispered.

"Because I knew she was pregnant and when I saw her in the snow that night, I could see she wasn't pregnant anymore. Abby, we had just been out in the fields delivering newborn calves. I knew a recently delivered female when I saw one, even if she was human instead of some other kind of mammal, and even if I was only a kid. Sarah had been pregnant, and she'd had the baby, and then she died."

"What happened to the baby . . . and who was the father?"

Abby was still whispering, as if she was afraid to ask such questions.

Rex tapped the first folder. "This is the child's DNA. I had it identified by comparing it with her DNA." He looked at her. "It's Jeff,
Abby. Jeff Newquist is Sarah's child. I got a sample of his saliva off a
cigarette he smoked, and I did that because of what I knew. I knew
Sarah was pregnant, I knew she stayed at the Newquists' ranch house
during her pregnancy, and then they showed up with a brand new
adopted baby. I thought there was at least a chance that baby was
hers." Once he saw that she had absorbed that information as well as
she could at the moment, he continued. "My next job was to identify
the father, so I sent in samples from the most likely suspects." He
tapped the second folder. "These are Patrick's DNA results." He
tapped the next one. "Mitch's."

"Mitch?" The single word was an anguished protest that gave away
her feelings then and now.

"I had his tested because Sarah had a crush on him."

"But that didn't mean that *he*—"

"I thought I should make sure."

"But how did you do that, how did you even get his DNA?"

"That part was easy. We shared a lot of clothes. I'd wear one of his
practice shirts for football, he'd slip on one of my basketball shirts."
Rex smiled slightly. "My mom keeps everything. And a teenage boy's
sweat is a long-lived thing."

Abby stared at the folders and then up at Rex.

"Does one of them match?" she said, looking afraid.

He nodded again. "Jeff has DNA that matches Sarah's and Mitch's,
Abby."

Tears flooded her eyes and she looked down.

He waited sympathetically for her to be able to look at him again.
When she did, he said, "I think that's why his parents sent him away,
so they could adopt Jeffrey as if he was a stranger's baby, and no one
would ever connect him to Mitch." He gave her a little more time to
absorb that, and then he said, "I think my brother killed her, out of
jealousy."

He expected her to look horrified again, but this time, she didn't.

"Oh, come on, Rex," Abby said, sounding the calmest she'd sounded since first showing up in his office that afternoon. "You don't really believe that, do you?"

His mouth almost dropped open. She wasn't reacting very dramatically to his momentous announcement of the terrible secret he'd been keeping to himself for all these years, that his older brother had probably killed a girl.

"Of course I believe it!" he protested. "I just said so. My God, I just called my own brother a murderer."

But she shook her head. "You two have never gotten along. Patrick would love to beat you any way he could and you'd love to believe the worst of him. It's true, Patrick is a jerk. He's a liar and a manipulator, but he's not very good at it, Rex. You know that. He always gets caught. If he had done this, he would have given himself away by now. No matter whether our dads were covering up for him or not. So, okay, he's all those things. But he wouldn't *kill* anybody, Rex."

When he looked at her as if she was naive, Abby said, "He wouldn't!"

Then, seeing him gathering the folders and getting up from his chair, she said, "Where are you going?"

"*We're* going out to the ranch."

"Why?"

"We're going to find out if my parents know anything that we don't know."

"Rex! You're not going to accuse Patrick to them!"

But he was already heading for the door. Abby jumped out of her chair and hurried after him. On her way out the door, she suddenly remembered the awkward moment in Verna Shellenberger's kitchen when Verna had seemed to falter in her own belief in Patrick. Abby's heart sank, remembering that, and suddenly she wasn't quite so sure of her own conclusions about him. And if she wasn't even sure about Patrick, who had been in and out of her life for all these years, then how could she possibly be so sure about the innocence of a man who had been gone for half of that time?

. . .

In his SUV, when she couldn't get him to talk about Patrick, Abby said, "We're a fine pair, aren't we?"

"We?" She had finally goaded him into speech. "What do you mean we? What's this we business?"

"You and me, Rex," Abby said. "Too much in love with other people to ever fall in love with anybody else."

Rex gave her an angry, puzzled look as he drove. "Huh? I'm not in love with anybody." Sounding reluctant, as though he hated to humor her even with a joke, he said, "Though I've probably been overfond of a horse or two."

"Sarah," Abby said, simply and directly. She looked over at him. "I know about the flowers, Rex. Every Memorial Day you give her flowers."

"How the hell do you know about that?"

"I maintain the cemetery, remember? I've seen you."

He tried being indignant. "Why didn't you say something?"

"It looked private."

"Well, so what? It doesn't mean I'm still in love with her, Abby. I'm just showing respect, that's all, and saying I'm sorry."

"Really? When's the last time you were in love with a woman, Rex?"

When he didn't answer, but only shifted uncomfortably in his seat, Abby said, "There hasn't been anybody, has there? Anybody you've loved, I mean. There hasn't been anybody since Sarah."

"She has nothing to do with it. And, anyway, you're a fine one to talk. Who have you ever loved since Mitch?"

"But that's what I mean, Rex," Abby said, without defending herself. "We're a fine pair."

They rode for two miles in complete silence.

Finally, he sighed, breaking it. "Yeah."

"I'm sick of it," Abby told him, taking up right where she'd left off.

He sighed again. "Me, too."

They were already driving alongside the fence line of his family's ranch. His parents' home was ahead on the right. "Look," Abby said, "your mom's waiting for us." Rex had called ahead to say they were coming. Now they both saw that Verna had spied them and was starting to run toward the gate where they would turn in.

"Rex?" Abby said, as they got closer and she could see Verna's face. "I think something's wrong."

When they pulled into the driveway, Verna hurried up to Abby's side.

Rex and Patrick's mother was weeping.

"Abby! Oh, Abby! I'm so sorry, honey! Abby, your dad's been shot!" She looked across at her sheriff son while Abby gasped, turned white, and grabbed for Verna's hands to hold. Verna squeezed them tight.

Abby almost couldn't get the words to come out. "Is he . . . ?"

"He's dead, sweetheart," Verna told her gently while the tears flowed down both their faces. "Your father's dead."

Chapter Thirty-nine

Two sheriff's deputy vehicles were already in the Reynoldses' driveway, blocking the exit by the other cars parked at the top of it. Rex
and Abby rushed into the house through the wide-open front door.

All Abby saw was her father lying on the living room carpet.

The wound was tremendous, fired at close range, opening up his
chest and penetrating his heart and lungs.

"Dad!" she screamed, while Rex held her back.

"I'm sorry, Abs, you can't go over there."

It was a crime scene now and he saw that his deputies were struggling to get it right.

She had called her sister, Ellen, from Rex's car, but she wasn't there
yet.

He took Abby out of the house again and then walked around to
the back and through the office door. Inside her father's little clinic
they found four other people huddled, waiting for somebody to pay
attention to them.

Her father's long-time nurse ran up to Abby and they sobbed in
each other's arms.

"We heard shouting," one of the patients said.

"Then we heard a shot," a second one said.

"What did you do then?" Rex asked them all.

"She tried to get into the house through that door—" The first one pointed at the nurse and then at the door that led into the Reynoldses' kitchen. "But it was locked from the other side."

All the patients were locals, older men whom Rex had known for years.

He realized they'd been scared, and who wouldn't be, hearing a sudden gunshot inside their doctor's house.

"We shoulda gone around to the front sooner than we did," one of them said.

Rex nodded. But they'd been frightened of what they'd find. It was a kindhearted town where people went out of their way to help one another, but it was also a town full of small-town fears of big-city problems, where an elderly nurse and three old men sitting in their doctor's office and hearing a shot might have imagined there were people wanting to steal drugs, or some such. He didn't blame them for being slow to act, but he knew they would forever blame themselves.

Deputy Edyth Flournoy walked in at that moment, carrying a rifle encased in plastic, which she displayed for Rex to see.

"That's it?" he asked her.

"This is it."

Rex looked over at Abby, then back at the rifle.

It was Mitch's childhood gun.

Rex, who had shot it many times himself, would have recognized it anywhere because of the heart and initials that Abby had scratched into the wooden barrel, an act of loving vandalism that might have infuriated another boy but had only made Mitch laugh and kiss her. Rex had been there to see it and he remembered thinking at the time, *it must be love.*

His cell phone rang. When he saw on the Caller I.D. screen that it was his parents' number, he answered, saying, "Mom?"

"Rex—" His mother's voice was shaky. "Mitch is here."

"Mitch is *there,* at your house? *Now?*"

Both the nurse and Abby looked up sharply at him.

"He's in our driveway, Rex," his mother said, sounding near panic. "With Jeff. Rex, he's got a gun."

"Where's Dad?"

"Upstairs."

"Can you get to Dad's gun case?"

"No!" Abby screamed, breaking away from her father's nurse. "No, Rex!"

Ignoring her, he continued giving instructions to his mother. "Get out one of Dad's rifles. You know how to use it, Mom. If Mitch does anything to threaten either of you, shoot the bastard."

"Rex, I can't! I couldn't do that!"

"Mom, it's his rifle that shot and killed Doc."

"No!" Abby screamed again.

Rex took the phone from his ear for just long enough to look his friend in her eyes and say, "Maybe it's about time that you and I believed the worst of Mitch Newquist."

• • •

She ran after him when he raced out to his SUV and jumped in before he could stop her. He didn't have time to argue with her or to force her out of the car. He had told his deputies to leave what they were doing and follow him. "But don't make any moves until I tell you to," he instructed them.

Rex flipped on his siren and his lights and left them on until they were close enough to be heard from the ranch. At that point, he turned them off again, but he continued to speed toward his parents' property, driving faster than any car Abby had ever been in before. He did it all with one hand, because his other hand never left his cell phone and his cell phone never left his ear.

When he got to the front gate, he heard his mother say in a calmer voice, "It's all right now, Rex. Your father has things under control."

• • •

Under control meant that Nathan Shellenberger had his own rifle leveled at Mitch Newquist's face as the four of them—Nathan, Mitch, Jeff, Verna—stood on the side porch by the kitchen.

When Rex and Abby walked up, Abby's heart betrayed her and lurched at the sight of the man she realized in that moment she would always love, whether she ought to or not, whether it was right or not, whether he had done the worst possible thing he could do to her family or not. She loved him, she had always loved him, she would always love him, *God help me,* Abby thought as she stopped in the driveway, exactly where Rex told her to.

"Rex, tell your dad to put his gun down!" Mitch yelled. And then to Nathan he yelled, "What is wrong with you? I'm Mitch! Remember? Mrs. Shellenberger, you know me, or you used to, and I know you know Jeff—"

"Where is your gun, Mitch?" Rex asked him, drawing nearer.

He did not tell his father to put the rifle down.

"Rex, my *gun,*" Mitch said in a tone of deep sarcasm, "is over there on the ground where I dropped it when your father came charging out of the house with his gun." To Nathan again, he said, "What do you think? That we're here to rob you? Or is this how far you'll go to keep me from telling what I know?"

"You show up with a gun at my house," the old sheriff said gruffly.

"After you've shot Quentin Reynolds," Rex said. "What do you mean, what Dad—"

Mitch turned so fast to stare at him that Nathan tightened his grip on his rifle, causing Verna to cry out, "Nathan!" Mitch interrupted, "*What?* What are you talking about, Rex? I haven't done anything to anybody. I haven't shot anybody. Are you telling me that somebody shot Abby's dad?" He looked at her. "Abby—"

"Do *not* move," Rex told him. "Jeff, are you all right?"

"Well, *yeah,*" the teenager said in sarcastic tones to match his brother's. "What are you talking about, Mitch shooting Doc? We were just over there, dude. Nobody shot Doc. Okay, they yelled at each other. I don't know what *that* was all about. But nobody fucking shot anybody." Belatedly, he realized Verna was standing there. "Sorry," he mumbled, with a glance at her. "But I mean, I was there the whole time, Mitch and me, we walked out of the house at the same time, and I'm telling you, Doc was just fine."

"Abby?" Mitch said, looking concerned and worried. "Your father?"

"My son told you not to move," Nathan warned him. "If you didn't shoot anybody then what the hell were you doing walking up to my house with a gun?"

Mitch ignored Nathan and talked directly to Rex. "It's Dad's old pistol, Rex. Remember the one he kept in the bed stand at the ranch house?" Then he remembered its history and turned back to look at Nathan. "You gave it to him, Sheriff. You and Doc, for one of his birthdays, remember?"

"I don't care who gave it to him, what are you doing with it here?" Nathan demanded.

"I had it," Jeff said, stepping forward. "Mitch made me give it back."

"*You* had it?" Rex asked.

"Okay, I took it. The other night, from the ranch house."

"We were arguing . . . talking . . . about it in the car on the way over here," Mitch said, "after we left Doc's house. Just now, when we got out of my car, I made Jeff give it to me. That's what your mom and dad saw." He looked at the older couple. "Verna. Nathan, that's what you saw, that's all it was. Now will somebody please tell me what's going on? Did something happen to Abby's dad after we left there?"

In spite of the arm that Rex put out to hold her back, Abby came walking up until she stood within a few feet of them. She looked at Mitch first and then at all of them and she began to cry again.

"Dad's dead," Abby confirmed for them. "Somebody shot him in the house."

"Abby," Mitch said for the third time, and started to move toward her.

"Stop!" Nathan barked, but then his arthritic arms gave way and he lowered the rifle.

"Will somebody tell us what the hell is going on?" Jeff said to all of them.

For the first time, Verna stepped forward and took charge. "We're going inside," she informed them. "You are going to clean up your language, young man," she said to Jeff, though her tone held affection as well as disapproval. "Come here, Abby." Abby ran forward into the older woman's embrace. With Abby enveloped in her arms and crying on her shoulder, Verna Shellenberger looked at her husband and then at each of the others in turn, and she said in tones that brooked no argument, "We're going inside."

The old sheriff gave her a wary look, but then something in his spirit seemed to collapse in the way his arms had, because he nodded, turned, and was the first to go into the house. All of them, looking at him, understood that that was the moment when Nathan Shellenberger really grasped that his lifelong friend was gone.

•   •   •

Rex remained outside for a few moments, warily telling Mitch and Jeff what was known about Quentin Reynolds's murder, and then the three of them went inside, too. "Can I pick up the gun?" Jeff asked, still sarcastic.

"I'll get it," Rex told him. "Go inside with your brother."

Then he sent his wide-eyed deputies back to the Reynoldses' home to continue dealing with the aftermath of homicide.

•   •   •

They gathered in the living room, taking seats on couches and in armchairs, with Nathan holding court from his leather lounger in the center of the room, opposite the television set. Nathan's hunting rifle was propped against his chair. The judge's pistol was in the kitchen, on the table. Rex's own gun was still holstered at his hip, and he kept his hand on it, just in case he needed it.

Abby sat as far away from Mitch as she could get, curling herself up against Verna on one of the two long couches where Rex and Mitch had used to laze and watch Sunday football when they were kids.

His father may have been center stage, but Rex took charge.

"All right. Mitch. What did you mean out there?"

"Yeah," his dad said in a voice that was still gruff from emotion. "What is it you think I'm supposed to know?"

Mitch shook his head. "Doc denied it, too."

"Denied *what*?" Rex said.

"The night Sarah died," Mitch said, still looking at Nathan, "I was in Doc's office, hiding. I saw you and Patrick bring her in, Nathan. I saw what Doc did to her body. I know the two of you covered up her identity."

Nathan Shellenberger couldn't have looked more shocked than he did.

Verna stared at her husband, while Abby stared at Mitch.

"My God," Mitch said, looked nearly as shocked himself. "You really didn't know that? What Doc told me, it's true? Neither of you has ever known? You didn't know I was there and I saw you?"

The old sheriff shook his head, seeming incapable of speech.

"Covered up her identity?" Rex said, taking a step forward. "Dad? What's he talking about?"

On the couch, still hugging Abby, Verna Shellenberger remembered the promise she had made to the Virgin . . . to Sarah Francis . . . to return the favor if Sarah could help Nathan with his pain. He was in a different kind of pain now, and Verna knew it was time to relieve that, too, and there was only one way to do it.

"Nathan," she said in the same firm voice she had used to corral them when they were all standing outside. "No more secrets. It's time for all of us to talk about it. Starting with you." In a quieter voice that was suddenly tear-choked, she added, "Do it for Sarah. Please, Nathan, for Sarah."

Slowly, and as if the effort hurt him more than arthritis ever had, Nathan began to talk to them. First he told them everything he remembered from the night when he and his sons had found the girl's body. And then he told them what he knew only from hearing it from Quentin Reynolds seventeen years ago.

Chapter Forty

January 23, 1987

In the late afternoon of January 23, 1987, Doc was in the middle of medicating old Ron Buck for an inner ear infection when his nurse stuck her head in the door and said, "Judge Newquist is on the phone, Doctor. He says it's an emergency."

Getting up quickly from his swivel stool, Quentin said, "Don't go away," to his patient.

The elderly man with his head bent over to allow liquid medicine to drain down into his ear canal, snorted with phlegmy laughter, and said from his bent position, "You pretty well made sure of that, Doc."

Quentin picked up the extension in his examining room.

"What's the emergency?" he said, right off the bat.

The deep voice of his oldest childhood friend filled his ear. "You need to come out here to the ranch, Quentin, you have to come out right now."

"What's the problem, Tom?"

"I can't tell you. Just bring your doctoring stuff and get out here as fast as you can."

Quentin started to snap, "It would help to know whether to bring a portable EKG or a Band-Aid, Tom," but the judge hung up before he could get the words out. Quentin glanced over at his patient, who still had his scrawny old neck cocked obediently. "You can put your head back on straight now, Ron. Slowly! Don't go all dizzy and faint on me." Then, as he glanced out a window at the weather—still clear, in spite of a forecast for what might turn out to be a doozy of a winter storm—he said, "I'm sorry, but I have to leave. Keep taking those antibiotics. Call me if the pain gets worse, or you get a stiff neck, or you develop a fever."

"Already got all those, Doc," the old man said as Quentin headed for the door.

Quentin turned around to give his patient a last moment of full attention. "I'll check in on you tomorrow."

Quentin Reynolds still made house calls, as he was about to do for Tom Newquist. He didn't even have to gather any supplies, since he kept a full medical bag in his car at all times, ready to go. All he had to do was let his nursing assistant know he was leaving. It would have been nice, however, to know if he needed any extras of anything, or anything special and unusual. Damn Tom Newquist for being such a goddamn judge sometimes, thinking he could order anybody—even his best friends, even a doctor—around like court reporters.

Just before he slammed his office door, he heard the old man call out from behind him, "What's the emergency, Doc?"

"I wish I knew, Ron."

* * *

Instead of somebody running out of the farmhouse to meet him as Quentin expected, Tom Newquist came running from the direction of the storm cellar. He was a big man who got precious little exercise—despite the nagging of his friend the general practitioner— and he looked awkward as he ran. But then Tom Newquist had always looked like a huge lumbering bear on the football field, too, even as he was mowing down an opposing line. He wasn't graceful, but he cleared a path, Tom did, he cleared a path.

Quentin, shorter, lighter on his feet, though not in much better shape himself now that they were both in their forties, grabbed his medical bag and hurried to meet Tom halfway. Before he was even that far, however, the big man turned, waving Quentin to follow him. When Tom broke into a run again, so did Quentin.

He was surprised they were headed back toward the storm cellar.

Its thick wooden door was wide open, revealing light inside.

Tom disappeared inside it first. When Quentin reached it and stepped in, he nearly recoiled in shock at what he saw there: Nadine, disheveled, bloody, staring toward the doorway with a look of horror that Tom had never seen on her face before. And there was Tom, staring at Quentin with hardly less dismay than his wife was expressing. And, most shocking of all, there was a young woman, a full-term pregnant young woman, writhing on a single bloody bed set up against a wall.

"What the hell have you done?" he said, but hurried to her side.

His brain had taken in other startling facts about the cellar that was appointed like an apartment: throw rugs to cover a cement floor, a toilet, a faucet and sink, a stove and oven. He also saw bloody towels that had been tossed to the floor.

The young woman turned wide, dark, terrified eyes to him.

He recognized her from somewhere, but couldn't think where.

Pleading eyes, Quentin thought, having seen them on women in the throes of nightmare deliveries before.

"What's your name?"

"Sarah," she whispered.

As he settled himself at the foot of the single bed, he suspected he already knew what he would find: breech birth, baby stuck in birth canal, mother losing blood, baby losing heartbeat, both of them threatened with losing their lives.

"Why is she here? Why isn't she in a hospital? Who's her doctor?"

Nobody answered him.

Quickly he determined the accuracy of his terrible diagnosis. He was going to have to turn the baby, and do it so quickly that there wouldn't be time to give the poor girl a shot to block the pain. Even as he began to do his delicate, violent work with the baby, within her torn body, he wanted to yell at the two supposedly intelligent people standing by doing nothing more helpful than wringing their god-damn hands. Instead, he talked to the girl, saying over and over, "I'm so sorry. I know this is terrible. We have to do it. I'll be as quick as I can. Hold on, hold on, hold on . . ."

And then he finally did yell, "Nadine, for God's sake, come hold her hand!"

The girl was screaming, screaming. Her blood was oozing all around them, around the baby, mother, and doctor. Over in a corner, Nadine Newquist didn't move, nor did her husband, who was now pacing like an expectant father.

When the baby finally turned, the mother screamed and did the one thing Quentin was praying she wouldn't. She fell unconscious.

"Wake her up!" he yelled. "She has to push!"

Neither of the Newquists moved to do his bidding.

"Goddamn useless!" he muttered. They might as well have dropped off unconscious themselves. Feeling nearly as panicked as they looked, he realized he was going to have to pull the baby from her body, like pulling a calf from a heifer, only harder, more danger-ous, and less likely to end happily.

But then, finally, Nadine sprang to some kind of life.

Suddenly she was at the girl's side, shaking her, screaming at her to wake up.

"Jesus, Nadine, I said wake her up, I didn't say kill her!" Quentin roared at her.

But it was working well enough to rouse the girl. When he saw her eyes flutter, Quentin didn't wait, but yelled, "Push, you've got to push! Push, Sarah! Nadine, tell her to push, push, push!"

Unbelievably, the girl did, though Quentin couldn't imagine how she managed it, as much agony as she was in and as weak as she was from loss of blood. From somewhere inside her, the girl found the strength to push until the baby's head emerged, and then its shoulders, until Quentin could finish the job of bringing it—a boy—into the world of its bizarre, cramped, delivery room.

And then, with the baby born, the girl passed out again.

He hadn't even had time to tell her she'd had a boy.

Quentin cut the cord, wiped the baby's eyes, slapped breath into its chest, and barked furiously for somebody to hand him some towels, which he wrapped it in. Then, holding the now-bawling infant in one arm, he snapped his other hand around Nadine's wrist like a vise, pinning her to where she stood, tall, thin, sharp-faced, bloody, and big-eyed in a way nobody would ever have dreamed Nadine Newquist could look.

"Who is she?" Quentin demanded. "What the bloody hell have you done?"

Nadine tried to pull away from him, but he wouldn't let her go.

Tom walked over. "Is the baby all right?"

"Probably," Quentin snapped at him. "Infants are tough little buggers, and this one has a tough little mother, to boot. Answer my questions. Who is she? What the hell is she doing delivering her baby here, and what do you two have to do with it?"

The girl moaned, and Quentin temporarily forgot his questions.

"Here," he said, handing the wrapped infant over to Tom. "Take him."

Tom tried to back away.

Quentin pointed to the girl on the bed, and said, "If you won't take the baby, then can you take care of her?"

"No . . ."

"Then take the baby, goddammit." Quentin handed the child over, and then began to examine the girl's pelvic area. Incredibly, there didn't seem to be any arterial flow. Nothing vital had been severed, as far as Quentin could determine. It had been rough, horribly rough, but she was probably going to survive . . .

"I want her in a hospital," he said, turning to look at the Newquists.

But Nadine turned to point out the open doorway, and suddenly Quentin became aware of two things that also shocked him. Cold air was pouring through the open doorway, and there was snow coming down outside, a fall so thick and heavy it looked as if it had always been coming down and would be falling forever.

The forecast storm had come. They had to leave soon, or they might not get out.

"Get moving," he instructed them. "You hold the baby, Nadine. Tom, you drive. We'll lay the girl down in my backseat, and I'll follow you to Manhattan . . ."

"No," Tom said, speaking for only the second time since leading Quentin there.

"What the hell do you mean, no?" Quentin demanded.

And then Tom told him why they could not take the girl and her baby to the hospital in Manhattan, or to a hospital anywhere.

"It's my child, Quentin."

"Your—?"

"We paid her to keep quiet."

"You had an affair with this girl?"

"You could call it that," Nadine said with deep bitterness. "Or you could call it rape."

Her husband's head snapped around. "It was consensual, goddammit, Nadine. I never raped anybody."

Quentin stared at his oldest friend, feeling the horror that had been on Tom's and Nadine's faces when he first walked in, although the horror he was feeling was of a different kind. He knew that they were horrified of the blood, and of getting into more trouble than even they could get out of. He was horrified by *them*. It wasn't the first time Tom Newquist had ever been accused of forcing sex on a girl, but the accusations had always been just gossip and his friends had always chosen never to believe it, they had always chosen to believe Tom, even though deep down inside they knew he was arrogant enough, felt privileged enough . . . Those other girls flashed through Quentin's mind as he looked back at the sleeping girl on the bed who had just suffered through so much.

And again, one more time, it would be Tom's word against hers.

A judge against a girl who cleaned houses, for Quentin had remembered how he knew her.

"We paid her to keep quiet and to have the baby," Nadine said with a vicious glance for her husband. "I want that child around for the rest of its life to remind Tom what a fool he is."

* * *

An hour later, after staying with the girl until she came to consciousness again and began to try to nurse the baby, and then remaining until he felt as sure as he could that both mother and son could get along without extraordinary medical intervention, Quentin realized there was nothing more he could do for them.

He washed his hands and arms in the sink and then washed them again.

Then he turned around to face his oldest friends. He had known both of them forever. Nobody could have claimed that he didn't know Nadine could be cruel or that Tom was arrogant beyond bearing sometimes. But they were smart, Nadine had wit, and they'd known him forever, too.

"I don't know what to do," Quentin told them, feeling appalled to his core.

"There's no need to do anything," Tom said. "It's done."

"We're making the best of a bad situation," Nadine claimed.

"But if you raped her, Tom . . ."

"It wasn't like that, Quentin. Maybe she thought it was, but it wasn't. I know what I did, and I know it wasn't rape. And even if it was, what good would it do anybody for me to go to jail for it? Think what it would do to our children." He pointed to the newborn. "To that child. This way he'll have a home, he'll have parents, he'll have a brother."

"And a rapist for a father."

"It was a mistake."

Quentin's rage exploded. "I'll say it was!"

"I mean," Tom said, "I thought she wanted me to, I thought it was mutual, I didn't know she thought it was rape until after it was done."

"You didn't know she thought . . ." Quentin trailed off. He wouldn't have believed it of almost any other man he knew. But Tom, Tom was just that arrogant to assume that a young girl wanted his advances.

The three of them argued about it while the snow fell outside the cellar.

In the end, he went along with it, but only because of the girl.

He heard her make a sound and hurried back to her bed to see what she needed. "Please," she whispered to him, "they'll give him a life I never can. I'll make a new start someplace far away."

"But he raped you . . ."

"Please," she murmured and then she closed her eyes again. He was the only one of them who heard her say one more thing. "I'll come back for him someday."

Quentin stood up, feeling undone by all of it.

"I'm going to try to drive back to town before this gets worse." He gave both of his friends a hard, penetrating stare. "You'll take care of them?"

"Of course," Nadine told him.

He believed them. God help him—as he told Nathan later, when it was all over and nothing could be taken back—he believed them.

He didn't know what a contributing, negligent, murdering fool he had been until the second devastating call came through, this time from his other oldest friend, Nathan Shellenberger.

"Quentin, we've found a body in the snow."

"Whose?"

He didn't connect it immediately, wasn't expecting the blow when it came.

"A girl. That girl who used to work for Nadine and Tom."

"What do you mean you found her in the snow?"

"We found her in the snow! Naked. Dead. *Dead*, Quentin."

He was a man who thought he could handle anything, but he found he couldn't remain standing and hear these words. Quentin sank down into the closest chair. He bent his forehead into his free hand and crouched over the telephone like a wounded animal. But before he could even say anything, Nathan blurted out words that made Quentin shut his own mouth. "Quentin, I'm scared as hell that Patrick had something to do with it. I heard him and Rex arguing about her, just in the last few days. From what I overheard, I think Patrick has been seeing her, Quentin. Rex was riding him about something to do with her, and Patrick was furious about it, like he was jealous. And he's not acting right, not since we found her. He hasn't even said he knows her. He acts like he doesn't care that she's dead! My son, Quentin! You know how he is, you know what people think of him. If they find out he had anything to do with her, they'll blame him. And if there's any evidence to tie him to her . . . I'm the sheriff! I can't turn my own boy into a suspect in a murder!"

"Murder! How do you know she was murdered?"

"Jesus, God, Quentin, are you even listening to me? We found her naked and bloody in the middle of a blizzard. What do you think, that she decided to take a naked walk in the snow? Of course it's murder, or if not murder then some kind of manslaughter, and what the hell am I going to do?"

"Bring her to me."

"I'm afraid to ask Patrick anything."

"Then don't. We'll figure this out. Bring her here, Nathan."

He didn't tell his old friend what had transpired earlier.

He allowed Nathan to believe that Patrick might have done it.

When they brought her into his examining room he made sure no one could ever identify her and bring all of their lives tumbling down around them. He said nothing while Tom and Nadine arranged an adoption of Tom's own biological child. He and Nathan both let Verna and Rex worry for years that Patrick might have done it, let other people wonder if Mitch was the guilty one.

And they let Jeffrey Newquist grow up without knowing the truth of his birth or the true nature of the people he believed had adopted him from strangers. In the years that followed, Quentin mentioned it only one time to Tom and once to Nadine.

To Tom, he said, "What did you do to her after I left?"

"I didn't do anything," the big man had said indignantly.

"Then what did Nadine do to her?"

Tom's eyes had narrowed, as if he was annoyed at his wife. "I went into the house to rest. I left Nadine in the storm cellar to watch them. When I woke up and came back out the girl was gone. Nadine said she had fallen asleep and the girl had wandered out into the snow-storm. We couldn't look for her, not in that weather, you know how bad it was. We couldn't even move the car."

Had Nadine fallen asleep and the girl just wandered away?

Escaped was more like it, Quentin thought.

Or had Nadine put her out into the storm to freeze to death?

Quentin could see that Tom didn't know the answer to that, either.

Either way, they had killed her.

To Nadine, Quentin said, "You locked her in that storm cellar! For God's sake!"

"She wasn't there the whole time, Quentin," Nadine had said, as if he were being unreasonable. "For most of her pregnancy we gave her the house to live in. We provided her with everything she needed! More than she had ever had before in her life, I'm sure. We only had to put her in the storm cellar when we found out that she'd had visi-tors. We couldn't allow that, so we put her in there for her own good so that she couldn't ruin our bargain with her. It was all to her bene-fit, after all." Nadine had smiled her cold smile, the one that chilled even her oldest friends. "I don't know what you're so upset about, Quentin. She was only in there for three months, and we made sure she had everything she needed there, too. She was only there until the baby was born."

"Did she escape, Nadine, or did you put her out?"

Nadine had given him a look with venom at the back of it, a look that told him all he needed to know about how Sarah Francis came to be found naked in a blizzard after wandering lost, weak, and bleeding from childbirth. And he also understood from that murderous look that Tom and Nadine would do anything, harm anyone, who ever divulged any of their horrible secrets.

Quentin told one person the rest of the story: Nathan.

Together they looked at the damage that had already been done, the damage that could still be done, and they came to the decision to let it be. The families involved were already broken up; telling the truth would only harm them further. The child Jeffrey was being raised by his real father.

They never spoke of it, not even to each other, again.

Quentin always thought that Nathan paid for it with the excruciating pain of his arthritis. Nathan always thought that Quentin paid for it in the loss of his closeness to his daughters. Filled with the guilt of what had been done to an innocent girl close to Ellen and Abby's age, Quentin Reynolds had never again allowed himself the pleasure of being close enough to his girls to feel loved by them.

But they went on with their "friendship" with Tom and Nadine. Because they had all known each other all their lives, because their wives didn't know anything about what had happened, and because it was a small town where relationships had to be mended in order for people to live together so closely, and because the sheriff, even the sheriff, and the town's doctor were afraid of the judge and of what he and his vicious wife could do to their own wives and children.

•   •   •

In the fraught silence that followed Nathan's recital, Mitch looked around the living room.

"Where's Jeff?" he said suddenly, breaking the mood. He stood up. "Where'd my brother go?"

Rex also jumped to his feet and looked over his father's head into the kitchen. The kitchen table was empty. Jeff Newquist had slipped away, taking his father's pistol with him.

He was gone, but somebody else had come into the house while

Nathan was telling his story and had propped himself against a wall to listen along with everybody else.

Patrick looked from Abby to Mitch and back again.

And then he said, "What happened at your dad's house, Abby? I saw the judge walk over there with a rifle."

Chapter Forty-one

The judge had observed his older son's car parked at the curb of Doc's house and then he had watched as his younger son followed Mitch inside. Push had come to shove again. He had lied to his son Mitch in many ways, but the pertinent one at the moment was the lie that claimed that he, Tom, had told Quentin and Nathan that Mitch had witnessed what they did to the girl's body. He had never told them any of that. They had no idea Mitch had been hiding in the supply closet that night or that he had seen the whole thing. They had never known, never threatened Mitch in any way.

But he had told Mitch they did, to justify getting him out of town.

And now Mitch was going over there, possibly to confront Quentin, who wouldn't know what the hell he was talking about but who might decide now was the time to tell certain other secrets.

Tom hurried to the gun case in his office.

He unlocked it and then pulled out Mitch's first rifle.

He might be able to get Mitch off of a murder charge, he told himself, but what he couldn't do was allow Quentin to talk about what he had known for the last seventeen years.

•   •   •

It was a quiet street with few cars on it at any time.

He knew that half of success in life was walking confidently and that witnesses saw what they wanted to see. If he walked with a sure stride across the street to Quentin's home and if he was carrying a rifle at his side, and if any neighbors saw him, they would see only who they wanted to see: Tom, their neighbor, the judge. And if they saw more than that, then it was their word against his and nobody's word ever stood up against his.

At the front of the house, the screen door was closed but the wooden door was open.

From within, he heard Mitch's voice raised in anger.

Tom stepped quietly through into the living room.

They were in the kitchen, arguing.

He heard Quentin saying, "I don't know what you're talking about!"

"The hell you don't!" Mitch retorted, and then he said, "Maybe Nathan Shellenberger will have a better memory than you do."

Tom stepped out of sight as his oldest son stormed through from the kitchen and slammed his way out of the house. He was followed by Jeffrey, who ran after him, yelling, "Mitch! Wait for me!"

Tom stepped around the corner, into the kitchen, before Quentin could go back into his clinic.

"What did you tell him?" he asked.

"Nothing." Quentin saw the rifle, then raised alarmed eyes to his old friend.

Tom nodded, believing him. But Mitch might not stop until he had answers, and Quentin was the only living person who could still provide them. Tom had already made sure that the only other person who knew about Sarah . . . his own wife . . . had been silenced. With a touch of poetic justice that he liked, he had led Nadine by the hand into the blizzard and watched her wander off, as lost and confused as that girl had been the night that Nadine took her, naked, into that other snowstorm. In Nadine's dementia, she had been starting to say things, little remembered things, that harked back to days that shouldn't be recalled or spoken of, so Tom had taken care of it by letting nature render judgment on her.

But nobody was going to render judgment on him.

He hadn't done anything wrong. The girl had wanted to have sex with him. She had wanted to have the baby. He had paid her fairly, taken care of her as well as Nadine would allow him to. And God knows, he had raised the troublesome child when he could have told her to have it aborted, or forced her to adopt it out to strangers.

He was, in his own mind, not guilty of anything.

Nadine had killed the girl, not him.

And Quentin was forcing him to take these measures, when God knew, he would rather not have raised the rifle and held it on his oldest friend.

"Lock the door to your office, Quentin."

The doctor did so. "Tom, you don't really—"

It was all he got a chance to say.

•   •   •

The judge put the rifle on the floor, took off the gloves he'd worn to carry and shoot it, and carried them out the front door with him. Then he walked with confident strides back across the street and into the house.

He noticed a red truck parked down the street, but paid no attention to it.

People saw what they were expecting to see. And his word was law.

It was only when he walked into his house that he found himself surprised by something. Or rather, by someone.

"Hey, Judge," said the disheveled-looking drunk who had walked in the front door that the judge, for once in his life, had left unlocked. "Remember me? You put me in jail a few times, right? Made me pay a few fines, right? Well, not this time. This time, I'm the one's come to collect from you."

Marty Francis stood weaving on the fine Persian carpet on the floor of the judge's living room. When Tom was able to figure out that the man was there to blackmail him to keep secret the identity of the girl in the grave, Tom said, "I don't have that much money in the house. Let's take a drive together and I'll get it from the bank for you."

Docile as a lamb being led by its own greed to slaughter, Marty followed the judge out to the black Cadillac in the driveway.

Once they were inside of it, the judge locked the doors.

He backed down his driveway and drove rapidly down the street.

When he reached the corner he turned left toward the highway instead of right toward downtown.

"There ain't no bank out this way," Marty objected.

"I keep my checkbook out at a little ranch we have."

A ranch where a person could be shut into a storm cellar and never be seen again.

"Oh," his passenger said agreeably. "Okay. But hey, slow down! You're kind of a crazy driver, Judge, you know that?"

*   *   *

Patrick was already gone.

He had been following Marty, wanting to see what the man would do next. When he guessed what Marty was going to do—try to blackmail the judge instead of spreading suspicions about Mitch—he knew his own plans were finished. The judge would never stand for blackmail. He would have Marty charged and tossed in jail, Marty would tell the story of how he had come to have the information about his sister, somebody would put two and two together, and Abby would find out that he had tried to betray Mitch.

Patrick drove into town and got a beer, and then he drove out to his parents' house to tell them he was sick of ranch work and he was leaving town again.

Chapter Forty-two

It was hard to drive when she felt so awful, but Catie was determined to make one last trip to see the Virgin. She hadn't realized she would feel quite this bad, but then it had been a couple of days since she had even attempted to drive her van. During all that time she had eaten almost nothing. Now she had pain and she had a fever that had been rising higher for the last day or so, but she felt light as air, ethereal, angelic. It was a beautiful night and Catie would have liked to be able to lean her face out the window and look up at it, but it was increasingly all she could do to hold the van on the highway.

She was veering across the center line, she knew she was, but she couldn't do anything about that. There wasn't much traffic and she always managed to pull the van back onto her side of the road when a car passed her going the other way. Catie didn't want to be a danger to anybody, she told herself; she didn't want to hurt anyone. She just wanted to park in the cemetery one more time and crawl, if she had to, up to the grave and lie on her back again and tell the Virgin how grateful she was for the gift of peace.

It hurt to turn the steering wheel when she made the turn onto Highway 177.

Once she got the van going straight again, it hurt a little less.

In another couple of miles, she would be there.

Catie felt excited . . . and also calm . . . at the thought of what she was doing. It just felt right. It was going to be the perfect ending to a miraculous trip. And then she could drive home and get into bed and stay there until she died, if that's the way things worked out. Or maybe she would have a miraculous cure of her body to match the one she'd already had of her heart, and then she would be able to flounce into her doctor's office and laugh and say, "Look at me!" She would even call that reporter back and say, "I told you so!"

In the moment when she first saw the cemetery she also saw something else.

"Oh!" she breathed, her palms relaxing on the steering wheel.

It was so beautiful . . . *she* was so beautiful . . . the vision Catie saw of a beautiful dark-haired girl who was smiling at her, just ahead of her. Catie knew immediately that it was the Virgin. She didn't know how she could be so lucky, but for some reason she was being blessed again . . .

As the vision filled her eyes, Catie's foot relaxed its pressure on the gas pedal; her hands dropped off the steering wheel entirely and fell into her lap. She just stared at the Virgin, smiling back into the beautiful face that was blessing her. The big van traveled straight down one side of the highway for quite a way, cresting one hill and then picking up speed on the other side. Halfway down the long hill, the van began to swerve toward the other side of the road, where a black Cadillac was coming from the other direction. But Catie didn't see the two men staring in horror at her in the front seat of the Cadillac. All she saw before she died was the most beautiful light she had ever seen, surrounding a beautiful dark-haired girl whose image vanished as the light accepted Catie into its warmth and glory.

Chapter Forty-three

Mitch stepped out of his car onto Abby's driveway with a birdcage in his hand.

When she saw who he had with him, she yelled for joy and came running. Mitch had already told her about finding J.D. in his father's yard and they hadn't even argued about which one of them would get to keep him. "He needs company," Mitch had admitted. "And Gracie misses him," Abby had said. "And, besides," Mitch had added, "it isn't as if I'll never get to see him again . . . is it?"

"It certainly is not," Abby had agreed with so much passion they had both grinned.

Now, with her running full-speed toward him, just to be on the safe side Mitch put the birdcage with the parrot in it down on the ground and braced himself. Sure enough, she didn't stop, but threw herself straight at him, nearly knocking him over, so that Mitch had to wrap his arms around her and lift her off her feet and steady his legs so they didn't both go tumbling to the ground and tear themselves up on the gravel.

And then Mitch found that in order to properly keep their balance he had to find her mouth and kiss it and that she understood the necessity of maintaining balance and so she kissed him back so hard they nearly melded into one body standing right there in her drive-way. Mitch felt his desire for her rise, and this time there wasn't going to be anything stopping it, and no misunderstandings about it, and no bad feelings or secrets afterward, there was only going to be loving Abby forever and ever, just as he was always supposed to do.

"Can you carry J.D., too?" she asked him breathlessly.

"No problem," he lied, but then they both laughed and she got down and walked, but she grabbed his arm that wasn't being used to hold the birdcage and she held on to it as if she were never going to let him go, which was just fine with Mitch. It was a damned good thing, he thought as they walked into her house together—with J.D. suddenly starting to squawk until their ears rang and her other bird, inside the house, starting to holler back at him—it was a damned fine thing that he had already started buying property in Small Plains so that his plan of moving back and helping to keep his hometown alive was well on its way to fruition. Granted, he had once thought he was doing it out of revenge, to take over the town his father's friends thought they owned, but it seemed revenge could turn into some-thing else entirely, something more like hope and love, for a town and a woman . . .

"And a bird," he said out loud.

"What?" Abby asked, looking up at him and smiling.

"Nothing." He kissed her. "You're going to love my son."

"I know I will."

The twinge of pain in her heart when he said that didn't last but a second before it turned to feelings that Abby recognized as the same ones she'd had as a young girl. Hope and love, that's what they were. The ache in her heart over her father's death was a more permanent pain, one that only Mitch could ever really understand, because he had lost his parents, too. Of the two of them, Abby knew she was the "fortunate" one, because she had always had her mother's love and she'd known her father's love, as well, before his own acts changed him. Mitch had only had other people's parents to truly love him.

And he'd also had Rex, Abby thought.

"And me," she whispered.

"What?"

"Nothing." She smiled up at him. "And your son will love me."

"Cocky, aren't you?"

"I have reason to believe," she said with confidence, and then Abby ran ahead into her bedroom, pulling Mitch along with her.

•   •   •

Rex crouched beside the grave and laid a dozen white roses in front of the stone.

A new gravestone was on order. Abby was paying for it. She'd insisted, saying she had promised it to Sarah. It would have Sarah's full name in big bold lettering, along with the dates of her birth and death. But it wouldn't be ready for several weeks, and Rex couldn't wait that long to come and say hello and good-bye.

"I guess I loved you, Sarah," he told her.

Maybe Abby had been right. Maybe he had been stuck ever since Sarah's death, but now that she was free, he thought maybe he could be, too.

"There's a lot of cleaning up to do," he told her.

His knees didn't like crouching, so he stood up, took off his hat, and held it in his hands while he talked to her one more time. "Abby and Ellen have to clear up their dad's estate and figure out what to do with the house. They're hoping to be able to attract a young doctor to town to buy the house and Doc's practice. Personally, I think they'll give it away if they have to, just to make sure we have a physician around here." He smiled a little. "They—Abby and Ellen—have this idea it should be a woman doctor."

He shifted from one foot to the other.

"I guess you know the judge is dead. And your brother. Your worthless brother, if you don't mind my saying so. Patrick thinks your brother was . . ." He stopped. "Oh, never mind. I suspect none of that worries you anymore, so I won't, either. My mom says you've been good to my dad, although I can't imagine why, so maybe you'll want to know there won't be any charges brought against him for covering everything up. Or against any of us, for that matter. The statute of limitations covers up a lot of things, too. And that poor sick girl took care of punishing Tom for what he did to you and other people."

Rex didn't like talking about that part of it, so he moved on.

"Mitch and Abby are back together again," he announced, with pleasure. "I know you may have mixed feelings about that, since you were pretty hot for him, but I think it's destiny, with them, I really do. Nobody else ever had a chance with either one of them. Oh, and Patrick's left town, which I hope is as okay with you as it is with me and Abby. She's convinced now that he tried to kill all of her birds. I guess we'll never know for sure, but of course I think it sounds exactly like something my brother would do. I think Abby's mostly embarrassed now that she ever had anything to do with him, but, hell, she was lonely, and it's not like she could ever let herself fall for anybody but Mitch. Pat was just a poor substitute, because that's all Abby ever had until Mitch came back.

"Speaking of whom—" Rex laughed. "You know his diabolical scheme to buy up downtown Small Plains? Turns out all he wanted to do was take it away from our fathers. I guess he had some nasty idea of letting the buildings go to hell, but I doubt he'd ever have been able to do it. Now he's ready to move back and live here and bring the properties back up to lookin' good. The mayor is thrilled, as you can imagine."

He remembered something else he wanted to tell her.

"With Patrick gone, that leaves the ranch in a bind, and I'm thinking maybe I should get out of sherriffing and take over for my folks. I wouldn't mind doing that. Hell, what am I saying, I'd love to do that. The only reason I didn't do it earlier was because I didn't want to have to work for my dad and be arguing with him all the time. But if he could trust Patrick to run it, he can sure as hell trust me."

He revolved his hat in his hands for a moment, thinking.

"We'll take care of Jeff for you, Sarah. I'm sorry we haven't all done a better job of it until now. He's living with my folks, I guess you know. It's not the best arrangement. He's too pigheaded and they're too old. But it won't last forever that way. I'm pretty sure Mitch intends to take him in, and once he and Abby get married, which they're sure to do, then Jeff will finally have a home with people who actually give a damn about him. I don't know what he thought he was going to do with that gun of his dad's when he ran out of my folks' house like that, but I shudder to think what could have happened. He was one hurt, angry kid, I'll tell you, after what he had heard about Tom and Nadine. And what he had heard about you. I think he was heartbroken on your behalf, Sarah. I think he wanted to kill the son of a bitch who had done that to his mother."

Rex took a deep breath, feeling upset all over again.

When he could talk calmly, he said, "About Jeff. I'll try to be more patient. Be like an uncle, or something, although I can't promise I'll be any good at it. You don't go from being the sheriff to being the uncle overnight, you know."

Rex gazed off into the distance, over the flint-topped hills now turning green with summer ripeness. "Well, I guess that's about it. I don't know if you ever actually cured anybody. My mom says you did, but I don't know. And I don't know if people will continue to come out to see you, now that you're not such a mystery anymore. But I'll tell you one thing—even if nobody else ever really got a miracle, I think I'm cured, Sarah, which should be good news." He grinned down at her gravestone. "God knows you must be sick of me still hanging around you after all these years."

Out of a still, clear day, the wind suddenly picked up.

It bowed the grass in his direction, unaccountably lifting his spirits and making him think that maybe she hadn't minded his devotion, after all.

About the Author

NANCY PICKARD is the creator of the acclaimed Jenny Cain mystery series. She has won the Anthony Award, two Macavity Awards, and two Agatha Awards for her novels. She is a three-time Edgar Award nominee, most recently for her first Marie Lightfoot mystery, *The Whole Truth,* which was a national bestseller. With Lynn Lott, Pickard co-authored *Seven Steps on the Writer's Path.* She has been a national board member of the Mystery Writers of America, as well as the president of Sisters in Crime. She lives in Prairie Village, Kansas. Visit her website at www.nancypickardmysteries.com.

About the Type

This book was set in Garamond, a typeface originally designed by the Parisian typecutter Claude Garamond (1480–1561). This version of Garamond was modeled on a 1592 specimen sheet from the Egenolff-Berner foundry, which was produced from types assumed to have been brought to Frankfurt by the punchcutter Jacques Sabon.

Claude Garamond's distinguished romans and italics first appeared in *Opera Ciceronis* in 1543–44. The Garamond types are clear, open, and elegant.